SO-ARH-716

SEARCH TO BELONG

SEARCH TO BELONG

By Christmas Carol Kauffman

HERALD PRESS

SCOTTDALE, PENNSYLVANIA

Dedicated to the fond

memory of

Sister Laura Umstattd

PREFACE

Search to Belong is based on an actual experience and has been written by permission. All the names are fictitious. The author has created some of the details.

This story has been written with the hope that it will:

1. Encourage foster children to respect and honor their foster parents.

2. Encourage foster parents to understand, love, and respect the adopted child.

3. Assure children of unfortunate circumstances that they can overcome every obstacle and make a fine contribution to society.

4. Remind workers in children's homes of the lasting impression they make on the children they work with.

5. Help the general reader to understand the needs of the foster child.

Christmas Carol Kauffman

CHAPTER 1

Where was he?

The strange big house frightened three-year-old Davy. Not because it was larger than the only one he had ever known, but because it was so utterly different. The high ceilings, the brown-knobbed doors, the long rooms, the unfamiliar rugs, and unfamiliar everything—the people, the oversize furniture, and most of all the lonely empty spaces, everywhere his sad searching eyes dared let him look—made it seem bigger.

And emptier!

No one his size in all this big strange house!

Davy bit the inside of his cheek and looked down at the toy wooden wagon the lady said he could play with. He didn't even touch it. The lump in his throat was getting bigger and chokier every second. He clutched at the top button on his blue plaid shirt. Tears filled his sorrowful brown eyes.

How kind they were, this man and lady who had come and talked a long time to Leon's papa, then had taken him for a ride in their car to this big house! So gentle too. So was the big girl with the blond wavy hair, the one they called Lesa. So was Janet, the girl in the blue jumper dress and long black braids, who sat beside him at the table and tried to coax him into eating supper he wasn't one bit hungry for. Freckle-faced Dennis acted neither kind nor mean. He just stared at him. Without words. He only made queer, wordy noises in his throat.

Not one of the five faces around the table looked familiar.

1

Not a single thing in the whole big kitchen (except the box of clothes they had brought along) belonged to him. Where were all his other very own things? Where were the chairs, benches, and low tables just the right size? Everything he looked at was too big, too high, too above, too strange and unknowing. Where were his own real children-people like Randy and Lester and Leon and the others?

Davy never knew before he had a heart that could be so lonely, so blowed-up-big with queer, scary feelings. This whole new world was frightening. Bewildering. The world he knew was a world of many busy little hands and feet, jolly children-talk, and suppers together—together with his own kind of people.

And Sister LoLo! How could there be a place anywhere without her?

Tears. Sister LoLo! Big tears.

The two were taking him across the living room toward the long open stairway, the girl Janet leading him by one hand, the lady carrying his box. The man called out pleasantly, "Good night, Davy boy. Sleep well. We'll see you in the morning."

The big girl likewise called cheerily over the dish she was wiping. "Good night, Davy boy. Sleep well. Lesa thinks you're cute. See you in the morning."

Davy did not answer. Nor did he look back. His frightened, teary eyes were fixed on that long, frightening stairway. Where, oh, where were they taking him?

He stiffened. He whimpered.

"Come, Davy," said the girl Janet. "We're going to get you ready for bed now."

Emphatically he shook his head and tried to pull his hand loose. "No," he panted. "Not up there."

"Why not?" Janet laughed playfully. "You'll like your room. It's all ready and waiting for you. It's right next to mine. And Dennis sleeps in the room on the other side. Come, honey. Aw, Davy, please don't cry. Lesa sleeps up there too."

In struggling to free himself Davy landed on the floor. Dennis, watching in the doorway, snickered.

2

"Here, Janet," said the lady. "You take the box if it's not too heavy for you."

The next thing he knew, Davy was being carried up the stairs, and with each step the lady was patting him and kissing him and saying soothing words that failed to soothe.

"We understand, sweet little boy. We knew this would all be strange to you at first. But you'll—"

Then the inevitable. Tears sprang and flowed the more in spite of the kisses and pattings.

"You'll be all right, sweetheart," the lady continued, squeezing him gently. "Dennis cried the first night, and he was older than you are. Janet did too."

"Did I Mamma?" asked Janet. "Did I really?"

The lady chuckled softly. "Of course you did, dear, but hardly for the same reason, because you were too little to know."

"I—I—" sobbed Davy, stiffening and struggling. "I want to—go back."

"Oh, you poor little boy." They were at the top of the stairs now. "We have your nighty things in your box. We'll put them on you, and tuck you in your own little bed, and look, Davy, here we are in your room. And tomorrow when you wake up, you can help Janet feed the chickens. And you can play on the swing with Dennis. And maybe you boys can both ride along to town with Papa Loomas. Won't you like that?"

"No," sobbed Davy. "I want to—go back—to Sister LoLo. I—want," he all but shrieked, "Sister LoLo to put me—in—my bed."

"Shall I come up and help, Mamma?" called Lesa from the bottom of the stairs.

"No, Lesa."

With much coaxing, more sweet words, plus considerable physical help, the two got the squirming child into his pajamas.

"Did Sister—" Mamma Loomas bit her lip. "Say, Davy, did anyone teach you a good-night prayer?"

If Davy heard the question, he did not answer. How could he think of uttering "If I should die" when all he could hear was

3

his racing, thumping heart screaming "no" to everything, including the horrid black bed the lady was lifting him into.

"No," he wailed. "Not—my bed." He refused to lie down. He was hot, panting hot.

"Honey, it's going to be from this night on." The lady planted another kiss on his damp forehead. "It's a nice bed, Davy dear. Dennis used to sleep in it until he got too big."

"But—but—" Brokenly Davy sobbed the objection. "My bed is—white. I—want—my—white bed."

"Poor dear. I'm sorry we don't have a white one for you. But, darling, black sleeps just as well. See, the mattress is nice and thick and soft. The pillow is nice and soft. Feel it."

"And it has a white cover on it, Davy," added Janet with a big sisterly interest. "And see, the sheets are white, if you like white best. And the top cover is white. Look, Davy." She held it up before him. "See?"

Instead Davy closed his eyes and hot scalding tears streamed down his cheeks to his quivering chin. He covered his face with both hands. "I—I—don't like—old—black beds," he cried. "I—I want—Sister LoLo to—to—come—and get me an' put me—in—my own white bed—beside—"

"Poor child," whispered Mamma Loomas, twisting one hand over the other. "What should we do?"

"Listen, Davy," exclaimed Janet with fresh intent. "I tell you what." She leaned over the edge of the bed and put one arm around him. "I'll go get my nighty on and—and—I'll come over here and sleep beside you. Huh? Shall I, Davy? Shall I? Can I, Mamma? Please say yes."

"Go get ready. It might help. At least he didn't shake his head. But, Janet, my dear, you'll have a hard time squeezing yourself into this bed. But you can try. We'll leave the table light on for a while. Maybe all night this time."

Ten minutes later, in the hall outside the door, Rose Loomas stood with arms folded and head bowed listening, smiling gently as she listened.

"Now put your head down on the pillow, Davy. Down just

4

a little more. Like that. See? It's nice and soft, isn't it?" Janet folded the sheet and coverlet up over the end of the bed. "It's too warm for covers tonight." Tenderly she wiped Davy's tears with a freshly ironed handkerchief. "I'll bet I can guess how old you are. You're three, aren't you?" No answer. "Three's a nice age to be. I think so. It's like three leaves of a clover. Huh? And three bears. You know that story? And like three things we use when we eat—a spoon, a knife, and a fork." She laughed ever so subdued a laugh. "And three things up in the sky—the sun, the moon, and the stars. We learned all that in the first grade. But I knew it before I went to school." She stopped long enough to make certain his sobbings were lessening. They were. She hurried on. "I think Davy is a very pretty name. You can say it three ways, too. Can't you? David. Or Dave. Or Davy. Sure thing. I like Davy best, like we call you." She laughed again, this time with real warmth. "My name is just plain Janet. But when I get older, folks can call me Jan if they want to. I like that better. I wouldn't care if you'd call me Jan now. It's shorter. Isn't it? Guess how old I am, Davy. I'm three and three and three and one. That makes ten. I'll be in grade five when school starts. The boy downstairs, Dennis, he's eight. That's him coming up the stairs now to go to bed, I think. He wanted them to bring home a boy more his size. But Mamma said they didn't have any at the Home eight or nine to let out. That's why," she whispered in his ear. "I think that's why he didn't talk at the table. But he can. He can talk plenty when he wants to. Papa and the schoolteacher tell him he talks too much sometimes."

Janet got up on one elbow and looked down into Davy's sober face. His big brown eyes, still moist, glistened in the soft light from the green shaded table lamp. "I think you're cute. I do. And pretty, too."

She touched his nose with the tip of her first finger. "I hope you stay here. I'm glad they couldn't get a boy of nine. I hope you are glad as I am. Papa Loomas, he's a real nice papa. And he gets us 'most everything we want; that is, if he and Mamma think we need it to make us happy. Did you bring any toys?"

Davy moved his head so slightly Janet wasn't sure, but she thought he meant no. "It really—" she hurried on, putting her head down beside his again. "It doesn't matter a bit, 'cause we have toys and a big sandbox out behind the house. And Papa made some nice little wooden wagons and a wheelbarrow. He knows how to make things little boys like. You know that? He does. And tomorrow, guess what, Davy? I'm going to show you a nest of baby kittens out in the barn. There's four. Two yellow ones and two gray ones. And their eyes aren't open yet. We'll be good friends. Won't we? We will. I wish you'd say something, Davy. I'll teach you how to jump rope, and whistle, and —and, oh, just lots of things. I don't know yet what your voice sounds like. I'll show you the sheep. And we have ripe grapes to pick. You like grapes? Say," she rambled on, "can you tie your shoes yet?"

The little head scarcely moved. But suddenly he turned and stared with wide, wondering, unbelieving eyes at this friendly, talkative girl snuggled so close to him in the horrid black bed.

"If you can't, I'll teach you how." Janet brushed her hand back over his damp glossy black hair. "Are you getting a teeny, tiny, little bit sleepy yet? Are you, Davy?"

No answer. Instead Davy drew a long broken breath and stared blankly at the high, meaningless, oyster-white-papered ceiling.

Where was he? The question struck his consciousness with a fresh dart. He took a sharp breath.

Why was he brought to this strange, strange place? So empty. So quiet. So unbearably lonely without his own world of many little people, and rows of white beds, and hooks he could reach. Davy clenched his fists. Tears started all over again.

"I—I want Sister LoLo," he whimpered. His aching chest rose and fell three times.

"But listen, Davy, she is most likely fast asleep already," suggested Janet. "It's sleepy time for everybody. Everywhere. So close your pretty eyes now—I saw they're brown—and I'll close mine.

6

Mine are blue. Close them. And away—away—away we'll float together into that happy nothing-land. Shall we go together?" She caught his left hand and squeezed it gently.

The smile that crossed Davy's sad little face was so faint, so delicate it could scarcely be called a smile.

"I'll sing a song for you about the happy bluebird family. If you close your eyes and keep them shut tight, you can hear it better."

"Rose," called Mr. Loomas from the bottom of the stairs, "someone wants you on the phone. Can you come?"

Carefully Mamma Loomas left the interesting conversation to tiptoe down the carpeted steps. She smiled all the way.

"Mrs. Loomas, this is Lora Wenzel at the Home."

"Yes, Sister Lora."

"How's my little Davy doing?"

"He's just falling asleep, Lora."

"Good. I couldn't help wondering. Maybe he doesn't—I mean I shouldn't expect him to miss me as much as I do him. You know—pardon me for saying this, but—it was pretty hard for me to see him leave, Mrs. Loomas."

"I can well imagine, Lora."

"You see, I've taken care of him since the day he was left here. I've never become this attached to any other child. From the start he was such a dear little thing. And so lovable. Different somehow."

"He was only about a week old, I understand."

"Yes. So you see he's never known anyone—" Sister Lora cleared her throat—"as a—a real mother. He seems almost like my own."

"I understand, Sister Lora. And I'll try my best to be a real mother to him."

"I know you will, Mrs. Loomas. I'm confident of that. He couldn't have been placed into a better home." She hesitated a moment. "Little Davy's such a dear child. Tell me—did he—did he mention me at all?"

"Indeed he did, Sister Lora. He calls you LoLo."

7

She laughed very softly. "What did he say?"

"He wanted Sister LoLo to put him to bed."

"Bless his little heart."

"He objected to our black bed."

"No." Sister Lora smothered another soft laugh.

"But Janet took charge."

"She did?"

"She lay down beside him. And talked. And sang."

"How sweet of her! How very sweet!"

"I'm quite sure he'll be all right, Lora. Come over sometime."

"No, Mrs. Loomas. Thanks, thanks a lot. Definitely my place is here. But when you think it's wise, please, bring him back to the Home to see me. I do want to keep in touch. Pardon me for being frank, but if I—if I were married and had a home of my own, no one else would have gotten little David Grant."

"You do love that child. Let me ask you a question, Sister Lora. Do you think his real name is David Grant?"

"I've wondered often. But that was the name I found in the toe of his little stocking. It was a wonder it didn't go into the laundry without being found. I wouldn't be surprised someday if we'll find out he's the son of someone very special and refined. I must run along. Some child is calling me. Did you start to say something?"

"I was going to say—he's like a sweet little mystery, isn't he?"

Rose Loomas jumped. There stood Janet at her elbow.

CHAPTER 2

Slowly Rose Loomas hung up the receiver. Sudden beads of perspiration appeared on her forehead.

"Janet," she exclaimed, gripping the girl's shoulder. "I thought you were upstairs with little Davy."

"I was. But he's asleep now and—well, I came down to ask you if I should stay in there with him all night. It's pretty crowded, especially when he flops his arms around."

"Of course. It must be. You'd better go over in your own room. Leave both doors open so if he does wake up, you'll hear him. I hope I will, but I'm not sure from down here. Janet," she smoothed back the girl's hair, "it was real sweet and nice of you to help me out the way you did. I'm glad you're kind to little Davy."

"I like to be. He's cute, I think. Mamma?"

"Yes, dear."

"Dennis came over to the door while I was singing and stuck out his tongue."

"My, my. I'll have to talk to that boy."

"I'm glad Davy's eyes were shut."

"So am I. Better go up now, dear."

"Mamma?"

"Yes."

"Isn't his real name David Grant?"

"Janet." Rose Loomas held Janet out at arm's length. "What makes you ask?"

9

"Well, I—I heard you asking Sister Lora. Why did you?"

Rose Loomas bit her lip. "His name is David Grant as far as anyone knows." She hesitated, fumbling for words. "Everybody—I mean nearly everyone—has a name given him at birth, and that's his name. David Grant."

"Doesn't he know his name?"

"Why do you ask?"

"I asked him what it was and he wouldn't answer. Maybe he's too little yet to know."

"It's Grant, Janet. Hop along now. Kiss me first. That's a girl. Sleep well."

"Grant," whispered Janet, climbing the stairs. "I guess I can remember that name for him."

"Come back, Leon. Come back, Leon."

Janet woke with a start. She sat straight up in bed.

"Leon, don't go."

She remembered. A small boy in the next room where the voice was coming from. She hurried over and found him on his knees clawing the air wildly.

"What's wrong, Davy?" she asked, clasping both his hands in her own. "You're dreaming, honey. Lay down. There now. It's all right. Everything's all right, honey. Janet is close by. Remember Janet?"

Quite out of breath, Mrs. Loomas came running up the stairs. "What's the matter with him?"

"Sh, I guess he was just talking in his sleep. Calling someone Leon. I don't know who he means, Mamma."

"Poor little dear. Leon. That's Kolbs' little boy."

"Kolb? You mean the superintendent at the Home?"

"Yes. Go back to bed, dear. He'll be all right. I think. I hope. Poor little dear."

In the morning Davy seemed much less afraid. He allowed Janet (to her delight) to fasten the shoulder buckles on his blue jeans, tie his shoes, and even comb his hair.

"Look in the glass, Davy," she beamed. "That pretty little

boy you see in there is Davy Grant."

Davy knit his brow. He shook his head doubtfully.

Janet laughed. "But it is. You funny, silly, little dear." She planted a smacking kiss on his temple. "That little boy right there—all slicked up for breakfast—smile at him. He belongs to you. Yes, he does. He's your own self, Davy Grant. We'll go find the kittens after breakfast. Shall we? Don't you know your last name is Grant?"

Davy stared mutely at the talkative girl.

"Mine is Chaveriat. You can't say that, I know. No matter. You don't have to. Just call me Janet. Say it. Say my name, Davy. Huh? Don't you want to? You know it anyhow, don't you?"

Davy smiled and nodded.

"Then come. Let's go down and surprise Mamma and Lesa. I smell yum-yum bacon. Sniff. Like that. Doesn't it smell good? I'm as hungry as a bear. Two bears. Three bears." She laughed. "Three bears. Do you know that story? I'll read it to you."

Dennis tore out of his room, shirttail getting tucked in as he sprang past the two on the stairs.

"Look out, Dennis Ray Forney," reprimanded Janet. "You might have knocked Davy right over. Mamma told you to be nice and polite. And here you forgot already. You bad Dennis."

Thus began little Davy's first full day in the home of Rose and Aaron Loomas, a prosperous farm couple in one of the lush "garden valley" spots of Lancaster County, Pennsylvania. Lesa, fourteen, was their only living child. A daughter, Raeleta Ann, had died when very small.

Their craving and wholesome love for more children prompted their frequent visits to the Millersville Children's Home a few miles distant. Rose and Aaron enjoyed a very close friendship with the superintendent, Melvin Kolb, and his wife Martha. Aaron Loomas had for years been a substantial and regular contributor to the Home. It was without any hesitancy that the careful-thinking Kolbs granted Rose and Aaron permission to take a child, little Janet Chaveriat, when she was scarcely a year

11

old. Five years later they asked for Dennis Forney, a five-year-old problem child.

"But," explained Superintendent Kolb to Rose and Aaron, "considering the boy's background and history, it's little wonder he has a hard time adjusting. If any two can help little Dennis, you folks can." The three were in the office near the big window.

"We want to try," ventured Rose with modesty as she watched the boy playing with several other boys on the lawn. "Don't we, Aaron?"

"I'm ready if you are, Rose. I often wonder how I'd feel if I had to be placed here because of a broken home."

"His has been *twice* broken," said Mr. Kolb.

Aaron was watching the boy from the window. "Let's take him, Rose, and see what we can do for him. To be truthful, I wouldn't mind taking several."

"Aaron." Rose pulled her husband's coat sleeve. "We'd better see first how we get along with one. But, bless your big sweet heart, I'm glad I didn't have to talk you into taking him."

"You may be very sure," tossed in Melvin Kolb, stroking his chin, "if that were the state of affairs, you wouldn't get Dennis Forney or any one of our children." He winked. "Parents must agree."

The trio laughed in good-natured understanding.

After three years of living and loving and giving, not to mention both playing and praying, Rose and Aaron Loomas were ready to admit that their success with Dennis had not been overwhelming. Without question they loved him. And they would keep him as long as he wanted to stay. Although they had not adopted either Janet or Dennis, they treated them like their own.

Janet's mother was dead. Her father's second wife had many children of her own and could not consider making room for one more. Grandma Chaveriat, so far, had kept in touch with Janet twice a year—on her birthday and at Christmas. Twice in ten years she had come to see her and seemed delighted with the good home she had "under the friendly Loomas roof," as she expressed it.

Dennis knew nothing of his father. His mother appeared unexpectedly one evening when he was playing in the Loomas yard with two neighbor boys. She came in a green Maxwell with the top folded back, and a strange man was driving. She bluntly informed Dennis that they were on their way to Michigan City to get married, and she didn't know when she would see him again. For days after that, Dennis was sullen and more easily irritated than usual. His mother's older sister, Marie, wrote him a hard-to-understand letter shortly after that experience, but Mamma Loomas had to read it to him (as she read between the lines), and also answer it for him. He received a second and a third such letter, but how could a boy of eight be expected to take an interest in writing to a faraway aunt in Chicago Heights, that he couldn't remember ever seeing? Mamma answered those two also.

"Rose," began Aaron one evening after Janet and Dennis had gone to bed. "What Dennis needs, I think, is a boy companion to share things with. Let's go over to the Home and look around. What say?"

"Just as you think best, Aaron. Dennis seems to crave something. Poor boy. I don't know, but maybe that's the answer. He acts unhappy so much of the time. Yet he wants to stay here. He says he doesn't ever want to go back to the Home."

"And we certainly won't take him back as long as he says that."

Then Davy came into the Loomas home.

It was the last day of August when Rose answered the phone.

"It's me again. Sister Lora. I don't mean to be intruding—but—please understand. I'm only interested. Little Davy—how is he doing?"

"Just fine, Lora. Just fine. He's well. He acts happy. Eats and sleeps good, and we all adore him. In fact, Lesa and Janet could easily quarrel over who's to do this or that for him."

"Dennis too?"

13

"Well—well, I'd say 'adore' is a bit exaggerated for him. They get along. You know what a problem Dennis has with jealousy. But we're working on it. It takes time. I hope Davy doesn't notice it too much."

"Has he forgotten me, do you think?"

"Indeed not, Sister Lora. And we don't intend to let Davy forget you. After all, Lora, I think you've instilled some of your loving personality into him."

"Now, Rose. I didn't ask to draw anything like that out of you! Really."

"I know you didn't, Lora, but I mean it. It's a month today we got him. And by the way, unless our plans fail, we're all coming over Sunday."

"Oh, good! You mean here to the Home?"

"Yes. And we'll bring a picnic lunch along, and you're going to eat with us on the lawn, or we'll go someplace not too far away. Can you be with us?"

"You mean it?"

"That's what I said, Lora. You'll see if Davy's forgotten Sister LoLo. Of course he hasn't. What makes you suppose he has?"

She laughed. "Is he still objecting to the black bed?"

"No, Lora. And say, we want little Leon in on our picnic too, so the boys can play together. Davy hasn't forgotten Leon either. I believe he misses him too."

"How sweet of you to think of that! You know, Leon cried and cried that first night Davy was gone. We had a hard time explaining to him."

"Sometime we'll arrange for Leon to come out to the farm and stay all day, and overnight if Martha and Melvin agree."

"How nice of you to think of it, Rose! The two always got along beautifully together. They grew up like brothers."

"I know. Call again, Lora. Call any time you wonder about anything."

In less than an hour Rose answered the phone again.

"Where's Davy, Rose?"

"Who's speaking?"

"It's Melvin. Where is Davy?"

"Outside playing in the sandbox. Happy as—"

"Listen, Rose," cut in Mr. Kolb. "I don't want to frighten you, but take the boy inside right away."

"Why?"

"A well-dressed man in a black Cadillac just drove away and headed south. I'm uneasy."

"What about? Tell me." Rose Loomas grabbed the mouthpiece.

"He came here and asked if we had a little boy named David Grant. I said we did, but not now. He asked where he was. I refused to tell. I didn't like his manner. He made me suspicious. I told him he was in a good home. No more. He said he was given orders to locate him, that it was extremely important. He wouldn't give me his name or address. He got quite indignant. Get that child and keep him inside, Rose. I'm afraid he might try to kidnap him."

"What! Oh, Melvin!"

"Well, there's been mystery surrounding that child since the night he was left here."

"Oh, Melvin! Pray."

"Yes. Are you there, Rose?"

"Yes."

"Sister Lora is in her room crying. Listen, Rose. Are you there? Don't tell Janet or Dennis. We *dare* not let them or the children here know anything about this."

"Of course not."

"Davy." Rose gathered the child up into her arms. "Come to the kitchen with me, honey. You can—can help me make some ginger cookies. You can put on—" She stumbled and all but fell. "Lesa, come inside a minute. I want to tell you something."

It was no illusion. A shiny black car *was* coming up the long lane.

CHAPTER 3

Fernaig B. Grant, prominent hotel manager in Glasgow, Scotland, had a second pride, his three attractive daughters. Shana, the youngest, was considered by many to display not only the sweetest disposition, but the prettiest face.

The oldest of the sisters, Bernice, married a well-to-do hotel executive, Lewis McCawlis. After touring the United States and Canada on their wedding trip they decided to locate in the States. In a surprisingly short time McCawlis was manager of not one but three large hotels in Columbia, South Carolina. Bernice's letters home always painted a glowing and growing success in business.

Hazel, second of the Grant daughters, did not need more than one invitation from brother-in-law Lewis to join them in Columbia and take a good-paying job in one of his hotels. Since Hazel was a sensible, levelheaded, intelligent young lady, her parents left the final decision to her. After all, they were confident of one thing: she would be in good hands and under careful supervision, for both Bernice and Lewis were natural-born leaders, and both had definite standards of living. Bernice would be like a mother to Hazel. So as soon as she obtained her passport and visa, Hazel sailed for America.

Seven weeks later came the surprise. Shana, then a budding fourteen, read the letter to her gasping parents, as the three sat at the dinner table.

"Dear Father, Mother, and Shana: I hope you receive this

16

letter before Bernice's arrives. I'm married. It all came about so quickly; that's why you didn't hear about a romance. I met Bruce at the hotel desk. It was love from that first meeting. No, I never believed in love at first sight before, but I do now. He is tall, has black, wavy hair, and is as handsome as it's necessary for a good husband to be. No matter what others say, it's so. Bruce is not rich—not yet—but he has a job as salesman for a farm implement company, and he loves me. That is the important thing, even if Bernice disagrees. He is kind and courteous, every inch a gentleman. And he makes me happy. We're going to live in Philadelphia, his home town. He's going to get a job that won't take him away from home.

"Bernice and Lewis are quite disgusted because I left them so soon. But when love strikes, that's it. And this is real. I'll soon be twenty, remember. We'll send you a picture before long. We had a simple wedding in a parsonage, performed by a nice minister Bruce knows. As soon as we get located, I'll send you my address. We are very happy. Love from happy newlyweds. Bruce and Hazel Middendorf."

Mrs. Grant tried not to, but cry a while she did, and hard.

She looked with disappointment at Shana. "Aren't you going to cry too?" she asked brokenly.

"Why cry?"

"Or faint or something?"

"Faint? Who wants to faint?"

"Well, react. Say something. There you two both sit and stare at me while I cry."

Shana shrugged her shoulders. "I don't know what to say, Mother," she began feebly. "I'm speechless. But it's done, and no matter what I do or say will make her Hazel Grant again."

Mrs. Grant turned to her husband. "React, Fernaig. What on earth are you thinking? Don't be a mute."

"I am thinking," replied Fernaig, tapping his fork nervously on the side of his water glass. "You just never know what your own daughter will do, once she goes abroad. But," he added after a pause, "if that's what she actually wants, and if she's happy,

why go into hysterics? It's disappointing, of course, but—well—"
His sentence dangled on that evasive swinging word.

"But so soon, Fernaig!" cried Mrs. Grant. "I can't imagine
why Bernice didn't stop this. How can a girl her age or any age
learn to know a perfect stranger that soon? And an American at
that! And a farmer! A cowboy, for all we know. Half the American young men are."

"You don't actually know," chided her husband gently.
"She'll live and learn," he added, wiping his trim, slightly gray-
ing mustache. "She'll learn plenty, I dare say."

"Bruce," muttered Shana in undertones. "Bruce Middendorf. What a name to be married to!" She gazed out the window
and watched a pair of happy robins hopping about. "Be it unto
her. Hazel is Mrs. Bruce Middendorf already. Whew!"

"What did you say?" asked Mrs. Grant.

"Nothing, Mother. Nothing."

Four years more and Shana, tall and strikingly beautiful,
was as efficient a hotel housekeeper as was her father a manager.
The two worked together as a team. Having grown up in the
business, Shana had never shown interest in any other type of
work. Because she loved her job, her pleased, proud father un-
grudgingly gave her the top wage she deserved. At eighteen
Shana knew how, when, where, and what quantity to order of
hotel linens, flatware, china, blankets, draperies, kitchen uten-
sils, or any item in the category. Best of all (much to her father's
admiration) she knew which salesmen to stall or tell off.

Lewis and Bernice never invited Shana (after what Hazel
did) to come and work for them. But they did quite tactfully
suggest it would be both profitable and educational (as well as
pleasurable) if she'd come to the States on a visit, primarily to take
back to Glasgow fresh ideas about hotel furnishings and manage-
ment.

The idea pleased Shana more than a little. In fact, she had
secretly been dreaming about just such a trip, but hesitated to
mention it for fear her parents would object. Now that the idea

was proposed by big sister Bernice, the ice was broken.

"Just think, Father," Shana began, "we'd all profit."

"It could be a profitable experience if you'd make it so," he replied.

"Oh! Then you mean I can go?"

"If you come back."

"Come back?"

"You would?"

"Of course I would. Why wouldn't I?"

"How about Hazel?"

"But I'm not Hazel."

"But—"

"But what? Say it, Father."

"Well, you just never know what a girl will do once she gets 'way over there."

"Well, Father," suggested Shana confidingly, "by the way Hazel writes she didn't do so bad. They're not rich like Bernice and Lewis, but they're happy, unless she doesn't mean what she writes. I can hardly wait to see her children."

All the while Mrs. Grant stood listening to the conversation. She could keep still no longer. "Shana, you don't honestly mean you think Hazel—"

"Please, Mother dear," interrupted Shana. "Don't imagine a lot of impossible things and get all excited. I promise you if you let me go to America I'll come back and come back single."

Fernaig Grant eyed his youngest daughter from head to toe. "Shana," he remarked, "you won't be the least attractive young lady that gets off the boat in New York City."

Tossing her head slightly, Shana laughed a rippling, musical laugh. Her blue eyes danced and soft waves of her auburn hair fell playfully around her high forehead. "I might even pick up a few American beauty hints." With gaiety she tripped across the living room and reached for her hat. "Maybe you won't recognize me when I get back." She laughed teasingly.

"You may pick up beauty hints if you like," blinked her father, "even if you don't need any. But remember now the main

19

reason for your going, young lady—you're to gather hotel hints. Understand?"

"You make me laugh, Father. You are so in earnest, aren't you? I'll come back simply loaded with ideas. Oh," she dashed toward the door, "I'm so excited! I'm going to write to— No, I won't. I'll surprise Hazel. Just walk up to Mrs. Bruce Middendorf's door and knock. Won't her eyes pop? And I'm not going to tell Bernice until I get there either. Call up. Oh, won't it be fun? Don't you write to them, Mother."

Four weeks before Shana's sailing date, lovely, attractive, active Mrs. Grant died, after an illness of only thirty minutes. The doctors said it was a heart attack. Although it was a severe shock, Shana's father insisted she take the trip as planned.

"It's just one of those fateful, unexpected things of this life," he told her. "Nothing but time will heal my broken heart. It won't be any easier for me to see you leave later. I want you to go ahead and tell the girls all about how it happened, and how sweet she looked in her casket. I'll get along. I'll keep busy. And don't you go and worry about me over there. I think July is the best month for an ocean trip, and I want you to go."

Shana was standing alone at the iron railing on the top deck of the "Pride of Glasgow" watching the changing splendors of the setting sun on the glassy ocean horizon when she felt a gentle tap on her left shoulder.

"Mr. Gray," she exclaimed.

"Miss Grant."

"But where— I—I—didn't know you were on this boat too."

"I got on at Southampton."

"Oh? Are you bound for New York too?"

"Yes, I am. You're not alone?"

"Why not?" smiled Shana. "My parents gave their permission. Surely you don't suppose I'm a runaway." She laughed softly. "Do you think I'm too young to go to the States alone?"

He leaned on the railing and looked with absorbing interest into Shana's pretty, wind-blown face. "Well, now," he began, measuring carefully each word, "if you want my honest opinion, little Miss Grant, yes, I do. You don't mind if I call you Shana, do you?"

She smiled and looked out over the water. "That is my name, Mr. Gray."

"And mine happens to be Brandon," he laughed genially. "You know that; so—well, let's be like good old-time friends the rest of the trip. I never dreamed when I last saw you in your father's hotel back in Glasgow I'd meet you like this. Tell me all about it. Is it a vacation?"

"Partly. Mostly an educational trip."

He never shifted his gaze. "Please explain, studious young lady."

"I'm going to visit my two sisters, of course, but primarily to learn how the Americans operate and furnish their hotels."

"I might have guessed."

"Now you're the very person who can give me some pointers on where to go, and what to take note of, Mr. Salesman Gray."

He took Shana by the arm. "Come. Let's go and sit in the lounge. It's getting a bit too chilly and windy out here, isn't it?"

They went inside together and found an unoccupied settee beside a handsome planted palm.

"I suppose you received that last order of tablecloths and napkins?" he began.

"Yes, and Father was pleased. He likes the lines you carry."

"He has taught you a great deal about the business, I see."

"I really love the work. It's practically all our family cares about. It's in our blood, I guess."

The two talked for an hour.

He found her the next forenoon among dozens of other passengers basking in the warm sunshine. He took advantage of the chair beside her as soon as it was vacated. They talked of countless unrelated things and subjects. They strolled the deck together; they sipped tea together, played chess, sat in the lounge, and listened to the orchestra play. Thus three pleasant days passed swiftly.

The fourth day it rained.

"You know, Shana," he began, easing closer to her on the settee in the lounge, "I can think of something very nice that could happen. Guess what I'm thinking."

"Give you another big order?" she asked, scarcely looking at him.

He chuckled softly. "Far from that, Shana dear."

She glanced up sharply.

"I—I always did think you were a pretty girl, Shana," he ventured.

"Mr. Gray."

"I thought I told you to call me Brandon. Don't start that Mr. Gray again after these pleasant days together." He smiled into her face. "What I must tell you is that you're a very, very beautiful young lady, Shana."

She turned.

"Don't look away," he said softly. "Surely you shouldn't object if I tell you. Don't you know that you're very attractive?"

She shook her head.

"But you are," he insisted, "and what's more, you're intelligent. And I think—" he touched her one hand—"I think a hotel salesman and a hotel housekeeper ought to do something special to celebrate before we get to New York."

"If you mean go to the bar, Mr. Gray, I don't drink."

"I didn't mean that, Shana. I—I don't drink either. Seldom. I meant—look at me, dear." He pressed her one slender hand between both of his warm ones. "I want to tell you I'm in love."

"With—with—"

"Yes, with you, Shana."

"No." She tried to draw her hand away, but he held it with firmness.

"Don't try to get away like a wild little frightened bird. Listen, Shana, we've known each other for years. I'm not a stranger. Why are you so surprised that I should tell you I love you?"

"I—I just never supposed," she stammered.

"But start supposing it now. Because I do. Every day you're growing sweeter and more beautiful. I just knew this morning I'd have to tell you today."

Shana's long lashes brushed her flushed cheeks.

"Does it seem so strange and improbable to you?"

She nodded.

"But it's not unreasonable, Shana dear. To me it seems only natural, and right. I—I wish we'd get engaged on this trip."

"Engaged?"

"You've never thought of such a thing?"

She made no answer.

"Or is there another?"

"Oh, no, Mr. Gray. I'm very free."

He smiled. "Then don't call me Mr. Gray, darling. Please. Listen. Love is the most wonderful thing in all the world. And when two people are interested in the same things like we are, it's only natural we'd be drawn together. Isn't it? I'm crazy about you. I'm wild about you. I know now I'll never be satisfied un-til— Shana!"

She was on her feet now. "Please, Brandon. Let me go to my cabin and—and be alone."

"All right, darling." He led her out of the lounge. "You go to your cabin and I'll go to mine, and we'll both think about love. And remember, this isn't the first time we've met. Your father knows me. Your mother knows me too."

"My mother is dead, Brandon."

"Dead? I didn't know, dear. Oh, I'm so sorry, Shana. So sorry."

"And my father. I—I promised him—"

She tore herself away, and hurried down the long corridor. Brandon watched her until she was out of sight.

23

CHAPTER 4

The instant he saw her the next morning, Brandon Gray felt more sure of his winning. Never had he seen Shana more radiantly beautiful, more ladylike, more inviting. He hurried to meet her, escorted her into the spacious dining room, and seated her at a table set for two at the far end of the room.

He launched discussions on this and that, and things he wasn't one whit interested in, before easing gently into the one uppermost in his thoughts. Shana was less timid, more responsive, and ever so much brighter than the day before. Brandon's handsome face glowed with enthusiasm. He was thrilled with his progress. He was thrilled with her growing loveliness.

"And I'm not one of those cowboy Americans either," he laughed heartily.

"No," agreed Shana, smiling sweetly.

He quivered with renewed boldness. "I'm a grown man who has been all over the world. And I've seen lots of attractive women, Shana dear, but never one to even compare to you."

She sipped her coffee.

"Tell me, darling," he said after beaming on her with vivid fortitude, "please tell me what you think of me."

"What I think?" She hestitated. "Well, Brandon, I'd say you are a very smart Englishman who has a most fantastic way of trying to charm a much younger person like—like me."

"To be sure," he admitted, winking. "What good is a salesman unless he can persuade, convince, sell? I'm bound to persist until I've sold myself to you. You've never been disappointed in any goods I represented yet, have you?"

She shook her head.

"Didn't you tell me your oldest sister married a hotel manager who is doing very well? Your father wouldn't object. He knows me."

Shana sat in deep thought. How could this be wrong? He was right. Salesman Brandon Gray. So handsome. So intelligent. So experienced. So at ease anywhere in the world. So efficient. And to think, of all the beautiful women and girls he'd met, he wanted her?

That day and the next the two were together constantly. Shana found herself living in a strange, new, tantalizingly sweet dreamworld. One moment she might be caught in a turbulent, disturbing crosscurrent of thoughts, but in the very next she was floating on clouds of fantastic ecstasy and bliss. She had never heard, read, or experienced anything like it. This *must* be love. The good fates had brought them together. No one had planned it so. How could it be a mistake to get engaged? Wasn't she next door to nineteen? Almost twenty? What if Brandon was seven years older? It should be so. Oh, to think he had chosen her! To be loved! To be wanted! This was true love, wonderful beyond any words to express.

Shana's new-found happiness was intoxicating.

"I'll get you the ring first thing when we get to New York," he told her. "Never has a happier man tasted of life."

"You know, I promised my father I'd come back single. He can't forget how Hazel did, you know. But he didn't say I couldn't come back engaged." Beaming, she snuggled close to him.

It was evening. The two were on the deck just outside the parlor door. The orchestra was playing the "Moonlight Sonata."

Brandon folded Shana in his arms and kissed her affectionately. "Darling," he said, "when we get to New York, I want to buy three rings."

"Three? For me?"

"No, dear. Two for you, and one for me."

"What do you mean?"

"What could I mean, sweetheart? I mean, let's get married."

Shana drew back. "Married?"

"Yes, married, Shana. Why wait? When we know we love each other. Wait for what?"

"But—but, Brandon," she gasped. "I promised Father I'd come back."

"That was a hasty, foolish promise, my love. Every girl makes a similar promise to her parents."

"But, Brandon," she insisted, "he's expecting me. He needs me."

"Not half as much as I do, darling."

"But you don't understand, Brandon. He does. Now that Mother is gone."

"But, darling, that's in our favor. He'll likely get married again."

"Never. Oh, how can you say those words? Mother's been gone only five weeks."

"But sooner or later he will, Shana."

"Never."

"Your father isn't an old man yet. Hundreds of women will be after him."

"You don't know my father, Brandon Gray. He's attached to Mother. I can't break my promise and disappoint him. He'd never get over—"

"Yes, he would, my dear little Shana. Listen to me." He held her out at arm's length and looked her straight in the face with eyes direct and expressive. "Your own personal happiness is what you can't afford to let slip. Your dear father, bless his heart, has experienced his term of married happiness. And you? You deserve yours. You're young only once, Shana. Right now is the best, the wisest, the greatest time in your life to start enjoying married bliss."

Shana caught her breath and held it. He tightened his grip on her shoulders and put his face closer to hers. "Forgive me,

26

precious, if I seem hasty, but I'm madly in love with you. There isn't one earthly reason why we couldn't and shouldn't get married when we reach New York. We can rent a furnished apartment. I can work the New York area and come home every night. I wouldn't think of leaving you alone in that big city."

"You wouldn't go back to Scotland?"

"Not without you, darling. Of course we'd go together sometime. I'd want to show you off."

"But my promise, Brandon."

"Is that all that stands in our way?"

"All? That's a big thing, Brandon. I'm all my father has now."

"Oh, you conscientious little angel," he said, pressing her to himself. "You'll make a wonderful wife." He kissed her. "Let me take all the blame. I'll call your father by phone and explain to him."

"No."

"I don't care if it would cost fifty or a hundred."

"Please, no."

"I'll send him a cable."

"No."

"Then let's keep it secret until we go back together."

To this Shana did not say no.

She was caught in the whirlpool of romance and there was no getting out. She was drenched, dizzy, dissolved in the delights of love.

Plans for their immediate marriage were settled before the "Pride of Glasgow" entered New York harbor. If Hazel had a quiet, simple marriage, why shouldn't Shana? Her father had taken that shock with grace and he would this one, if and when he learned of it. She would write to him her interesting, new, profit-making findings. Shana steeled herself, refusing to dwell on the broken promise.

At the desk, after she had signed her name for the license, Shana felt a sudden weakening inside. She grabbed the edge of the desk.

"What's wrong, dear?" Brandon eyed her closely. "You look pale."

She shook her head. "I don't know what's wrong," she whispered feebly. "Just excited, I guess." She caught hold of his arm. "I feel sort of wicked." She tried to laugh.

Brandon looked hurt. "Wicked? Shana! Why should you? Don't tell me you'll back out now?"

"Oh, no. I didn't mean that. We've got to go through with it. I—I love you." She cleared her throat. "Believe me, I do. And I'd never be happy without you. Not now. But can't you understand why?"

He frowned. He fumbled awkwardly for an answer to this insupportable question. Suddenly he found one. "We're going to start a family of our own, darling," he tried desperately to sound calm, "the way the Almighty intended. We're going to be a new family of Grays."

For a moment Shana felt herself floating on a lonely, un-anchored, unclaimed island. But Brandon's eyes so close, so direct and serious, and his strong arm around her brought her back to a confident standstill. She watched him pay the clerk.

"Come, my precious. I said I'd take you back to Glasgow someday to show you off, and I will."

The third-floor apartment was small and moderately furnished. Far from what Shana had been used to, but she didn't expect to start on that level. She was happy and satisfied. Brandon came home each evening, jovial and pleased over his commission totals, and if this continued, they could soon move to a better apartment. Six times in three weeks they ate out in hotel restaurants where Brandon had sold accessories, and each time he took her on a tour of the buildings. Every Saturday night he brought her lovely flowers from a nearby florist.

Shana did send her father a cablegram to let him know she arrived safely. Nothing more. She could not bring herself to it.

"Brandon," she began one evening. "I just must write to Hazel. I'll break the news to her first and wait for her reaction before I tell Bernice."

"Are you afraid of your sister Bernice?"

"Not afraid. Not that," she repeated as if trying to convince herself. "What could she do to me? I'm married to you."

"That's the way I like to hear you talk," commented Brandon. "Don't ever allow anyone to disturb our happiness. Remember, we're a family unit of our own now." He looked up from the *London Daily News* he was reading. "How soon will dinner be ready?"

"As soon as you get washed, dear."

"These articles each day about Churchill are fascinating. Listen to this. Though he began his parliamentary career as a Conservative, he won great renown in the House of Commons as a Liberal. Undersecretary for the Colonies. Today the Right Honorable Winston Leonard Spencer Churchill is the youngest man ever to hold the office of First Lord of the Admiralty in the Asquith Ministry."

"Go get washed, dear. You'll have to explain to me what all that means, my very right honorable lord Brandon Gray."

In exactly one week Shana had a reply to her intitial newsbreaking letter. Brandon found it in their first-floor mailbox when he came home for lunch.

"No secrets now," he said teasingly as she tore it open. "Read it out loud."

"Of course I will. I don't believe in secrets between husbands and wives."

Brandon tossed his hat across the room. "Neither do I. Come. Sit on my knee to read."

"Very well, my love." She perched herself and drew a long deep breath. "Dear little sister," she began.

"Well," remarked Brandon. "That starts out sweet enough."

"Now please don't interrupt me again." She pressed her fingers on his lips and laughed. "Now I know how surprised you were when I wrote home I was married. I'm very happy for you and I'm sure you have a good husband. But I didn't even know you were coming over. You and Brandon must come and see us soon. We will have a room ready for you. The children danced up and down and clapped their hands when I tried to explain what your letter was all about. Barbie talks everything and Vicky is learning fast. Little Darlene is a doll."

"What?" exclaimed Shana. "Darlene? Hazel has three children already?"

"Read on." Brandon squirmed impatiently.

"She's two weeks old Sunday. Looks like you, Shana. Bruce is terribly anxious to meet you and your husband. Brandon sounds like a high-class name. But no wonder, coming from England.

"Bruce has a good job and gradually we're getting ahead. Of course these three children haven't been small items to pay for, but they're worth every sacrifice. We are one happy family. You just must come soon.

"Have you heard from Bernice? She must be quite a society fan. She seldom writes, but when she does, her letters are full of parties and entertaining, and trips she takes with Lewis. They stopped here once for ten minutes on their way to a convention in New York City. You should have seen the car they had. Even a chauffeur. Bernice favors Mother more all the time. What does Father have to say about your marriage?

"Now please, let's keep in touch. And do come soon. We plan to get you a gift."

"Well," said Shana, eyes glittering, "that's your sister-in-law Hazel."

"Nice letter. Very nice. Doesn't sound as though you've cut yourself off from your family."

"How soon can we go see them?"

"Maybe next year."

"Next year?" exclaimed Shana.

Brandon picked up the *London News*. "I meant next month, honey." Promptly he began scanning the paper.

CHAPTER 5

Sister Bernice let her feelings have a respectful cooling-off period before she answered Shana's shocking announcement. This she did, however, only upon her husband's insistence.

"But, Lewis," fumed Bernice, "that child is either out of her mind or she's lost all respect for her family, or she's cruelly disillusioned, and I mean to find out which."

"Let her find it out herself."

"Oh, Lewis, I could scream. I could pull my hair. Am I the only daughter of Fernaig B. Grant who married a decent man?" The cords in her neck stood out. "I call this a disgrace to the family."

"But you can't call Bruce an indecent man. Modify your words a little, Bernice. Give Shana a chance. If she's happy with Gray, let her keep on believing she's happy. Maybe she really is."

"She just might have a raft of children too, like Hazel's starting out to have."

"Now calm yourself," admonished Lewis McCawlis. "Somebody has to replenish the earth. If every woman liked children as much as you do, think of all the doctors and business concerns that would have to go out of business."

"You're surely not sticking up for my sisters," Bernice said with sullen sentiment.

"I'm neither defending nor condemning. It's somewhat disappointing, I'll agree, but we'll live our lives and let them live

31

theirs. Better not write back to Shana until you simmer down."

"I'm going to answer at once."

"Make her wait," blinked Lewis. "I'd make her wait."

"All right," consented Bernice. "Wait and wonder she will. And in the meantime I'm going to write a few other letters."

A month, then two, rolled by, but Hazel and her family did not entertain the much-looked-for newlyweds from New York City. Shana wrote to explain that Brandon's business was taking him now to cities beyond New York and he couldn't always come home over weekends. But they would be coming some happy day. It was unbearably lonesome when he was gone, and so she sometimes went along with a little, old widowed neighbor to her church.

But Shana was really glad Brandon was away when the letter came from her father. It was not a mean letter. It wasn't sarcastic. Nor denouncing. Not one word of disapproval could she find anywhere on the single sheet. But for some reason his few tender words made her curl up in a ball on the sofa and cry like a child. He did not as much as infer she had broken a promise. She was confident he had restrained himself. What pierced her so sharply were the unwritten thoughts that she imagined he was thinking. Oh, if she could only have a good, long talk with Hazel and find out who had told him!

Then, after seven more weeks, the letter came from Bernice. Shana opened it with an uneasiness Brandon could not help noticing.

"Shall I read it to you?" he asked. She held the letter without unfolding it and after a brief silence handed it to him. She tried to rub the foreboding notions out of her mind with the palm of her hand.

"Do you have a headache?" he asked.

"A little. Never mind. Go ahead."

"Dear Shana," he read. "I guess you thought you'd go one better than Hazel, didn't you? Mother always wanted her girls to have nice big weddings and write-ups in the paper like I had.

32

When Lewis goes to New York on business, I'm going to come along and drop in to see you. So if you change your address, be sure to let me know at once. Bernice."

"Well," scowled Brandon with indignation, "that's short and icy. Your sister Bernice," he grabbed Shana by both shoulders and faced her squarely, "is not coming here to give you any of her advice, my little lady."

"No, Brandon," faltered Shana. "No, of course not."

Another month passed.

It was on one of those weekends when Brandon was out of town that the second letter came, postmarked Columbia, South Carolina.

"Dear Shana. You had better get your marriage annulled at once." Shana shook. "That Brandon Gray you say you married has a wife in London." She turned white—white as the paper in her trembling hands. "And he has not been granted a divorce. I got this information straight."

Shana crumpled in a heap on the floor.

Years could have passed before she came to herself. Gasping, struggling, moaning, she managed to pull herself to a slumping position on the sofa. Everything in the room was madly out of balance, out of proportion. Even the clock on the shelf was ticking out of rhythm. Rain splashing on the windowpane behind her sounded like the tears from a million brides waking from a fool's dizzy paradise to a horrible reality of life. Her blue eyes became hot volcanic pools of scalding misery. She tried to move her arms. They felt heavy, immovably heavy. Her whole body felt as though it had been cut on, hammered on, chiseled on by ruthless, heartless sculptors.

The letter lay on the floor where she had fallen. It looked dirty, black, scorched by cruel fire. Every object she tried to place, every thought she tried to think ran together into sordid senselessness. Ashes. Everything turned to ashes before her eyes. How long she sat there she did not know. Nor did it matter. She did not want to go into the bedroom. That corrupt bed would hoot at her now with maddening hootings. She did not want to look at his clothes. Brandon's detestable clothes some other wife had a right to look at and handle. She did not want to look at the chocolate cake she had baked with such joyful anticipation of his eating. She would give it to the neighbor's dogs and cats. Or the rats on the city dump would fight over its sour, smelly sweetness.

She stared at the two rings on her finger. Hollow bands of lies. One melted to the other. Transparent hopes. Vanished dreams. Shattered life. Slowly she pulled both off and let them drop into the crack at the end of the sofa. Bare finger. Bare hand. Bare heart and soul. Shana Grant, stripped bare of everything worth living for.

She was still sitting there at three a.m. when Brandon came in. He stood stock-still in the doorway, mouth gaping.

"Shana!"

But before he could say more, something unexpected, a power, a mysterious strength she never knew she possessed came over Shana. She got to her feet, and with eyes burning she pointed to the crumpled letter on the floor.

"Pick that up." Her voice was frigid. "Read it. Read it," she repeated.

Stunned, Brandon obeyed.

She could see the paper shake in his unsteady hands.

His glance was grim when he raised his eyelids. A smitten expression erased the first blank one.

"Answer the charge." Shana spoke in a low, dry tone, almost inaudible.

Brandon's shoulders sagged. He bit the inside of his cheek until blood oozed from one corner of his mouth. All the color left his face. He stared at her several torturous, clock-ticking seconds. His chest rose and fell three times before he spoke, and when he did, his voice was cracked and unnatural.

"I—" he stammered. "I cannot—deny it."

Shana stood erect. She slightly raised her head and her voice.

"Then get your things and leave," she said. "I mean at once. I am not staying in this place with you for one single moment

34

longer than it takes for you to pack up what belongs to you."
She did not move an inch. "You brought me here and I'll stay
until I see you out."

"You mean—" he gasped, "you mean—" he stepped closer—
"we can't even talk this over!"

"What is there to talk over if it's true?"

"But—but she's crazy," panted Brandon. "She's—she's in an
institution. She's the same as dead."

"The same as?"

"Yes."

"I'm the one who is the same as dead." Shana fed him the
words from her closely set jaws. "You've killed me with your
poisonous love words and cruel promises. Get out of my sight
before I call the law."

"Oh, Shana! You wouldn't!"

"I wouldn't want to, Mr. Gray. But I will if I have to."

He lunged toward her with outstretched arms. "But, Shana,
my dear. I love you. Margarit is crazy, I tell you. I had to put
her away. She's a doper. She was driving me insane. I had to."

Shana backed away. "Don't you dare touch me with your
little finger. You've deceived me, Brandon Gray. If you've deceived me about this, how do I know you don't have women in
other cities too? Is that why you're away on weekends?"

"Never," he shouted. His face got red, almost purplish red.
"Don't you ever accuse me of that. Margarit is the only other
woman I ever—ever had anything to do with. But the doctors
said she's incurable. You don't know what I put up with—with
her—for five horrible years."

"But why didn't you tell me about this? You're deceitful.
You lied. You—"

Brandon wilted. He shook with sudden sobs. "Darling, I
couldn't bring myself to tell you. You were so sweet, so young, so
innocent and beautiful." He stepped closer, holding out both
arms.

"Don't you touch me, Brandon."

He cried the harder. "Oh, Shana, darling. I—I don't know—

I can't explain. I—I should have told you. I'm sorry you found out. I—I thought if we lived here—well, no one would ever know. Oh, that dirty, snooty sister of yours. How did she—"

"Stop," cried Shana. "Don't say it." Her voice was clear and definite. "It's a good thing my snooty, snoopy sister did discover your dirty trick. You had no right to marry me. It's not even legal, and you knew it all the time. Go get all your things together and get out of here."

"You mean you won't even help me pack?"

"I don't want to touch any of your things."

"But, Shana," cried Brandon, "have a little pity. If I go back and get a divorce, won't you take me back?"

She stood frozen. Speechless.

"Oh, you little tiger," he said. "You awful little tiger. I took you for a lamb. How can you be so cruel to me? I loved you. In spite of everything you think I am. I never loved Margarit. I never loved anyone but you. It's all a horrible mistake I ever met her. I admit I did you wrong. I admit I should have gotten a divorce, but they're hard to get in England."

He waited. His hot breath came in great bunches. "Life won't be worth living without you. I'll go back and try to get a divorce."

Silence.

"Then won't you take me back, darling?"

"I doubt if I could ever trust you again."

"We'll have a real wedding. Get married all over, darling. Anywhere, anyway you say. Surely, surely you care a little, a little for me yet."

Shana swayed. Her lips quivered.

"No matter what you say to me, I still love you. I trust *you*. I've been bad, but I want to be a good, upright man. Believe me. That's why I love a good woman like you."

He stepped closer. She stepped back.

"All right. I won't touch you if you hate me so. But by God's help I'll get that divorce and I will take you in my arms again. You little tiger, you."

Heavily Shana sank on the sofa and buried her face in both hands.

CHAPTER 6

Shana did not look up. She could hear him cross the room and enter the bedroom. She could hear dresser drawers being opened and closed. She could hear emptied wire clothes hangers clanking against one another. She could hear his low, pitiful moans. She could hear Brandon blowing his nose. She knotted her feelings tighter.

With a bag in each hand he finally came out, and stood at the door, haggard, dejected, but still handsome. "Won't you come and open the door for me, dear?" His voice sounded worn, old, uncertain.

Without a word Shana crossed the room and opened the door.

"You realize I'll have to find a place to stay until I can sail? You realize how cruel this is?"

"I—I know," she whispered without looking up. "I'm sorry for that."

He stood there, eyes swimming in tears. "The rent," he said, trying to control himself, "is paid until the fifteenth of next month. I put a hundred dollars on the dresser for you."

A moment of dead silence elapsed before Shana glanced up. Sudden, uncontrollable tears blinded her.

"We must keep in touch, Shana." His voice was unsteady, low, hurt, but tender. Meltingly tender.

She lowered her gaze to his feet. She bit her lip.

He dropped both bags and moved very close to her.

Shana gripped her shaking hands behind her.

"Darling," he cried. "I realize now I've wronged you, but—" he shook with sobs—"as heaven's above me," he clenched both fists, "I'm not all wicked. Surely you love me a little bit yet. Won't—won't you take me back and marry me again when I get back?" Hot tears streamed down his sullen cheeks.

Shana backed against the door casing. All her strength was leaving. Her entire body shook. No. No, she would not let him touch her. But blinding tears streamed uncontrolled.

Suddenly she cried out. "Don't ask me that. I can't think straight now." She shook with sobs.

All at once she found herself crushed against his shaking body. She felt his hot tears drenching her hair. She felt him kissing her forehead again and again.

He released her. He picked up the bags.

She caught his arm. "Brandon," she cried, "I'll take you back if—if you bring a divorce. I—I mean a legal paper to prove and to show me. Then we'll get married all over. I mean a real church wedding."

"Darling." He grabbed her in his arms again. He kissed her on the lips. "Oh, darling, I love you. I love you. I love no one but you."

"Then hurry back," she sobbed. "Oh, Brandon! You've been so awful mean to me. This shock is killing me! I—I don't want to—I don't want to—I *don't want* to love you at all now but—I do—I do—I still love you. I can't help it, I do. I do. Oh, go away quick before I go crazy. I love you so."

Brandon stumbled down the dimly lighted stairs. He all but fell. All the way he could hear Shana sobbing convulsively.

After he was out of sight, her great fountain of tears broke loose. There was no stopping all night.

Shana told her inquiring neighbors that Mr. Gray had gone to London on important business and wasn't sure when he'd return.

"My dear, you're pining away from loneliness," ventured the

little widowed neighbor one day. "You're more peaked every time I see you."

She could not bring herself to telling anyone. Not even Hazel. She would bear this awful shame and grief alone. Alone. As long as possible. Alone.

Every day she scanned the *London Daily News*, searching with special care for a court column on divorces asked and granted. For three long months she searched frantically, but found no "Brandon Gray vs. Margarit Gray."

Twice in the three months Shana received an international money draft of fifty dollars. Both came by registered mail. No letter accompanied, preceded or followed either. Then at long last one did come. With mingled hope and dread she opened it.

"Dear Shana: Divorces in England, as I told you, are very hard to get. [Shana could not hold the paper steady.] My chances are very slim. [Shana found a chair and sat down before she'd fall.] I've enlisted in the army before they draft me. [Shana burst into tears.] I'm terribly sorry for everything. I still love you. Brandon."

That same evening between heartbreaking sobs that racked her whole body, Shana penned a short letter to Hazel. "Let me know if it would be suitable for me to come and stay with you for a few months. Brandon is in England and I'm awfully, awfully lonesome."

Hazel did not write an answer. She sent a telegram.

Bruce would have been at the depot to meet Shana, but they did not know which train she was coming on. Two days passed and no Shana, no letter, no call. Hazel instructed Barbie to play by the front window to watch.

"I have a funny feeling something is wrong," Hazel told Bruce. "Why did Brandon go to England to be gone for several months?"

"I hope we find out for your sake. Do try not to fret so. It could upset the children."

No one was watching at the window when the taxi stopped at 1357 Pinewood Avenue at 2:45 a.m.

40

"Is this the place, Ma'am?" asked the cab driver.

"I was never here before," said Shana. "If it's 1357, it's supposed to be the house I want."

"Looks like everyone is in bed, Ma'am. They expecting you? Shall I wait until you find out?"

"It would be kind of you, sir. It's kind of you to carry my bags up too. Thanks, sir."

Timidly, fearfully Shana pressed the doorbell. Her hand shook. Nervously she pulled her coat together. A dim hall light was burning and then—then through the glass pane in the door she recognized her, the one coming. The door opened.

"Shana," cried Hazel throwing her arms around her sister and kissing her. "At last—at last. Thanks, mister, we'll take care of her bags. Oh, Shana, it's wonderful to have you come—why, Shana—Shana—here, give me your coat. You never told me. How soon?"

Shana lost control of her emotions. She covered her face with her handkerchief and cried as though her heart were broken.

"Something wrong?" asked Hazel. "Sit here on this chair and tell me, Shana." She put her arm around her sister's shoulder.

"Oh, Hazel," she sobbed. "It's worse, lots worse than—than being left a—a widow."

"What do you mean, Shana?" gasped Hazel.

"Hasn't Bernice told you?"

"No. Nothing. I can't imagine."

"Someway—Hazel, I don't know how—but Bernice found out Brandon has a wife back in London."

"A wife? Living? And you never knew it?"

"Of course I didn't know it," she sobbed brokenly. "I—I told him to go back and—" She shook with sobs. She could hardly talk. "And get a—a divorce—and now he can't."

"You poor dear child! My dear. My dear." Hazel was crying now almost as hard as Shana was.

"And now—and now—my baby's due in May. And—and—" she bowed her head to her knees and cried, "and now it won't

41

have a father! I—I thought I was married—Oh, Hazel," she sobbed. "I thought I was married to a good, an honest man. I loved him. We were happy. We were—until Bernice wrote. Oh, Hazel, it's all like a horrible dream. I'm ruined—for life. I've disgraced the family! And my baby! Hazel! My poor baby. I think I'll lose my mind."

"Please, Shana, don't talk like that. It's breaking my heart too. Oh, I'm so sorry, Shana. I can hardly believe it."

"You'll hate me after you know everything."

"Hate you? I will not hate you, Shana."

"Maybe Bruce won't want me here in your house."

"He will too, Shana. You don't know Bruce. He's kind—kind as a man ever was."

"If—if I can only stay here till the baby comes, it's all I ask. I'll get a job then—and—and a room somewhere. I'll never, never go back to Glasgow and disgrace Father. Oh, please, Hazel, you won't write and tell him, will you? Or Bernice? Please."

Hazel did not answer. She was crying too hard to speak.

"I thought of hiding away somewhere until—"

"Shana, you did the right thing to come to me. I'm glad now you came at night while the children are asleep. Please, dear, I know how hard it must be, but try not to cry too often in front of them. They wouldn't understand."

"I'll try—I'll try, Hazel. Oh, it's sweet of you to take me in like this. I'll try to help you with your work all I can. Thanks for letting me come."

"It's no more than you'd do for me in a like situation," said Hazel, helping Shana up. "I'm putting you to bed. You poor, tired child. Let me get you a glass of warm milk first. It will help you sleep."

The two talked on and cried for another hour. The clock struck five before Shana finally fell asleep.

Hazel's tenderness was more than Shana could comprehend. With each passing week her sister's kindness and sympathetic understanding seemed more sincere. And Bruce was every bit as thoughtful and courteous as Hazel had said he'd be. The children endeared themselves to their new aunt and she to them.

To be sure, alone in her room, Shana shed many a bitter tear. The tyranny of the brief, sweet past haunted her, tortured her, was crushing the very heart out of her. Melancholy accompanied a growing dread as her last days of waiting grew heavier. She could feel nothing but the sickening failure of her happy young heart's expectation. And now so soon, disgraceful, husbandless motherhood. The contrast between her own deplorable situation and Hazel's happy one was maddening. She lost her appetite.

Bruce saw to it that Shana got the *London News* each evening. Her sad hungry eyes, bloodshot and burning from salty tears, searched every page every night before she went to bed. It brought no ray of hope, no amount of comfort, not even a tiny feeling that anything would or could ever be rectified. The papers were saturated with nothing but depressing news. Wealths shrunken, hunger of all kinds, failures, crimes, promises broken, suspicious hates, unrests, and fears between statesmen and races and nations. Fresh terrors, new unheard-of accusations, and new preparations for war in any fearful, likely event. Shana shuddered.

Did Brandon enlist because he knew he couldn't get a divorce? Did he want to enlist? Did he actually enlist? Would she ever know? Would she ever hear from him again? Would he ever find out he was the father of her baby? These and hordes of other frustrating questions kept piling up to hound her, sixty minutes of every waking hour.

"Shana," began Hazel one morning in early May. "You must consult a doctor. You're puffy under your eyes and look—your feet—even your hands—"

Shana shook her head emphatically.

"But, my dear," said Hazel concernedly. "I'll have a neighbor come in and sit with the children and I'll go with you. To my doctor."

Again Shana shook her head. "I don't want to go until I have to."

"The doctor may hesitate to take you at the last minute. Let me call and make an appointment. It's best, Shana."

"No, Hazel. Please, no. I have just so much money." Shana began to cry.

"But your health, Shana. It's more important than—"

"Not that important," interrupted Shana. She turned and went into her room and softly closed the door.

Just before midnight on the twenty-third, Hazel called a taxi and accompanied Shana to the hospital.

Shana was crying all the way.

"Why are you crying, dear?" asked Hazel.

Shana shook her head. "Don't ask me. I'm too terribly confused to talk about anything. And please don't write and tell Bernice about this. And please, please, Hazel, don't act surprised when I give my name, because I'm—I'm not going in as Shana Grant or Mrs. Gray. Oh, I'm so upset."

At 5:45 the next morning the baby was born. "You have a nice little boy, Mrs. Monson," the nurse told her. "A perfect baby."

Shana closed her bloodshot eyes and turned her drawn, pale face to the wall.

Hazel stayed with her for an hour. "Would it be all right if I go home now, so Bruce can go to work? I'll come back this afternoon." She bent over and kissed Shana's one hand.

Shana nodded. Tears oozed and trickled down both temples to the white pillowcase.

Hazel bent over again and kissed her quivering lips.

The supervisor met the chaplain in the elevator. "Reverend Holcome," she said, "I wish you'd stop in Room 421 and talk to Mrs. Monson. She's very depressed about something, and eats practically nothing. Her baby is doing fine, but she's crying most of the time. All we can get out of her is that she was married ten months ago. No one has been in to see her except a sister, and she has been here over a week."

"I'll stop in. Thank you, Miss Sosbee."

44

Shana was robed and sitting in an armchair when the chaplain tapped gently on her door. "May I come in?"

Shana gave a startled "Yes."

"Mrs. Monson?" He greeted her with a cheery smile.

Shana hesitated. "Yes," came her feeble answer.

"I'm John Holcome, the hospital's Protestant chaplain, Mrs. Monson. I'm making my rounds, and I thought I'd stop in and congratulate you on the birth of your fine little son."

Shana stared at the stranger with sad, unbelieving eyes. She did not smile a trifle. "Who—who told you?" she asked.

"The nurse. I'm glad to hear the Lord's been so kind to you. Children are a wonderful gift from God, aren't they?"

Shocked, Shana made no reply.

"Every time a baby is born, it's another miracle of God, and it's His way of telling us He has faith in human beings, and is anxiously longing for that soul to prepare for His kingdom. Your husband must be very happy too."

Shana looked up in utter astonishment.

"Tell me, Mrs. Monson." The chaplain stepped a trifle closer. "Are you having a problem I might help you with?"

Shana's only answer was a prolonged silence, a prolonged stare, then a dropping of her head—then tears.

CHAPTER 7

"I didn't come here to make you sad, Mrs. Monson," said the chaplain with tender sincerity. "My duty is to help people. Evidently something is distressing you. I'd like to help you if I can."

She shook her head. "My case is too awful," she cried. "It's too great, too tangled. I'm sure you can't help."

"Nothing is too great or hard or tangled for God to untangle. Would you care to tell me what it is that's troubling you?"

He waited.

"I realize I'm a perfect stranger to you," he said at length, "and perhaps I have no right to be prying into your personal life. But I'm certain God wants to help you. I'm here to help you find comfort and peace of mind."

Again he waited.

"Some patients I call on in the hospital here cheer me, while others like you, need my help. I'm simply one of God's ministers to try to bring Him and troubled hearts together."

"You—you mean," she faltered, "you've helped others in a mess like—I'm in?"

"Whatever your case, Mrs. Monson, I'm confident there have been others who have gone through the same. There's nothing new in suffering, or grief, or sorrow, or disappointment, or heartache. You are not alone in this. What's more, Christ is acquainted personally with every kind of grief and suffering."

Shana sat in troubled thought.

"Whatever your heartache, my friend, it evidently is new and very painful to you, but not to God. He's well acquainted with grief."

She looked up, but did not speak.

"He knows all about it. He understands every minute detail. And He cares. He sympathizes. He feels for you. He loves you. And best of all, He has a solution."

Patiently the chaplain waited. "I do wish I could help you," he said.

Shana twisted the belt on her robe. After taking several deep breaths, she began slowly to unload. Brokenly, briefly, she told her story, careful not to mention any names. Her bloodshot eyes gave him a glance of affrighted reprehension.

"And now," she cried, "what have you to say?"

"There have been thousands of other innocent young girls in this same plight," the chaplain stated with reverence. "My heart is deeply touched by your sad story. So is the heart of Jesus Christ. He came to earth to cheer, to comfort, to forgive, and redeem just such as you. He did not come for those who never make mistakes, for those who feel self-sufficient."

"And what will I tell my son when he is old enough to ask?" Shana repressed the scream that rose in her throat.

"Tell him the truth, my friend," answered the chaplain. "Of course he will ask. Never tell him anything but the truth."

"Tell him his father was—was bad and deceitful and dishonest?" she cried.

"Tell your son the truth. But the truth about his father's good points also. You told me he had some."

"And—and then supposing someday—he wants to know why I refused to live with him? How will he understand? Every boy needs and wants a father." Hot tears streamed down Shana's sad, tired face.

"Of course every boy wants a father. But you did the right thing. If you explain all this to him when he is old enough to understand, your son will agree you did. Don't wait too long to tell him."

47

"And," Shana looked up into the face of the chaplain with a most pitiful glare of despair and fresh agony. "And what if— if my son—wants to know—whether or not he's legitimate? What will I tell him?" She cried outright.

The chaplain bent over and gently placed one hand on Shana's trembling shoulder. "Never lie to your son, my friend. He will wonder if he is a normal boy. He may ask you that very question someday, but never tell anything but the truth. In one sense your son is illegitimate, and yet you say you didn't know. You were taken advantage of. Your innocent little child can't help this situation, any more than you can help it that you're his mother."

"Will he hate me for this?" sobbed Shana. "Will he curse me someday? And shun me?"

"You love your baby, don't you?"

"Love him?" cried Shana. "Of course I love him."

"And you want him to grow up to be a good, honest, God-fearing man, I trust. Don't you?"

"Of course," panted Shana. "I want him to grow up to be the best man that ever lived."

"Then never let him feel inferior because of what has happened. Give him the best love and care and the best Christian teaching any mother ever gave a son. Would you be ready today to give your little son over to God—to let God handle the situation?"

"How? What do you mean?"

"I mean, would you be willing to dedicate your tiny innocent baby into God's loving tender care, to let God lead him, guide him, direct his life, use him in any way He sees fit? In spite of this situation that he can't help, and that you can't change?"

"Oh—if it would help and I knew how, yes, I would. I'm afraid I'll never be happy again, but I want my son to be. I want him to grow up to be good—and—and strong, and handsome, and happy—and to never get mixed up in a mess like this. But my task frightens me. Just frightens me to distraction. I think I'll lose my mind over it."

"Listen to me. I'm going to tell you something that I've told but very few people in my life. I am one of those illegitimate children."

"You? No! Not you?"

"Yes, it's true. I well remember how I felt the day my mother told me in tears. But she told me in love. She loved me just as you love your little son. She told me the truth even though it was hard to tell. But from that moment on we loved each other more than before. Yes, my mother loved me then and still does. She wasn't to blame any more than you are for your situation. Listen to me. In whatever way you yourself have erred or sinned, confess it to God. He is more than happy to forgive. Your heart can be cleansed white as the whitest driven snow, my friend. What I really believe your greatest problem is, is that you can't forgive yourself. Isn't that so?"

Shana studied. "Maybe," she said. "But I just can't think straight any more. I feel so—so let down. I feel like nothing."

"I can see you are physically weak, but how about it if I pray for you just now, you and your little son?"

"I wish you would. And please—please baptize him too. It may help. My future looks so lonely and dark and hopeless, but I want the best for him."

"God can make your darkness light, and life meaningful to the most hopeless. I'll baptize your baby and give him into God's hands."

"Please do. And pray for his father too. In spite of everything I've told you, I still think I love him."

"But if he never comes back, are you willing to give him up?"

"I—I just don't know," answered Shana, "if I'm willing down deep in my heart. You don't know how I feel. I hate him one minute; I love him the next. I can't separate my love and my hate. To be honest, I want him back. Maybe I shouldn't. Oh, I'm so confused. I can't think straight."

"Pray God to take all hate out of your heart. That man most surely did wrong you. He was dishonest. My, my, the

49

tragedy of it! I realize how you must feel and the hundreds of thousands of other young girls, so many of them innocent, who are suffering as you are."

He baptized the baby. He prayed. He shook her hand. He left her crying.

"Mamma," called Barbie. "Some lady's at our door."

"Hi, Hazel. Can you tell me anything about Shana?" Bernice shifted uneasily from one foot to the other and fumbled with the gold chain around her neck.

"Why?" asked Hazel in surprise. "Where did you come from?"

"We were in New York last week on business and I couldn't locate her. Has she moved? Hello, Barbie. My, you kids grow like weeds. Hi, Vicky."

"Bernice," began Hazel. "Come in. Sit down." She pointed to a chair. She looked out the door, and saw the chauffeur in the car at the curb. "Where's Lewis? Isn't he along?"

"At the hotel resting. I'm uneasy about Shana, Hazel. I thought perhaps you knew what's become of her. I told her if she ever changed locations to let me know."

"Bernice," Hazel cleared her throat. Her cheeks colored. "Shana is to be pitied. She's in the Mercy Hospital."

"Hospital? Since when?"

"She has a baby boy, Bernice."

"A baby? When?"

"Eight days ago. It's darling, just a darling."

"Darling? Oh, my stars, Hazel."

"She gets to come home with it today."

"Come home? You mean here?"

"Where else could she go, Bernice? She's been here with us for over three months."

"Three months!" exclaimed Bernice, with indignation. "Why didn't you tell me? I can't understand these secrets."

"She didn't want me to tell. Shana's been going through something, let me tell you. I could cry my heart out for her."

50

"You cry? Why didn't *she* cry for herself months ago? You say she's in Mercy Hospital?"

Hazel nodded.

"I'm going right over to see her. Do you know what room she is in?"

"She's in 421. But please take it easy, Bernice. She'll be terribly surprised. She's upset enough. She looks haggard and sick."

"I'll take it easy, don't worry. Does she have any clothes or things for this baby?"

"A few. I'll loan her what I have. Remember, Bernice, she's awfully broken up. Brandon went back to England."

"Well, he should have, the low-down rascal. Give me the credit for doing some quick detective work. And what will she do now?"

"Get a job to support herself and her baby, she says."

"Oh, Hazel! Mother would simply turn over and scream in her grave if she knew all this. Why didn't she get rid—"

"Bernice! Please," whispered Hazel. "Never! Remember Barbie has ears. I'm going over in a taxi to get her this evening after supper while Bruce is here to stay with the children. Why don't you and Lewis come back and eat with us?"

"No, thanks, Hazel. We must drive on part way tonight yet. Lewis is a busy man. All business. Let me see your baby before I go."

Hazel led Bernice into the bedroom where eleven-month-old Darlene was sleeping in her crib.

"Well, look at that red hair," is all Bernice had to say. "I'd better be going. Guess I'll stop in town and get a blanket or something for the baby before I go up to see her. Mercy Hospital? Say—I'll bring Shana here and save you the trip. Has she named the baby?"

"David."

"David? I always liked that name before. But mercy sakes! David sounds much too high and too fine for such a common little brat."

"Bernice! How can you? That little David is as dear and beautiful a baby as ever I laid eyes on. Even the doctors and the nurses all say so. And he might just grow up to be something far from that awful character you just said. Shame on you." Hazel's face got red. "Maybe I'd better go along to the hospital. Don't you talk like that to Shana when you get there."

Flippantly Bernice laughed. "Don't worry. I was just talking. Forget it. But honestly, it gets my dander up to know you two have kept this from me. It's not one bit nice. And how about Father?"

Hazel shook her head.

"He doesn't know either? Well, maybe it's best he doesn't know this. He'd die of a stroke. But you might as well know I've told him about Brandon. Yes, Hazel. But if Shana is willing to listen to me now and take some big sisterly advice, she can soon rise above this and start life over. Now don't object, Hazel."

Abruptly Bernice left. Her jaw was set.

Shana pressed her baby closer to her as the door opened.

"Mrs. Monson?"

The instant she saw the woman with pad and pencil, Shana knew she would have to face the thing she had been dreading for days. She looked past the woman at nothing definite as the unnerving weakness she could not get accustomed to swept from her finger tips to her toes. She sucked in her breath before the first question could stab at her already wounded heart and bleeding conscience.

"I'm to complete your baby's birth certificate, Mrs. Monson; so your maiden name, please, and your birthplace."

Shana's heart hammered out of reason. "Shana Grant." She cleared her throat, and bit the inside of her cheek. "Glasgow, Scotland."

"And your husband's first name?"

Even though she knew it was coming next, she wanted to scream loud enough for all the world to hear it. She hesitated. In her shifting glance there was both fear and tragedy. "I—I—" She picked at the edge of the blanket. She shook her head.

52

"Oh, I see. Just tell me, please, Mr. Monson's first name."

"The baby's father's name—" Shana's lip parted just enough to let the words slip out—"is Brandon, and his last—"

"Just a second, will you spell that name, please?"

With lips pressed tightly, Bernice McCawlis stepped out of the elevator on the fourth floor. She hesitated, looking first to the right, then to the left.

"May I help you?" asked an attendant.

"I'm looking for—for a Mrs. Gray."

"Gray? You must be on the wrong floor, Ma'am."

"Well—well—or perhaps it's—is a Mrs. Grant on this floor?"

"Grant? No, Ma'am. Not that I know of."

"Well, who *is* in room 421?" demanded Bernice.

"I'll look on the register, Ma'am. If I recall, it's—yes, it's Mrs. Monson. You may be on the wrong floor, Ma'am."

Bernice walked past the attendant and stuck her head inside the door with number 421 above it.

Shana was sitting in the armchair, head lowered, looking intently at the tiny blanketed infant in her arms. Her lips were moving.

"Shana." Bernice closed the door behind her.

Shana jumped. Her mouth opened, but only a startled throaty sound came out.

"You're surprised to see me, aren't you?" blinked Bernice.

"Yes—very," answered Shana. She could feel her heart pounding in her throat. She gripped the bundle in her arms closer to her. "Please," she said to the lady with pad and pencil, "come back later, won't you?"

"It was true then. Wasn't it?" bluntly asked Bernice as soon as the woman was gone. Triumphantly she found a chair, and triumphantly sat upon it.

Shana looked at the floor. "He's gone," she said with bitterness. The lifelessness of those words was mirrored in her lifeless eyes.

"We're all glad of that," stated Bernice. She did not ask to see the baby. Nervously she looked around the room. "You're about ready to leave, I hear."

"Hazel's coming for me tonight."

"No, she's not," corrected Bernice. "I am taking you."

"You?"

"I was out to Hazel's. We made out together I'd come and save her the taxi. Lewis is resting at the hotel and my chauffeur is waiting below. What will you—" Bernice twisted her handbag strap round and round her two fingers. "What will you do with that baby?"

"What will I do with him?" asked Shana. "Why, what any mother would do with her own baby. I'll love him, and—and love him, and work hard to support him. And give him a good education. That's what I'll do." Her eyes got so misty she could scarcely see.

"But I have a better suggestion, Shana," Bernice began, sitting on the edge of the chair and waving her one hand back and forth as though she were very warm. She reseated herself. "You are still young." She waited to let that fact soak in. "You are much too young to be burdened down with a child you have no obligation to keep."

"Obligation?" gasped Shana.

"That's exactly what I said, Shana. This child was cruelly forced on you, and by all kinds of human reasoning, it's for your own good and his too that I have a plan worked out."

"*You* have a *plan?*" gasped Shana. "But he's mine. My own flesh and blood. I have my own plans."

"True, you gave birth to him. But society has a responsibility here too. Look now. You are going to— (thank heaven, Shana, you didn't come in here as Shana Grant)."

"How do you know? Did Hazel—"

"No, the girl in the hall said a Mrs. Monson was in this room. That at least was real clever, I must say. But when you get out, you're Miss Shana Grant again."

Shana looked down. Her lips quivered.

"Of course you are," said Bernice tersely. "Surely you don't intend to go around dragging that filthy Gray name with you, do you?"

"Bernice!" Shana began to cry.

"Now, Shana, don't get hysterical. I came here to help you. Listen to me. You leave this all up to me. I'm older and I know a few things about this life in America you haven't learned yet. Now you must spruce yourself up. Get some pretty clothes; go to a beauty parlor. Put on some class and get yourself a job in a hotel. You can. And then start life all over. Forget the past. Forget that Brandon Gray ever existed. Don't tell a single living soul you ever had a baby."

"But I do," cried Shana. "He's right here in my arms and I'm not going to lie to him or anyone else about it."

"Silly," snapped Bernice. "You're not following me. You won't need to lie to him or anyone else. Just dismiss it. Act as though it never happened." Bernice stopped to get her breath. She fanned herself with her handbag. "I can't help you unless you let me, Shana. I'll take that baby. I'll place it in a good home. You wash your hands of the whole dirty mess."

"Give up my baby!" cried Shana. "Never! Never!"

CHAPTER 8

Bernice frowned. She got up and paced back and forth across the room, watching the closed door with anxious eyes.

"Calm yourself, Shana," she said admonishingly and trying to modify her tone. "Some nurse will pop in here and wonder what's going on. I came to help you and you're too stubborn or— or weak to see it." Her voice was cold, sharp, yeasty.

Shana cried the harder.

Bernice went over and pressed one hand firmly on her knee. "Listen, Shana. Are you listening to me? You aren't."

Shana shivered. She did not look up. The baby squirmed and yawned. A delicate smile played around his tiny mouth. Shana planted a kiss on his soft warm forehead. Two big tears fell on the blue and white blanket.

"Look, I brought you a blanket fresh from the store." Bernice took it out of the paper sack. "See?" She held it up a second, then tossed it over the end of the bed. "Now this is how we'll do it, Shana." She hovered over her, pressing her hands with each word. "You keep what money you have and I'll pay your hospital bill when we leave."

Shana shook her head.

"Yes, I will, Shana. You keep what you have to get things you'll need to get started. I'll pay your bill. I'll have Jasper drive us back to Hazel's and you start fresh from the very minute you step out of my car. I'll do all the rest for you."

"What do you mean?" Shana looked horrified.

"I'll take complete responsibility for that baby. You won't need to worry about one thing."

"What?" Shana looked aghast, ashen, appalled.

"I'll deliver him safe and sound to a good home. I promise you, Shana."

"Deliver him! Where?" Shana's breath all but choked her.

"I can't tell you now. But I'll find a good place. You simply cannot, dare not, disgrace yourself and the Grant name by owning a child born like this one. Think now." She pointed to the bundle in Shana's trembling arms. "Just look," she said. "This is making an old woman of you already. You look awful, Shana. It's too much. You can't bear the responsibility of a son. Why, they're ten times harder to raise than a daughter. And he wouldn't appreciate all you'd have to do to slave and slave and sacrifice and sweat for him all your life. All your life! Shana. Think. What have these foundling homes been established for? Why, for just such unfortunates as you have there. People who want children and can't have any of their own can go there and get them to adopt. Listen to me. Stop crying, Shana. Take hold of yourself. He'd probably land in a good home and be far better off than what you could provide. I'd take him myself, but children make me nervous. I shouldn't say so, but I might as well admit it. Look, your nerves are practically shot already. What if you'd keep him and break completely? Do you want to land in a crazy house, Shana? Of course you don't. Then they would take your boy from you for sure, and put him in some institution. And who would you get to take care of that baby if you'd hold a job? A trustworthy day nurse is mighty hard to find here in America. I wouldn't trust one for thirty minutes, Shana. You are a stranger here yet. I know what I'm talking about. What's more, you couldn't afford it. I'm going down to the desk right now and pay your bill. Monson? Is that the name?" She backed toward the door. "Mrs. Monson? Room 421?"

Shana buried her face in the baby's blanket. "I wish I were dead," she sobbed. "Yes, Mary Monson. Oh, I want to die right now."

57

"You'll snap out of it," said Bernice unfeelingly.

"I—I don't—want—to—live," cried Shana. "I wish we had both died together. I do. I do. Oh, why didn't we?"

Carefully Bernice latched the door behind her and hurried toward the elevator.

An hour later the girl, still on duty, took Shana down on a wheel chair. Bernice carried the baby.

"She has a mighty sweet little one," ventured the girl to Bernice. "About the cutest one we've taken out for a long time."

No answer. Bernice looked steadfastly at nothing.

"I do hope you all can cheer Mrs. Monson up a little," she ventured further. "She's shed 'way too many tears of late. Poor thing."

"She's nervous," glumly offered Bernice. "She'll be all right. Guess the first one," she cleared her throat. "She's young. That's in her favor."

"Yes-sum, yes-sum, you're right." She wheeled Shana outside, where the pleasant warm June air blew across her wan, tear-washed face.

"That car there, Ma'am?"

Bernice nodded and motioned for Jasper to drive up closer to the walk.

"Good-by," said the girl, helping Shana into the back seat of the handsome black limousine. "Good luck to you and your sweet little baby. Take care of yourself."

Shana did not answer.

"Go back to 1357 Pinewood," Bernice told Jasper. She got into the back seat beside Shana and closed the sliding glass partition behind the driver's seat.

"Let me hold him," said Shana.

Bernice handed her the baby. What was happening to her? Was she losing her mind completely? Already? Shana pressed her baby close, closer to her breast. She put her face down against his tiny pink one. His eyes were closed in peaceful sleep. "My baby—my baby," she sobbed. "Oh, what am I doing to you? I love you—I love you—oh, my darling—I love you, my dear little

58

David. What will happen to you? Will you grow up to be a good boy and a good man? Your father wasn't all bad. Oh, David, my precious little son—my darling—your mother loves you—like no other mother ever, ever loved her little son. In my own heart—I'm not—I'm not giving you away. It's not my doing, darling—oh, my David—my love will follow you to the ends of the earth. But I'm afraid we'll never, never see each other again," she cried out convulsively, in sobs that shook her whole body.

Bernice sat rigid, unmoved.

They were nearing Pinewood Avenue.

"I'm doing the best I know, darling," she sobbed into the blanket. "I'm so distracted I think I'm losing my mind. I'm glad you don't know this. You don't even know who you are. You'll never know how your mother has suffered. Oh, baby dear." Shana held her breath— "Here." She handed the baby to Bernice. Quickly she found a pencil and a small piece of paper in her purse. She jotted something on it.

"What are you doing?" asked Bernice.

Shana folded the paper. "I wrote his name," she answered between sobs. "I gave him one. I—I want him to own that much of me."

"Well, I certainly hope you wrote Gray," said Bernice.

"I lied about mine but—" She bit her lip. "Give him back." Reaching inside the blanket Shana tucked the slip of paper down into the baby's one stocking. He squirmed and smiled as though having a very pleasant dream.

Jasper was stepping on the brake pedal. Shana's heart pounded until she feared her chest would burst wide open. She must be going completely mad! This was worse than childbirth—worse than death. Worse than murder! What right did Bernice have to come and order her around? Why didn't she stand up straight and fight?

Shana could not understand herself, her terrible weakness, her fate, her dying. The whole mad world was nothing but madness and grief and injustice. She had no strength at all. She was going blind. Her sight, her blood, her breath, her feelings were

59

ebbing from her with every inch closer to the house.

Oh! There it was! 1357! A light in the window. A shadow of someone at the door. Hazel? Hazel with a kind husband—love—a home—and children—not one illegitimate! Not one. Why? Why? Why was *she* destined to such crushing partiality?

"David," she all but screamed his name. She kissed his tiny warm pink face over and over and over, passionately. His forehead, each cheek, his nose, his chin, his lips. "You're mine—mine —all mine, no matter who gets you. You'll always belong to me. O God—God, if you hear at all, hear me now. Go with my baby. Watch over him. Be good to him."

Jasper stopped.

Shana's heart stopped. Then raced.

"O God," she sobbed. "Let some very kind people care for my baby. Oh, Bernice! Bernice!"

Bernice almost snatched him out of Shana's arms.

"Let me know where you leave him," sobbed Shana feebly.

"Don't be foolish," chided Bernice with cold calm. "You can't know that. You're beside yourself. Go in now and rest. Rest for a week or two. You'll be all right soon."

"Oh, Bernice!" screamed Shana. "This is killing me!"

"Sh, Shana. Remember, here's Jasper. There's Hazel now, coming out to meet you." She opened the sliding glass. "Drive on, Jasper. At once. Turn left at the first corner. Hurry."

"Where's the baby?" exclaimed Hazel, astounded.

"Take me in." Shana could scarcely speak. "I'm—Hazel— I'm going to faint."

Bernice bent forward. "Now listen, go 'way north, Jasper," she said; "drive around through that part of town until I tell you to stop. Don't drive too fast then, but fast now. Till you get over north."

"Yes, Miss McCawlis. Any certain number?"

"It's not a number I want. It's a building. I'm not sure but a building with a—well, a certain sign. I don't know exactly myself."

60

She sat on the edge of the seat. She kept biting her lower lip. It was almost dark and they had driven at least ten miles up and down streets, many streets, across streets.

"Stop. I think I see what I want. Jasper, you drive up there and park around the corner and wait there till I come."

"As you say, Miss McCawlis."

Slowly and with dreadful uncertainty Bernice McCawlis got out of the back seat and started toward the gray brick building with the sign above the door. "Gospel Mission. Everybody welcome." She clutched the infant in her trembling arms. She walked past the building. She looked in. She saw lights. Someone moving about. She retraced her steps. She tried to swallow. Her throat was uncomfortably dry. She stood, a sickening while, then walked on half a block.

Then she saw a young girl coming toward her. She stopped her. "Little sister, will you do me a favor?" she asked.

"What kind of a favor?"

"See that place there with that mission sign on it? Above it? See?"

"Yes."

"Will you take this baby and deliver it for me to the lady that lives there?"

"You mean the preacher's wife?"

"I think so."

"That's where a preacher lives, I think."

"Oh, yes. That's the place. Will you do it for me?"

"Whose baby is it?"

"I can't tell you that, dear. It's to be delivered to the people that live there because—well—they're—they're good people. See? Here. Take the baby. I'll give you two dollars. Now. Here you are. Thank you, dear."

The girl stared at the strange woman completely dumbfounded. Without saying another word or asking any more questions she walked toward the mission. Bernice watched from a distance, holding her breath, biting her lip, eyes bulging.

She saw the girl knock. She saw the door open. Her one

hand grabbed her throbbing neck. She saw the girl nodding in her direction. Bernice began to walk. Fast. She stopped only long enough to glance back once. The girl and the baby had both disappeared into the house.

"But where did this baby come from?" asked Mrs. Warren, the minister's wife.

"I don't know," insisted the girl. "A woman that was dressed rich stopped me down there about half a block and told me to deliver it here to you because you're good."

"Good?" Mrs. Warren took the baby and opened the blanket. "Well, the little dear!" she exclaimed. "Who'd ever give away a sweet little thing like this? John," she called to her husband. "Come here. Look what we have."

"A baby? Just out of the blue?" exclaimed Mr. Warren. "But we aren't running a foundling home. Why was it brought here?"

The girl had no explanation.

"Sweet as it is," said Mrs. Warren, "we just aren't fixed to keep babies here. I don't know what to do with it. My, what a pretty baby!"

Friends of the Warrens called later that evening and the baby was the only topic of discussion.

"Say, I have an idea," finally suggested Minister Warren. "Supposing you folks go home by way of the Millersville Children's Home and take the baby there. Would you do that?"

It was finally agreed upon.

Melvin Kolb answered the doorbell. It was late Saturday night and all the fifty children in the Home were sound asleep. Sister Lora was making her final rounds before retiring.

"We have a baby for you, Mr. Kolb."

"Where from? Whose baby is it?"

"We don't know. Some young girl brought it to the mission in Philadelphia this evening. It's a complete mystery. She said a strange woman paid her to deliver it."

"Huh. Well, we can't say no, can we? It's a soul. And a

soul is worth more than all the world. Sister Lora," he called. "Come down here. Looks like you'll be having a new charge. Martha, come here. See what we got by special delivery."

Sister Lora took the baby and placed it on the office table. "Why, you dear little cherub!" she exclaimed. "Who are you, anyhow? Mrs. Kolb, did you ever see a prettier baby? Wonder how old it is. Are you a little girl, or a boy, or an angel?"

She started undressing the baby by pulling off one stocking, then the other. She felt something crackle in the toe of the second. She turned the stocking wrong side out. "Look," she said, unfolding a small crumpled paper. "David Grant, May 24, 1913. Mother—Shana Grant, Phila."

"Why, you darling little David!" exclaimed Sister Lora. "So that's your name? Who could give you away? I'm going to claim you if no one else does. You're hungry, aren't you?"

In the morning Melvin Kolb got busy on the telephone. First he called the mission. They had no new light on the mystery. He called every hospital in Philadelphia. Not one could report the birth of a baby boy Grant on or during the week of May 24.

"We might as well conclude," he told Sister Lora and his wife, "the baby was not born in a hospital. All we can do is keep him and hope the mystery will be solved, somehow, someday."

"And in the meantime," said Sister Lora, holding the tiny soft face against her cheek, "you can be sure of one thing, you pretty, precious, little baby Grant, that Sister Lora will love you just like your own mother ought to if she doesn't."

Three years—and little Davy had grown fonder and dearer to Sister Lora every day. She taught him to walk, to feed himself. She taught him how to talk, to laugh, to play, to love. She taught him songs and prayers and little children's rhymes. She was as much a part of Davy Grant as he was of her.

Three years—and Shana, thin and sad, was working in the Blackstone Hotel in Philadelphia. She still read the *London Daily News* faithfully. That's how she learned it. In bold headlines she read the front-page news on August 19, 1916. "Entire squadron of Scottish Highlanders annihilated in French mountain." And below in the list of known dead was the only name she was personally concerned about. Brandon Gray, of Leeds.

CHAPTER 9

Morning worship in the Loomas household was as much a part of each day's schedule as the seven-fifteen breakfast. Papa Loomas usually launched the morning table conversation by asking each of the children if their night's rest had been a pleasant one, and without fail commended each one on looking so chipper and bright or neatly combed or whatever he noted was worthy of personal praise. After all heads had bowed and after grace was said, Papa would invariably report on any new thing he had noticed on his early morning rounds about the farm or in the barn: a strange bird call, a baby calf, a nest of newly hatched ducks, a gopher trapped, a first flower in bloom, a sign of good fishing, a rain cloud, a ripe tomato, or an ear of corn ready to eat. This was interspersed with questions from Dennis or Janet or Lesa or Mamma Loomas. And Papa always had the answers. Next he shared the planned outline of his day's activities and Mamma would give hers. Plans were often altered, or adjustments made without fuss or fume. Long before Davy Grant became a part of the family, Janet and Dennis had learned that things ran smoothly in the Loomas home, not by rod nor harsh words nor by the domineering of one spirit over another. It would have been next to impossible for either of the children to give an honest answer (if asked) as to who was the head of the house. Rose and Aaron Loomas thought, taught, worked, planned, prayed, and lived as one.

Little Davy soon learned that the eggs and toast were never

passed until each one seated at the table wore a relaxed, pleasant expression. He also learned that after breakfast slender, gentle-faced Mamma Loomas handed calm, kind-voiced Papa Loomas a black leather-bound book called a Bible from which he read some hard-to-comprehend words about God and people. Then they all folded their hands and bowed their heads while Papa talked to "Dear God, our Father in heaven" about each of them and many other things, and people in need.

This worship period every morning was not an unheard-of experience to Davy Grant, for in the Home Leon's papa had done the same. Only, at the Home there were many children, seated on low benches or chairs the proper size around many tables, and he always sat next or close to Sister Lora. And there they sang before and after the prayer and sometimes the older children read from the Bible or quoted verses they had memorized. Papa Loomas did ask Lesa to read once in a while.

By the time Davy was transferred to this private home his knowledge of God, vague as it was, was above that of the average three-year-old. Sister Lora had often chosen Bible stories for her storytelling hour. She had taught Davy a bedtime prayer and three-word verses—"God is love . . . God is light . . . Follow thou me"—and a five-word verse—"The Lord is my shepherd." To be sure, he did not even begin to fathom the meaning of these phrases he spoke so distinctly, so free from any babyish accent. But Davy, at three, did not doubt there was a strange, mysterious, loving being somewhere in the great high unknown called God, who could see all things, hear all noises, and do whatever He chose. He knew no doubtings because he heard this from the lips of Sister Lora. To him she was the embodiment of truth and rightness, of love and uninterrupted security.

After he learned, the first morning in his new home, that these people also knew about Sister Lora's God, Davy felt a degree of security. He could not have defined it had he tried, but he detected a mystical sameness in the gentle details of Mamma Loomas's face and Sister Lora's, although they looked nothing alike. There was that sameness also in the softness of their voices, although they were distinctly different in tone. To learn also that Mamma Loomas and his beloved Sister LoLo were good friends quelled many of his initial inward fears.

The church they attended was not new to him. Leon was there too. Davy went to his class without hesitancy. Miss Morgan, the teacher, made him feel welcome and wanted. Even necessary. With pride he put each Sunday's small attendance card away in a special box up in his room.

"Now everything you put in this box will be your very own, Davy," explained Mamma Loomas, when she gave it to him. "It belongs to no one but you. See?"

Davy ran up the stairs all smiles and put the beloved box, all his very own, in the safety of the bottom dresser drawer.

One forenoon another quite different incident made a lasting impression on Davy. Dennis was performing his daily task of walking out the long lane to get the mail, and Janet was setting the dinner table. Lesa was frosting a layer cake. Davy slipped off to the barn to do some exploring. At the foot of the haymow ladder he saw Papa Loomas on his knees, head bent low. Davy stopped short.

"What's the matter?" he asked in a frightened voice as he stepped close.

Aaron Loomas looked up in surprise. He got to his feet. "I—I didn't hear you coming, Davy," he said. "Have you been in here long?"

Davy shook his head. "I just came now. What you fixin'?"

"Nothing, Davy," answered Mr. Loomas, lowering himself on one knee. He reached out and gently pulled Davy over to him until the boy was seated on his one leg. "I was just having a little talk with God."

"Why?"

"Well, because I needed to."

"Why?"

"Because He knows so much more than I do, Davy."

"What about?"

"About everything, my boy." Mr. Loomas closed one big

hand over one of Davy's small ones. "I have lots of problems I could never solve by myself."

Davy stared into Papa Loomas's face with eyes wide open and lips parted. His eyelids fluttered.

"You don't understand, I know," observed Mr. Loomas, "but once you're a grown man you will. Thank God, little boys your age don't need to be troubled about jobs or crops, or wars, or raising children, or anything. Just eat and play and go to bed and sleep and be happy. Not a worry or a care. That's what fathers are for, to handle the problems—with God's help, I mean."

"Is He?"

"Is He what?"

"Helpin' you?"

"Yes, indeed, Davy. Yes, indeed."

"He can even hear you in barns, can't He?"

"Yes, indeed, Davy. In barns or out in the field, or anywhere. I wouldn't own a barn if I couldn't pray in it whenever I wanted to."

A faint smile played around Davy's lips. He took one long breath.

"What's more, Davy. We wouldn't have a nice little boy like you if we hadn't prayed about it."

"Why?"

"Because we didn't have a little boy of our own."

"Why?"

"God never sent us any."

"Who did?"

"I—I mean of our very own, Davy."

Davy's eyebrows twitched. He drew back and looked bewilderingly into Aaron Loomas's smooth-shaved face. "Well—who—whose own—is—me?" asked Davy.

Sudden surprise raised Aaron to his feet. He swung Davy over his left shoulder and trotted him across the back yard past the garden plot to the sandbox. He dropped beside the boy and began running his right hand aimlessly through the warm white sand. What should he tell this child? What could he tell him?

This miniature man-child too young to have such far-reaching concerns. Aaron scolded himself for so stupidly (unintentional as it was) leading the child on. To completely ignore the question (though feebly asked) would be both crude and cruel. As he remembered it, Rose had handled the situation with Janet and had done a beautiful job.

"I'm so glad we found you," said Aaron, lazily filling the little wooden wheelbarrow with handfuls of sand.

"Was—was I losted?" asked Davy.

"No, Davy. Remember we found you at the Children's Home?"

He nodded. "I was there. I remember. Did you find Dennis there?"

"Yes."

"An' Janet, too?"

"Yes."

"Are you going to go find more childrens there? There's more."

"We don't know yet, Davy. Not for a while anyhow. We hope you want to stay here and be like our own."

Davy answered by throwing both arms around Papa Loomas's neck.

That same afternoon both boys went along with Aaron to town. Janet stayed home to help Mamma and Lesa pick raspberries.

While Aaron went into the hardware store, the boys agreed to stay in the car.

"I hope Papa buys us candy," began Dennis.

"I hope so, too," echoed Davy.

"Once my mother brought me a whole bunch of candy. Just for me."

Davy shifted his gaze from Dennis to two fat ladies walking by. He said nothing.

"Did your mother ever bring you candy?"

No answer.

"Where is your mother?" Dennis pulled on Davy's sleeve.

Davy had never been asked such a question before. He simply looked into space.

"Haven't you got any?"

"Huh?" Davy blinked.

"I said, haven't you got a real mother?"

Davy didn't answer. He bit the end of one finger, then two fingers.

"Haven't you got any father either?"

Davy looked blank, then confused. He never knew before a boy had to have a mother when there was one like Sister Lora. Much less a father when there were two like Melvin Kolb and Papa Loomas.

"Where did you come from, anyhow?"

Davy couldn't answer that either. No one had ever asked him so many hard questions. He frowned.

"You got to know all that stuff when you start to school," said Dennis, grinning with a sense of happy superiority. He played with the steering wheel. "You've got to know your name an' how old you are, an' your birthday, an' what's your father's name, an' a lot of junk like that when you go to school. I know you do. Leastways, to our school you do. But you're not four yet. You can't know much when you're only three. 'Cause you're almost a baby yet when you're three an' babies don't know much. You don't even know if you got a mother. Ha Ha. Or a father. Ha Ha. You must be nobody."

Davy tried to swallow the lump that started growing in his throat. His eyes were wet with tears when Papa Loomas returned.

"What's wrong with my Davy?" he inquired.

"He's cryin' for candy, I think," answered Dennis, grinning to hide his own disappointment.

Davy shook his head.

"Dennis isn't right?" asked Mr. Loomas.

Again Davy shook his head. "He—he," he faltered, pointing to Dennis, "said I haven't any mother an' I'm nobody."

"Dennis, did you say that to Davy?"

"I jus' asked him where she was. I was only teasin'."

"But, Dennis, you musn't tease Davy like that. Of course he has a mother, or had a mother the same as you did. Cheer up, Davy. Here, I'll give each of you boys a penny, and, Dennis, you take Davy into that grocery store right there, take him by the hand, and let him spend his penny for whatever kind of candy he chooses in the penny case."

Both boys were smiling when they came out.

"Rose," said Aaron after supper, "before Davy goes to bed you'd better tell him a few things. It's a shame, but Dennis has been questioning and tormenting him already."

"Oh, no."

Rose Loomas took the child on her lap after he was in his pajamas. She sat close to the window in his room. Davy's head rested on her left shoulder. "Once about four years ago," she began, "a very kind man and lady at a Children's Home had a tiny baby given to them. The people who brought the baby said it needed a good home. So the man and lady said, 'Fine. We have a good home right here.' Everybody loved that little baby. But he didn't stay a baby long. Soon he was walking and talking and by the time he was three he was quite a little man. A man and lady who love children very, very much visited at that Home and saw this nice, pretty, bright little fellow. They asked if they couldn't take him along home so they could be near him and love him all the time just as though he were their own."

Davy sat up very straight. "Was—" He touched her cheek with his finger tips. "Was he like me?"

"He most certainly was, darling. That sweet little boy *was* *you*. Nobody seems to know exactly *where* you were born, Davy, but that doesn't matter. We all love you because you are you. We like to say God sent you to us from heaven. And listen, darling, if anybody ever asks you any questions that you can't answer, you come and ask me. Will you?"

Davy smiled and snuggled closer, and Mamma Loomas kissed his cheek and held him until he was sound asleep.

71

CHAPTER 10

Shana had learned his name months before he introduced himself. R. Anthony Drextell had checked in and out of Hotel Blackstone many times. He had occupied a seat in the Blue Room at various conventions. His step, his manner, his voice were familiar.

Bernice had overpowered Shana in one thing, but only one. Shana did not spend her money, as Bernice suggested, for stunning clothes nor did she patronize the beauty salons. Shana possessed a natural beauty that required only time, rest, and nature to restore.

R. Anthony Drextell was not attracted to her because she tried in any way to make herself particularly attractive to men. Certainly not because she made any advances. He came back one day, after he had checked out, to look for a lost fountain pen. Shana was in the vacated room checking the drapes, the spread, the chair covers.

"Pardon, Miss," he said. "You're too pretty to always look so serious and sad. How about a date next time I come to town?"

"Thanks." Shana smiled a little, but shook her head.

It was not because Mr. Drextell appeared to be a man of wealth that she finally, after repeated invitations, accepted a dinner date. Shana was lonely. Now that she knew Brandon was out of her life forever, she felt more keenly than before the pain of her mutilated life. Constant emptiness. Her soul never knew anything but craving, coupled with an unhappy tinge of guilt.

"I wish I could know exactly how you feel, Shana," Anthony told her some weeks later on their fourteenth date. "I am sad because I lost my wife. Why can't we join hands and try to cheer each other? You always look sad. Have you lost a lover?"

"Anthony," Shana picked at the corner of her handkerchief, as her head dropped. "I'm sad—because of—something worse than losing a husband or a lover. You'd never guess."

"Tell me." He caught her hand.

"I have a little—a little son, Anthony. It—it shouldn't have been."

"You never told me."

"I'm telling you now. He's not four yet."

"Where is he?"

"That's what kills me, Anthony. I don't know."

"Why don't you know?"

"Because my sister in South Carolina came here to the hospital when I was ready to be released and took charge." Her eyes filled with tears.

"I don't understand."

"Neither do I. Why I ever allowed her to lord it over me I don't know. But I was so distracted, so grief-stricken at the time, and so weak physically, I just gave in. I must have been— oh, I don't know. But it's haunted me every day since. I can't forgive myself."

"What haunts you? I don't understand at all."

"She took my baby, Anthony, and put him in some home, down South, I guess. She absolutely won't tell me where. I've written to her repeatedly and it's no use. You don't know my sister Bernice, Anthony."

"Bernice who?"

"Mrs. Lewis McCawlis in Columbia, South Carolina."

"She's your sister? Mrs. Lewis McCawlis?"

"Do you know her?"

"I know McCawlis. In Columbia, South Carolina. Sure I know Lewis. So his wife is your sister? Well. You mean she took your child against your will?"

73

6

"I must have been out of my mind," cried Shana. "I—I— Listen, Anthony. You go and talk to my sister and—and get her to tell you where my son, David, is, because I want him back."

"Want him back?" Anthony's shoulders sagged.

"I mean, that's the only condition on which I'd ever agree to marrying—any man."

"Why, Shana Grant!"

"If you want me for your wife, Anthony, you must let me have my David in the home. That's final."

"Well—well, my dear," panted Anthony. "I guess, if you really mean that—I'll—I'll have to try. I'll do my best. I'll even make a special trip to see your sister." His hands played nervously with the steering wheel. "You should have told me this long ago, Shana. You'll marry me if I get your boy back?"

"Yes," answered Shana. "I promise." And her head fell on his shoulder.

Bernice ushered R. Anthony Drextell into the lush living room after looking at his card.

"I came on a special errand, Mrs. McCawlis," he began, molding one hand around the brim of his Stetson hat. "I'll—to be frank, I'm in love with your sister Shana."

"Oh," exclaimed Bernice, "how lovely, Mr. Drextell! How delighted I am!" She clapped her hands in her excitement.

"She told me about her little son David."

Abruptly Bernice's countenance underwent a drastic change. She grasped the edge of the mahogany table. Shame, disgust, and anger were written in every line on her face.

"She tells me you know where he is," he continued.

"But I don't," puffed Bernice. "I do not, and she told you wrong."

"Can you tell me anything about him?"

"No. Not a thing." Bernice squirmed uneasily.

"Mrs. McCawlis, did you take him when he was a baby?"

Her eyelids twitched. "I never had that baby."

"But didn't you take him and give him to someone?"

74

"Why do you ask me all these questions, Mr. Drextell?" interrupted Bernice, reddening.

"Because Shana wants him back."

"Wants him back?" Her voice was near panic.

"She does. She says she will not marry me unless I find him. I've got to, Mrs. McCawlis. So I came to you for help."

Bernice studied the pattern in the red Oriental rug until her face was almost as red. She got to her feet, picked up a vase, then set it down.

"If you weren't a friend of my husband, Mr. Drextell, I'd never take you seriously." She paced back and forth before the fireplace. "I'll tell you this. But maybe I shouldn't." She hesitated. "I left that child at a—some—a—a kind of religious mission somewhere on the north side of Philadelphia."

Anthony dropped his hat. "You mean he's been right there in Philadelphia all this time and Shana never knew it?"

Bernice fumbled irritably. Her pulse went on a rampage. "Well," she said at length, in a tone of self-defense, "she agreed to it. It was for her own good. She's been far better off without him. I think it's clear out of reason she requires you to get that child back. Why, he might not want to go back to her. She's a perfect stranger to him now. Why—why—" she panted.

Anthony got to his feet. "What street is that mission on, Mrs. McCawlis?"

"I couldn't tell you that, Mr. Drextell. I never paid any attention to the street names."

An awkward pause was punctured only by Anthony's heavy breathing.

"Well, thanks for this much information. I'll do my best. And please know this, Mrs. McCawlis, I'm willing to make a—a home for the kid if it will make Shana happy. I never had any of my own, and I think perhaps I'd sorta enjoy the experience. He wouldn't go in want, let me tell you, if I looked after him."

It was days before R. Anthony Drextell knocked at the little

75

mission with the Gospel sign. He plunged to the point without an introduction.

"Yes, a tiny baby was left here on a Saturday evening," admitted the minister. "Yes, sir, some over three years ago. We well remember. No. No. By a young girl. No, we didn't know his name—or where he came from. Never knew. We sent the baby to the Children's Home in Millersville. We never did keep children here."

Another week and R. Anthony Drextell stopped at the Children's Home to interview Melvin Kolb. "We did have a little Grant boy here for a while, yes," nodded Superintendent Kolb. "But he's not here now. He's been placed in a good home."

"Has he been adopted?"

"The people who took him would have to answer to that, sir."

"Where is the home he's in?"

On that point Melvin Kolb stood his ground. He would not tell.

Vexed and panting, Anthony Drextell wheeled around and stalked away, slammed the door of his Cadillac, and sped south, muttering disgust. Halfway up the long Loomas lane he stopped abruptly, picked up a map on the seat beside him, and frowned over it.

There were certain places and objects and spots about the farm that soon had definite attractions for little Davy. The sandbox now was one. The feel of the warm white sand on his bare hands and feet gave him a happy sensation of being wanted since the day Papa Loomas sat there with him. That is where he was playing when Rose got the frightening phone call from Melvin Kolb.

In her excitement and alarm she had forgotten both the sugar and spices, as she quickly clapped the ginger cooky ingredients together. Frantically she stirred, then rolled dough, watching with one anxious eye down the long lane and at the same time trying to talk sense to Davy.

76

"See," she said, giving him a handful of raisins. Several dropped on the floor. "You put one here for eyes—one eye, no, he's to have two eyes—then, yes, one here for a nose—then four for a mouth."

"What are we making, Mamma?" asked Davy.

"Ginger man cookies, I guess. Yes, we'll bake him. Oh," she cried, dropping her spoon, "there comes—oh, yes, it's Papa coming already."

Davy scrambled from his stool. "I want to go meet him."

"No, dear," cried Rose. "Not this time. Come back. Help me put the cookies in the oven. Papa's hungry for cookies—he's —he's talking to—oh, yes—next, Davy, we put them on a pan—I mean a cooky sheet—first. One leg fell off? Oh, we don't care. Stick it on again."

Already Rose was perspired wet. What was the man in the car in the lane saying to Aaron? Oh! What was Aaron telling him! She wanted to run down there and find out. Stop him.

"Davy, Mamma forgot the oven isn't hot yet. Go ahead. You can eat some of the raisins, precious. Play in the dough. I don't care."

The phone rang. She ran to answer.

"Yes, Sister Lora. Yes. Yes. I have him in the kitchen with me. Yes. Yes, right now. In our lane! I will. I will."

Aaron Loomas drove up beside the man in the black Cadillac and greeted him. Dennis and Janet were in the seat beside him.

"Looking for someone, sir?" asked Aaron.

"Well," answered the stranger, scratching his head. "Guess I was," he laughed with embarrassment, "sorta rattlebrained, I guess, and got off the highway without noticing it. The—the party I'm looking for, I suppose, would be as hard to find as a needle in a haystack."

"Don't know. Could be," pleasantly replied Aaron from his car window. "Be glad to assist if I can. I've lived here for over twenty years, and I think I know about everyone in this valley."

Squinting, the man glanced at the two children beside Aaron. "Just tell me, sir, how to get back to the road to go to Philadel-

77

phia," he said. "Something tells me I'm wasting my time as well as yours." He mumbled some complaining phrases Aaron didn't comprehend.

"Go into the bedroom a minute," Rose whispered to Aaron as soon as he came in. "I want to talk to you."

"What you so excited about?"

"Janet dear," said Mrs. Loomas, "you and Davy finish putting those cookies on that sheet if you want to. I have to talk to Papa. Dennis, you can eat some of those raisins there. Lesa, take charge till I come out. And remember now."

Rose closed the door. "Who was that man in the lane, Aaron?"

"I don't know. What's wrong, Rose?"

"What did he want?"

"I really don't know. Said he missed the road to Philadelphia. Why? What's wrong, Rose?"

"Melvin called and said a well-dressed man in a black Cadillac stopped at the Home a while ago and asked where Davy Grant was. Melvin wouldn't tell. Said he's afraid he might try to nab him."

"No."

"Said he acted—well, gruff and sort of mad-like."

"No."

"Told us to watch Davy. What do you think? Was that the man?"

"How do I know? It was a Cadillac, and the man was well-dressed. But he never mentioned Davy's name."

"Well, what did he say to you?"

"He did say who he wanted to locate would be as hard to find as a needle in a haystack. But he didn't say who it was. Honestly, Rose, I can't believe. . . . Oh, no, Rose. He didn't look like—you mean we've got to be afraid someone will try to take—oh, no, Rose—surely not. Why, haven't we been asking God every day to keep His hand over our children?"

78

"But, Aaron, Davy's—special. You know he's always been—a mystery."

"But surely anyone who would give a child away wouldn't try to kidnap him later."

"You never know. Maybe he was kidnaped in the first place. Listen, Aaron, you've got to be on the watch. And be careful what you say to strangers."

"I made a special trip to Columbia to see your sister, Shana," Anthony announced by telephone.

"Oh," exclaimed Shana. "Would she tell you anything?"

"Yes. I'll give you a full report tonight, my love. We're going to the Dewberry Inn for dinner. I'll be seeing you."

All day Shana lived in a dream and her heart was in a strange flutter. She pictured a child's room, equipped with lovely furniture, toys, pictures, a tricycle, storybooks; but most of all a little boy on her lap, snuggled in her arms, calling her Mother.

"Shana, my dear," began Anthony, drawing her close to himself in his car. "I traced him to a beautiful Children's Home." He parked beside the Dewberry Inn. "Let's sit here and talk a bit."

"Oh, Anthony! Did you see him?" cried Shana in excitement.

"No, my love." He caught her face in both his warm hands. "I'm sorry to have to tell you this, but he's gone, Shana."

"Gone? Gone where?" She pulled his hands away.

"Your little baby died, Shana dear."

"Died! Oh, Anthony! When?"

"He didn't live long, honey, my love."

"Oh," cried Shana, in tears. "Then—then I—I should have kept him. It's my fault. All my fault. They didn't take care of him."

"Now wait. I wouldn't say that, dear," said Anthony. "Maybe the good Lord wanted to take him before he grew up."

"I—I can't understand," sobbed Shana. "Why I—I gave him to God in the hospital. I had him baptized too. I thought God would watch over him—and—and keep him safe from harm, and

79

danger, and sickness. Why, Anthony, I gave my baby over into God's hands—to—to lead him—and direct him just as the chaplain said He would and now—now he's—he's dead? Oh, no. I don't understand God at all."

Anthony sniffed. He blinked. Nervously he cleared his throat. "I don't either," he remarked with stupidity. "In fact, I never did. Shall we—shall we go inside?"

"I don't feel like eating now."

"Oh, come, come, dear. I'm sorry I had to tell you this. Don't blame yourself, Shana. Please be a brave girl. I tried so hard to please you. I wouldn't want you to think I didn't at least try to locate him for you."

"What home was it, Anthony? Was it down in South Carolina?"

"You wouldn't want to know that, Shana. It's best you don't." He caught her hand in his.

"Why is it best?" She pulled away. "I want to know."

"It'll be much easier for you to forget him if you don't know that, darling."

"Forget?" Shana all but shouted. "What if I don't want to forget?"

CHAPTER 11

Anthony rubbed one unsteady hand across the back of his plump neck with caution. "How can we be happy, darling," he ventured, "and dwell on our past sorrows? We want to start a new life—a clean slate together. Let's talk about a pleasant subject now. Look how long I've been kept waiting. I'm lonely. You're lonely."

"But I don't feel like talking about anything else right now. Anthony, please tell me this. Where is my baby buried?"

"I never asked that, Shana. The man in the office I talked to was curt and I'd say quite impolite. He didn't seem to want to tell me anything, really. I doubt if he even knew. Maybe he was new there in the office."

"Then are you sure it was my David Grant—that died?"

He cleared his throat twice. He shifted. "No mistake about it," stated Anthony. "It was the only Grant child they ever had there."

"Well, how long did he live?"

He sighed. "Oh, a—a week or two, I believe he said."

"My baby," sobbed Shana. "Oh, Anthony, he was so sweet, so dear. I loved him something awful. I was out of my mind to let Bernice take him. It just haunts me to death. Do you know sometimes I could have crawled over live coals on my bare hands and knees to find him. I can't forgive Bernice and I can't forgive myself. Oh, Anthony, take me to that Children's Home. I want to hear with my own ears all about him, and what happened."

"Now, sweetheart," he protested.

"I want to know. Did he take a cold? Did he starve? Did he—oh, he was so tiny, and so helpless. Did they neglect him? I'm his mother, Anthony. You've never been one. You don't know."

"Shana dear," began Anthony, breathing with heavier heaviness, "I'd take you there, but—but that would be positively cruel of me. Listen to me. He's gone and he's happy. He couldn't have suffered. Tiny babies—they—they never know suffering. God wouldn't let an innocent little baby suffer. They simply—just—fall asleep. He wasn't supposed to live or God would have let him." His tone was next to desperation now. "Shana dear, listen to me." He toned down a bit. "If I didn't go out of my way, and if I didn't try my level best to please you and to prove my love for you, God can strike me down. I'm giving you God's truth."

"Oh, Anthony," cried Shana. "Please, I—" She caught his arm. "I didn't mean to infer you didn't try. Forgive me. I'm sorry. I *know* you did. And I do—I do appreciate it. I *know* you've told me the truth. But it's such a shock. It's such a disappointment."

"I realize, dear," he said, trying to calm himself further, "but look at it this way. You can remember your son as a sweet, innocent baby. If he had lived and—and someone had adopted him, you couldn't get him back, no matter how much you wanted him. And if he wasn't happy with whoever adopted him and you knew it—that could be possible, Shana—then you really would be unhappy and upset. Then you really couldn't forgive yourself. Have you thought of all that?"

"No. No, not all that," sighed Shana, wiping her eyes. "I know you're right, dear Anthony. I'm sorry I caused you so much trouble. But I'm glad I know now."

"Then let's talk about our love and our home. You'll soon be Mrs. Drextell, my own beautiful wife. No longer drab, sad Shana Grant. You'll never work another day of your life, my love, except in our own home. And even there you can have a maid if you say the word. Mrs. Drextell is to be a fine, happy, satisfied lady of leisure."

"No, Anthony, no. I wouldn't be happy if I couldn't work. I wouldn't want a maid."

"I'll get you beautiful clothes, and a nice blue mink coat. And we'll go places. To Niagara Falls—to Florida—to California, and even to Columbia to call on Mr. and Mrs. Lewis McCawlis."

"No," objected Shana with resentment. "I'd never want to go there."

"But your sister was tickled when I told her I was in love with you. She even clapped her hands, she was so delighted."

"Just because you have means. Bernice doesn't associate with people beneath her social standard. I never want to go there. I want to take you to meet my sister Hazel. She's altogether different. You'll love her. And her husband Bruce too. He's refined and cultured, yet common and humble. They have six adorable children."

"Six children?"

"And Hazel is a wonderful mother to all six."

Melvin and Martha Kolb and Sister Lora kept a watchful eye on every car that passed or stopped at the Home. One of them called Rose Loomas at least once every day. The safety of little Davy Grant was a special request sent heavenward in every inaudible prayer the five adults prayed.

"Sister Lora," said Rose on the phone one afternoon, "you know we've never had that picnic yet. Rain spoiled our first attempt, then this scare. I wish we didn't need to be thinking of it so much of the time. Davy is such a happy little boy, I wish we didn't have to be concerned like this. It's a wonder Janet doesn't ask why I'm so careful. Let's plan to have our picnic this Sunday. Here he comes now. Wait a minute. Davy, honey, come here. Climb up on this chair. Sister Lora is on the phone. Say hello to her. Say it right in there."

"Hello."

"Hi there, Davy. It's nice to hear your voice. What have

you been doing?"

"Playin'."

"Who with?"

"Wagons an' things. An' Janet."

"Having fun?"

"Fun." Davy nodded.

"That's fine. You know who this is talking to you?"

"Sister LoLo."

"That's right, Davy. You be sure and come to see me soon."

"I want to."

"I want you to, too. Come Sunday. Will you?"

"I want to."

"Bless your heart, Davy. Be a good boy for Mamma Loomas."

"I be good."

"I know you're a good boy, Davy. Mamma Loomas tells me real nice things about you. She tells me you like Janet to read to you. And I hear you helped bake cookies. Was that fun?"

"They didn't taste good."

"They didn't? Why not?"

"We let Rover an' the chickens eat 'em all."

"Well," laughed Lora. "The next time tell Mamma to put more sugar in."

"I will," laughed Davy.

"Tell Mamma I'd like to talk a little more with her now."

He sobered. He handed over the receiver and hurried across the room to rejoin Janet on the long, low one-step back porch.

"Couldn't you find it?" she asked.

"What?"

"I sent you after a storybook."

"I forgot." Davy squatted beside Janet. "I want—" he pulled her one arm with both hands. "You take me to see her."

"See who?"

"Sister LoLo."

"It's too far, Davy. I couldn't. What made you think of her?"

"She wants me."

84

"No, she doesn't, Davy. She has other children to take care of."

A look of dismay crossed his face. "Yes," he repeated. "She wants me."

"No, she doesn't, Davy. She's too busy."

Dolefully he shook his head. Tears came to his big brown eyes. All at once he broke into sobs.

"What's wrong with Davy?" inquired Mamma Loomas, appearing in the doorway.

"I don't know. He just started to cry," said Janet. "Wants me to take him to see Sister LoLo."

"Where's Dennis? I thought he was out here playing with him too."

"He said Davy's too little to play with him. He went over in the field to play ball with Joey and Ron. We don't care if he did go. He pinched Davy twice."

"Why?" Mamma Loomas came out on the porch.

" 'Cause he wanted that wagon there. The one Papa finished for Davy last night. He said he might hide it where Davy can't find it. I think that's why Davy wants to go see Sister LoLo."

Davy put his face against the side of the house and cried.

Mamma Loomas gathered the forlorn child in her arms, carried him over to the big porch rocker, and held him on her lap. "Now let's see what we can do together," she said with tenderness. "Go find a storybook, Janet. I'll read to him."

Davy shook his head.

"No? Not a real good story?"

He shook his head the more.

"Well, you know," she began, rubbing one hand very lightly up and down one little arm, "sometimes just 'talk' stories are the best anyhow."

Janet returned with a book and seated herself on a low stool close by. Mamma Loomas motioned for her to lay the book down.

"One time a mother had a sweet wee little baby boy and a very bad wicked king didn't like the baby one bit. The mother was afraid some harm would come to him, and she fixed a little basket all up nice and safe so it wouldn't leak and put a blanket inside and put the baby in the basket. Then she hid it in the rushes in the—"

"What's rushes?" asked Davy.

"Those are tall stems that grow in still water, honey. That way the basket with the baby in it couldn't be seen by passers-by. But to be on the safe side, because she loved her baby very much, the mother had the baby's own big sister stay around on the bank to keep an eye on him and hear if he cried."

Davy looked up. "Was it Sister LoLo?"

"No, dear," she kissed his forehead. "This wasn't Sister LoLo, but another big sister that was kind to little children like she is."

"I wanna go see her now."

"We'll go see her on Sunday. We'll see Leon, too. Day after tomorrow. Don't you want to hear the rest of this story about that little baby and the big sister?"

"Who was she?"

"Her name was Miriam."

"Who was the baby?"

"His name was Moses."

"He could sleep in my bed with me."

"He could?" Mamma Loomas smiled.

"Don't let him be in those old stems all by himself in a basket," frowned Davy.

Janet burst into laughter.

"Sh." Mamma Loomas shook her head. Desperately, as she caressed the child on her lap, she tried to gear her adult understanding into his young thought stream. Janet had listened to this same story often at Davy's age and had not once asked any of these questions. Nor had Dennis at five. He wanted to capture the bad king and lock him up tight in jail.

"Tell it again," musingly said Davy, "but let him be my brother an' sleep in my bed. An' play with me. I wouldn't hide the wagon so he couldn't find it."

"I'm sure you would be nice to the little Moses boy," com-

86

mented Mamma Loomas, fondling his one small hand. "Instead of telling that story over, how about another one?"

She told not another, but others. For well over an hour she told stories. And with each tick of the clock on the wall inside, and with each beat of the heart in the breast of the child in her arms, his delicate web of simple childlike trust and confiding love for her was becoming ever stronger.

The lawn picnic on Sunday was as enjoyable as the day was perfect. Before and during the dinner Sister Lora beamed on Davy as he told her about the kittens, the sheep, the chickens, Rover, and the wagon Papa had made for him. After dinner he and Leon romped all over the lawn together, while Janet and Dennis played with the older children. Lesa found Helen, a girl near her age, and they had a chatting session on the front steps.

"Davy seems happy, doesn't he, Rose?" asked Sister Lora, "and well adjusted already?"

"We think so. He and Janet get along beautifully. And I think when he's old enough to start to school Dennis will be more of a pal to him. He's still a little resentful because we didn't get an older boy. But Aaron and I don't feel we should let Dennis know we see this. And we can't scold him about it all the time. Davy's very sensitive and tenderhearted, but not peevish. We're sure Dennis will make up to him later. We must be patient. No two children are alike."

Out by the swings Dennis was confiding in Nathan, a robust towheaded niner. "Wish they'd leave that Davy Grant here and take you along. Would you go if they'd want you?"

Nathan shrugged. "I don't care if I stay here. We get good things to eat."

"We get lots better things over there where I live. Ham. I mean thick slices, an' steak, and all the eggs for breakfast we want. And homemade bread. And real good everything."

"Are you adopt?"

"No."

"Why not?"

"I don't know. Guess my mother said not to."

"Did they adopt him? That little kid?"

"Guess not. They're just tryin' him out."

"Did they adopt that girl what lives there?"

"How do I know? Quit askin' me them dumb questions. Come on. Go with me. Let's ask Papa Loomas if you can go along home with us."

"I don't want to. My grandma's coming to see me next week. She's bringing me a present."

"What is it?"

"How do I know? It's a surprise. If I knew it wouldn't be. Let's go inside. I'll show you a card she sent me."

The two tiptoed up the back stairway. As they passed the door to the boys' nursery, they heard voices. "It's Davy and Leon," whispered Dennis. "Let's scare 'em."

"This one is my bed," Davy was saying, clasping with both hands the side railing of one of the white iron beds.

"Not any more," Leon was saying. "Tony sleeps in that one now."

"But it's mine," insisted Davy. "I know it is, because it belongs to me."

Leon shook his head.

"I'm going to go ask Sister LoLo," said Davy. "She knows it does."

Dennis stuck his head in the door and let out a boisterous tormenting laugh.

Davy jumped.

"Go ahead, Davy," he shouted, "and see what Sister LoLo says."

Davy stood for a moment terrified, then ran down the steps and across the lawn as fast as his legs would take him.

CHAPTER 12

"We really should be going," Rose remarked to Sister Lora as she picked up her two picnic baskets. "But those two little boys must be having the time of their lives. Look, here they come racing. Watch it, Davy," she called. "You'll stumble and hurt yourself."

Davy ran panting past Mamma Loomas to Sister Lora. "It's—it's my bed, isn't it?"

"What bed?" She read both alarm and consternation in his hot, uplifted face. She drew him closer.

"Up there," he pointed. "In my room. The white bed *is* mine. Isn't it mine?"

"But I told him," interrupted Leon, short-breathed and perspiring, "Tony sleeps in it now. But he says it's his."

"You boys weren't up in the nursery room?" she asked admonishingly.

Davy nodded. "Isn't it my bed, Sister LoLo?"

Perplexed, Sister Lora rubbed one hand over Davy's shoulder. "Well, now," she remarked, "I wonder what you two have been doing up there. Leon, you know—"

"We were only looking," said Davy, "at—at my bed."

"Only looking? Well, now, Davy, my boy, I know you loved your little white bed, but now," she added with tenderness, stroking his hair, "don't you think we should let Tony sleep in it when you're not there? And when you have a good bed all your own in your new home?"

Davy stood thinking and panting. His eyes got misty.

"You can still call it yours if that makes you happy, Davy. We all want you to be happy." She hesitated. "Listen, Davy." Sister Lora put his chin in the cup of her one hand and looked down into his distressed eyes. "Just last evening I told Tony that that was your bed when—" Suddenly she got down on one knee and caught the child in her arms. Then through a mist of tears Davy laughed softly, and she laughed with him.

"Go tell Lesa it's time to go home," said Mamma Loomas.

"Rose," began Sister Lora as soon as the boys were out of hearing, "just why is the child so attached to that bed?"

"Well, now, I'm no child psychologist," began Rose Loomas thinkingly, "but I believe Davy unconsciously connects that white bed with you. You're the most important person in his life."

"Rose Loomas," Lora Wenzel blushed.

"You are," insisted Rose. "You're the first person he ever trusted, because you loved him first. You loved him into that bed and out of it. Didn't you? He found security in you, and that white bed is only a symbol, a reminder of that security."

Sister Lora laughed a little. "And where did you learn all this philosophy, pray tell?"

"I didn't," answered Rose. "I'm just surmising. If you'd tucked him into a green or a black bed, he would react the same way, I think. If you'd whipped him to bed, I dare say, he wouldn't insist it was his. I've learned already that little Davy is a child who craves just a little more love and security than the other children do. And I wonder why."

"Rose," remarked Lora, with a pondering faraway gaze. "I hope I've been good enough to little Davy. And understanding. He's so alone in the world. I—I only hope my love and caring for him won't make it hard for him to break away. I know I'll always miss him and love him, and be interested in him, but I don't want to ever, ever," she turned abruptly and faced Rose squarely, "interfere with his loving you more and trusting you more. I mean that. I want him to be completely happy, and feel secure in your home now."

90

"I'm sure you mean it, Lora."

"Truly I do want him to love you like a real mother, Rose. I know that's what the child needs above all else."

"I believe you. If I were little Davy, I'd undoubtedly feel the same about you. I'm glad, believe me now, and for the remainder of your life believe this"—Rose reached over and touched Sister Lora's hand—"that I'm glad you're the one who taught Davy what love is. You are responsible for his earliest impressions. As long as we have him, I won't let him forget you either."

Sister Lora smiled and drew a long breath. "I have much to learn about understanding children," she said. "I must try to find some good books on the subject."

"If you do, please let me read them too. I'm the one who has a lot to learn, Lora. No one knows how often I have to slip off to my secret place and talk to God about each of our children."

"I wonder how many authors suggest that?"

"Well," answered Rose softly, "whether they do or don't, it's absolutely necessary with me."

Before going home Aaron and Rose decided to chat a bit with Melvin and Martha in the Home reception room, and the agreement was made that twice a month Leon would spend a day or two with Davy at the farm and at least once a month Aaron would bring Davy to the Home to spend a day and a night.

With great anticipation both boys looked forward to these visits. Mamma Loomas gave Davy a personal calendar and marked with a red circle the days Leon would be coming and with blue the ones Davy would be going to the Home.

"Mamma," said Lesa one afternoon in late August, as she came into the kitchen with her arms full of dry clean wash, "step to the window and look out. Davy and Leon remind me of those two little bear cubs we saw at the zoo in Philadelphia, the way they hug each other and roll around on the grass. Isn't it cute the way they play? Wonder what they talk about. Don't you?"

"I'd like to be an innocent little bird sometime and sit in a tree above them," laughed Mamma Loomas.

"Janet said she heard Leon telling Davy he'd like to come and stay a whole week sometime."

"Well, I'm glad he likes to come here, but we'd better not wear out a good thing. Now, Lesa, I was thinking perhaps we could consult his parents about staying here the first week or two of school. He'll miss Janet something awful."

"Please do it," said Lesa. "Please, Mamma."

"And why are *you* so concerned?"

"Because I—well, I just can't bear to think of him being home and lonesome all day long. Isn't that what you're thinking about?"

For some reason her feet, her legs, her entire body suddenly felt years younger as Rose Loomas started dampening the clothes on the kitchen table. A fresh glow of warm and tender appreciation for her only daughter was readily defined on the sweet simplicity of her face.

"I'll quit school and stay home if—if you want me to," suggested Lesa.

"Indeed you won't," answered her mother with consternation. "Miss graduation? Lesa Loomas. My dear child. I'm glad and thankful that you love Davy that much. But listen to me. You're going on to school. And what's more, we dare not spoil or pamper that little boy just because we love him."

As Thanksgiving Day drew near, Martha and Melvin Kolb planned a special dinner for the children with the sumptuous food donations goodhearted farmers brought in. Janet, Dennis, and Davy each received an invitation to the dinner. Rose discussed the matter with Martha over the phone.

"It's a nice idea, Martha, and, to be sure, all three want to come. But isn't this something out of the ordinary? And Christmas Day just around the corner?"

"I'll tell you, Rose—it's like this. Leon has been begging for Davy to come. And Melvin and I felt that if we invited him we should invite Dennis and Janet too. We don't want them to get the impression we're partial to Davy."

"That's sweet of you to feel that way, Martha. Aaron and I both appreciate it. Dennis gets quite jealous at times."

"For several mornings now in our worship period, Melvin has been having the children tell what they are most thankful for, and every morning Leon says the same thing. Davy."

Rose chuckled ever so softly.

"Some of the other boys here would like to come over to the Loomas farm too."

"I imagine," commented Rose.

"Hazel, this is Shana. I'm calling from Mercy Hospital. Anthony is quite a sick man."

"What's the matter?"

"The doctors are going into consultation with a specialist as soon as he gets here." Shana's voice was unsteady. "This morning after breakfast he fell just as he was getting up. Blacked out. Scared me, Hazel. I called the doctor at once and he said to have an ambulance bring him here to the hospital."

"You think it's something serious, Shana? Do you want me to come over?"

"There's nothing you could do, Hazel. Anyhow you couldn't leave, could you?"

"I'd have to arrange for the children. You think that bump he got on his head a while back has something to do with this?"

"I don't know. I told the doctor about it, but he rather doubted. But he's been complaining of more headaches since that happened. But even before that he didn't feel right. He couldn't ever seem to relax for some reason. He's been so restless at night, he often got up about two and would try to doze in the easy chair in the living room. Said he had such crazy dreams when he lay down. I wish I knew what's wrong with him."

"Was he feeling all right when you were here last week?"

"No, he wasn't, Hazel. But he tried hard to hide the fact. On the way home I unwisely remarked how I wished my little David had lived. It just slipped out, because I always think about him when I see yours. Anthony stopped the car and acted so queer and sort of dizzy like, it frightened me. He said if I mentioned my baby once more, he'd have a stroke or something."

"Why?"

"He says he's afraid I don't really love him. He says it makes him jealous and that he couldn't help it he couldn't bring him back to me."

"Well, of course not. And I know you do love Anthony. And he knows it too, Shana."

"Of course," agreed Shana with a sad, feeble tone. "Of course he does. I told him so over and over. I can't understand it all."

"Let us know how he is tonight."

"I will." Shana's voice faded into a whisper.

"Bruce will want to come over, I'm sure. Please tell us if we can help in any way, Shana. You poor dear."

"I will."

For weeks Shana's reports to Hazel gave little or no improvement in Anthony's condition. He still suffered headaches, ran irregular fevers (not alarmingly high), couldn't sleep without sedatives, and his thinking was getting sluggish.

"Hazel," Shana called one day in early spring. "It just seems like I'm destined to have nothing but disappointments." Her voice dripped with tears.

"You mean Anthony is worse?"

"He's not better, that's certain. I—I have a feeling this *is* something serious—but the doctor doesn't tell me. I'm so upset and lonely, Hazel."

"I think of you all alone in that house every night. I know you must be lonely, dear."

"Hazel, no one knows." Shana's voice broke.

"You can come here any time you feel like it, Shana. You know that, don't you?"

"Yes. I know, but—but, oh, Hazel, I can say this to you

94

and I've got to say it to someone—if only I'd—never given my baby to Bernice," she sobbed brokenly, "he might still be with me. I'd at least have him."

"Listen. Shana—you—Shana! Shana!"

But Shana had hung up.

Months before Davy started to school he began to be more and more puzzled over remarks he heard about himself, directly and indirectly.

Rose and Aaron Loomas were blessed with a host of friends who enjoyed, as they did, demonstrating old-fashioned hospitality. This meant there were few Sundays in the year when the Loomases didn't either entertain dinner guests or were entertained.

Without exception this included first of all a round of hand-shaking. Davy began to dread that.

"And whose little boy is this?" (Typical question number one.) Davy got a prolonged handshake.

"He belongs to us," Papa Loomas would say with a grateful smile.

"And your name, little man?" (Question number two.)

"Davy." He wanted to squirm loose, but hardly dared try.

"Davy Loomas?" (Question number three.) Still holding Davy's hand.

He could do one of two things. Shake his head—act stupid, too stupid to answer, or speak up and say, "No, sir. Davy Grant" (as he had been told to do).

"Grant?" Then turning to Aaron or Rose (typical question number four), "and where did you pick up such a nice boy?" or "where did you find him?" or in an undertone, "orphan? parents separated?"

Davy dreaded these experiences more and more. And once he overhead a lady remark to Mamma, "Why is it that so often *that* kind [and she nodded at him] are the cutest of all? It happens over and over."

"That kind?" All afternoon that remark went through

95

Davy's mind. He wondered what "kind" she meant he was. "That kind." He began comparing himself to all other boys. His hands and arms. His legs and feet. His teeth, his hair, his ears. As far as he could observe, he was made like other boys. He liked to eat, and play, and run like the others. His clothes were like those other boys wore, as nice if not a bit nicer.

"Janet," began Davy, at the top of the stairway, one Sunday evening. "What is the cutest?" He ran one hand back and forth over the banister.

"Cutest what? What do you mean?"

Davy shrugged his shoulders. "I don't know. Cutest anything."

"It means the nicest. The best, or the prettiest. Why?"

"I don't know." And Davy hurried to his room and, after closing the door, looked scrutinizingly again at his image in the framed oval mirror. He frowned, he scowled, he made faces, he wiggled his nose, he did everything but smile at "that kind." He couldn't decide he was the nicest and prettiest.

The first cruel pinching thoughts followed Davy after the next annual Christmas celebration at the Home. The whole Loomas family was invited.

CHAPTER 13

Excitement rode high. People of all ages and descriptions milled through the Home. Laughter, hugs, kissing, handshakes, and introductions seemed to have no end. Nathan was leading a fat but pleasant-faced lady around by the hand, calling her his grandma. Jerry had two trailing beside him, his daddy and his big sister, a pretty girl with black hair and red lips and cheeks. Rodney had a grandma and a grandpa. Craig had a pretty mother—his real mother, he said she was. Dian—Jeffery—Lois—Alvin—Barney—Phil and Brenda—all had someone they were taking around and introducing as a mother or a father, an aunt, uncle, or cousin. Fay even had a father and two brothers that looked alike. Twins. Janet's very own grandmother arrived a little late, but she did arrive. And with a present wrapped in pretty green paper and tied with bright red ribbon. Even though Dennis didn't act completely thrilled (he was a little), a lady did appear later who said she was his Aunt Marie (don't you remember, dear?) and brought him two presents. One from his mother. (She said she was sorry she couldn't come this time.)

Davy sat forlorn and dejected in the far corner of the gaily decorated assembly room, his lonely heart pounding and his sad, hungry eyes searching for someone to come in and single him out. No one to claim him as a relative? He recalled now with genuine unhappiness all the times Dennis had reminded him (when they were alone together) he must not have a real mother or father and that that made him a nobody. But Janet told him emphatically that he *did* have a mother; that he *had* to have a mother somehow, somewhere, someway.

He wished he knew for sure that Janet was right. Janet wouldn't say something unless it were true, would she?

With disappointment and dismay, Davy watched forty-two children enjoying the company of at least one relative and opening presents. In his troubled thoughts ran the frightening refrain, "I don't belong to anyone. I don't belong to anyone." Why? Why was he the only one who didn't receive a present? Why was he the only one who didn't have one single relation? Yes, Mamma Loomas had said they would have Christmas at home tomorrow with gifts and a turkey dinner, and oranges and nuts and crackerjack in the evening. She and Papa and Lesa were all in the kitchen now, helping Leon's mother and father prepare the refreshments to be served. And Leon must be out there too. He wasn't one of the Home children. He was different. He belonged to Martha and Melvin Kolb. He slept with them in their own private apartment. Why did Mamma Loomas tell him to sit in the assembly and watch all this merrymaking he had almost no part in?

A gentle tap on his shoulder. Davy looked up sharply. There stood Sister Lora, a special radiance about her gentle face and smiling eyes. Davy thought he had never seen anyone so beautiful. His heart skipped a beat. She sat beside him and closed his one hand snugly between her own. "I wondered where you were," she said, bending to look into his face. "I—" she noted the sad expression in his eyes change to relief. Or was it gratitude? "I have a gift for you." His eyes almost sparkled. "I'll send it along when you go home, so you can open it tomorrow when you have your own Christmas."

Suddenly Davy's shoulders drooped. "You see, dear," Sister Lora added quietly, and with particular tenderness when she saw his lip quiver, "I haven't gifts for all the children. Only you. That's why it would be best to open it at home. Don't you think?"

Davy drew a long breath.

"You're someone extra-special to me," she whispered.

He felt the warmth of her breath on his temple. He smelled the sweet fragrance of delicate perfume about her person. Davy wanted to get closer to her. He wished she were his own big sister. Why wasn't she? Maybe—maybe she was. Maybe she really was, but never told him. Why did she tell him he was an extra-special someone?

"Sister LoLo," ventured Davy, with timidity. "I—I mean Sister Lora." He glanced down at his feet with abashment.

"You're growing up, aren't you, Davy?" smiled Sister Lora pleasantly. "What were you going to say?"

"Don't I," he twisted—he turned, "don't I have—" For some reason Davy could not bring himself to the finished question that was racing through his mind and demanding an immediate answer.

Lora Wenzel tried to sense Davy Grant's problem, the problem she herself dreaded would someday possess this child. She had hoped not so soon.

"You have lots of things to be glad for, Davy," she said with compassion. "You have Mamma and Papa Loomas, who both love you, and you have a good home; you have Lesa and Janet. And Dennis and Leon. You have lots of—"

"But I—I mean—"

She waited. "Can't you tell me?"

Mr. Kolb entered and was clapping his hands. "Now, friends—" he was saying.

Davy's eyes filled with sudden, unbidden tears. "You have me," quickly added Sister Lora. "I'll sit here and eat beside you if I may. Or would you rather have Leon?"

"You stay by me," he whispered. Sister Lora slipped Davy her handkerchief and with it he quietly and quickly wiped his eyes.

Before the refreshments came, Davy's feelings had been somewhat soothed. Of one thing he was certain: no boy or girl in the big circle had a sweeter or more dearly loved partner than he had that day.

99

Once a year the Home staff and board of directors announced a summertime reunion, which brought back people from many near and distant parts: professionals, farmers, parents, preachers, missionaries, students, and children of all ages. Anyone who had ever lived in the Millersville Children's Home was invited, as well as all interested friends and donors. Of course Rose and Aaron would be there with their Lesa and three Home children.

It was most interesting to see how many of those former Home youngsters had grown up and become useful, substantial men and women in society, in business, and in some church program. All these enjoyed coming back to meet each other again, and the new children. It was a great event, getting greater each year. But with all its gaiety, there was one thing about the reunion that made Davy sad. Not one person came to him and said, "I'm your cousin, or your uncle, or your mother." Not one person said, "I knew your father or grandmother.' Not one person said, "My name is also Grant."

Davy was lonely in the crowd. The larger the crowd grew, the lonelier he felt. He wondered if anyone else felt the way he did. He couldn't tell.

Davy was assigned the job of going for the mail. It was not a hard chore, walking down the long lane. But every time he went, he hoped there would be a letter for him. Once in a while Janet got one, and she jumped and squealed with delight over it. Not because it contained much of news or importance, but because it was addressed to "Miss Janet Chaveriat." It made her feel cared-for and a little important. Even Dennis Forney occasionally got a letter or a post card.

"Why don't I ever get a letter?" Davy asked Lesa one day.

"Who would write to you?"

"I don't know. Maybe somebody would, but they don't know I'm here."

"Who doesn't know you're here?"

"Anybody. I just wish somebody would send *me* something once. Do you think I have a grandma, Lesa?"

"I just don't know, Davy."

"Or a cousin, or something like that?"

"I have no idea, Davy dear."

"I wish I knew."

The first term of school brought Davy some very unpleasant experiences. He liked classes well enough—reading, writing, and especially number work—and he liked all the other six first-graders. (Leon was a grade ahead.) He enjoyed the tasty dinners Mamma packed with care, in his personalized red lunch bucket. He sat beside Leon to eat.

One part of schoolgoing Davy did not enjoy, and as time went on he disliked it worse and worse. It began the very first day during recess. Two husky sixth-grade boys called him aside. "Not you, Leon. You stay where you are. Come over here, David. We want to ask you something." Edwin stood grinning sheepishly while Gilbert did the talking.

"What's your dad's name, little kid?"

Davy stepped back, shifting his glance nervously.

"Yours is Grant, isn't it?" Gilbert asked, with an air of boldness and looking very big and wise.

"Isn't it?" he demanded. "Isn't it?" he repeated in a merry-go-round voice. Edwin jutted his jaw and raised his eyebrows inquisitively.

"Yes," admitted Davy feebly.

"Why isn't it Loomas?"

Davy was suddenly seized with an unexpected density of thought. He felt limber like a rope. He turned to run back to Leon, but Gilbert caught him firmly by the arm and held him.

"We heard you tell the teacher your name was David Grant." This Gilbert spelled out with an air of certainty and finality.

"Well, it is," said Davy in a frightened voice.

Gilbert laughed. "Then you told her your father's name was Aaron Loomas. How come?"

"Well," blinked Davy, almost puffing. "So what? I—I live there. It's my home. And—and Papa Loomas," tears welled up

101

in Davy's eyes in spite of every effort to squeeze them back, "he's just as good a papa as yours is."

Gilbert was eager to argue the point, any point in fact, to start a fracas. Such a statement from a little first-grade brat was fit for an explanation and a full one.

"You didn't answer my question, little smarty. And you'd better not say anything you can't prove about my father, you little bas—"

At that instant Edwin clapped one dirty hand over Gilbert's mouth, for there at his very elbow appeared Janet. She had been watching unnoticed behind the big oak tree.

"You boys let Davy alone," she said with fiery intent, "or I'll report you to the teacher. Come," she said, and with her arm around his shoulder, she escorted Davy back to Leon.

Janet was always ready to protect or defend Davy. He always walked to and from school with her while Dennis dashed ahead. On rainy days Papa took them.

Miss Scott called him David from the start, and so the majority of the scholars did likewise. Dennis consistently called him David Grant (with emphasis) only on occasions when he reveled in disdainful superiority. He found, or manufactured, such an occasion about once or twice a week and always when the two were together alone about the barn or in the close proximity of the bully-type boys, like Gilbert and Edwin and Nick. Dennis seemed to get a degree of enjoyment in watching Davy suffer humiliation or frustration concerning his parents and name.

One day on the playground Nick put the question to Davy with crushing bluntness. "Where do you think you came from? Some baby factory? Did they pick you out of the catalog?"

Davy wanted to run and run to the end of the world and hide where no one could ever find him.

Another time Reah, a seventh-grader, said to him, "You don't look like you belong to the Loomas family. Did your real mother have black hair like yours?

After that Davy never heard the word "mother" without enduring a secret spell of wondering and baffling ideas. Once when he was at the Home with Leon he almost confided in Sister Lora. Many times he was on the very verge of asking Mamma Loomas if she couldn't tell him something, anything, at least one thing about his birth. He could go to her about any other thing. But this—he just couldn't. With every passing month, however, he felt more closely knit to both Papa and Mamma. And Lesa— why, he learned she was almost as sweet and kind as Sister Lora. He loved all three. He called it home. It *was* his home. Although he was well, although he knew he was loved, although he was well supplied with toys and clothes, although he was happy most of the time, Davy often hid in the barn to think and wonder and cry in secret.

Above the blackboard in school Miss Scott kept a loaded revolver. A new road was under construction running parallel to the schoolhouse, and she had told the school board she was afraid of some of the men in the construction gang. No one ever heard that she used it, but to the pupils it was an ever-constant reminder of her determination to have authority and order.

"David," blurted Gilbert one day at recess. "Did you or Janet tell your Papa Loomas a bunch of stuff about me? Huh?"

"No," answered Davy.

"Well, you'd better not either. You know that revolver in there is to scare people with. An' I know how to use it, too."

Davy cringed under the big boy's glaring eyes.

"I know something you don't know," Gilbert added. "My father found it out. And it's about you."

Davy was too frightened to ask. He ran away.

The black bed he so much hated at first had been stowed away in the attic and replaced by a handsome, single oak bed. Davy liked his own room very much. One night as he knelt to say his usual memorized prayer, he added two sentences of his own. "Could you somehow find out, dear God, if I belong to someone real? I don't know how to tell you, but I hope you know what I mean."

103

CHAPTER 14

The next year Miss Eloise Ranger taught the one-room school. Davy liked her at once. The neatly dressed, soft-voiced lady had a smile that came out of a face vivid with life and human understanding. She had no revolver above the blackboard, not even a strap in sight, even though Gilbert was bigger than she was. So were Nick and Edwin.

Davy tried his best to avoid being attacked with questions. The sight of Gilbert almost nauseated him. But it happened. The second day Gilbert picked Davy up bodily and carried him across the schoolyard and planted him behind the big oak tree. "I'm glad I'm not what you are," he said in a cocky, teasing manner. "You're one of those illegitimate kids."

"No," cried Davy frantically. "I'm not either."

"Yes, you are," insisted Gilbert, showing his big teeth. "My mother said so, and she knows."

"No," cried Davy tearfully. "Let me go."

"O.K., go," said Gilbert. "The whole school ground is yours. But everybody on it knows it."

Davy was horrified, horrified to weakness. He had no idea what—what that awful word meant—but it must be something bad. Oh! What was it everybody knew he was? How did they know? How did Gilbert's mother find out? "That kind—that kind," that lady said he was. What kind?

Davy ran to Leon. He would ask him. But—but already he forgot. A big word, a hard word. He had never heard it before.

"Leon," he choked, panting, "am I—am I—one of those real—real bad—oh, Leon," he sobbed, "do you know what that means I am?"

"What do you mean, Davy?"

"I—I—Gilbert said every—everybody in school thinks I'm—I'm—" He couldn't say another word.

Janet, ever-protecting Janet, noticed Davy crying. She ran and put her arm around him. "What's wrong, honey? Did you get hurt?"

He shook his head. "I—can't—say it." He tried to control his tears. Across the yard Gilbert and several other boys including Dennis were eying him and grinning. "It's a bad word—I think—and I—I want to go home."

"No, honey. Let's go in and tell Miss Ranger about it. What happened, Leon?"

"I don't know."

"Don't cry, Davy," begged Janet. "Those big boys are naughty. Awful naughty."

"Mamma," said Janet that evening while Dennis and Davy were out helping Papa with the chores, "some of the boys at school and even a few girls, too, make Davy feel bad sometimes."

"How?" Rose Loomas stopped beating the corn-bread batter in the big brown bowl. She frowned.

"They tease him because he doesn't know who his mother and father are, and say snippy things at him."

"Like what?"

"And Dennis just laughs."

"Like what do they say, Janet?"

"Today he cried. Hard."

"Tell me, Janet. What snippy things—who says it?"

"He wouldn't tell me. I asked and he wouldn't, but I'm pretty sure it was Nick or Gilbert. Gilbert, I think."

"Has this happened before?"

"I think quite a few times."

"You should have told me, Janet. You should have told me."

"I thought maybe Davy told you himself. I'm telling you the truth, Mamma. He cried today."

"Does Miss Ranger know this?"

"I don't know," answered Janet. "Shall I tell her? Davy wouldn't."

"No, dear. I'll have a talk with her myself."

After supper Davy played on the floor with his prize possession, the electric train Papa had given him for Christmas. Out of the corner of her eye Mamma Loomas watched his every movement and expression. She detected no sign of unhappiness or nervousness, but twice she noticed he sat as though in deep study.

The following evening Aaron and Rose took Davy into their bedroom.

"You've been with us four years now, Davy," began Papa Loomas, "and we have grown very fond of you. You know that, don't you?"

A delicate smile played around Davy's slightly parted lips.

"We hope you want to stay living here with us." Papa patted Davy's shoulder.

Davy nodded.

"We'd hate to see you leave."

"Do I have to?"

"Oh, no, no," answered Papa Loomas, "but we would like to ask you now, would you rather your name would be Loomas, or do you want it to stay as it is, Davy Grant? You may choose. You see we could adopt you; then by law you'd be our very own and you would change your name to Loomas. Would you like that better?"

His eyes widened. "Did—did my mother tell you to adopt me?" he asked.

"No, Davy. We never heard from your mother."

"Never?"

"Never, Davy."

"Or my father?"

"Never."

106

Speechless and almost motionless, Davy looked first at Mamma, then at Papa Loomas, then at his trembling hands.

"You don't have to decide tonight, Davy," put in Mamma Loomas.

"I—I think," he said at length, "I will keep my own name till—"

"Till when, Davy?" asked Papa. "Don't be afraid to tell us."

"Till my mother says—says she—" Davy hurried out of the room. He ran upstairs. No one followed him. Only God and the angels knew why he cried himself to sleep.

Rose met Eloise Ranger in the post office on a Saturday forenoon by prearrangement.

"I want to talk to you about our David," began Rose. "How is he doing in school?"

"Excellent, Mrs. Loomas. Bright as a tack. He really is capable of doing third-grade work."

"Does he ever seem sad?"

"Sad? I hadn't thought so. A little sober at times. Is he sad at home?"

"No. Not really. But Janet tells me some of the older pupils question him and tease him because he doesn't know where he came from. And about his name being Grant."

"How cruel, Mrs. Loomas. I'm indeed sorry. I didn't know this was going on. Why, the poor child. Why, he's a perfect dear, Mrs. Loomas. I'm surprised no one has adopted him. Do you intend to?"

"We're giving him his choice, Miss Ranger. We're ready the day he says he wants to be."

"You mean? I don't believe I'm familiar—yes, I've heard of it, I believe. So you're leaving it up to him? You could be very proud of such a child, I'd think."

"We do dearly love him, Miss Ranger. And we are proud of him. I sincerely hope you will do what you can to protect him from insulting or discouraging remarks. Perhaps the pupils are thoughtless or ignorant or haven't been taught to respect the feelings of others. But we are concerned that Davy won't develop any feelings of inferiority because he doesn't happen to know who his parents are."

"I'm glad, real glad, you told me about this, Mrs. Loomas. By the way, I'd like to find another place to room and board in the community if I'm hired again next year. Could you suggest a place? Don't tell anyone, but I'm not exactly satisfied with my present situation."

"We have an extra room," said Rose. "You may come and look at it any time. I'm quite sure you'll be rehired."

"It's settled. I'll take it without looking. Now I'm glad for two reasons we met here today. I'll keep my eyes and ears open from now on."

A week later the teacher was watching from a window when she saw Gilbert grab David and say something to him that appeared to be impudent. At least she saw David pull back, shake his head, and whimper. Miss Ranger took her chance to speak, not to Gilbert, but to the entire school.

"I have a story to tell you this morning," she began. Davy, in the third from the front seat to her far left, folded his arms and sat erect. "When I was in the fifth grade in school in southern Indiana, a new pupil by the name of Erick Wolf enrolled in the second grade. He was a newcomer, a very nice-looking boy and intelligent. I'm not sure who started the report, but someone did, and soon it was on the lips of every one in school that, because his name was Wolf and not Williams like the people he lived with, Erick was an unwanted child and that someone had left him, as a tiny baby, in a basket at a fish market." Davy cringed. Several pupils snickered behind tightly pressed lips. "I remember hearing some of the pupils referring to Erick as the little fish." Gilbert laughed outright. Miss Ranger continued. "Can you imagine how that hurt Erick? Can you imagine, children, how *you* would feel if someone called you an unwanted fish?" No one laughed this time. Davy blinked. Maybe "that word" meant a fish.

"I remember how sorry I felt for Erick. And when I told my

108

parents about this, they were deeply grieved and horrified. Now my father was acquainted slightly with the people who had taken this boy to raise. And one day during a business transaction my father had occasion to talk to Erick's foster father. I'll make a long story short because," she glanced at the wall clock, "we have to be going to our lessons, but the day came when that ugly bit of gossip about Erick was proved false, and I was glad for Erick. It was years later that he actually learned the truth about how he got separated from his parents when a tiny baby. But today Erick Wolf is a highly respected citizen, a teacher in a big high school, and assistant to the pastor of a church in Illinois."

Janet raised her hand.

"Yes, Janet."

"How did it happen that he got separated?"

Davy looked back at Janet.

"I'm not sure of all the details," said Miss Ranger, "but perhaps some other time I'll tell you more. All I want to say now is this: Never tease or make fun of anyone who doesn't know who his real parents are. He can't help it any more than you can help who yours are. I know how it feels, because I myself was tormented sometimes." She cleared her throat and gazed a long moment at the blackboard. When she spoke, her voice was low and mellow. "I may never know," she said, "who my real parents were. But," she bit her lip, "I will always thank God for the good, kind people who took me and loved me like their very own."

A gasp, then a hush fell over the entire schoolroom. Davy's eyes filled with sudden tears. He wanted to go forward and throw his arms around Miss Ranger's neck and say something gentle and sweet in her ear.

"Fourth-grade spelling class stand, please."

From that day on school took on new meaning for David Grant. From that day on Mamma and Papa Loomas were more dear to Davy than ever. Dennis treated him with near respect. They even had enjoyable times working and playing together. Papa got Dennis a bicycle, which, to Aaron's glad observation, he shared quite willingly with Davy.

109

Stanley Wingard (a boy two years Davy's senior) lived half a mile "short cut over the hill" from the Loomas farm. He took a special liking to Davy and frequently spent part of Saturday afternoon with the "two Loomas boys," as his mother called them. Stanley also had a bicycle which he seemingly enjoyed letting Davy try out in the long lane. Weather permitting, the three (and sometimes more) roamed the hills and explored the woods together. They played ball, climbed trees, fished, went nutting, flew kites—in fact, did anything that normal healthy boys on a farm would do. Each season brought new games, new thrills.

Weeks, months, and not a reference, not a question, not a word of teasing came to David Grant's ears after Eloise Ranger had told her short story. Janet's reports to Mamma were that all was going smoothly.

The school year was almost over when Gilbert, with Nick at his side, drew Davy aside on the playground. "Why did you tell Miss Ranger we teased you?"

"When?"

"Long ago when school started."

"I didn't."

"You sure? Now you tell the truth, David. Someone must have told her."

"I didn't."

"It's a sin to tell a lie, David." Gilbert took Davy by the shoulder. "You remember that story she told one morning about—"

"I remember."

"Well, she's going to stay at your house next year, my dad said. So don't you go tellin' her a bunch of bad things about me or Nick or any of us big guys. We were just in fun about you not havin' another name an' all that junk about not knowin' where you came from. Understand? Don't you go an' make it hard for us. Will you?"

Davy shook his head.

"An' you still say you never told her nothin'?"

"I know I never," answered Davy.

"Did she ever ask you a bunch of questions then?"

Davy shook his head.

"Have you found out anything yet?"

"What about?"

"About who you are an' your own folks." Gilbert's eyes snapped, mean and tricky.

Shocked and appalled, Davy stood speechless.

CHAPTER 15

Eloise Ranger, the pretty, young, genial schoolteacher, soon seemed like one of the family. What interesting table conversations they all enjoyed! There was much to talk about, from the trivial to local and world events, or the newest inventions. The radio was fast becoming one of the marvels of the day. Davy's face became vivid with wonder, excitement, and a desire for adventure. Depending on the topic discussed, sometimes his expression spelled perplexity, apprehension, or reverence.

In each of Papa's morning prayers, after the reading of a short Scripture passage, he thanked God for the privilege of living in America, for freedom of worship, and for "sparing our lives." Davy realized that included him. "And we thank Thee that at last war has ceased. I pray also that our boys may never have to become involved in destruction of life." Davy caught every word, and wondered why Papa always said that. "And we thank Thee that Lesa and Janet have made their vows to Thee. Help them remain true, dear Lord. And when our sons"—here Davy's heart always beat a little faster—"come to the age of accountability [he wasn't just exactly sure, but he was beginning to speculate on what that meant] give them the courage to take their stand for Thee also." He wondered if Dennis knew what Papa meant. He should. He was older. But Davy never felt prompted to ask him. Whatever accountability was, it somehow made him feel warm and trusting toward Papa.

"Papa," ventured Davy one evening, "will we get a radio?"

"It depends, Son." Papa looked up from the pages of his *Farm Journal*.

"How long will it depend?"

"I can't tell you now, Son. I won't say we'll never get one. We'll see. There's something else I'd sooner get."

"What?"

"I'll surprise you someday. And by the way, Davy. I'm going to give you and Dennis each a calf next week."

"A calf? Why?" Davy stepped closer. Close enough to lean against Papa's chair.

"For your missionary project. Then next spring you can give what they sell for."

"Papa," cried Davy, pulling at his hand, "you're the best papa in the whole world."

"Thanks, Davy. I want to be," answered Aaron.

"Listen, David," began Lena Mae, another fourth grader, one day at recess. "I'll bet," she waggled her forefinger in Davy's face, "just because Miss Ranger lives at your house she gives you the highest grades. You're her pet."

Davy backed away from her. "No, I'm not her pet."

"I'll bet she drills you at home on spelling," added Lena Mae, wriggling her upper lip.

"No, sir. I drill myself," returned Davy. "If you don't believe me, go in and ask her."

"Are you going to come to this school again next year?"

"I suppose. What do you have to know that for?"

"I thought maybe you'd go back where you came from." Lena Mae arched her arms on her hips.

Davy reddened. "What do you mean, where I came from?"

"I just hope you do, David Grant—teacher's pet. I mean wherever they found you, smart boy."

Davy clenched both fists as he stepped closer to her.

"Don't you dare touch me," she snapped. "Just because you spell me down, you don't have to have the big head," and at that she ran away.

"I see," said Miss Ranger one evening before supper, "David has already given you the valentine he made in school today."

There it was, tacked on the wall beside the kitchen sink. "I'm so proud of it," Rose said. Then she read out loud the four carefully printed lines:

I love you for so many things

I don't know where to start;

So I'll just say, I love you, Mother,

From the bottom of my heart.

"He made two. I suppose he gave you the one he thought was the nicer."

"Well, I'm proud of it," commented Rose with feeling. "I noticed he went upstairs with something in his hand. I don't believe he came down yet."

Miss Ranger moved close to Rose Loomas and spoke in a sub-dued tone. "Don't you think maybe this is an indication he'd like to be adopted?"

"Oh," exclaimed Rose, delight glinting her gentle eyes, "I wonder. But as I told you, we're letting him make the decision."

"He understands it's that way?"

"Yes," replied Rose, "he understands. I'm sure he does. And," she swiveled her one hand on her wrist, "either way, it makes no difference with our affection for him. We think of him as our own always."

Davy found himself confiding more and more in Leon about his personal problem. It began one Saturday when Aaron left Davy off at the Home while he went on fifteen miles to a mill for feed.

A man and lady in a shiny green car came for little Georgie Frederic. All three acted overjoyed, and, my, oh, my, such crying and laughing and kissing Davy had never witnessed.

"What's it all about?" he asked Leon.

"Oh, Georgie's mother and father got married all over again.

So now Georgie gets to go live with them again. They sure do all act happy, don't they?"

"I say," agreed Davy. "Do very many do like that? Get married again all over?"

"Naw," answered Leon. "I don't think so. Lots get married, sure, but not to the same one. I sure hope they stay together this time, 'cause when Georgie's father brought him here he nearly cried his eyes out. He wouldn't play or eat for two days. An' Papa almost had to call the doctor. Georgie about had a convulsion."

"What's that?"

"That's when you cry too hard and lose all the breath you got. An' I guess you get stiff too."

"Yeh?"

" 'By, Georgie," called Leon. All the children were waving and shouting, "Good-by, Georgie."

When the shiny green car was out of sight, Davy turned to Leon. "Say, do you think," he asked confidingly, "maybe my mother and father are like that?"

The two were walking toward the swings. "Like how?" asked Leon.

"You know. Like separated and might—you know—get together again and come get me?"

"I don't know. Could be."

"Do you think your father would know?"

"How could he know that, Davy? Let's swing a while."

"Did he ever—I mean, how does he get children to come here?"

"He doesn't. People bring 'em. You take this swing an'—"

"Why do they bring 'em here?"

" 'Cause sometimes people don't want their kids. That's why. Some do, but they have to bring 'em anyhow."

"Why?"

"They can't afford to pay for 'em, I guess. Sometimes people say that. There's all kinds of reasons, Davy."

His eyes opened wide. His breath came fast. Davy stopped

115

short. "Do you think that's why they brought me here?"

Leon frowned. "Davy," he said, "I can't answer all these questions. I don't even remember when you came." He grabbed a swing. "I know who does remember, though."

"Who?" asked Davy.

"Sister Lora. I heard her talk about it already."

Davy caught hold of the chain and stopped Leon from swinging. "Who to?"

"Different people. Different times."

"What did she say?" he demanded.

"Well—just that you were cute and tiny. And left here. In a blanket. Come on, let's swing. That's all I know."

"Who left me?" Davy bit his lip. Easy tears were ready to flow if he wasn't careful. "Was it my mother who left me?" His voice was insistent.

"I—I don't know, Davy. Come on, let's swing a while."

"I wish," said Davy, "I was like God and knew everything."

The following week in school Leon confided in Davy. "Papa said it's true, that *nobody* knows where you came from. I think it sounds awful mixed up, don't you?"

"Oh, Leon," fretted Davy. "I—I had to come from somewhere. How would you like to not know where you came from?"

"I wouldn't like it," admitted Leon sympathetically. And that expression of brotherly love and understanding bound the two boys closer than ever together.

The weeks passed and for David Grant it was a never-ending series of baffling ideas. Little did those closest to him know the maze of bewildering and frustrating emotions he was constantly fronted with. He continued to make top grades in school. He was a sharp quick-to-answer pupil in the Sunday school. The teacher mentioned the fact to Rose more than once. He seemingly enjoyed feeding the chickens, going for the cows, even carrying in wood. Papa got him a secondhand (like new) bicycle, which made him very happy. By the aid of a picture with instructions in *Popular Mechanics,* Papa helped him build a raft that floated in

116

the creek. What fun! Many a boy could have envied David Grant, and some actually did. Especially after Papa Loomas came home from town one Saturday with the surprise.

"Come, my boys," he called, "here you are. You've both been good workers; so I bought each of you a watch."

Davy whistled. "Thank you, Papa," he exclaimed, gazing with admiration at the gift in his hand. "Thanks a lot."

"Yes. Thanks," echoed Dennis, glancing first at the watch in his own hand, then at Davy's. "Yours is bigger," he observed with a tinge of disappointment. "I—I like yours the best."

"I'll trade with you," said Davy. "I mean if you don't care, Papa."

"If you want to trade, it's all right with me. Only—" Aaron stroked his chin. "I really bought the smaller one for you, Dennis. But if you like the bigger one better and Davy's willing—"

"It's shinier too," observed Dennis.

"Here," said Davy. "I'll take that one."

The trade was made. Dennis smiled triumphantly.

"Since you're older," remarked Papa, "I paid more for the smaller watch."

"Oh," cried Dennis, smitten with sudden dissatisfaction, "then I want that one back, Davy." He reached to take it.

"No," stated Papa in a tone of finality. "You keep the one you said you wanted. The exchange has been made."

All the way up the stairs Dennis scowled and grunted his sickening defeat. After that, it was quite easy for him to disregard any particular fondness for the younger boy who was carrying the smaller, more expensive watch. In fact, his was more often in the dresser drawer than in his pocket.

"Dennis," began Papa one morning when the two were alone in the barn, "have you thought it over about going to high school?"

"I've decided I'd rather not."

"It would never come amiss, Dennis," remarked Papa.

"I'd rather get a job so I can buy a car when I'm eighteen."

Papa Loomas hung up his pitchfork. "It costs quite a bit

117

for upkeep on any car, Dennis, especially on a used one," he commented.

"I s'pose so," blinked Dennis. "But," he added with confident expectancy, "I'll be able to make it. When I'm sixteen I—I—" He hesitated.

"And that won't be long now," observed Papa concernedly.

"I know," agreed Dennis, straightening his shoulders, "Then I want to see if Mom won't say I can go to the city and get a job. I wish she'd write to me."

"You're not—" Papa Loomas cleared his throat. "Are you quite anxious to leave the farm?"

Dennis thought a moment before he spoke. "I—I like the farm okay and all that, but—well, pretty soon Davy will be big enough to do my work, an' you won't need me then, will you?"

"I'll make a need for you as long as you want to live here, Dennis. But I won't insist you stay if your mother gives you permission to leave. I wonder if she wouldn't like to see you go on through high school."

Nonchalantly Dennis shrugged his shoulders and walked away.

It was not difficult for Davy to take a special liking to Clifton Dunbar, the tall, handsome young man who for months had been calling on Lesa every Sunday evening. Clif always took occasion to chat at least a few words with Davy (whenever in sight) and once he took him for a three-mile ride in his blue disk-wheeled Overland coupé.

"It's great," remarked Davy admiringly when they returned. "I don't blame Lesa for—well—" he fumbled, half embarrassed, for the right word, "liking you. Guess she does."

Clif laughed. "I hope she likes *me* a whole lot more—a *whole* lot more than this old chariot, Davy. You see, cars never make the man. And what's more, they wear out awfully fast. Then you have to trade them off or junk 'em and buy another." He slapped Davy on the knee. "See what I mean, my boy? Sure thing, Lesa's a wonderful girl, and I hope she likes me."

118

There was something indefinable about Clifton Dunbar's manner that made Davy anxious to become a man. He was always held spellbound for a while by the sincerity and exuberance of Clif's deep voice.

And when one morning Lesa announced at the breakfast table that she and Clif were going to get married in six months, Davy didn't know whether to laugh or cry. He felt like (but did not) doing a little of both.

CHAPTER 16

It came reunion time again at the Home. Davy dreaded going, but how could he explain to anyone why? Who would understand?

He had played with the idea for days. It simply had to be right. Before they got there he thoroughly and convincingly arrived at his conclusion.

The crowd was larger than ever. New faces, familiar faces, almost forgotten faces, people shaking hands, asking and answering questions. "Who's who?" "Yes, to be sure." "I remember." "So nice to meet you again."

His turn. Davy tried to move from Leon (momentarily).

"And your name?" the bright-faced lady inquired in a sweet musical voice.

"David Grant, Ma'am. And yours?"

"David Grant? I'm Sally McAllestor. I worked here for four years. That was back in 1910 to 1914. I remember when you came, a wee tiny baby everyone went wild over. My," she exclaimed, "you're a handsome young man already. Did they ever locate any of your relatives?"

Davy was quite taken aback. He gulped. He had thoroughly made up his mind and he was not going to back out now. "I have a sister," he stated with forced calmness.

"Oh, how glad I am for you," smiled the lady graciously, still holding his hand as she beamed on him. "And how about your mother?"

Davy shifted. He tugged to pull loose. He bit his lip.

"I know it must be hard," she said softly. "But your sister, is—is she younger and perchance—"

Davy blinked. "No, Ma'am," he answered. "She's older."

"How precious! I can't tell you how glad I am for you. Just what you need, I'm sure. What's her name?"

"It's—it's—" Davy's heart missed a beat. He felt a little giddy-headed. "It's Sister Lora," he swallowed.

"Sister Lora?" exclaimed Sally McAllestor in such an un-believing tone Davy jumped. "This Sister Lora here in this Home is your sister?"

Davy lost his voice. He nodded.

"Why, why, it's like a story, David." The lady pressed two fingers against her lips and studied the grass. "Grant and—and hers is Wenzel. Well—well," she mused, "anything these days is possible, it seems. But it's like a story in a magazine, really now. Glad I met you again, David."

As she glided on to meet others, Davy felt hot, feverishly hot. He hurried to the fringe of the crowd to think and collect himself. He had declared it once and he was not going to un-declare it. He knocked his two fists together. He would have one relative or die. Sister Lora *was* his sister from now on, Wenzel or whatever her name.

He declared it again that day, this time to a sweet old lady who looked shocked and almost unbelieving. Sincerely he hoped she would forget it and not go and ask Sister Lora. Anxiously his eye followed her throughout the crowd.

"I wish it was time to go home," he said to Leon, attaching himself again to him.

"But we haven't had the ice cream and cake yet."

"Oh," remarked Davy, "that's right. Let's go and find a nice, cool spot to sit down a while. I'm getting tired meeting people."

Davy scrambled frantically around in his mind all the way home to find the answer. He could not fit himself comfortably on either end of the teeter-totter. This strange feeling inside—like tremors—was it delight or guilt, satisfaction or apprehension?

Up—down—up—down it tossed him until he was dizzy. Once in his room, Davy studied himself in the mirror. His brown eyes searched every line of his face until he was almost embarrassed and even disappointed. Pulling at the reins of his conscience he prepared for bed and knelt to say his prayers. He started to thank God for his sister Lora. Surely sisters do come from God. But that didn't sound right for some reason. Confused and bewildered he finally found the words, but offered them apologetically and with an explanation. "Dear God," he cried in tears. "You know I've just got to have someone real to belong to. Like everybody else has. Please try to understand how it is. And please don't let her be angry with me if—if she ever finds out."

For a long time Davy lay in bed looking out the window to the star-studded sky, before he fell into a dream-broken sleep.

Not once more, but several times, Davy loosened the reins, brushed away the annoying thread of doubt, and declared (to strangers) those sweet impassioned words for his own salvation. "I have a sister. Her name is Lora." They were soothing ointment that gave at least temporary relief to the smarting of his never-healed wound.

But one day Davy ran into an unexpected sickening snag—namely, Bud Bonebeak, a very talkative clerk in a small grocery store—while Papa was shopping in another store in the village. Conversation flowed easily on and on from one thing to another, even to relations.

"You're kidding," said Mr. Bonebeak, smile changing to surprise.

"No. I'm not kidding," asserted Davy. "Lora is my own sister."

"Sister Lora Wenzel up at the Children's Home? Is that lady your sister?"

Davy batted both eyes as he nodded his affirmation.

"But you just told me you were the boy Aaron Loomas took from the Home."

"I am."

"Well now, Son, I wouldn't accuse you of being untruthful, but that Lora up there is my second cousin, unless I've been misinformed all my life." Mr. Bonebeak laughed heartily. "Either you or I have some wires crossed."

The dart was sharp that pierced Davy between the eyes. He was smitten almost flat.

"I—" he finally managed to stammer. "I came in for ten pounds of sugar, sir. Have you?"

"You betcha, Son," said the smiling Mr. Bonebeak, leaning over the counter. "We got sugar."

Two nights later Davy woke with a start. The whole house seemed to be rocking on its foundation. Terrified, he sat straight up in bed. He held his breath. A blinding light filled his room and seconds later a terrific clap of thunder shook the house again. Rain was slashing against the windows and roof like a million sharp nails. The wind split the air with a weird howling sound. Another horrifying zigzag bolt of lightning, a flash of fire, and Davy squirmed to the edge of his bed. Breathlessly he crossed the room, then half stumbled, half slid down the stairs. For a moment he stood frozen as another flash of light blinded him. The entire house looked on fire.

Davy made his breathless way to the bedroom where Mamma and Papa slept. The door was open. Trembling, he slipped inside and gripped the door casing behind him. Could they be sleeping?

Another fiery flash. Papa sat up. Then Mamma. "Davy," said Papa, holding out his one hand, "come. Crawl in here beside me."

Hesitatingly Davy neared the bed. "I—I don't want to—be a baby," he said.

" 'Course not," said Papa. "Come on in." He moved over. "I remember at your age I didn't enjoy such storms either." He reached out, caught Davy by the hand, and drew him toward the bed.

"I—I—didn't know whether to come down or not," said Davy apologetically.

"It's all right, Son," said Mamma with sympathetic understanding. "It's a bad storm."

Another bolt of lightning—another heaven-clapping thunder.

"I was just about to come up," Papa remarked, "to see if you were sleeping through all this." Davy was in his warm arms.

"I'll go back up when it quits," commented Davy.

"It's only four o'clock," observed Papa. "Tell you what. I'll go up with you, and stay till the worst is over. How about that? We can both get several hours' sleep then."

It was too dark for Aaron Loomas to see the comforting smile that spread over Davy's face, but he did hear the big sigh of relief. All the way upstairs he kept his hand on the boy's shoulder.

"Aren't you afraid it might strike our house?" questioned Davy.

"Well, I can't say I never think of it, but at times like this we put our trust in God, Davy."

"Doesn't God ever let—good people's houses burn or good people get—killed?" Papa noted the tinge of anxiety in Davy's voice.

"Sometimes He does, Son, but good people are ready to go, any time, any way, anywhere. So the safe way to live is to always be ready all the time."

"But I can't see how anybody can be that good all the time," reasoned Davy. He covered his face with both hands when the next flash lighted the room.

"You're right," said Papa, "absolutely right. Nobody, of himself, no matter how hard he tries, could be good enough to go to heaven and live with God. So that's why Christ died in our place. And when anyone believes that with all his heart, he's good enough. Every sin is gone."

The two lay down together. "You think this bed will hold both of us?" chuckled Papa, stretching out beside Davy.

"What's goin' on over here?" There stood Dennis in the semidarkness in the doorway.

"I just came up to keep Davy company until the storm subsides," replied Papa. "I hope we haven't disturbed you."

124

"Who could sleep with all this goin' on? Sounds like the devil is really mad tonight. Why didn't you come over with me, Davy?"

"Well," he answered, "I didn't know you wanted me to."

"Does the devil make the storms?" asked Davy after Dennis returned to his room.

"Sometimes I'm inclined to think he does. But he can't do anything unless God lets him. Remember that."

"Why does God let him do such things?" Davy shivered, for that very instant another bolt of lightning was accompanied by a rocking, nerve-racking crack of thunder.

Papa, comfortingly close, waited a moment before he answered. "The only reason I can think of is to cause people to check up on themselves."

"What?"

"A few people when they're scared or think they might die begin to confess their sins. God uses all means to try to speak to sinners."

Davy lay motionless.

Papa continued. "But I think the best time for anyone to get right with God is when he is calm and can think it through with a clear mind."

Out by the barn the next morning Davy questioned Dennis. "Say, were you scared last night too?"

" 'Course I was. Who wouldn't have been?"

"If Papa was, he didn't let on," remarked Davy musingly and with a glint of admiration on his face.

Sister Lora and Bud Bonebeak met on the village street.

"I hear you have a new brother," said Bud.

"What's the joke this time, teasing cousin?"

"That David Grant that Aaron's have—he told me you were his sister."

"Come now, Bud. He didn't mean it."

"He said it in all seriousness. But I knew it was only his wishful thinking. I could hardly keep my face straight."

"Well," exclaimed Lora, "it doesn't exactly make me feel like laughing. The boy craves something. Poor boy. I hope he hasn't told anyone else that. But to be honest, Bud, I wouldn't care if I were his real sister. I'm glad," she added, "that he and Melvin Kolb's boy are good chums. That way I get to see him pretty often."

"He's a handsome and intelligent kid, he is," remarked Bud. "Please now, don't let him know I told."

It was on a balmy Sunday afternoon in May, and Davy was again at the Home with Leon. By this time everyone knew they were inseparable friends. They sat on the concrete steps facing the broad green lawn.

"Do you suppose someday we'll have to go fight in a war?" asked Davy.

"What made you think of such a thing?" asked Leon.

"I don't know. Just thought how it would feel to fly one of those big airplanes. Or run a machine gun."

"Papa says history repeats itself and that means there might be a war again someday."

"Well, in ten years I'll be twenty," remarked Davy. "Next week I'll be ten. Dennis says he's going to learn to fly someday."

Silence.

"Leon?"

"Yeh."

"How do I know I'm going to be only ten? If nobody knows where I came from, then who decided when my birthday is and how old I am? Huh?"

Leon studied. "Maybe it's on the record."

"What record?" Davy faced Leon.

"In the file."

"What file?" Davy grabbed Leon's arm.

"In the office. That's where Papa keeps such things."

"About me?" gasped Davy, tightening his grasp.

"Yeh. About every child who comes here."

Davy leaned forward. He grabbed Leon by both arms almost fiercely. "Could we?"

"Sh." Leon looked around. "Come," he whispered, "let's go see if anybody's in there."

The two tiptoed across the portico and carefully, slowly Leon opened the door. The office door was closed. With great caution he noiselessly turned the knob, and, yes, the room was empty. Not a sound of anyone near. There stood two tall, green metal files with brass handles. The boys crossed the room on tiptoe.

Couldn't the answer be in there somewhere? Davy almost squealed. He closed his tightly pressed lips over his teeth, lest an exclamation would burst out. "You," he whispered, motioning.

Leon pulled on the middle drawer. It made a rolling, gliding, ball-bearing sound. Both boys shivered as they cast anxious glances toward the closed door.

Leon's right hand thumbed folders. "These are all H's and K's," he whispered. "G's must be in the drawer above."

Again both held their breath and eyed the door as Leon pulled on the drawer. "G. Gable, Galley, Garber, Gardner, Gray, Gerber, Ginther."

Davy's heart thumped violently. "Hurry, Leon," he panted.

"Glassburn, Golden, Good, Goodman, Graham, Grant! Here it is, Davy! David Grant."

From the folder Leon took out a single white card on which was clipped a small, once crumpled, paper. He handed it to Davy.

His eager eyes burned as he read: "David Grant. May 24, 1913—Phila. Mother—Shana Grant."

"My mother!" he whispered. "I have a mother! I—I do." He could hardly keep from shouting. He pressed the card against his chest. "It's mine," he gasped. "It's mine. I'm gonna' keep it."

"You can't," objected Leon. "Why, then they'd know we've been in here. Put it back, Davy. You've got to. Quick. We're not supposed to come in here."

"I—I won't put it back," cried Davy. "It's all I've got. I need it."

"But you darsen't take it, I tell you. Put it back before we get caught."

Davy glanced at the desk. "Paper. There. Give me that piece of paper. Quick. Give me that pencil. Leon, quick."

Davy's hands trembled. He put forth every effort to hold them steady. Carefully he traced the seven words and the date, then tucked the paper into his inside coat pocket. "Here, put it back."

The task completed, the two slipped out unnoticed.

"Why didn't you tell me long ago it was in there, Leon?" whispered Davy.

"I never thought of it before. Honest, I never."

CHAPTER 17

The two sat facing each other on the concrete steps. Fifteen minutes slipped by and neither had spoken.

"Let's shake hands on it," whispered Davy, puncturing the prolonged silence. His heart was still thumping. He glanced in every direction. "You know—never to tell a single soul. Will you?"

"Shake," agreed Leon, extending his hand, "but I'd never tell anyhow. Look. There comes Papa Loomas."

"Well," smiled Aaron, "guess you boys had a good time, didn't you?"

"Sure," answered Davy. " 'By, Leon. Be seein' you."

Going directly to his room Davy carefully tilted a high-backed chair and wedged it under the doorknob. Seldom did anyone intrude, but he wanted to feel secure. For nearly half an hour he studied the paper in his hand. With pains he creased, then trimmed it down to about four inches with his pocketknife. Then loosening the lining of his left shoe he planted it safely and securely underneath. No one would guess. He put on his shoe. He walked around in the room. No one would ever find his priceless treasure. "Shana." Over and over Davy repeated the name, spelling it each time.

From the dresser drawer where he kept his Sunday-school tickets and papers and valued things he took out the valentine. He read the four-line poem. Then with meticulous care he printed across the top, "To my mother, Shana Grant," and put it back in the drawer underneath everything else.

There was the little notebook and pencil, his reward for perfect attendance in Sunday school the past year. In it he wrote, "Found paper Sun. Sept. 22, 1923."

The grass suddenly looked greener. The water tasted fresher. The cricket's chirp sounded happier. Davy felt like running. Like skipping. Like flying. He sprang down the steps and shot out across the back porch.

"Davy," called Papa from the door. "Where are you going? It's nearly suppertime."

"I'll be back," he answered. Like a young deer, he ran all the way to the creek. Leaning hard against a willow tree, panting, he flung his arms open wide and looked up at the cloud-dabbled sky. He laughed—laughed out loud. "I have a mother," he cried with audible joy and he listened for, but did not hear, his echo.

Like a deer, he ran all the way back. Laughing—squealing.

"What is it, Son?" inquired Papa. "You act all excited over something. Let us in on the secret. What's down there at the creek?"

"Just the creek," answered Davy. "Same as always. Just the creek."

Hazel drew Shana to the far corner of the hospital lobby, and put her arm around her shoulder. "Please, don't cry so," she said. "I know how hard it must be."

"You can't know," sobbed Shana. "I was so hoping he'd be all right. To get to come home, then have to come back here. Oh, it's so much harder." She shook her head as she sobbed brokenly. "I fear this time it's for good."

"No, Shana. Please, try to brace up."

"I haven't told you what he did, Hazel. He got into my box! My box of personal things, while he was home. The only picture I had of Mother and Father, and my graduation picture, and a little tiny one I had of Brandon. He tore them all to shreds—to shreds, Hazel!"

"Why?"

"He didn't know what he was doing, I guess. I didn't see what he had gotten into until it was too late. He acted awful. and said things that didn't make sense. He's in terrible shape, Hazel. Whatever this sickness is, it's already damaged his mind. I feel so crushed and forsaken. I feel so—so disgraced."

The week following, Hazel called Shana, but very, very reluctantly. "My dear, I hate to have to tell you this," she said, "but Bruce has been transferred."

"What?" Shana all but screamed into the mouthpiece.

"The company has ordered him to move to Des Moines, Iowa, to take over a new assignment."

"Hazel!" cried Shana. "No. Oh, no, Hazel! Who will I have to go to if you leave me? Oh, Hazel, the whole world is caving in on me!"

"Mamma," ventured Davy one evening as he stood beside her at the kitchen stove. "What's that you're making?"

"Brown flour potato soup. How does that sound for supper tonight?"

"Yum. It's the best in the world," smiled Davy. "I wouldn't care if we had it twice as often."

"And in the oven is green tomato pie." Rose pulled gently on Davy's one ear.

"Oh, goody. Two things I like best of all." Davy rolled the palm of his hand over the nickle rod across the front of the stove. "Say, Mamma, do you know anybody who lives in Philadelphia?"

"A few people. Why?"

"I just wondered. It's a pretty big town, isn't it?"

"Philadelphia is a city, Davy. Over a million, I'm sure. Are you studying about big cities in school?"

"No. Not right now. I just wondered if we'd ever go there sometime. You know, to the zoo or something like that."

"We might sometime," answered Mamma, stirring the soup. "I don't know."

"How many miles is it?"

"About a hundred. You can go tell Papa and Dennis supper's almost ready."

Rose Loomas pondered a few things as she stirred the soup.

Although he could not feel it, he was constantly aware of the reassuring paper in his left shoe. Even in school Davy frequently lost himself in his thoughts. In every secret corner of his tablet he practiced printing "Shana" and "Philadelphia."

Never did he go to bed now without first looking to make sure the paper was still in place and readable. To his dismay, by the end of the second week it felt limp and damp.

It was a balmy Saturday afternoon in early October. His fishing pole propped between two rocks, Davy sat alone on the creek bank completely enveloped in daydreams. Finally he took a sheet of paper from his hip pocket and using the side of his tin bait can (he first dumped the bait) for a smooth solid surface, he penciled the letter.

Dear Mother,

This is your son, David, and I'm writing to find out where you are and why I am here where I am. I just found out two weeks ago what your name is. Please write to me at once. I never got a letter from anyone in my life yet, and I'm going on eleven. I am living with Mr. and Mrs. Aaron Loomas, Lancaster, Pa., R.R. 4. Please answer this, and I will write to you again. I am glad I know now I have a real mother. Write *soon*. I made you a valentine in school and I still have it. Is my father also there? Tell him hello.

Lovingly,
David Grant

That much accomplished, Davy lay on the creek bank, and gazing long and hopefully into the steep hazy blue heavens he tried to figure out where and how to get a stamp and an envelope without anyone knowing it. Mamma? No. Janet? No. Lesa? No. Clifton? Hardly. Leon. Leon must be his only confidant.

132

"I know," said Davy after sharing his secret. "Ask Sister Lora if she won't give you a stamped envelope. Huh? For a very close friend? Don't tell her who it's for unless you just have to."

To his glad surprise Leon brought the stamped envelope to school on Monday.

"Did Sister Lora ask questions?"

"I just asked her if I could borrow it."

"Did she guess it's for me?"

"I hope not. She just looked surprised and gave it to me."

"You won't tell her, will you?"

"Didn't we shake on it? 'Course I won't tell."

"But now I don't know where to mail it so nobody will see it."

"Let me," offered Leon. "I can stick it in between all the other letters that go out from the Home in the morning. No one will look at it."

"You're the best friend a fellow's got," whispered Davy.

Anticipation.

Eager expectancy started after the third day. "Maybe tomorrow the answer will come," he told himself. But the tomorrows ran on into weeks, with daily disappointment. Davy confided in Leon every day at school.

"Are you sure you mailed it?"

"Davy, I know I did."

"Do you think it got to Philadelphia?"

"It had to, Davy. But Philadelphia's a big place and you didn't know what street. It might take them a long time to locate her."

A new thought startled Davy. "What if there's more than one Shana Grant? What if the wrong one would answer? Then I would be in a mess, wouldn't I?"

"I tell you what I think," suggested Leon. "Philadelphia on that paper, I'll bet, meant you were born there. But it might not mean your mother lives there now. Maybe she never lived there."

Fresh perplexity, with added disappointment, clouded Davy's forlorn face.

133

Miss Ranger called him to her desk at recess. "Aren't you feeling well today, Davy?"

"I feel all right."

"Has something happened to make you feel sad?" She put her hand on his shoulder and looked him full in the face.

Davy flinched. "No, Miss Ranger, nothing, nothing new at all."

"Has someone been tormenting you?"

"No, Miss Ranger."

"Good. I hope you're not worrying about anything, Davy."

Nervously his eyes shifted from the floor to the windows. "I'm all right, Miss Ranger. Leon's looking for me. May I go outside?"

"Run along, Davy. Run along, and put on that happy face if everything is all right."

This incident convinced Davy he would have to do a better job of hiding his feelings, not only in school, but more so at home. He sincerely hoped Miss Ranger would not mention this to Mamma. He therefore put forth special effort to act happy the remainder of the day.

Six weeks. Davy despaired of ever receiving an answer.

"What else can I do, Leon?" he fretted.

"Sometimes Papa gets letters back stamped 'unclaimed' or 'unknown.' But you have to put your name and address up in the corner to get them back. You know, like we learned in English."

"I know," admitted Davy thoughtfully, "but that way whoever gets the mail would know then. I only go after it on Saturdays."

"I could put my name on it for you," suggested Leon.

Davy shook his head. "Then somebody would ask you why you wrote to Shana Grant. No, Leon. What if—what if—" Davy rubbed the toe of his shoe in the ground— "what if maybe she did get it—but just—just doesn't want to claim me?" Two hard-pressed tears crept to the edge of his eyelashes and hung trembling. "Maybe—maybe—I—I—wish I knew my father's name. I'd write to him."

"Maybe they're—they're both dead," whispered Leon hesitatingly and with a sorrowful tone.

Davy chilled. A new fear swept over him. A new loneliness with gnawing pangs of hunger started to torment him. In classes that day he was so preoccupied he could scarcely concentrate at all.

But more penetrating, more disturbing was the wound inflicted on him, not by a schoolmate, but by a mature woman in the church yard the following Sunday morning. Davy had just left a group of boys and was walking toward the family car when he overheard his name.

Three women were in lively conversation. "He's that good-looking boy Aaron's got at the Home," one said.

"But he's illegitimate," another added.

As if shot, Davy stopped. Only for a second.

Illegitimate! Illegitimate! That was the word. He'd heard it once before and it had given him a most unhappy feeling. He remembered. A cloud of misery nearly blinded him, but somehow he managed to make his way to the car. He felt like crawling under the seat where no one could see him. He didn't want to look at anybody until—until he knew. After what seemed like hours Papa and the rest came. The ride home was extra long.

To add to his misery they had guests that day. Visitors from some distant church Mamma invited to come along home. Davy didn't feel like shaking hands with any of them, least of all the two teen-age girls in the party, but he had to.

His face burning with fear and bewilderment, he found quick refuge in the seclusion of his room until dinner was ready.

Food almost choked him. He could scarcely look up. After dinner, quivering all over, he approached Miss Ranger's door. She was in her room reading.

"I would like to ask you something, please, Miss Ranger," he ventured.

"What is it, Davy?"

He cleared his throat. "Could I borrow the key to the schoolhouse?"

135

"What for, Davy?"

"I—I need to go down there for something."

"You don't study on Sunday, do you?"

"No, Ma'am,' he answered. "Not that. I just want to take a walk that far and—go inside a while."

"Well, now, I guess that will be all right." She got up to get the key. "Are you going alone?"

"Yes, Ma'am. Thanks."

"Be sure you lock it when you come out. Try the door to make sure."

"I will, Miss Ranger."

Illegitimate. All the way, Davy tried spelling it. Ili—illi—ilig— He wished with all his soul no one had ever invented the word.

The door seemed unusually heavy and squeaked on its hinges. The shades were drawn so that the room was dark. It smelled musty inside. The floor snapped and creaked with almost every step. Davy raised the shade at the window nearest the big dictionary.

His breath came in bunches, as he turned two pages past "hy" to "I." Feverishly his eye followed his forefinger down six colunms. "Illegal—unlawful or unauthorized." Then he found it. There *was* such a word. "Unlawfully begotten, not legitimate—a bastard." What? What? Shaking frantically Davy turned the pages back until he found that word. "Bastard—an illegitimate child or one of bad origin—questionable or not genuine."

Incensed, Davy pounded both fists on the dictionary. "No!" he cried. "No! I won't believe it. I'm not a bastard and I'm not illegitimate! And I will *not* believe it! Nobody has a right to say I am. Nobody!"

Yet, overpowered with a crushing, smothering, haunting fear, Davy crumpled in the nearest desk, and burying his face in his arm, he cried convulsively.

136

CHAPTER 18

Oh! To be despised—unwanted—unnecessary—smeared—outcast. He would not confide in anyone, not even Leon, about this disgraceful thing. A shabby, humiliated bundle of pain, Davy finally gathered himself together enough to wash his face. He glanced, half ashamed, in the cloakroom mirror. His eyes, red and bloodshot, frightened him. He washed his face again, patting cold water on his eyes. He locked the door and headed for home.

Davy felt an urge to run away. Far away. But where? Where? Yet something was pulling him on home—home to gentle Mamma and kind Papa. To Janet and Lesa. But was their love and kindness really genuine? Did they believe he was illegitimate? The grass lost its greenness. The air was polluted. The birds were crying, because they were lonely. Suddenly everything smelled bad and Davy hated everybody in the world, especially that woman who blotched his name. He kicked every stone in his path. He picked up a stick and broke it against a fence post. The whole world was against him. He hated everything in sight. Yet, as he neared the house, Davy never felt a stronger drawing to get inside its shelter, to be near those he had learned to trust. He wished he could call up Sister Lora or, better still, he wished he could go see her and tell her how kind and sweet she'd always been to him. Surely she would not condemn him.

This duel going on inside, pinching, pulling, tugging, urging —it was all so confusing! It was like two voices, each trying to outtalk the other. No other boy had to feel like this, of that Davy was certain. Why was he the only pupil in school, the only pupil in the Sunday-school class, the only child at the Home, who did not have one single relative? Why was he the victim of such gross unfairness? The grossest now of all, to be branded of bad, low-down, unlawful origin!

In the midst of his deep, deeply hidden hurt, Davy's sensitive mind never lay idle. Constantly the question stared him in the face, never answered, always tantalizingly unsettled. "What do they know about me? What does she say about me? What do Leon and Sister Lora and my Sunday-school teacher believe about me? Do they know, but out of mercy or pity never let on?"

Davy resented being pitied. He tried to act tough. He tried not to care. He whistled more. Played ball harder. He'd overrule this inner feeling of desolation. The paper in his shoe was worn to small scraps and the words illegible. He stuffed them in the far corner of the dresser drawer.

But David Grant did care. It swooped with full reality over him when preparations were in the making for Lesa's wedding. He heard several discussions on who all would be invited. There seemed to be no end to Clif's relations. They were all such lovely, highly respected people, and Rose and Aaron were anxious to meet them all.

Davy was plunged into fresh uncertainty. What girl would ever want to marry an unlawfully begotten? Who could his bride's parents be introduced to? Highly respected? Well thought of? He without one single measly cousin?

On the north side of the barn, out of sight of the house, lay the field of half-grown corn. Davy knew where Papa kept his corn knife. He picked up the long-bladed, wicked-looking instrument and looked at it fiercely. Muttering under his breath, he dashed into the field and started slashing corn.

"I will kill every last one of you," he shouted, his eyes flash-ing vengeance. "You hated me first; so I hate you to the death." Corn fell to the right and to the left. "Every one of you is a bastard; so down you go. Dead. You, and you. You too." Davy was almost out of breath. In fury he slashed on and on, shouting

138

phrases of retaliation and murder. "You're as bad as the Germans."

Just beyond the fence stood Aaron Loomas, stunned at what he was witnessing. He did not call or whistle. He waited quietly until the dramatic slaughter was finished.

Panting and sweating, Davy started back toward the barn.

He saw. He stopped. His arms dropped limp.

"What were you doing out there, Son?" inquired Aaron, unruffled.

In blank numbness Davy just stared at Papa. No rebuke? No sign of anger? No consternation?

"What were you trying to do, Davy?"

"I—I don't know, Papa." He looked at the ground. His lip trembled.

"What has made you so angry, Son? Have I provoked you?"

Davy looked up. In Papa's face he read nothing but compassion, tender compassion. "Oh, no, Papa. It's—it's not you I'm mad at." His red face burned.

"Mamma?"

"No. No, not her." He wanted to run away. Far away to the farthest end of the earth. And jump off.

Papa stepped close to Davy. "Was it anyone under our roof?"

Davy shook his head. He bit his lip. He tried desperately to control his quivering chin.

He felt Papa's hand on his shoulder. "Well, do you feel better now, Son?"

Two big tears trickled down Davy's cheeks. "I—I don't know." he cried. "I'm sorry I ruined the corn, Papa, but," he sobbed, "I'll give back my watch to pay for it. I—I just don't know what to do." Davy dropped the corn knife. It lay on the ground beside his feet. The next thing he knew he was leaning against Papa and crying as though his heart would break.

"There, there, Son," he heard Papa say. "We'll figure out some other way for you to pay for the corn. There's something I'd hate a lot worse to lose than that much corn, Davy."

Davy looked up. "What is it?"

139

"Your confidence, Son. I only wish I knew what caused you to go out there and demonstrate such fury. Something has upset you. Why, this is not like you at all, Davy. I maybe should whip you for this, but before I do I have to know what's at the bottom of such an action. Can't you confide in me?"

Surprise merged into amazement as Davy looked up into Papa's gentle smooth-shaven face.

"I heard somebody call me something ugly an' bad."

"But was it true, Davy?"

Davy looked away. "I—I don't know. I wish I knew." He started to run.

"Wait," called Papa. "Let me tell you something. Listen, Davy." He caught the boy by the arm. "I'm making a guess what it was. But remember this, nobody can ever ruin your character. Your character is what you really are. Not what anybody calls you. And we don't want you to fret or be so upset like this by what people with bad manners say. Some folks called Jesus bad names too, but that didn't make Him bad. Some of His own people turned against Him, but never fear, Davy, we won't turn against you. Mamma and I couldn't love you more if you were our very own."

"Really?" Davy drew a breath of tremendous relief.

"That's a fact, Davy. Now put the corn knife back where you got it. And the next time you feel like exploding, come explode to me first. Then we'll cut corn together. Huh?"

With that Papa Loomas resumed his previously planned work.

In spite of that memorable experience and Papa's expression of kind human understanding, Davy's inner battles were not all won. There were countless secret broodings, frustrations, and fears hinging on the point of his personal connection. True, he felt loved and wanted in the Loomas home. Nor was there the slightest doubting that he loved, trusted, and greatly respected both Mamma and Papa. They and Sister Lora were the dearest, the best, the purest people on earth. Leon was almost like a real brother. And Stanley Wingard was another good friend. They were together more and more in the coming months, in ball games, bicycling, fishing, rafting, skating.

"My mother says you're to come along home with me for dinner," said Stanley one Saturday.

"Why?"

"Because she likes you."

Davy looked baffled. "Why does she like me, I wonder?"

"Because I do. And she says you always act like a perfect gentleman in church. She likes me to be with you."

Davy smiled faintly. "I'll have to go in and ask Mamma."

The Wingards were a closely knit family of seven. Years of happy living and growing up together enveloped the home like a warm blanket. Quick to observe, Davy sensed this as soon as he stepped inside.

On the piano were two pictures of Stanley with his brother Gregory, taken when they were very small. On the table were photographs of each one of the children. After dinner Stanley showed Davy through several big albums.

"This is my mother holding Gregory and that's me on Papa's lap. That was taken so long ago I can't remember. And this picture was taken when I was four. I remember that day, because Papa slipped and fell in the water and got all wet." (Laughter) "We were at the lake. And this is our family at Grandpa's place—" and on and on. "Our family—my sister—my mother"—until Davy felt himself dangling alone again.

Incidents piled high. But his best friends never realized how, why, or when David Grant was made aware of the pending stigma on his life.

Accountability. Papa was still using that word in prayer. One day when Davy was using the school dictionary to look up the word "acclaim," he found accountability in the next column. It meant what he thought it did. "State of being capable to answer and give account, or state of being responsible."

All through the sermon Davy felt a tugging at his heart. Every word the evangelist said seemed to fit his need. At the close

141

of his message he extended an invitation for "anyone to confess Christ before God and all these people by standing to your feet."

It was not an easy thing to do, but Davy stood.

"God bless you, young man," said the minister. "You may be seated."

Davy trembled. Not from fear, but from a joy and peace that swept over him. It made him tingle from the top of his head to his feet.

"And God bless you and you and you," Davy heard the minister say. "I would like to meet you four in the basement after the service."

He spoke first to Leon and dismissed him. Next, to Stanley, then to Dennis.

"Now it's your turn," said the minister, shaking Davy's hand. "How old are you, my boy?"

"Eleven."

"It hardly seems fair the youngest should be interviewed last."

"It's all right," answered Davy.

"Well, at least I can't accuse you of following the older boys, because I remember you stood first. I don't know your name."

"David Grant."

"Well, David, do you feel you're old enough to take this serious step?"

"I feel I'm old enough to be—to be lost and to be punished for my sins if I would die, sir," said Davy. "I feel I've come to the age of accountability. And I want to be baptized."

"I see," remarked the minister. "Can you explain to me why you stood then?"

"Because I want Christ to forgive all my sins, and make me His child, like you said in your sermon He would."

"Very good, David. I see you were a good listener. And you've committed sins?"

"Yes, sir. Some pretty big ones."

"And you're sure Christ will forgive you if you confess them and tell Him you're sorry?"

"Yes, sir. I already confessed them and told Him I'm sorry."

"When did you do this?"

"Well," answered Davy, "just about all evening and again just before I stood up. I've been thinking about doing this for some time."

"And now you feel forgiven?"

"Yes, sir. I do."

"Do you come from a Christian home?"

"Yes, sir. I live with Mr. and Mrs. Aaron Loomas and they are good Christian people and pray every day."

"They are not your parents?"

"No, sir," answered Davy. "I—I—" he looked away— "I never had a real home—I mean I—" he hesitated.

"You mean a broken home?" The minister bent forward and touched Davy's arm.

"I don't know. That's—one of my—my sins." Davy bit his lip. He didn't intend to tell this.

"What do you mean?" The minister's voice was extremely mellow and kind.

"Well—well—it makes me mad because I don't know where I came from." He fought to keep back the tears. "I don't really belong to anybody, then how can I know who I am? Somebody wrote my name on paper that it's David Grant, but I can't prove it, because I don't know if there really is that person." A lone tear fell on Davy's coat front. "Then something big comes up inside of me an' makes me feel like being mean."

"Yes," said the minister. "I understand. But the people you live with, are they good to you, David?"

Davy brushed a tear away. "They treat me swell," he said.

"As though you were their own?"

Davy nodded. "Yes, they do."

"Then listen to me, David. If these people treat you swell and as if you were their own, wouldn't God, who is much kinder and much more tenderhearted and understanding, love you even more? Because you took Christ you are born into God's family. You belong to Him. It's the best family to belong to. And re-

143

member, another thing I said in my sermon is this, that Christ said He'd be your father, your mother, your brother, and your sister, if you ask Him to be."

A smile lighted Davy's sober face. "Yes," he said, "I heard you say that. And that was one reason why I stood up."

"And now Christ, your big brother, will help you overcome this temptation to get angry, David. He knows how you feel. So God bless you, my boy," said the minister, clasping Davy's one hand in both of his. "I believe God has big things planned for you. And because of your experiences you may be able to help hundreds, maybe thousands of other boys someday. Girls too. Who knows? I'll pray for you right now, and your pastor will instruct you for baptism."

Papa Loomas didn't talk much on the way home. Neither did Mamma. But when they were all inside, Papa said, "There is great joy in this house tonight, my boys. And joy in heaven too."

Dennis hurried to his room. Davy lingered to get a drink. Mamma folded him in her arms and kissed him. "You did a wonderful thing tonight, Son," she whispered.

CHAPTER 19

The next two years brought many changes, both the expected and the unexpected. Naturally Lesa was missed, but it was a satisfying vacancy, for she had done what the good Lord intended most young women should do—help establish another Christian home. And she was not so far away that she and Clif couldn't come home occasionally.

Dennis was the next to leave. It wasn't a trivial matter for Aaron and Rose to see him go, after wrapping years of love and concern around that boy. His mother sent him the train ticket (he begged for) to Detroit. There he could be close to her (he and she reasoned) and find quick employment.

Mamma, Janet, and Davy all went along to the depot to see him off.

"Be sure and write to us," begged Mamma, teary-eyed, but calm. "We do want to keep in touch with you. And please come back to see us whenever you can."

"I will, Mamma," Dennis replied. "And thanks for all you've done for me. You've really been good to me, even when I was a pill at times."

"And be true to your baptismal vows," were Papa's final words. His voice was a little husky. "That's the only thanks we want, Dennis. Detroit's a big city and a wicked city. But God is there too. Do find a church to attend. Let me know if you ever get up against it. And remember, Dennis, our latchstring is always on the outside."

"Thanks, Papa. I may surprise you all sometime when I get a car. 'By, Janet. Bet you'll be married the next time I see you."

Janet blushed. "You may be yourself before long. Who knows?"

" 'By, Davy." Dennis slapped Davy's arm. "You be good now. And don't work too hard. Why don't you sell my bike and get yourself a radio? You can as far as I'm concerned. Ask Papa to let you."

"You may want your bicycle if you come back in a car," suggested Papa.

"We might as well take a leaf out of our table," Mamma said to Janet the next day. "And we'll have to learn how much less to cook. Well," she added, "we have two husky appetites left to be satisfied or I wouldn't bother to bake pies today."

Not many weeks later Rose watched the beautiful tender bud slowly unfolding before her observant eye.

"My dear," she remarked one afternoon as Janet was cleaning. "I want to tell you how grateful we are you are going out with a respected young man like Clare. You've been a good girl and a good worker and you deserve a nice sensible boy friend."

Janet beamed. "I'm glad you like Clare," she said. "I wouldn't want to go with just anyone." She finished dusting the rocker. "I turned down several I thought you wouldn't want me to date."

"You never told me that." Out of the corner of her eye Rose watched Janet as she continued with her job. "You know," she said, "we'd better go to Lancaster this week or next and get you a new coat, and shoes, and," she added, "you need gloves, don't you?"

"Oh, Mamma," and Janet dashed across the room and gave Rose a kiss on the cheek. "You're so good to me, Mamma dear."

Before the year ended, Janet was happy, radiant Mrs. Clare

Rupert. Mamma and Papa Loomas gave her a lovely wedding. Of course there weren't as many guests as at Lesa's wedding, but Grandma Chaveriat, all aglow, was there, and the living room was filled with Clare's kinfolk from near and far, and Janet's well-wishing friends.

"And now," remarked Mamma to Aaron and Davy the next day, "shall we take another leaf out of our table? or get more children? What do you suggest, Davy?"

"Me? Well, this isn't my home. I have no right to suggest."

"But this *is* your home, Son," corrected Papa. "You have a right to suggest if we ask for it."

"Well," said Davy contemplatively, "if you two want more children, why should I object?"

"That's all we wanted to hear you say," smiled Papa. "Now we know," he hesitated, "that you're very unselfish." He glanced over at Rose, dropping eggs into the hot skillet. "We've been talking things over, Mamma and I, and we're ready to put the farm up for sale."

"For sale?" Davy looked up with surprise.

"Yes, Son. Since you'll be ready to start to high school before too long, you'll need your evenings for study. There's just too much farm here for you and me to look after and do it right. And I don't like to have a farm unless I can keep it in tiptop shape."

Davy's brown eyes widened. "Where would we go? I must say this sounds pretty exciting."

"We're not sure. But we'll start looking around. There are a number of nice towns in Lancaster County. Above all, we want to go where it's best for you."

"For me?" exclaimed Davy. "For me?" he repeated.

Later as he walked across the yard, Davy could not begin to fathom the import of Papa's statement, but greater esteem and fresh adventure put a new glint in his eyes.

By the end of the school year the farm had been sold and the big event—the public auction of machinery and stock—was history. A comfortable six-room house in Landisville (just what

Rose had been looking for) had been purchased. The moving day was set.

Then came the unexpected.

Clare called before daylight. His voice was near hysteria. "Janet just died."

"Janet!" gasped Rose. "Dead! Oh, Clare," she cried, "we'll come at once."

She ran to the hall where both could hear. "Aaron," she cried, "Davy. You won't believe it. Our Janet is—dead! That was Clare on the phone. Get up. We must go."

The whole experience was a profoundly moving and lingering one for Davy. Janet had been like a sister. A dear sister. Every kind word she had ever spoken, every smile, every loving deed kept flashing before him all the way. He lived again the first night when he so feared that long stairway and that horrid black bed and Janet soothed his fears. Every square foot of the house and yard and long lane reminded him of something pleasant they had done together. He heard her singing; he heard her reading to him, and laughing the singular rippling laugh he liked so much to hear. And now she was still! Songless! Speechless! Laughless! Janet dead? Janet who loved life and work and hated no one?

It was Davy's first experience with death. There it was. Real as life. Janet so young, so pretty, so happy, so healthy, cut down like green, half-grown corn. What cruel injustice! And her baby. Her wee helpless son. What will become of him? Who will take him to mother? Will Clare? Or will he give him a name on paper and leave him at the Children's Home? Then disappear? Never come to claim him?

Wild, stark-naked thoughts went on a rampage to torture Davy. Could it be that's what happened to his mother? To Shana Grant? If so, would Janet's spirit go to be with hers? Would she tell his mother he was all right, and growing up? Do people say such things to each other in heaven? Where, oh, where was a God of love in this? God taking pleasure in breaking Clare's heart? And leaving a tiny baby motherless? Bitterness was push-

148

ing Davy into a jungle again, this time from a new unexpected angle.

"Who will take the baby?" he whispered to Mamma as soon as he considered it polite. He pulled her to the corner of the living room.

"Clare says his sister wants to," answered Mamma, wiping her eyes. "Don't worry, Davy," she sobbed, "he'll have a good home. God loves him. He's so tiny. Don't fret, Davy. Someone will take him."

"Why didn't—God take the baby with her? I'd think it—" He bit the inside of his cheek.

"Our thinking is not always God's thoughts," whispered Mamma, tears streaming down her stricken face. "He may grow up to make some home as happy as you've made ours. Don't fret, my dear."

Davy went outside and sat alone in the car to think. He tried to reason through this enormous injustice. He relived his earliest frustrations. Memory took him back to that ride to a strange house, and the pangs of being torn away from Sister LoLo.

Davy listened. At the funeral the minister said, "Death is in itself a sad word. We all shrink from it. But death to the aged and suffering Christian spells relief. To the faithful hard-working servant of God, reward. But you are all asking today, What could death spell to this young sister? Janet Rupert, the young, happy wife and expectant mother with all the joys of married life and home before her. What could death spell to her? Friends, to us it spells loss, but to Janet it spells gain. She simply stepped from one room into a bigger, brighter room where God and angels dwell. Let's not say Janet is dead. She has stepped into that place no tongue can describe, where the fullest meaning of living has started a bit sooner for her than for many. Janet wouldn't want to return. I hear you asking, Why did God call her? If I could tell you why, I'd be God. Clare, let not your heart be troubled. Take all the *why's,* all the tangled strands, and place them in God's hand. In time He will lovingly unravel all the *why's*—if we let Him. When we try, the tangles only get more tangled."

Davy pondered those remarks for days. It helped him out of the jungle into the clearing again.

He took great pleasure in helping to move into the new home in Landisville.

"Here, you got a letter," announced Papa one day, handing it to Davy.

"For me?" Davy ran up the stairs two at a time. He closed the door to his room and leaned hard against it. What? From Millersville? Not Philadelphia?

Dear Davy,

I want to, in some way, express my personal sympathy to you since I know you thought a great deal of Janet, even though she wasn't your real sister. She was very sweet and thought a lot of you. [Davy felt goose pimples coming out on his arms.] Since you have moved to Landisville, we won't get to see each other as often as we used to. So I decided to write to you. Know this, I will never stop praying for you as long as I live. [As long as she lives? His forehead wrinkled. He sincerely hoped she lived as long as he did.] Be sure you come to all the reunions.

Sincerely,
Sister Lora

Davy read it again. His thoughts began to whirl as he stood there. Finally he wrote on the envelope, "My first letter," then tucked it deep in the dresser drawer with his other prized possessions.

"Guess Leon's going to miss you," ventured Papa at the dinner table.

"I miss him already," answered Davy. "But the letter," he took a slice of bread, "wasn't from him. It was from Sister Lora."

"I see." No questions were asked and Davy offered no more information. Conversation soon turned to job possibilities.

"I want to apply for a paper route right away," began Davy. "If you don't care, I'll do it today."

"That's a fine idea, Son," agreed Papa. "Many a succesful

150

businessman started with a paper route, so I've read. I want to show you how to keep a financial record." He laughed good-naturedly. "I'm serious, but it may sound funny to talk about finances before you've earned your first dollar. It's the thing to do—mark down everything you earn and everything you spend. I hope you begin to save too. It would be a fine thing to set aside a tenth of what you earn toward your missionary offering. I can't give you a calf this year, you know."

"I already decided I'd do that," nodded Davy. "I noticed across the street where those two old ladies live, there are high weeds in their back yard. Guess I'll go over and ask them if they wouldn't like to have them pulled, and when winter comes I hope I can clean walks."

"Hold on now," laughed Papa, trying to conceal his pride. "You'll be the busiest fellow on this street if you're not careful. There won't be anything left for the other fellows to do."

Davy wrote three words: "Dear Sister Lora." He bit on the end of his pencil. For two years he had been trying to dodge and evade the matter. Why did such a little sin flare up so often and unbalance his peace? Especially at reunion time? How could he tell her without making her disgusted? He wrote. He erased. He jostled words. It was past eight when he went downstairs and hesitatingly asked for an envelope and stamp. "Just one, Mamma. I'll pay for it after I start earning money."

"Davy, you'll do no such thing. Go to the desk drawer and help yourself."

Little did Sister Lora guess how hard and how long he had labored over those few lines. But she could readily see he had tried more than once. In some places the paper was worn thin. The words blurred before she reached the end.

Dear Sister Lora,

The letter you sent me made me happy, but now I must write something I am afraid will make you disappointed. I know it is wrong to tell a lie. I told some people you were my sister, because I wanted somebody to belong to me. I asked

God many times to forgive me. I thought He did, but it still bothers me sometimes; so I'm not sure if He did. If it's not too hard I hope you can forgive me, because I want to be your friend as long as I live.

Davy

In less than a week he held her answer in his trembling hand.
Dear Davy,

If I would write it a thousand times, "I forgive you," I would not mean it any more than when I write it once. Yes, you are forgiven. God forgave you the first time you asked Him. Don't ever let it bother you again. I wish it would not need to be a lie that you are my brother. I wanted to be at church the morning you were baptized, but I had a sick child here to take care of. I wanted to shake your hand and tell you how happy I am you made your decision to accept Christ. So I will tell you now. You will have temptations as every normal young Christian has, but when you do, remember I am praying for you just as if I were your real sister.

The summer breeze coming in his bedroom window was suddenly exhilarating, full of dancing needles on Davy's flushed face. It smelled so clean, so fresh, so strangely invigorating. He marked the letter, tucked it away, and bounded down the stairs two at a time.

The weeds pulled with far more ease that hot August afternoon.

"Here, David," said one of the little old ladies, finding him beyond the grape arbor, "have some lemonade."

"Thanks. Thanks a lot." He took a swallow. "It's real good, Miss Salome."

"You shouldn't work so fast in this heat, my boy. You might keel over."

Davy laughed. "I don't think so, Miss Salome. I don't mind the heat like you would."

"Your father must have taught you how to work. Want more?"

He let her refill the glass. "Ah—yes, he did. I—I like to work.

Thanks, Miss Salome."

"How old a boy are you?"

"I'll be thirteen in May."

"I have a nephew your age, but he's no hand at pulling weeds. He'd rather play ball all day or go swimming. His ma can't hardly get him to do a lick of work about the house. Aren't you much for sports?"

"Oh, sure," answered Davy. "I love to play ball. And I like to swim too. Where we lived on the farm I built a diving board and a raft. I haven't gotten acquainted with any boys yet since we moved here."

"Well, in that yellow house over there next to yours is a boy near your age. A little older I judge. Duggie Yonkers. They're gone on a trip now, but they'll be coming home before long. Duggie's a right nice boy when he's in good company. He's the only child Yonkers have. I remember when they took him."

Davy blinked. He handed Miss Salome the empty glass. "How does it look," he asked, "where I've gone?"

"Fine, David, just fine. I see you know weeds from flowers. Guess we'll have you mow our grass too."

"I'd be glad to."

"If you get thirsty again, just whistle."

"Okay, Miss Salome. I will," smiled Davy. And his smile accompanied her all the way to her back door.

The two met on the sidewalk the following week.

"Hi. I'm Dug. Please don't call me Duggie like my mom still does. Seems she can't realize I'm not a little kid any more. You're Dave, aren't you?"

Almost abashed, Davy stepped back. "How did you know my name?"

"My mom was talkin' to your mom. She still calls you Davy, doesn't she?"

Davy shifted the paper bag on his shoulder. "Yeah," he admitted. "Sometimes she does." He glanced toward the open door. "When did you get home?" he asked.

"Late last night." The boy advanced closer.

"Where were you?" asked Davy.

"All over the West. 'Way out to Kansas, Missouri, and Colorado. Ever been out there?"

"No. I've never been out of this state."

"Then you haven't seen much."

"Well," agreed Davy after a respectful pause, "not yet. But that's not saying I never will."

"Got yourself a paper route already?"

"Sure. I got to run in and eat some supper now, then finish delivering. I do the rest on my bike."

"See you later, Dave."

"See you later, Dug." He hurried up the steps.

"Come on over when you get done," called Dug over his shoulder. "We got some new records."

"Thanks," answered Davy. "I—I might. I'll see if I have time."

CHAPTER 20

Davy was hanging over the back of Mamma's rocking chair, watching her sewing a button on his white shirt.

"What's on your mind, Son?"

"Oh, that boy next door."

"What about him?"

"He asked me to come over a while."

"Do you want to?"

"Is it all right with you if I go?"

"Well, I wouldn't know why not," came her pleasant answer. "Of course, you know how tired you are, and how soon you ought to go to bed. You worked plenty hard today, didn't you?"

"I'm not awful tired," answered Davy. "I won't stay long."

"All right then. I hope you have a nice time."

"Thanks." Davy dropped a quick kiss on the back of Mamma's neck. "You too, Papa," he called back at the half-open door. "It's all right if I go next door for a while?"

Aaron looked up from the evening paper. "If Mamma said so, of course."

"You know, Rose," remarked Aaron, folding the paper, "I was just wondering how that boy would ever get along without Leon and Stanley. Looks like he's making out all right so far."

"I think he seems especially happy since we moved here. He takes such interest in his paper route. Yard work too. Now if he finds a boy friend right next door, what could be nicer?"

Aaron leaned back in his chair and folded his hands behind

his head. "They'd better not get chummy too fast. What sort of people are the Yonkers? How do we know that Duggie is the kind of a boy we want Davy to make up with?"

"Well, Mrs. Yonkers talks to me like a Christian. She says they all go to church regular."

"That's fine."

"And she said Duggie was hoping some nice boy near his age would move into this house."

Aaron put his feet on the ottoman and stretched. "How old?"

"Fourteen, I believe she said. Did you know he's not their own?"

"No."

"They got him when he was six months old."

"Adopted?"

"Yes. You know, Aaron, I wonder if it isn't about time we approached Davy again."

Aaron shook his head. "Rose," he said, "that boy knows how we feel. We don't need to hint any more. The thing that bears on my mind is why he holds off. He knows full well we'd adopt him whenever he says he's ready to give up that name."

"I wonder if he actually thinks he'll discover someday who his parents are?"

"Has he ever mentioned it?"

"Not to my knowledge, Aaron, but that's not saying he doesn't think about it."

Aaron sat thinking. "I tell you," he said at length, "maybe he's better off not knowing. I wish we had some way of knowing what's in his thoughts. I mean without prying."

"Well, we won't start that," said Rose.

"Of course not. But listen now, if you were in his place, wouldn't you wonder sometimes who left you and why?"

"How about yourself? Wouldn't you?"

"Of course," admitted Aaron. "I'd think every normal child would, and Davy's intelligent. Supposing he would ask me some-time to help him start searching. What would I say? Where would I begin?"

156

"Wait till the time comes, Aaron."

"Well, you can be sure—unless he mentions it first, I keep quiet on the subject. As I said, he might be a lot happier living in ignorance."

"Mrs. Yonkers said Duggie's parents were both killed in an automobile accident. And Duggie was thrown clear over the fence into a clover field and never hurt. That's what the agency told them."

"What else?"

"That's all."

Aaron got up and walked across the room. "Well, at least the boy knows they're dead and—" he fumbled with a plant leaf— "I find myself wishing Davy knew the same of his."

"Aaron Loomas," chided Rose, half smiling as she cast him a sidewise glance. "I find myself wishing the same, but I never intended to admit it out loud. We should both be ashamed of ourselves."

"Yes, Mamma Loomas, we should be ashamed." Aaron walked to the open door. "How about it now? Isn't that Yonkers boy plenty bold to be making up to Davy so soon?"

"Bold?"

"Why, they've scarcely seen each other and now he's over there in his house already. Won't they have things to talk about and notes to compare?"

Rose put Davy's shirt on a hanger and picked up a pair of socks that needed mending. "I think Davy can judge what sort of a boy Duggie is. If he doesn't appeal to him, he won't soon go back."

"Listen," Aaron put his head closer to the screen. "They've got either a radio or a phonograph over there. Hear that? I'll venture to say Davy will come home all excited and want one too."

"He could wish for something a lot worse," remarked Rose, threading her needle. "We want Davy to learn to appreciate good music, don't we?"

"Sure," agreed Aaron, running both hands deep into his

157

trouser pockets. "Good music. You hear that? Call that good music?"

"Yes, We Have No Bananas. Ever heard it?" asked Dug.
"No," answered Davy.

"Turn it down a little, please," called Mr. Yonkers from the other side of the room. He never looked up from the magazine he was reading.

"Sure, Dad," answered Dug, turning it down. "He doesn't care for this one," he whispered to Davy. "Yes, We Have No Bananas! Sorta crazy, isn't it?"

"I—I guess it is," agreed Davy in an undertone.

"It's not my favorite, but I wanted you to hear it. I hardly ever put it on when Dad's at home, because I know he doesn't like it. But, well—"

"Then don't think you have to play it just for me. I thought you said you got some new ones."

"Sure thing. I'll put one of those on next. This is that song about Floyd Collins. You know that guy who got caught in that cave?"

"I read all about it. Was awful. Sure did feel sorry for him, didn't you?"

"It's kinda sad," said Dug. "Kinda creepy like. But I sorta like it anyhow. Listen."

Neither spoke a word until the record was finished.

"How about that one? Like it?"

"Well," began Davy. "Just as you said, it's sorta creepy an' sad. I doubt if I'd want to listen to it every day. Would you?"

"Guess not. Now I'll put on these two pretty records. This one is the Missouri Waltz and the other is The Blue Danube. These aren't crazy or weepy. Just the opposite. They make a guy feel good. Listen. You'll soon know what I mean."

Davy sat spellbound, eyes glittering.

"Agree?" asked Dug.

"Yes," smiled Davy. "I like that kind much more. If your father doesn't mind, I wish you'd play them both again."

158

"Oh, Dad won't mind. It's just that banana one he can't stand." Dug laughed. "I smell popcorn. Don't you? That's Mom for you. I guess that means she likes you and she's glad you came over."

Very soon into the room glided beaming, pleasant-faced Mrs. Yonkers, a rounded bowl of hot, buttery popcorn in each outstretched hand. "Here you are, boys," she said. "Boys like this kind of white stuff, don't they?"

"You bet," shouted Dug.

"Thank you," said Davy. "But I hope you didn't think you had to go to this bother just because I came over."

"It's no bother, David," came her cheery voice. "I like to do things to make our boys happy."

Davy smiled. "Our boys?"

"Me too," reminded Mr. Yonkers. "Dont forget—this boy likes popcorn."

"You shall have all you want, my dear," answered Mrs. Yonkers, hurrying to the kitchen.

"Let's go up to my room to eat ours," suggested Dug.

He led the way. "I want to show you my models. It's a hobby I've started. I like to put ships together on rainy days when we can't play ball. I finished those two there, and I'm working on this big one now. Do you like to mess with stuff like this?"

"Sure do," answered Davy. "But I like airplanes best. I have one model about half done. I made a twin engine plane of my own that I whittled out of wood."

"Yeah? I'll have to see it."

"Sure thing, Dug. Some evening you come to our house and I'll take you up to my room."

"You the only one they've got?"

"You mean child?"

"Yeah. I'll call you Dave if you don't mind."

"I don't mind, Dug. They had a child that died. They have Lesa, married to Clif Dunbar. They live twelve miles from here. I'm—I'm not theirs, Dug."

"You're not? How long you been living with them?"

"Since I was three."

"Where's your home?"

Davy flinched. "I—I—" he faltered. "Well, that *is* my home, Dug."

"I mean before you went there. Where'd you come from?"

"Well," Davy squirmed. "I can't tell you, Dug. Wish I knew. Miss Salome told me they got you too."

"Yeah. They did. But I'm adopted."

"Since when?"

"I can't remember. I was a baby. My parents are both dead. They seem like my real mom and dad. I guess they don't to you, do they?"

"Oh, yes, they do," answered Davy. "Just about," he added. "Only I remember being in the Children's Home and Sister Lora. It sorta makes you feel sorta creepy like, not knowing if yours are living or dead, or where, or anything, or if you have the name they gave you, and all that."

Dug stared at Davy as he munched his popcorn.

"Don't ever mention it that I wonder all this, will you?"

"No," answered Dug. " 'Course not if you say so. But I'm glad you have a good home. I'm real glad for you, Dave. What does your dad—I mean Mr. What's-His-Name—work at?"

"Aaron Loomas. He used to farm, but now since we moved here to town he's going to start doing carpenter work. He's real good at that. Especially fine finishing. My dad can do about anything. Just anything. When you come over, I'll show you the wagons and tractors and trains and things he made. What does your dad do?"

"He works in a machine shop. What are you going to be? Are you going on through high school?"

Davy got up and slowly worked his way toward the door. "I haven't decided yet what I'll be. Sure thing, I'll finish high school. After that I can't say. All depends. I've got to go now."

By the time school started, Dave and Dug had become close friends. To be sure, they were not together constantly, for Dave

160

had found several additional yard jobs that he worked at with diligence. But after his evening papers were delivered he and Dug (Dug worked part time in a greenhouse) found time to practice ball together, or play on a neighborhood team, or play checkers, or listen to records at Dug's house. Little by little Dave confided in Dug some of his secret fears and longings, for Dug seemed to understand, or at least in a measure.

But that one fear, the fear of being illegitimate, no. Never would he share that with anyone, not even his closest friend Leon. Although he and Leon would not be attending the same school now, they did see each other almost every Sunday at church, and at least once a month Leon was invited to go along home with Dave for Sunday dinner.

"Come," said Dave one Sunday. "I want to show you what I've got up in my room. There," he pointed, "on the dresser. That."

"A radio!" exclaimed Leon. "Man, oh man! Does it work?"

"Of course it works." Dave turned the knob. "Listen to that orchestra music. Say, how about that?"

"Yeah," shouted Leon. "How about it? That's pretty swell. Who got it for you?"

"I got it with my own money I earned," beamed Dave. "I sold that bicycle Dennis didn't take along and put that toward it."

"You mean Papa Loomas said you could?"

Dave nodded. "I had a letter from Dennis and he said he didn't think he'd get back for a long time to pick up the bike and I should sell it. Papa said I could; so I did. Dennis has a car of his own now."

"Yeah?"

"He has a job working at the Ford plant."

"Yeah?"

"I asked Dad—"

"You call Papa Loomas Dad now?"

"Well, it's like this, Leon. Dug, the boy next door, he calls his father Dad since he's older, and one day it just slipped out an' I called Papa Dad before I thought. He looked at me a little

161

surprised and funny like. I quick apologized. I certainly didn't want to hurt his feelings or have him think I was being disrespectful or anything like that. And you know what he said?"

"What?"

"Well, he said, 'Davy, it's not what you call me; it's how you say it that matters. If you think Dave sounds as kind and loving and warmhearted as Davy, we can call you Dave if you want us to. And if you can call me Dad with the same feelings in your heart as when you say Papa, it's all right with me.' Oh, I'd never call him Dad if he didn't like it. I couldn't, Leon. Not him."

"And he was in favor of you selling the bike an' getting this radio?"

"Well," explained Dave, "we all talked it over for quite a while first. He didn't say yes right like that. Neither did Mother, but they agreed or I wouldn't have gotten it."

"You call her Mother now?"

"I'm starting to. I'm getting at that age, Leon. It sounds more dignified and grown-up. Especially when I talk about her to the other fellows. Mamma Loomas, no, not at my age. But just the same, Mamma or Mother, either one sounds nice to me because I love her just like she was my own. Listen now, isn't that beautiful music, Leon?"

"I'll say. I could listen all day. Wish I had one."

"They told me I couldn't ever neglect my studies to listen to it, and I'm not to listen to any silly trash, or have it on after 10:15 p.m. So I promised. That's fair, don't you think?"

"Guess so. Sounds fair to me."

"I wouldn't want Papa an' Mamma, I mean Dad an' Mother, to just let me do any old thing I might get into my head. I can get wild ideas sometimes," Dave laughed.

"You don't think they're too strict with you, then?"

"No. Not really. I sorta wanted to get a record player like Dug's folks next door have, but Dad said not yet. Said they cost too much. And the records cost too much. I know he's right. But someday I'm pretty sure I'll have one."

"You will? When?"

"I don't know when. But someday, when I'm old enough to be on my own, I'll get one, and some real good records. The prettiest they make."

"Dinner is ready, boys," called Aaron from the bottom of the stairs. "Are you hungry?"

"Coming," answered the two in unison, and they bounded down the stairs.

One evening in early May of the following year, Aaron knocked gently on Dave's door.

"Come in." Dave looked up from his biology textbook. "Hi, Dad."

"Son," began Aaron, stepping over to the radio, "may I turn it down a little?"

Dave bit his lip. "Why, sure. Go ahead, Dad."

"Do you actually enjoy that kind of jazz, Son?"

Dave fumbled a moment with his pencil before he spoke. "Why—yes, Dad. I do," he answered. "If that's what you call jazz. Once in a while I like it. Not all the time, of course. Why? Don't you care for it at all?"

"Well—" Aaron evaded the question; he stroked his chin. "I'm a little surprised. I thought you were up here studying. And I thought your taste was for higher class music than that. And you agreed not to have it on while you were studying, didn't you?"

"Turn it clear off, Dad," suggested Dave, shifting on his chair. "I hope it hasn't been disturbing you downstairs."

"Well, I just wondered how you could concentrate on your studies with that on. Since you're in high school, don't you have to study a lot harder?"

Dave leaned back in his chair and pushed the small table away from him a few inches. He ran both hands back over his black, curly hair. "Well," he began with some hesitancy, "it's like this, Dad. What I'm studying," he coughed nervously, "has me so—well, so crazy mixed up and confused that—that music doesn't make it any harder to concentrate."

163

"What's this?" asked Aaron, leaning over the table.

"Well, Dad, I—I don't know how to say it, but I don't know what I believe about anything any more." He slapped his hand on the open book and threw his pencil down.

"What?" exclaimed Aaron. "I don't understand. Explain to me what this is all about." He bent over the table and looked Dave full in the face.

"Oh, all this deal—this crazy stuff we've been studying about evolution."

CHAPTER 21

An awkward pause followed.

Aaron Loomas swallowed hard and Dave could hear his heavy breathing.

"Evolution?" Aaron asked. "You mean that theory that we came from apes and—and—"

"Sure, Dad. It's all here in our textbook. We've been on evolution since school started, seems like. I'm about fed up on it."

"You never told us, Son."

"Why bother you? It's required of me, not you. Tomorrow we're to hand in our outlines on the theories of Lamarck. And also one on the Darwin theory, the most logical of all the theories ever written."

"Logical?" Aaron's face spelled sudden concern.

"I have to make my grades, Dad."

"Yes, but you said this has you confused until you don't know what you believe."

"Well, Dad, it has. Seems to me it would anybody."

"I imagine. But you, Son. To the extent that you don't know now what you believe? Why—why, Davy, this is serious."

"Please, Dad, don't get so worked up. I shouldn't have told you."

"Yes, you should have, Son." Aaron walked across the room.

"I had no idea—no idea this would be thrust on you so soon. I supposed you'd—why, Davy, I planned to open the subject to you someday—and prepare you for this. I feared it would be coming. That book there? Read me a paragraph." Dave heard distinctly the hurt, startled tone in Dad's voice.

"Sure, Dad." Dave picked up the book and began to read. "There is an ever-increasing wealth of data today to fully support the fundamental assumption on evolution, that all forms of life have come from previously existing forms. Few today hold to the belief that living beings of any kind were created separately. Modern scientists emphatically discredit the Biblical theory that man was created by a supreme being or a God. We have sufficient evidence to prove that all forms of life, both plant and animal, living or extinct, high or low, including man, have evolved over long, extended periods of time from previously existing forms. We have at our command, in orderly classification, well over three million different species of living things described to substantiate this theory. In the past some conservative and conscientious historians launched fiery battles over this. We will not go into that here."

"Son!" Aaron's voice was a trifle too unsteady. He cleared his throat. Reaching over the table he placed one hand firmly on the boy's shoulder. "You—you surely—surely don't take to heart what you've just read there."

Dave sat in quiet thought before he spoke. "I just don't know, Dad," he said. "I—I'd hate to think that—well, that you," he looked up, "or Mother, or Leon," he looked at the wall, "or Sister Lora," he shoved the closed book across the table, "came from a—a monkey or tadpole. But," he stood up abruptly and pushed the chair under the table and clasped the back of it with both hands, "it really doesn't make much difference about myself."

"It doesn't?" gasped Aaron. "Why doesn't it? It certainly does to us."

Dave made no answer. He simply looked at the floor and shook his head.

"Let's sit down and talk this over, Son."

Dave looked up sharply. "Tonight?"

"Right now. Yes. I—I had no idea. Why didn't you confide

166

in us about this when it first came up?"

"Please, Dad." Dave bit the inside of his cheek, as he glanced up apologetically. "Maybe I should have," he said. "But Dug and I—we decided we'd figure this out ourselves. We didn't want to bother our—anyone else with our assignments."

"But if this is undermining your belief in God and the Bible, David—Davy, this is serious. Soon you'll lose belief in everything, once that's gone. Dug's in your class?"

"Yes."

"And you two decided you'd figure this out together?"

"Well, something like that, yes."

"But you said you're all mixed up and confused. Then he is, too?"

"Sit down, Dad. I'll tell you. It's like this." Dave seated himself across the end of the bed, his one leg curled up under him. He twisted on his shoestring. "How can anybody know who is right? How can anyone actually *know* anything?"

"Davy," called Rose from the bottom of the stairs. "Dug is here and wants to know if he can come up."

Dave saw the sudden look of distress and disappointment cross the face opposite him. "Sorry, Mother," he called back. "Tell Dug to come back after while. I'm busy right now."

"Thank you, Son," whispered Aaron. "I really appreciate that. I hope Dug won't get peeved at you."

"Well, if he does, he can get unpeeved."

"Tell me this, Dave," began Aaron. His voice was low and quite calm. "Did those questions bother you before you started studying evolution?"

"Perhaps a little once in a while."

"Could you tell me why or how or when?"

Dave shook his head.

"Does it make any difference to you what I believe?"

Dave rubbed his one hand over the toe of his shoe. "I suppose it does. Why, sure it does."

"Would you want me to be disturbed about this matter of where we came from?"

"Well, no. Not you, Dad."

"Why not?"

"Well, I'd rather you'd keep on believing what you always have."

"Why?"

"Because I—I think it makes you happy and satisfied."

"Why does it?"

"Well—because you think it's the right way to believe, I guess. You have faith in what you believe and it makes you happy, I guess."

"Anything else?"

"Well, if you believe it was God who created the first man, then I suppose you believe God had a hand in creating all your ancestors."

"And so?"

"Well, then, so in you too."

"And so?"

"Well, I guess that makes you feel good. And—well—sorta important." Dave rubbed his hand over his shoe again. "As though you had a good reason for existing. I don't know. Guess you think that sounds queer, and I guess you think now I really am confused, don't you?"

"Son, I think you have excellent reasoning. You've told me a lot. I'm glad I came up here tonight. You're just beginning to face some of the problems every young man must face sooner or later. And as long as God allows you to live under my care I want to share with you every problem that confronts you. If you'll let me. If I can help you realize this, that 'God is no respecter of persons,' I want to do that much right now. Man can write millions of books to try to prove God did not create him, but no one can really prove it. The Bible is true and God cannot lie. I'm no theologian, Davy—Dave—I'm not even a good Bible student, but I'm just simple enough to believe that the Bible is the infallible word of God. Heaven and earth shall pass away, but God's word never. And just as surely as Abraham and Moses and David and the Apostle Paul and Christ were all born for a purpose, so was Sister Lora Wenzel, and Melvin Kolb, and his son, Leon, and Dug, and Mother, and you, David Grant. You!" Aaron reached over and shook the boy's arm.

In Dave's troubled eyes came a faint gleam. A muscle quivered by his right temple.

"Does what you've been reading there give you any inspiration to live to discover and fill your special place in life?"

"Not if I just happened. No. That's just it, Dad." Dave's face got hot. He pulled his shoestring. "Who are the accidents of creation?" he asked. "And who aren't? Who knows?" He got up and walked to the door. "Don't you think," he said, "I'd better go over and see what Dug wanted?"

"Maybe so. But maybe I'd better go along over and have a talk with Mr. Yonkers. And together we try to set our sons thinking straight on this."

"Oh, no. Please, Dad." Dave caught him by the arm. "Please don't do that."

"Why not?"

"That's the very thing Dug wouldn't want. I know. He's afraid if his folks know about all this they might go talk to the principal. Or they might even make him quit school. Oh, Dad, I hope you won't make it hard for Dug."

"Then you've been discussing this with each other at some length?"

"Every day. Sure thing. We're in the same class."

"Son," Dave felt Dad's arm across his shoulder. "If I had never believed before in the eternal, inspired, holy Word of God, and that God has a purpose for the existence of every human individual, I would have come to believe it now. But Mother and I were sure of it from the day you came into our home."

Dave stood speechless. A strange, strangely warming feeling enveloped him, possessed him. For a prolonged moment he was carried away to some far-off foreign place, so lost in thought he was. Then sudden gratitude brought him back and with head erect and eyes shining he said, "Why, Dad, I never knew before that you could make such speeches."

Aaron smiled. "I'm going to leave it to you then (if you don't think I should go over) to help your friend, Dug, get settled on this."

Dave nodded.

"I know neither of you wants to lose your faith."

"That's true, Dad."

"I'm pretty sure Dug's parents would sooner have him quit school than—"

"Sure. I know what you mean."

"I hope you've kept up your reading." Aaron nodded toward the little stand beside the bed.

"Well," Dave colored a bit, "I will tonight," and he ran down the steps ahead of Dad.

Months later Mrs. Yonkers was talking to Rose Loomas across the back yard fence.

"I want to tell you how much we appreciate the influence your boy has been having over Dug."

"What do you mean, Mrs. Yonkers?"

"Well, before you moved here Dug sometimes got in the wrong gang and we didn't approve of what all went on. I like to know where my boy is when night comes on. When he goes out to play ball with your boy, I know he's in good company and he'll be home when he says he'll be. He's been more courteous too. And I've noticed he has his Bible beside his bed. So I figure he's been reading it. And, do you know, he told me yesterday that he and Dave were both pretty well shook up some time back over evolution. Did you know about that, Mrs. Loomas?"

"Yes. Not at first, though. But after Dave told Aaron, we had some interesting discussions with him about it. I'm sure it made all of us do some honest thinking on the subject. Young people want reasons for what they believe."

"Oh, Mrs. Loomas. I was just shocked. I do hope Dave is thoroughly settled on it now, because Duggie thinks what Dave thinks about it. They seem to be quite confidential."

"Well, Mrs. Yonkers, I'm sure we have reason to appreciate

170

your son too. We're glad Davy has found a good friend right here next door. It's what he needs. I'm sure we can't imagine what all goes through the mind of a boy like David. Or any boy for that matter. It's no small task to be real parents without getting preachy and that simply is not the method, to our way of thinking."

"I'm sure you're right, Mrs. Loomas. I've overheard bits of their conversation at times and I think you and your husband have made a tremendous influence on Dave."

"Well, I only hope it's for good. I have bread in the oven, and I'll have to excuse myself."

It happened the next week right after basketball practice. Among the two dozen girls who flocked in to cheer and watch the boys was the pretty blond Kalene Flemming. Everyone in the entire school knew Ted Brown walked her home every evening. Dave knew it too and it was no concern of his. He and Dug walked home together and let the rest of the world alone.

Kalene waited by her locker until Dave walked by.

"Hey, there," she called. "How about a real handsome Mr. Grant helping a girl into her coat?"

Surprised, Dave stopped short. "Here, handsome," she dimpled, holding out her brown tweed.

Blushing Dave stepped over and held it for her. No girl had ever approached him like this. In fact, he could count on one hand the number of girls he had said a dozen words to since school started.

"Thanks, Dave," the girl whispered, and turning around she pinched him under the chin. "Why don't you walk home with me tonight? Please?"

Around the corner came Ted just in time to see Kalene reach up and touch Dave. He scowled. His eyes shot fire. He stepped up and in a torrent of rage clenched both fists and jammed Dave back against the wall.

"You low-down rascal," he snarled. "You leave your filthy hands and eyes off my girl. Understand? I mean what I say. And

171

I mean I mean it. Get me?"

Dave made no answer.

"He wasn't flirting with your girl," puffed Dug in defense. "She was flirting with him. I saw the whole deal. You go on and take your Miss Kalene home and see who cares. She asked him to hold her coat. I heard her call him handsome Mr. Grant. Didn't she, Dave? Come on, let's get out of here."

Ted was furious. He turned to Kalene and grabbed her by both shoulders. "Listen here," he said. "You stay away from that disconnected crud. Don't you know he's—" he lowered his voice two steps —"illegitimate? Don't you ever let him touch you or your coat again."

Kalene's mouth opened wide. Ted wheeled her around and scurried her down the hall, but she looked back long enough to give Dave one questioning glance that stabbed him through.

Humiliation left him weak, appalled, crushed. Dug was not the only one who had heard. Two boys and at least one girl were close enough to catch every word Ted had said, even those in padded tone. Sudden indignation overwhelmed him and sent Dave racing after Ted.

"Hey, there," he shouted. "Stop! Listen. You don't know what you're talking about. You're the one who has filthy, dirty hands and eyes." Dave was trembling now. "What's more," he panted, "you've got a filthy mind too. And I'm no more an illegitimate crud than you are. And I'll prove it."

"Shut your—"

Mr. Harding, the coach, stepped out of a side room. "What's this racket going on here?" he demanded.

"I have no idea, Mr. Harding," answered Ted. "Ask Dave," and he shoved Kalene out the nearest side door.

Dave hurried out the second door, Dug after him.

The incident not only shocked Dug, but Dave sensed it and it sent him into a sudden pool of shame and misery. "I don't suppose you'll care to walk home beside me now," he said under his breath. "I'll run on."

"No." Dug caught Dave's arm. "We'll go together as always."

172

The two walked in silence to the first street crossing.

Dug spoke first. "I'm not going to believe what Ted said about you."

"I hope you won't." Dave's voice was dry, parched, and broken.

"How do you suppose Ted heard such a thing?"

Dave bit his lip. "No idea." He brushed away a tear.

"Bet he never heard it. Just made it up. Sure wasn't one bit nice either."

They walked on in silence. Hideous, tormenting thoughts sneered at Dave and mocked him with long claw-like fingers. He could see hundreds of eyes, girls' eyes, teachers' eyes, boys' eyes, dark and accusing, piercing him the next time he entered the school. How could he ever face anyone?

"You going to tell your folks?"

"No," cried Dave. "Please, Dug, please. Oh, don't tell yours. If you do, I'll never come over again."

"Okay, Dave. I promise. Sure was mean of Ted. Even if it had been true, it was nasty of him. I never heard you speak up like that before."

Dug heard Dave sniffle. A minute later he thought he saw him wipe his eyes, but he didn't try to look. "You come over after supper and we'll play your favorite records."

Dave shook his head. "Not tonight. I—I feel sorta sick on my stomach."

"Ah, you mustn't let this upset you," Dug consoled him. "Goodness gracious. Why, I'll bet there's thousands, maybe millions of that kind of kids in the world. It's not their fault and they go on like it was nothing at all. And as long as you know it's a big lie—well, then, why feel so bad? Nobody believes it."

"You don't understand."

"Understand what?"

"It's a lie, Dug."

"Of course it's a lie. Be glad it is."

"You don't understand, I said."

"Understand what?"

173

"I—well—" Dave stood there in front of his house, a bundle of bewilderment and pain, and with a smarting, stricken conscience.

"I can't prove it," he cried brokenly. "I can't prove anything." Without looking back he ran up the steps and into his house.

CHAPTER 22

Rose was at the door, about to open it to shake the rug in her hand.

"You're a little late, aren't you?"

"A little. Basketball practice." He hurried past her, avoiding her glance as much as possible.

"Everything all right, Son?"

"I'll—I'll just have to hurry with my papers." He tried to act calm.

"There's fresh cookies there on the table."

"Thanks." Dave stuck one in his pocket, grabbed his paper bag, and shot out the back door.

At the supper table Rose noticed he wasn't taking his usual helpings.

"Is something wrong?" she asked, eying him anxiously.

"I'm just not very hungry tonight," explained Dave.

"You're not getting sick, are you?"

"I guess not. Don't worry about me, Mother."

"Maybe all this ball practice and your paper route are too much for you," suggested Aaron.

Dave shook his head.

"You look a little pale," observed Rose. "Maybe I should make you some boneset tea."

Dave shook his head.

"You'll drink it if I make it, won't you?"

Dave shrugged. He forced a smile. "You worry too much over me," was his comment.

"We want to take care of you, Son," added Aaron, concernedly. "Maybe the best thing you can do is get to bed early tonight. You look tired in your eyes."

"We're invited to the Home for six-thirty supper tomorrow night," announced Rose. "It's to be a surprise for Sister Lora's birthday. Clif and Lesa are to be there too. We want you to be feeling well for that. I'm sure we won't go unless you're able to go along."

Dave glanced momentarily at Mother, then at the water glass before him. Sister Lora. Her sweet, sincere face, so radiant, so gentle, so undefiled, seemed to be looking at him with eyes clear and direct. Does she—does she think— "May I be excused?" he asked.

"Of course, Son," answered Rose. "I'll bring up the tea after while. If Dug comes over, I'll tell him you're not feeling well."

He closed the door securely.

"O God," Dave dropped on his knees beside his bed, and buried his face in the spread, "how can I prove it's not true? I'm afraid I've done wrong. What can I do about this awful temper? Is it really true? Oh, no, God. Isn't there some way you can help me? I don't want to be one of those meaningless accidents."

To the best of his ability Dave tried to pour out to God his soul anguish. Words, sentences, phrases, simple phrases, senseless phrases ran into groans. He came to his wit's end. Exhausted and still troubled, he got up and went to his dresser drawer and found the letter he had received from Sister Lora over two years before. His sad, troubled eyes, almost bloodshot, read the comforting words: "If I would write it a thousand times, 'I forgive you,' I would not mean it any more than when I write it once. Yes, you are forgiven. God forgave you the first time you asked Him. . . . You will have temptations as every normal young Christian has." Dave drew a long, long breath. "But when you

176

do, remember I am praying for you just as if I were your real sister."

"O God," cried Dave, "forgive me for every lie. I mean the one I'm not sure about. O God, you know what I mean and can't express. Just help me walk straight and be an honor to Dad and Mother and Sister Lora—and my own parents if I do have any."

On the table by his bed was his Bible. He opened it at random, near the center. "Why art thou cast down, O my soul?" he read, "and why art thou disquieted in me? hope thou in God: for I shall yet praise him for the help of his countenance." Dave felt a faint wave of relief. He read on. "O my God, my soul is cast down within me: therefore will I remember thee."

He heard the gentle tapping on the door. "It's Mother with the tea."

He hurried to the door and opened it wide. "Thanks, Mother. You go to entirely too much bother for me." And he planted a kiss on her warm cheek.

"How could that be, Son, when you're the only one we have to look after? Drink it while it's good and hot. And go to bed early."

"I will. I promise, Mother dear."

The next evening Dave came home from his paper route with a package done up in green paper. He put it on the dining room table with extra care. "It's for Sister Lora, Mother. An African violet. Do you think she'll like that?"

"She'll love it, Davy—just love it, I know. My, I'm glad you're feeling well enough to go. Can you be ready in ten minutes?"

"I think so. You can call me Dave tonight if you want to," he reminded her.

"I'll try to remember that, big boy," smiled Rose.

The planned surprise was a real surprise. Everyone had a good time. The chicken supper, served in the Kolbs' private dining room, was super-delicious. No one, not even Leon, de-

177

tected that Dave was putting forth any special effort to hide his personal perplexities. Across the table Sister Lora smiled at him time and again, and each time he returned a smile

"How's school at East Hempfield?" asked Leon.

"Okay."

"Studying hard?"

"Not too hard."

"Making all A's?"

"Just about."

The months dragged into years, and Shana continued going home from the hospital with the same disheartening report. "Sorry, Mrs. Drextell. No improvement in your husband. We're doing all we can for him. He was rational only for a few minutes today."

The night was dark and a hard, freezing rain was slashing against the windows of her two-room apartment. On the end table beside her chair lay two letters. Shana picked up one and held it listlessly for a long time, while she gazed bleakly at nothing in particular. She felt chilled and agonizingly empty, yet not hungry. Her face wore a taut mask of misery that both time and sorrow had etched about her delicate lips and once-sparkling eyes.

Slowly she unfolded the letter and read what she had read twice before that same day:

Glasgow, Scotland
Dec. 6, 1927

Dear Shana,

It is a long time—too long a time I have waited to write to you. I must admit I have fought many bitter feelings toward you. You did not write and tell me about yourself and all your troubles. Why, Shana? Why? Are you afraid of me? Hazel finally wrote about your having a baby boy and losing him. Then later about your marrying again. And now recently about Anthony's serious illness. Shana, I am still your father. Why haven't you confided in me? I am not so well the past year. It will soon be sixteen long years since you left Glasgow.

Why don't you come back and work for me? Let bygones be bygones. So many things I simply cannot understand. Not even Bernice's actions. I wish you would write. No matter what has taken place, please write. I do not understand why our family has been torn apart like this. I am sad and very lonely. I do sincerely beg of you to consider my offer to take you back. The way Hazel wrote, your husband could pass away almost any time. All will be overlooked if you will only come back to me and help me keep our home.

Father

One lone tear crept to the edge of Shana's eyelash and hung trembling, before it fell on the paper. She wiped it listlessly with the back of her hand, and folding the letter, placed it where it had been on the table. She buried her face in both hands and groaned out loud. At long length she unfolded the second letter, drawing a deep breath as though she were very tired.

Des Moines, Iowa
Jan. 12, 1928

Dear Shana,

We haven't heard from you for so long, I am quite worried about you. How is Anthony? We are all well and Bruce continues to like his job. He got another raise. We bought a better, bigger house and moved into it two weeks ago. The children will have a nice big yard for picnics, croquet, or whatever. We are all anxious for spring to come.

We had a Christmas greeting from Bernice and Lewis. No letter. Not one single sentence. She almost never writes to me any more. I can't understand her. She lives in a world of her own. Shana, I had a letter from Father too, and he says he's not well. He wishes you'd come back home. I'm sure he means it. Of course I'm certain he means in case Anthony does not get well. I wonder if you've ever thought of going back. We only wish we were close so we could be of some comfort to you in all your sorrows and disappointments. I think of you every day even if I don't write often.

We have started attending church and Sunday school and

enjoy it very much. Remember this, Shana, we do pray for you every day. It's all we know to do, but if there is something more we are not aware of, please, please, be free to tell us what it is. Could you come on the bus or train for a week or weekend, if Anthony is so you can slip away? It would do you good. Please write soon.

In love,
Hazel and all the
family

The freezing rain continued slashing against the windowpanes. Sudden, scalding tears streamed down Shana's sad, troubled face.

She draped a red sweater around her shoulders, and for half an hour she held the pen in her hand before she started moving it across the sheet of paper. Drearily she wrote, wiping tears that nearly blinded her.

Dear Hazel,

I have no good news to write. Anthony's condition is gradually getting worse. Sometimes he scarcely recognizes me. Sometimes he has to be restrained and that is harder on me than on him. I rented our nice, big house because I was too sad and lonely in it. I moved into a small apartment close by. I'm working in the Mayfield Hotel four days a week, mostly to put my mind on something else. Anthony wouldn't like it if he knew. I take a taxi to the hospital every evening. This endless suspense is almost killing me.

Thanks for your prayers. I wonder sometimes what God thinks of me, or does He take time to think of me at all? I have but one request to make of you, Hazel. You may not be able to do it, but please, if you can think of a way to find out where my baby is buried, do it. I see him in my dreams so often, my sweet, innocent little David in that blue and white blanket. Why did I ever let him go? Oh, why? It drives me mad some days.

Thank you for your invitation. I will never leave as long as Anthony is in the hospital, if that is a lifetime. I had a letter from Father. Bless his heart. I feel sorry for him, but I'll never go back to Scotland even if Anthony should pass away, unless I find my baby's grave first and put a marker on it. Can't you please find out someway from Bernice where it is? Do try again, Hazel. This is my only request.

Love,
Shana

The unpleasant incident with Ted and Kalene was never repeated. In fact, the remainder of the school year passed without any reference to it. At first Ted ignored Dave, but as time passed and the two rubbed elbows on the same basketball team, they spoke as though nothing had ever happened. Ted may have forgotten completely. But not Dave. He tried his utmost not to show it, but the haunting, silent stigma swung over his head unceasingly. The label "uncertainty" was branded with permanent letters on his consciousness. There was no getting away from it. The older he got, the deeper the branding.

"Son," stated Aaron when Dave handed him his final report card of the year. "I'm real proud of this. God has blessed you with brains and the ability to use them. Have you thought what you'd like to prepare for? It's probably a little soon, isn't it?"

Dave scratched his head. "I think I'd like to be an electrical engineer, or an airplane pilot."

"Well, I tell you, Son, we'll talk about this again someday. For the summer what do you have in mind?"

"I suppose I'll keep on with my paper route. But Dug thinks I might get a job at the greenhouse where he worked last summer. I could make more there than doing these yard jobs in the neighborhood."

"Well," smiled Aaron, "I see you have an eye for business."

"I'd like to go talk to the manager right now, if you don't care."

"Run along, Son. Mother will hold supper until you get back."

It was the last week in June. Dave and Dug had both been working faithfully and hard at the greenhouse—watering, planting, transplanting, weeding, delivering, building, remodeling, painting, and spraying.

More and more as the two worked together their confidings increased. After the incident with Ted, Dave found it easy to tell Dug things he didn't suppose he'd ever tell anyone.

"Dug, I think sometimes I've just got to find out."

"Why don't you save up your money and hire a lawyer to help you?"

"Maybe Dad and Mother wouldn't approve of that."

"Why not? That's what lawyers are for, aren't they?"

"I'm afraid it would cost more than I've earned. I wonder if my real dad is tall. I wonder how old he is." Dave rambled on because Dug was a good listener.

"I've often wondered all that too," remarked Dug.

"Have you really?"

"Sure I have. But I know it's no use. So I try to dismiss it. Do you know what your dad's name is?"

"Grant, I hope. But I've no idea what his first name is. But I do know my mother's first name."

"What is it?"

"Shana."

"How'd you find that out?"

"I found it in the file in the Children's Home where I was before they got me."

"Shana. Never heard the name before."

"I think it's pretty. About the prettiest name I ever heard. I keep wondering if I look anything like her and what she's like and where she is."

"Bet you do too."

Dave took fresh courage. "The paper with her name on it said Philadelphia."

"Well, then," exclaimed Dug, "why can't you find her?"

"I've been thinking for a long time about going there sometime and hunting until I do."

"Well," said Dug, "take hold of that end of the table. Let's move it this way. Listen, I'll go with you."

"To Philadelphia?"

"Sure I will. I've been there quite a few times. It's only sixty miles on the train. Let's go on the Fourth of July."

"The Fourth?" Dave whistled softly, ever so softly. His heart pounded. "What would we tell our folks we're going for?"

"Wouldn't we tell them why?"

"Oh, no, Dug. Never. Don't you dare tell your parents anything I've been telling you."

"Why?"

"Why, Dug, because. Because. Can't you understand? If I'd find her and—and—" his heart was pounding so violently now, he could scarcely control his breathing, "what if—oh, I've imagined all kinds of things. It nearly scares me to think of it. Yet I want to. I have no idea what to expect. What if she doesn't want to see me? Or what, just what if she wouldn't even own me?"

"Well, Dave, don't get so worked up. You're jumping to conclusions. While your imagining anyhow, I can make up some wild ones too, such as, what if she's a movie star? Or a great musician? Or a millionaire? That's possible. Maybe you were kidnaped. Maybe in the hospital you got exchanged for another baby. You know. Got swapped? That's happened. Maybe you have a twin. Maybe your mother knew she was about to die and gave you to someone. Maybe there is a big fortune waiting for you. I can't understand why, if you had her name, you didn't tell someone and go there long ago."

"Sh, Dug. Don't get so loud. I don't want anyone to hear this. I wasn't old enough to go before. If you go with me, you've got to keep mum about the whole thing or I won't tell you anything more."

"Okay. Okay. I'm your true friend. Honest. We could tell our folks we just want to go to be going someplace. Hard as we've been working, looks like we could both stand a little vacation."

183

"What would it cost?"

"I don't know. Something like three-fifty round trip. We'd need money to spend for eats. We could go to the zoo and the Independence Hall. There's things enough there to spend several days."

"Do you think your folks would approve?"

"Well, that depends mostly on what your folks say. If yours approve, I'm pretty sure mine will."

"I'm going to ask mine tonight. I don't know when I've been so excited, Dug."

That evening Aaron Loomas called on Mr. Yonkers. "Sounds like our boys have a little adventure in their veins."

"So I hear. They're growing up fast, aren't they? I wouldn't want Dug going to the city alone, but with Dave I see no harm as long as they mind their own business and come back the same night."

"We're invited to a picnic and a big ball game with the Home children on the Fourth, but Dave insists he'd rather go to Philadelphia. He's been a good boy, obedient and respectful. I hate to refuse him. Now understand, Mr. Yonkers, we don't give in to all his whims and wishes, but I aim to be reasonable with the boy."

"Same here, Mr. Loomas. We can see Dave has a good influence on our Dug. So I'd say let 'em go to Philadelphia and see what's right and educational."

The sun was just coming up over the top of the gray stone depot when the train pulled into Philadelphia. Dave went straight to the telephone booth and looked in the directory. "My soul!" he exclaimed. "Look, Dug. Why, here's pages and pages of Grants."

184

CHAPTER 23

His hand trembled. His whole body trembled. Slowly Dave's eyes, eager and expectant, followed his forefinger down the first column of Grants. A. B—Abby—Abel—Abner—Allan—Allison—on and on through the A's and B's, the C's. "Dug, did you ever dream there were so many Grants in one city?"

"You may have lots of relations and don't know it," laughed Dug.

"This is something. Why, look, here's several David Grants, and Harold, and Howard, and three Jameses, and look at all the John Grants, Grants, Grants."

"Turn a page," suggested Dug, getting impatient.

"Lewis Grant—Lory—Lyon—Mable—Mason." On and on he scanned names, his breath coming faster, faster. M's, N's. Olson—Palmer — Parks — Pauline — Peter — Prudy — Randy — Rawleigh—Robert. "Look, would you?"

"Hurry up, Dave. Move along faster."

"Well, be patient, Dug. I don't want to miss a name. Sam Grant. Now we're in the S's. Sanford—Sally—Schaeffer—Schmitty—Shad—Shaffer—Shalmar. Oh, it's got to be here someplace." Dave was almost prancing. "I'm excited, Dug. Here's a name. Shannon M. Grant. Maybe that's close."

Dave copied the name and address. Shannon M. Grant, 2612 Teal Avenue. "Do you think that could be them?"

"Not the slightest idea, Dave. Look, why don't you go through the list once more, since it's early yet? Folks are hardly getting up here in the city. Let's get a glass of milk and a dough-nut or something, pretty soon. I'm hungry."

Dave went down over the list again more carefully. "Looks gigantic to me," he remarked with a big sigh. "Here's David A. Grant. I'll copy his address. 1602 Foster Avenue. And here's a David C., 451 Rosedale. They might be able to tell me some-thing at least." Then his eye caught a name he had overlooked. "Here, look what I found! Mrs. S. Hana Grant." He almost jumped with glad surprise. "I wonder now. This must be my mother. Mrs. S. Hana. Say, maybe it was to be that way on the card in the file. 949 South Neptune." He copied it, scarcely breathing lest he make a mistake.

"Maybe that's her and you didn't copy right," suggested Dug. "Hana, seems to me, is a more common name than Shana anyhow."

"You may be right. Let's go across the street and eat in there. It's open. We'll have to get a map of the city, won't we? Or ask someone where these streets are. I'm sure I haven't the slightest idea."

"Wowie, Dave, this is a bigger city than you know. Now where can we buy a map?"

"Let's ask the man in the restaurant. Come."

"This is a bad day to buy much of anything," said the dirty-aproned restaurant operator, stroking his brown mustache. "Don't you know this is a holiday?"

"Well, can you tell us how to find—" David glanced excited-ly at his paper—"Neptune Avenue?"

"Neptune—Neptune." The man scratched his round bald-ing head. "Sorry, but I can't help you on that one. It must be clear on the other side where I'm not familiar. Ham and eggs? Oatmeal? Sausages and pancakes? What'll you have?"

Dug glanced at Dave. "Let's order ham and two eggs and milk. I'm about starved."

Dave nodded.

"Sit right up to the counter here, boys, where you can watch how I do it. How do you want your eggs? Sunny side up?

"Easy over once," answered Dug.

"Mister," said Dave. "We're strangers here. Rosedale. Do you know where that street is?"

"Well, now, just a second here." He placed the ham on the hot grill and got out four eggs. "Rosedale? You go—let me see now, I think it's ten, yes, ten blocks west of the square—turn right and go north till you come to it. You'll find it on a post."

Write it down, Dave. Ten west of square, turn right and go north."

"Then, please, sir, do you know where Foster Avenue is?"

"Looks to me like you boys are in for a merry chase. Foster is close to Windom Park and for that you go east, maybe a dozen blocks. Could be fourteen—better catch a trolley. Foster runs parallel with Lawndale. You'll have to ask someone when you get out there. I thought I knew this city pretty good, and I could go to it all right, but to tell someone else, that's a different thing. My business is cookin' an' nothin' else."

The two started out much refreshed after the hot breakfast.

"Wait," exclaimed Dave, glancing at his paper. "I forgot to ask him where to find Teal Avenue where Shannon M. Grant lives. I'll go back."

"Listen, boy," remarked the man, somewhat irritated. "You think I'm some walkin' directory or encyclopedia? Well, that I ain't. Teal Avenue used to be on the south side, close to the tracks an' I s'pose it's still there, though there's been talk of fellin' those apartments to put in a new highway. Teal—Teal—you find the trolley tracks over here three blocks west, an' follow them south to Teal. If that don't get you there, ask someone who knows mor'n I do."

"Thank you, mister," said Dave. "I realize I've asked an awful lot of you, but it's terribly important."

"Must be," said the man, leaning halfway over the counter. "Well, run along now, an' I hope to the good Lord you find what you're lookin' for that's so terribly important," and with that he smote the palm of his hand on the top of the cash register.

"Let's go to this Shannon M. Grant first," suggested Dave.

"We go three blocks west and follow the tracks south, he said."

The tracks were easily found. The two walked south with quick brisk steps, saying little, expecting much. They must have covered well over a mile when to their glad surprise Teal Avenue greeted them from the top of a light post.

"Now we must find 2612. How do these numbers run? Do you know, Dug?"

"Not me. But I guess we can soon find out. Whew. It's going to get warm today. Here's 602. That means many blocks one way or the other. Here, we go this way."

Eagerness hastened their steps. In due time they found the number. What's more, the name Shannon M. Grant on the mailbox. A small printed card said, "Bell out of order."

Dave rapped.

"Rap louder," whispered Dug.

They waited.

"Let me try." Dug pounded on the door.

A little old lady in a black lace dust cap stuck her head out of a next door window. "What you want?" she called in a high shrill voice.

"We're looking for Mr. Shannon M. Grant," explained Dave.

"Well, he ain't to home. He's gone for three weeks to California; so don't pound his door no more. But if you got a special delivery fer him, I can tell where to send it on to."

"No," answered Dave. "It's not a special delivery. Thanks."

"Now what?" asked Dug.

"We've got to figure out which is the next closest place to get to from where we are."

"Yeah. But that won't be easy. Hey. Ask this man coming here."

"Oh, sir, please, mister," said Dave. "Can you tell us where to find Foster Avenue?"

"Sorry," he said, walking on. "I'm a stranger here."

Together the boys studied the directions the restaurant man had given them.

Two hours later, after walking what seemed all of five miles, they arrived at 1602 Foster Avenue, only to be informed David A. Grant no longer lived there and the man who answered the door had no idea where he had moved to.

Too soon it was high noon. The sun beat down mercilessly and the scorching pavement was blistering to their already tired feet. The ice-cream cones purchased from a corner vendor only added to their thirst. They drank long and again from a fountain they spied in a public park, but the lukewarm water tasted disappointingly rusty and quenchless.

"I'd give a dime or even a quarter for a good cold drink," said Dug an hour later as the two trudged on their way toward Rosedale. It was close to three o'clock and the man at the filling station told them 451 was all of thirteen blocks farther west.

"That means against the sun too."

Dave detected a whine in Dug's voice. "How about you resting here till I go on and come back? You're tired."

"Let you go alone? No, sir, Dave. I'm not that kind of a friend. I'm no more fagged than you are. And it was my suggestion we come, wasn't it? Don't pay any mind to me if I fuss and grunt because it's hot. I just can't help it. What's more, I want to be right there when you do find her, or him, or them."

"Then you're not getting disgusted?"

"I'm disgusted these crazy streets are so crazy long," admitted Dug. "Just wish we could afford a taxi. Come on. I'm not ready to give up unless you are."

"I'm in no notion to give up now," asserted Dave.

The two climbed the concrete steps to the stately vine-covered white stone house. A well-dressed young man with a violin in his left hand answered the doorbell at 451 Rosedale.

"Is this where Mr. David C. Grant lives?" asked Dave, trying desperately to control his emotions.

"It is," blinked the man, printing his face with question marks.

"Is he at home?"

"He is. Step in." His icy voice made both boys, especially Dave, tense and uneasy.

"Thank you." Dave felt his heart beating in his neck. Quickly he slicked back his hair. He wet his lips. The grandeur of the inside of the house amazed, even startled, him. Beyond the first room he could see a beautiful lady seated at a grand piano.

"Stay right here," ordered the man. "I'll see if Mr. Grant is available."

He came in due time from some room beyond, a sprightly, well-groomed man with snow-white hair and a huge sparkling diamond on his left hand and a smaller one in his yellow necktie.

"You wish to see me?" His voice was not exactly indignant, not exactly resentful, but perhaps a bit friendly. At least it gave Dave a spark of confidence.

"My name is David Grant." He shifted on the thick red carpet. "This is my friend Dug Yonkers. We are both students from Landisville."

"I see," remarked the man without any change of expression.

Dave wet his lips. "I'm trying to locate my parents."

"Your parents? You mean you don't know where they are? Where they are?" He repeated in a louder voice.

"That's right, Mr. Grant. I was left when I was a very small child at the Millersville Children's Home. All I have ever been able to learn is—is that my mother's name is either Shana or perhaps Hana. I believe she lives here in Philadelphia somewhere."

"Well." The sprightly old man wriggled his lower lip. "What is your father's name?"

"I don't know."

"Who left you at the Home?"

"I don't know that either, sir."

"Huh. Well, do you know what your mother's name was before she married Mr. Grant?"

"No, sir. I don't know that either."

"Well, now," said the man, squinting and wriggling his lower lip again. "I have heard some very strange stories in my day. I won't say I believe or disbelieve this one. But there are a lot of Grants in the United States. Some are a very fine breed of Grants. Some are not so fine." He straightened his yellow tie as he scrutinized Dave. "I'd say you appear to belong to one of the better breed, perhaps." He glanced at Dug. "Is this your brother?"

"No, sir, he's a neighbor, Dug Yonkers."

"Yes. Yes. Well, some Grants are Scottish. Are you?"

"I—I don't know, sir. I hardly think so."

"Well, I happen to be. I doubt very much I can be of help. But you can give me your name and address. And when and where you were born and your mother's name. And if I find out anything, I can drop you a line, or call you collect."

"Oh," gasped Dave. "A—a—thanks—but I'd rather you'd write. It wouldn't suit for you to call me, sir."

"Well," said the man, "write on the paper I'll give you."

The sprightly old man hurried away and returned with a sheet of paper.

"You may think this strange," he said, "but I have a purpose for all I do. Now write very plainly on this paper. Do you know that twice in the past six months, strange men have called on me here? Yes, here, trying to claim to be some relative of mine?"

"No. Really?"

"It's so," answered the man. "I ran an ad in the paper, also on the radio, a while back for a lost nephew of mine by the name of Clark Handley. Strange what some people will try to prove if they think there's money in it. Now I want to make sure your name is actually what you write down. Yes, go ahead. Write it. I can have—" He waited until Dave had finished, then took the paper and looked. "I have your fingerprints here if I need them." He smacked his lips and grinned.

Dug looked at Dave. Dave was too scared to look at Dug.

"You say your mother's name is Hana, as you have it here?"

"Or Shana," corrected Dave. "I'm really not sure. I—I know it sounds queer to you."

"She's not in my recollection," remarked the man, shaking his head. "But if you're genuine, and if I can, I'll help you out. I have ways. You bet I have."

"Thanks," Dave managed to say. "Thanks for your time, sir."

As the two were going down the steps, they heard the old man laughing.

Neither looked back.

"What do you think of him?" asked Dug, when they were out on the street again.

"I don't know," answered Dave. "He's either a smart, rich old man, or kinda cuckoo. That would be something if I'd ever hear from him. But I think he's touched in the head. Really I do. The way he laughed. He's making fun of me. Shall we go on and try to find the one on Neptune? I don't like being made fun of."

"Whatever you say, Dave. You know we've got to catch that 7:30 train, and it's a long tramp back to the depot."

"Let's go there yet. Then get something to eat on the way back. I'm beginning to feel funny in my stomach."

Walking wasn't getting any easier. But on and on they trudged, following the trolley tracks south as the old man had directed them. The two-story frame houses on Neptune were anything but attractive. Dave's determination to go on all but failed him. Would he find his mother in one of these shabby-looking dwellings? Poor soul. If he did, he'd maybe want to offer to take her along home with him. Mother Loomas would be kind enough to take her in until he could earn enough to buy them a decent, comfortable home. What wild ideas! What crazy ideas! Dave scolded himself.

He looked at his paper. 949 South. "It's that house across the street, Dug. I'm so nervous and excited now, I can hardly walk. My legs are wobbling." He tried to laugh for a stimulant.

Half fearfully he pressed the broken doorbell. Did it work? He pressed it harder. He heard scurrying inside. Voices. From two screenless windows on the second story faces appeared. Two from each window. Small faces. And dark! All four looking down at them and grinning.

"Yes, sir?" In the doorway stood a plump green gingham-aproned colored woman, a white kerchief tied around her head. "What is it?"

Dave winced. He stood paralyzed. His power of speech left

him for the moment. Dug pulled on his belt and muttered something Dave didn't understand.

"Is—is your name Mrs. Grant?" he finally managed to say. His voice was unnatural.

" 'Tis. Been dat fer near nineteen year."

"Do—" Dave fumbled. Frantically he tried to select words, the right words for this, the unexpected. He was not only hot, but almost dizzy. "Do you have a son?" he asked.

"A son? You mean sons. Der's Hal and Jeth—Travis, Alek, and Sumpter. All my sons. I got three daughters too. But listen now, what's this all 'bout?" The woman twisted her hands nervously in the corner of her apron.

Dave twisted his hands too behind him. "Is *your* name—" he began. He tried to clear the phlegm in his throat, "by any chance Shana Grant?" Beads of perspiration came out on his forehead and started trickling.

"Yes, some calls me Shana," blinked the woman. "My name was Anna when I marry Henry Arnett. Folks begin callin' me Hana, 'cause there were too many Annas. He die an' I marry Sam Grant. So folks begin callin' me Shana 'cause I weren't any longer Hana. Understand? So now I come to answer to all of 'em if necessary. I'm Mrs. Sam, yes, S. Hana Grant."

He had a strong urge to turn and run, but something held Dave fixed. "Did you by any chance—receive a letter from a David Grant?" he ventured half afraid.

"Letter? When?"

"Oh, in the past four years I'd say."

The woman shook her head. "I jes wonder what dis is all 'bout. You askin' me sech questions. If I'd get a letter from David Grant, I'd think heaben open up fer sure."

"You would," gulped Dave. "Why?"

" 'Cause I would. But firs' you tell me what you all up to? You some kine a secret detective?" Her smile faded and a serious expression crossed her face.

"Oh, no, Ma'am," politely answered Dave. "Please don't let us frighten you. I—I—we're just trying to locate a—a lost party—

193

a Mrs. Grant—and I found your name in the phone book—so—"

"Who is de los' party?"

Dave sobered. He unbuttoned his shirt collar. "Her name—we think—we thought—was Shana Grant." He looked at the door casing. It seemed to be moving. "And she has—is supposed to have a son, David, who is living," he hesitated, "and we're trying to locate her for him." He backed unsteadily to the edge of the porch. "We sure do ask you to pardon us for this interruption, Mrs. Grant," he said feebly. "I fear it's your suppertime. We must go."

"Dat's perfectly all right, sir," smiled the woman. Her whole face became radiant. "An'," she beamed, "I jes wish I could be a help to you all. I even wish I could be dat Shana Grant, an' some angel—white—" she looked straight in David's eyes— "or black—" she shifted her glance and looked straight at Dug— "could fetch my David back to me jes for one blessed day. Hallalu."

Dave stood dumfounded.

"I know you all thinks dat soun' silly. But I jes sits an' dream silly dreams like dat sometime. It done do me or nobody no harm. Funny thing, I was jes dwellin' on my sweet little baby what die when you all knock. No matter how many a mother's got she miss one dat's flown."

"We—we must be on our way, Ma'am," Dave heard himself saying. He felt giddy-headed. He blinked.

"Now wait," the woman said, stepping out on the small porch. "I do recollec' as I hear 'bout a Miss Grant who live in wid her sister on Vine Street somewhere. Now I do believe her real name is Shandy Mae. She done had a baby she give 'way right soon as he were born 'cause she weren't married at de time an' couldn't afford to keep him. Now I's only been tole all dis. I met her only once. I can't prove nothin'; so don't use my name."

"Is she—" Dave bit his lip. Twice he wiped his forehead with his handkerchief. "Is—is she a white woman?" he stammered.

"She ain't real white, as I remember, an' she ain't so dark either. Jes in between. An' right pretty. I wouldn't know fer sure, but I believe she done marry. Is dis here David you all tryin'

194

to help a Negro boy?" She looked at Dug when she asked the question.

Numbed, Dave stood speechless. "No, he's white," answered Dug. "Come on. Let's go." He pulled at Dave's hip pocket.

"Thanks," mumbled Dave in a daze.

"Now what next?" asked Dug after they had gone several blocks in silence.

"Next? There won't be a next," answered Dave gloomily. "I'm done trying. I know now it's no use and don't you dare tell one single soul anything. Anything," he repeated almost in tears.

Once on the train Dug fell into a ready and sound sleep. But Dave sat wide awake with stark and startling fears. New fears he had never feared could be his fears. All the way home he studied his hands. He found himself comparing them with every other hand in sight on the train.

CHAPTER 24

Disappointment, uncertainty, defeatism intensified as the train ground homeward. With a heaviness which bordered on mockery, Dave listlessly watched the moving landscape as it darkened. He regretted he had gone to Philadelphia. Especially with someone. He regretted now each confidence he had shared with the sleeping adopted one beside him.

Before the train reached Landisville station, David Grant realized that, in order to live above his former dismay, plus these fresh suspenses, and still to act happy and at ease, he would need an extra amount of maturing will power, as well as spiritual fortitude. It would mean acting older than he really was.

He cast an apprehensive glance at Dug as the two neared home. "You'll most certainly keep everything we did today to yourself," he said.

"I give you my word, Dave. How often must I say it? Stop worrying." Dug's voice had a tinge of impatience in it.

"I'm—I'm counting on you to always be my friend, Dug." In spite of his determination, Dave knew at once there was childish supplication in those words. He tried to apologize by adding, "I mean no matter what develops."

"Why wouldn't I?" returned Dug.

"Well," began Dave, "just supposing someday I really would—" He cleared his throat with nervous sensitiveness. "You know, discover I am part Negro."

Dug laughed dryly. "Yeah," he said, "a lot of wild ideas have whizzed through my mind already too."

"Like what?" Dave's voice was husky.

"Like what? Like about myself, that's what. Not you, Dave. Look at me. I'm a lot darker than you are. I've even been teased about it. You've got nothing to worry about."

"You think?"

"Think? Of course, Dave. Look, now. Supposing I discover someday I'm part colored? I can't prove where I came from or anything."

"But your parents wouldn't have adopted you if—"

"How do you know? What if I am and they didn't know it? Seems to me if we really want to fret about something, I have a head start on you. Wish we hadn't gone to that last place. But," Dug added quickly, "I'm not going to let it take the fun out of life for me. You can be sure of that."

Dave got hot. "Nor me," he mumbled with suppressed apprehension. "But those names," he went on, "is what's got me all woolly. And that—that Shandy Mae giving her baby away. I'll be wondering the rest of my life who gave—" Dave stopped short. "Look," he said. "There's Dad at the door watching for us—dear Dad Loomas." He lowered his voice to a whisper, "Wish he really honest was. So long, Dug."

Aaron swung open the screen door. "Hi, Son." He slapped Dave on the shoulder. "I heard the train pull in. How was the big day in the big city?"

"It was hot. Terribly hot," panted Dave, wiping his forehead.

"Mother's gone on to bed. But she made lemonade for you. It's in the icebox."

"That sounds good," smiled Dave, "and I'm thirsty too."

"Well, did you get to see all you wanted to?"

"Why, Dad," remarked Dave, opening the icebox door, "that would take a week. I never realized how big Philadelphia was." He got out the pitcher and poured a glass of cold lemonade.

Aaron laughed. "I figured you'd say that and want to go again."

He emptied the glass. "This sure hits the spot." Dave forced

197

a laugh as he shook his head. "I'd rather save my money and go west sometime."

"West? What big notions are these? Dug's, I suppose."

"We were just talking." He shrugged his shoulders. "You know, like boys do. He's already been part way west, you know. Maybe someday we could buy a car together and—don't look shocked, Dad." He patted Aaron on the arm. "It won't happen until we're through high school, and not even then unless you'd give your consent."

"Well, then, there will be plenty of time to talk about such a venture."

"Sure, Dad. Lots of time."

Tired as he was, Dave scanned through a short psalm before he snapped out the light. His legs ached, he ached all over, but sleep he could not. He tossed. He relived all the happenings of the day, the anticipation, the conversations, the shattered dreams, the blasted hopes, the long, long walks, the new inroads to new misgivings. He found himself trying to talk to God, himself, and countless characters he knew, and some he'd never met, explaining, reasoning, pleading—all in one tangled, overlapping conversation. Forlorn and exhausted, he got out of bed, snapped on the light, and opened his Bible.

"Judge me, O God, and plead my cause against an ungodly nation." He drew a deep breath. "O deliver me from the deceitful and unjust man. For thou art the God of my strength: why dost thou cast me off? why go I mourning because of the oppression of the enemy?" He took another long breath. "O send out thy light and thy truth: let them lead me; let them bring me unto thy holy hill, and to thy tabernacles. Then will I go unto the altar of God, unto God my exceeding joy: yea, upon the harp will I praise thee, O God my God." He rubbed his hand across his forehead. "Why art thou cast down, O my soul? and why art thou disquieted within me? hope in God: for I shall yet praise him, who is the health of my countenance, and my God." He read the last paragraph again. Then again.

Dave heard the clock downstairs strike three. He dropped

on his knees beside his bed. "O God," he prayed, "please look deep into my heart and forgive any sin you find there. I'm in trouble. I've been fretful and impatient, and I know it. I don't know how you do it, but please, plead my cause. I think that's what I need. If I do have living parents, please bless them tonight. Wherever they are, do take care of them, especially my mother. Whatever her name is, remember her someway with happiness, and be kind to her. If it is Thy will, let her live and let me live to meet her sometime. Or help me forget all about it. O God, whoever I am or wherever I came from, lead me, O God, by Thy light and Thy truth, like I just read in this Bible. Bless Mother and Dad downstairs. They've been so good to me. Help me show them how much I appreciate all they've done for me. I can't deserve all I enjoy in this nice home. You've been very kind to me. Help me not to care—I mean not to fret about all this mix-up I'm in. I know I do care. But, please, help me to believe you do have a place reserved for me, like Dad insists you have. And help me hide these feelings that come over me."

Dave woke with a start. Dad was by his bed. "Oversleeping, Son? Aren't you going to work this morning?"

"Why, yes. Yes, of course." He sat up.

"Then you'd better be getting up. Mother is sick, but I have your breakfast ready."

"Sick?" He jumped out of bed. "What's wrong with Mother?"

"I don't know. I'm going to call the doctor soon."

Dave dressed as rapidly as possible and hurried downstairs. He tiptoed to Mother's bedroom. He hesitated.

"May I come in?" he asked.

She held out one hand.

He bent over her. He touched her hot cheek with the back of his fingers. "Why, Mother," he whispered, "what's wrong with you?" She saw his look of alarm.

"Don't worry about me, Davy," she said. "Whatever it is, I'll get over it."

"Are you sure, Mother?"

199

"The doctor will know what to do. And better than that, God knows how to master every situation."

"Oh," whispered Dave. "I'm glad of that."

"You just ask God to help me, Son, and He will. Go eat your breakfast before it's all cold."

"Shall I stay home?"

"Oh, no, Son. Of course not. Go on to work. I just hope whatever I have, you won't get it."

He pressed her one hand against his cheek. "Please, please get well. Oh, Mother, I don't know what I'd do if anything real bad would happen to you."

"It's going to be a scorcher for ball tonight," said Dug that evening on the way home from work.

"I'm not playing tonight," answered Dave.

"Not playing?"

"Not when Mother is sick in bed. I have to help Dad with the housework."

"Did he say you had to?"

"No, he never mentioned it, but I want to, and I'm not playing tonight."

"Goodness, Dave. How sick is she?"

"Sick enough that I'd rather not play ball tonight."

The doctor called it a hard-to-conquer virus of undetermined origin that could be contagious. Dave was given orders to stay away from Mother's room and her dishes were to be kept separate from the others.

Dave asked about her every time he came down in the morning and every time he came home from work.

"Here, Dad," he said one morning, "give Mother this note. Is she able to read?"

"If not, I'll read it to her."

The note read: "Dear Mother, I miss you something awful. Hurry and get well. I pray God is mastering the situation."

A few days later he handed Dad another: "Dear Mother, I

miss you more and more. I pray for you many times while at work and at night. Please get well soon."

Sister Lora called every evening around 8:15 after she had the children in bed. Dave answered the first time and each time thereafter. He anticipated hearing her gentle voice, so sincere and caring. It did something for him he was scarcely aware of. Mother Loomas was in bed three weeks. The entire experience—Dad's tender care and devotion to Mother, Sister Lora's calls, and Dave's own prayers—all had a maturing, growing, enriching impact on his life. His personal fears and frustrations were, at least for the time, pushed well into the background. It was a day not soon to be forgotten when Mother was able to come to the table again.

"Dave," she said, "tonight you go play ball."

"Okay, Mother. I will. And when I get home I'm going to turn up my radio to celebrate."

By the time school started, Rose was almost her usual vigorous, glowing self again. Dave found himself thanking God repeatedly for answering his prayers.

He and Dug both enrolled at East Hempfield High School. Across from Dave in his citizenship class sat Hugh Latimer, a soft-voiced, shy, but nice-looking Negro. Dave studied him closely. Hugh was smart, courteous, and clean. Cleaner about his person than some of the white boys. His shoes, though worn, were usually polished, his fingernails trimmed, and his teeth brushed. As the weeks passed, Dave took a special liking to Hugh. They played on the same basketball team and Dave admired the boy's hard, honest playing. He talked with Hugh every chance he got. In fact, he frequently went out of his way to make chances.

One evening Dave looked up from his *Popular Mechanics* and said, "Say, Mother, would it be possible for a person to be part Indian and not know it?"

"Why, I suppose so. What makes you ask that?"

"I was just wondering."

After a few minutes he looked up again. "Would it be possible to be part Negro and not know it?"

"Why, yes, I imagine so. Why are you asking?"

"Oh, I don't know. I just happened to think of it." He turned a page. "Do they have ways of finding out such things?"

"What do you mean?"

"Well, let me see. Well, for instance, Dug over here. He's pretty dark, isn't he?"

"Yes."

"Well, just supposing he'd want to find out just for anyhow, no reason at all, whether or not he's Negro or just part Negro. Would there be a way of finding that out? I don't mean I think he is. I just wondered."

"Well, David Grant," chuckled Rose. "You surely can think of the things to wonder about. I have no idea—no idea. If there is, I never heard of it. Now don't you ever mention such a thing to Dug," she chided. "Why, he'd be terribly embarrassed. He can't help it he's so dark."

"I know he can't," came Dave's ready answer. "And even if he really was—well—I'd think just as much of him as I do now."

"I'm sure you would and I'm glad to hear you say so," stated Rose. "In God's sight we're all one color."

Dave picked at the corners of the pages.

Weeks later he approached Rose with another question.

"Mother," he began, looking up from another magazine. "I have a good friend in school. His name is Hugh Latimer. I sorta wish I could—maybe bring him along home for supper some evening. He's a good student and we could work on our lessons together. Would you care?"

"That would be all right with me," answered Rose. "You and Dug are together so much, I think it would be a fine idea to be sociable with some other boys too once in a while."

"How about next Thursday night? That is, if he'll come. I haven't asked him yet."

"It's all right with me. Shall I have chicken or steak? You help me decide."

"Whatever you feel like fixing, Mother. He'll like anything you cook."

"How about your paper route?"

"I'll take him with me."

Rose took special pleasure in preparing a chicken and dumpling supper for this new friend of Dave's. She put her pretty rose pattern cloth on the dining room table and got out her best dishes and silver.

"This does my heart good to see Dave making new friends," Rose remarked to Aaron as she stirred the batter into the gravy. "I am anxious to see what kind of a boy this Hugh is."

"Why, Aaron, look," she exclaimed a few minutes later. "Look out the window. There comes Dave with a colored boy. Could that be Hugh? Why didn't he tell us?"

"Well," said Aaron, peering through the lace curtain. "If that's Hugh, let's not show any surprise. Let's act as though he's as white as we are."

"Or we're as dark as he is," added Rose, smiling. "Must be. He's bringing him in. I'll go dish up the supper."

"Wait," said Aaron. "Meet the boy first."

After supper and after the boys had gone upstairs, Aaron and Rose sat on the sofa talking.

"I wonder," began Aaron, "why he's taken a liking to him."

"We must admit he acted like a perfect gentleman," observed Rose.

"That's true," agreed Aaron. "But for Dave to invite him to eat here sorta surprises me."

"Listen, Aaron," remarked Rose. "I just have to wonder now why he asked me that question the other night about Dug being so dark. I tell you, Aaron, that boy's not always reading when he sits with a book or magazine. Sometimes he's just sitting there pretending. And he looks as though his thoughts are on something fantastic, something serious and far away. And, do you know, this morning when I took his shirts up to his room, I took along a clean scarf to put on that stand by his bed, and when I took the other scarf off, there was a paper under it with a bunch of names and addresses on it. All Grants. Streets and numbers, but no towns or states."

"Where'd he get them?"

"I've no idea."

"We'll ask him."

Rose shook her head. "Then he'd know we found it. We wouldn't want him to think we were snooping around in his room. Just wait. He'll tell us sometime."

"No. You ask him. You're the one who found it. It's not like Dave to keep things from us."

"Well, he didn't tell us about evolution at first, remember? And look, he didn't tell us Hugh was a Negro, did he?" reminded Rose.

Aaron rubbed his one hand over the other. "I think," he said, "Dave is going through something you and I don't know about. He may have the feeling we wouldn't understand. And it's possible we wouldn't. But we've got to let him know we want to understand. We've got to somehow. I'm not deaf. I'm not blind. I can sense it when he's trying to figure something out. He's trying to find himself, I think. Find his place—his strength, his beliefs. Don't you see? And we've got to help him. But, no, we can't force ourselves on him. Dave's different from Dug, or Leon, or most boys. Seems to me at times he craves our advice, yet, well, just like those names you say you found. That proves he doesn't always confide in us. Now, Rose, there's a reason. What is it? Is it me? Is it our age? I tell you, I wonder about some things."

"So do I. But he's an individual, Aaron." Rose pressed one hand on his arm and faced him as she spoke. "He's growing up. And so fast. Why, he won't be a boy much longer. He wants to think for himself." Rose sat in meditation, then continued. "You know, it would simply break my heart if someday he'd get a letter —like Dennis did from his mother—and away he'd go to Detroit or some other big city. You know, blood runs thicker than water, and if a Mr. or Mrs. Grant from somewhere would show up and claim him—O Aaron! We couldn't act as though he's been adopted. We must be careful, Aaron, not to do anything to make him lose confidence in us. I think if we just keep on praying and wait and act as though we trust him, in due time we'll find out everything we need to know. I shouldn't say *act* as though we trust him. I mean trust him. We don't have to know everything he thinks and feels and dreams about. Our part is to make him feel accepted."

"That's what we've been doing since the day we got him," reminded Aaron.

"I know. I mean we've got to keep on accepting him and loving him while he's going through this growing-up period of his life. We can't treat him like a child. Why, he's as tall as you are."

"That scare we had back there on the farm. The black Cadillac in the lane. Could those names and that incident have any connection, do you suppose?"

Rose shook her head. "Who would know? I'd hate to mention this to Dug's mother."

"Better not," said Aaron.

"Say, Dave," began Hugh, closing his civilization textbook. "How come you invited me to come along home with you?"

"How come? Well, because I wanted to."

"But why? I don't understand."

"Do you wish now you wouldn't have come?"

"I don't know what to say, Dave. I appreciate your kindness. Your father and mother were very courteous to me. Your mother's supper was wonderful, but I won't ever be able to return all this."

"I don't expect you to, Hugh. That's not why I invited you. I asked you because—well, just because I wanted to get better acquainted with you." Dave closed his book. "I just admire you for some reason."

"Admire me?" exclaimed Hugh. "I can't imagine what I have you admire."

"I just admire your size, your playing, your brains. Your personality. I guess everything."

Hugh covered his face for a moment with both hands.

"Look," he said, pressing two fingers against Dave's shoulder. He glanced around the room. "You have a lovely home. Real nice parents. A nice room. Nice clothes, a nice bed. Everything I see is very nice. I have none of these things."

"I didn't know," said Dave.

Hugh got up and walked across the room. "I—I guess I should tell you," he said, running both hands into his pockets. "It embarrasses me. But I don't think I should stay any longer. I guess I'll be going now."

"No, Hugh. You don't need to feel embarrassed."

"But can't you see how I feel coming in here?" Hugh looked distressed. "Here where everything is so ideal-like? I've enjoyed your kindness, but," he hesitated, "when I hear you say Mother and Dad, it cuts me pretty bad in here." He pressed one hand against his chest. "Not that I'm jealous, but—well, yes, I guess I sorta envy you. I just can't help it, Dave, but something inside makes me want to scream."

"Scream?"

"No one ever called me son in my life, Dave—and I feel like screaming loud."

"But, Hugh, I—"

He brushed Dave off. "I know you can't understand a guy like me, because we're just not on the same level. I'll bet if your folks knew—" he looked away, avoiding Dave's glance— "I don't even know who my parents are or where I—"

Dave jumped up. "But, Hugh, we're more on the level than you think. They aren't my real parents. I don't know where I came from either."

"What?"

"That's true. They got me at a children's home. Their name is Loomas, Hugh."

Hugh stood speechless, mouth gaping.

"It's true, Hugh."

"Well," panted Hugh, "at least you—you have a decent place to live. And they call you son. You don't need to know anything else. What does it matter? They treat you like you were their own. Boy, Dave, you don't know how lucky you are. All I've ever had is Aunt Vi, and she's no kin to me. I just call her aunt so folks will think I have somebody. But I hate her. And don't you ever come to her place. Now let me go."

"No, Hugh. Don't go. I want to talk to you."

CHAPTER 25

Dave finally persuaded Hugh to stay. The two sat facing each other across the table.

"If you'd care to," said Dave, "I'd like you to tell me about yourself."

Hugh sat for some time with eyes downcast. "There's not much to tell, Dave," he said at length. "I don't remember when Vi got me." He looked up. "She's told me so many different stories about where I came from that I don't believe any of them."

Dave's expression seemed to give Hugh courage to go on.

"That used to bewilder and haunt me to no end. It made me afraid of her and then suspicious of everybody. I soon hated Vi. I felt so unnecessary and in her way. It's terrible to learn you've been shoved onto someone who doesn't really want you— just looks after you because they get paid for it by the county. I used to cry myself to sleep nearly every night." He looked down. "I mean when I was small, like from four to seven." He looked up again. "Then it made me mean inside. And hateful when I got older. Sometimes I felt like killing her," his voice rose with emotion, "and everybody. Then," he continued, calming himself, "one day when I was especially blue and downhearted, I was sitting on the steps of the Public Library when Miss McClure, my seventh-grade teacher, came along with some books to return. She stopped and asked me if I would like to read a good book she had with her. I told her I might. She let me borrow the book on her card. I've often wondered why Miss McClure took that much interest in me. She was always nice to me. I read half that night. It was *The Redemption of Charles Barton.* Ever read it?"

Dave shook his head. "Go on."

"It's the story of an orphan boy who had a very unhappy life in the home where he'd been placed. One day when he was about sixteen (I'll skip hurriedly over it, Dave) someone told him that his mother was white and his father was Negro."

Dave held his breath.

"Boy, that smarted. He felt horrible. He ran away. He wandered all over. It's a sad story, real sad." Hugh cleared his throat before he continued. "One evening while walking through a woods this Charles came to a small schoolhouse in a clearing. He heard a man inside talking. He eased up beside an open window and listened. The man was practicing his first sermon. Just talking to the empty seats. I won't tell it all, but when the young preacher came outside, he saw Charles standing there crying. He talked to him, then took him along home. There's a lot more to the story, but Charles fell in love with the minister's younger sister Emily, even though he knew he could never be worthy of her. But he determined to be somebody worth while, because the minister talked to him and that helped him feel that in spite of everything against him, God Almighty could help him make good. He had a long hard struggle, but in the end he and Emily were married."

Dave had been listening spellbound. "Then what?" he asked. "I mean about you?"

Hugh leaned back. "Well, when I finished reading that book I made up my mind if Charles Barton could make good, I would at least try. When I took the book back to Miss McClure, she and I had a long talk. Lots of times I felt like running away. She got me to promise I wouldn't do that, but go on through high school. Miss McClure's a real nice lady. The next day she brought me a Bible."

"And you read it?"

"Yeah. Sometimes. I can't understand all I read, that's for sure."

"Well," said Dave, "I didn't know why—but somehow I thought there was something about you that—that made me want to know you better." He picked up his pencil and rolled it between his hands. "Do you think—you'll—ever try to find out where you came from?"

Hugh shook his head. "What's the use? As long as Vi can't or won't tell me anything, what could I go on? Miss McClure told me that's not too important as long as God knows. But it bothers me. Especially like tonight when I see how nice you've got it here. Do they get paid for keeping you?"

Dave dropped his pencil. "It never entered my mind. I have no idea."

"So then they really care for you?"

"Why, yes," answered Dave. "They sure make me feel that they do. I can't believe they're only pretending. They've offered to adopt me more than once."

"Well, then, why haven't they?"

"I've been hoping and hoping someday I'd find my real parents. At least my mother." Dave twisted his hands. "It's been my decision to wait. I'm seventeen. I'm more baffled now than ever. I wouldn't want to go and say to them now, 'Please adopt me after all.' It wouldn't be fair to them, I don't think, after waiting so long. Say," he said, "in that book you read, did that Charles ever find out whether or not his father was a Negro and his mother white, or the other way around?"

"In the story he never found out. I guess his worries were all for nothing. Someone lied to him, I guess. He would have been upset all the rest of his life if it hadn't been for that preacher."

Dave reached across the table and grabbed Hugh by the arm. "Let's be friends," he said, "and help each other. I'm going to get that book and read it too. I'm glad you stayed and told me this. I hope you come again sometime. And I'd like to take you along to church with me some Sunday too."

"Now hold on." Hugh stood up and stretched. "Go easy, Dave," he said. "After all, I'm plenty shy about going to a white man's church. Pardon me for saying so."

"Okay, Hugh. I won't insist."

"Now it's your turn to tell me about yourself."

"I—I will next time, Hugh," said Dave. "What little there is to tell. It's not fair at all."

"What's not fair?"

"Why, that I've had someone to love me as far back as I remember and you've had no one. I feel awful about this, Hugh. It just isn't fair."

"You needn't feel bad about me," said Hugh, "but there's sure a lot of things in this world that's not fair."

Long after Hugh had gone home, Dave sat thinking.

Throughout the remainder of the school year the two boys continued being friendly. One time Dave did persuade Hugh to go along home for a wiener roast in the back yard, but only once.

"Sometimes," frowned Dug one evening on the way home from school, "you have me wondering if you don't think more of that Hugh Latimer than you do of me."

"No, Dug. That's not so. I think as much of you as I ever did. But Hugh's lonely. He's never had anyone who cared for him. Don't you understand?"

"But he doesn't want your pity."

"I'm not a friend to him just because I pity him. I like him for who he is. And what he is. And I admire the way he tries to live above all his—well, his problems. Hugh's had it tough."

"Sounds like he's been telling you things."

"A few things. Yes."

"And you've been telling him things too."

"What do you mean?"

"You know what I mean, Dave."

"I've never told him all I've told you, Dug. No, sir."

"Not about our trip to Philadelphia?"

"No, indeed. You're the only person who knows that."

"Honest, now?"

"Honest, Dug. And you promised to keep it, too. Have you?"

"Yes, I have."

"I'm banking on that promise."

"Just the same, I don't see why you take so to Hugh Latimer."

It was the middle of July when Miss McClure answered her doorbell.

"I'm Aaron Loomas, Miss McClure. May I speak to you a few minutes?"

"Come in, Mr. Loomas."

"Our foster son, David Grant, has befriended himself to a boy I understand you know. Hugh Latimer."

"Yes, I know Hugh."

"David brought the boy home with him twice. He's talked about him quite a bit and feels sorry for him. He seems especially anxious that the boy has a chance to go on to college. What can you tell me about him?"

"Well, Mr. Loomas, just what do you want to know? Something about his capacity for learning, or what? Won't you take a chair?"

"Thank you. I'm interested in anything you can tell me about the boy."

"Well, to begin with, Hugh was extremely retiring when he came to my room. Intelligent, but very apprehensive. He always looked afraid or hurt. He would get tears in his eyes over the least little embarrassment. I felt sorry for the boy. So one day I asked him to stay after school to help me with some work. He seemed glad and willing. I got next to him after several such efforts. Very gradually I learned something about his home life and background. I suppose, of course, you know he is an orphan."

"That's all I know, Miss McClure, and that he lives with his aunt."

"Well, she's actually not his aunt, Mr. Loomas. She's no relation. She's not the kind of woman I'd have chosen to make shelter for the boy. He can't call it a home. I've never been there, but from what I've learned from Hugh, it's far from a pleasant situation, and I wish someone could get him out of it. The boy needs someone he can confide in who can understand his frustrations and problems. I feel it should be a man. How much has he confided in your son, Mr. Loomas?"

"That I can't tell you. We let David tell us what he wants to, but we never try to pry."

"Well, the boy's greatest problem stems from the fear— Really, Mr. Loomas," said Miss McClure, rubbing her right hand over her left arm, "I have no right to betray the boy's confidence. He told me in tears things he said he overheard that woman telling someone else about himself. She was half drunk. He's lived since with a sense of shame and inferiority. I shouldn't repeat it. But it's worked havoc on the boy's mind and nerves. Thank God, one day he finally confided in me. I don't know when I ever felt so sorry for a boy. But what could I do? Nothing, but lend a sympathetic ear, and tell him to try to close his mind to what he'd heard, and hold his head up, and study hard, and walk straight, and dream of someday being a good, upright, respectable father to children of his own. I think I helped him a little. I saw a different expression come over the boy's face. I think he's been trying. Mr. Loomas, there are thousands of children in this United States, not only among the Negroes, but whites as well, who are confused and distressed, because they can't place themselves. Always wondering who they really are, where they came from, what life is all about. Who cares? Nobody wants me; nobody would miss me. When I was in State Teachers College, a classmate of mine, a very attractive young woman, told me this very thing has plagued her all her life. She told me she never walks the streets or rides a bus, or enters a store or church that she doesn't ask herself the question, 'Could that man possibly be my father? Could that woman by any chance be my mother?' But the thing that bothered her most, and I remember how she sobbed when she told me, wasn't that she feared she wasn't all white, or that she was illegitimate, but the fact that no one ever claimed her as their own. It must give a child an awful void not to feel attached."

Aaron nodded. "Yes," he said. "It must." He sat thinking,

213

studying the distance between his face and the pattern in the carpet.

"As I said, Mr. Loomas, I am not led to betray Hugh's confidence. And I didn't mean to infer anything by what I've just related. But I think it would be the part of courtesy and wisdom for you not to tell your son of this interview with me, since he and Hugh are friends. Hugh must tell himself what he wants told. Shattered confidences have caused more lasting damage than any other thing I can think of."

"I agree, Miss McClure. I won't repeat to David what you've told me about Hugh. I'm quite sure—well, Dave's a very tender-hearted boy. He might fret even more over Hugh. Besides, I wouldn't want to repeat anything that might start him imagining. He's too good at that as it is." Aaron rubbed his chin. "I called on you because David has told me Hugh said he liked you very much. So I thought you might simply give me your opinion of the boy. I was wondering if you'd think it advisable if a group of interested persons could go together and give Hugh some financial help to go to college. Say, for a year, and see how he gets along. Now he doesn't know I'm doing this. Neither does David."

"I think that would be wonderful—wonderful, Mr. Loomas. I would even be ready to help a little."

"I'm not ready yet for David, or anyone but my wife, to know I came here to talk to you. I'd want to study and pray this matter over considerable before taking further action."

"Of course, Mr. Loomas. There are so many angles to consider."

"Personally, do you think the boy worthy of help?"

"I'm inclined to say yes to that or I wouldn't have said I'd help. Now I don't mean I'd give hundreds, you understand, but I'd help what I could. What college would you be interested in seeing him attend?"

"I'm not sure. We've been discussing colleges with David and I think it's about decided he'll be enrolled at Eastern Mennonite in Virginia. Hugh could choose, if it comes to that. Do you think the boy is honest?"

214

"I've never known him to be dishonest. In fact, I think he's trying to live as upright as he knows how. I think he's one in a thousand, and if Hugh doesn't make a worth-while contribution to society someday, I'm going to feel I've failed to inspire him. But I haven't seen him for months. I wonder what he's doing this summer."

"David helped him get a job at the greenhouse where he worked last summer. He's doing all right, I hear."

"And David?"

"He's working at the Mountville Manufacturing Company. We almost dread to see September come, my wife and I. Even though David's not our own, we love him as much as if he were and it's going to leave a big empty hole in the home when he goes away."

"But you wouldn't want to deprive him of the privilege."

"Oh, no. Never. I thank God every day he has a desire to go on and prepare himself for the job I'm sure the Lord has planned for him."

"You mean he knows what it's to be?"

"No, hardly at this point, Miss McClure. But we're sure God does. But coming back to Hugh again. I didn't come here to talk about our boy."

"Yes, I was just thinking while you were talking, Mr. Loomas, what a world of difference in the parental support of the two boys. And yet they're friends! I'm glad for Hugh."

"Something must have drawn them together. It would be interesting to know who made the first move."

"Knowing Hugh as I do, I can't believe it was he. But evidently the two have something in common."

Aaron picked up his hat. "Is there someone else I could consult with, who knows the boy well?"

Miss McClure shook her head. "I can't think who it might be. He's so alone in the world. That Vi might raise objections. You'd better clear first with her and the Welfare Agency, before you start raising any money. She's a character. But I've never talked with her."

"Can you tell me where she lives?"

"Go up that outside stairway on the building west of the mill. I think that's the place. I've never been there. She may not be at home. I'll be interested in learning what you find out. Hugh said she peels potatoes at the Dixie Doodle Café. It's best you go there when Hugh's not at home."

A small bleary-eyed woman answered the knock. Her features were definitely Negro, but her skin would have readily passed for sun-tanned white.

"I'm Aaron Loomas, David Grant's foster father."

"Never heard of you," she hacked.

"My boy and Hugh are good friends."

"Since when's Hugh been mixin' up with whites? Your boy white?" She placed a hand on each hip.

"Yes. The boys were in high school together."

"That may a-been. But I've allays warned Hugh not to mess with anyone white, girl or boy, 'cause it allays comes to a bad end. Them whites takes advantage every time an' I don't mean maybe. I know."

Aaron groped for words. He stood fumbling with his white straw hat.

CHAPTER 26

Miss McClure had said Hugh was an honest boy. Hadn't he told this woman where he had been when he was at their house? Baffled, Aaron weighed what to say next. It might be best to forget the whole idea.

The woman eyed him severely, impatiently.

"Well?" she blinked with evident irritation. "If you've come to report somethin' ornery that rascal's gotten into, I'm no mind to listen to it. I've got my own troubles and can't be puffin' around with anybody else's."

Aaron thought he smelled liquor on her breath, even through the dusty and corroded screen door.

"Hugh enjoyed his schoolwork, didn't he?" ventured Aaron.

"Reckon he did. Why? Made grades nobody could sneer at, 'less he copied."

"I'm sure he didn't do that. I was wondering if he's ever mentioned anything about going on to college?"

"College!" exploded the woman, with mounting indignation. "No, an' he'd better lay off any such stupid ideas. An' if I find out it's your boy or any other white trash stuffin' such rot into my boy's head, I'll pinch it, I'll nip it, I'll smash it dead, so I will."

"Is Hugh your son?" asked Aaron after a brief pause.

"Now listen, mister—whatever your name is," panted the woman quite out of breath. Her eyes shot angry darts at Aaron. She reached up with an unsteady hand and hooked the screen

15

door. "It's none of your business who I am," she said, holding her head high with effort, "or where Hugh comes from. I don't come aroun' to your place askin' no questions 'bout you an' your kid or how many you got or had or how many you los', or what you named 'em or nothin'. I mind my own affairs an' I 'spec you to mind yourn. Some youngsters knows all 'bout themselves an' go on not kickin' a hoop. Well, Hugh ain't wound up that way. No, he wants to know every little smidgen 'bout every measly thing, an' he ain't findin' out nothin', or he'd fly the coop. An' you're not findin' out anythin' either."

"I see," said Aaron, trying to remain calm.

"No, he would not get away, but he'd try it," corrected the woman; "so you'll be good to yourself, mister, by goin' on down those same steps you came up while you can go nice an' easy without fallin'."

Aaron turned. No! There came Hugh, his one hand bandaged, and he was holding it in the other.

"Hi, Hugh," called Aaron from the top of the stairs. "Something happen?"

Hugh's lower jaw dropped. He stood stock-still.

The screen door opened and the woman bumped into Aaron. "I beg your pardon," he said, stepping down.

"What now?" she called out with a gruff voice and scowling.

"I cut my hand on a piece of glass, Aunt Vi. Mr. Gregory told me to go see the doctor. It may need a few stitches."

"You awkward boy," she yelled. "Let me see first what it needs. We ain't got money for no doctor, an' you know it."

"I'll take you, Hugh," said Aaron, hurrying down the steps.

"Shall I?" called Hugh. "Mr. Gregory said he'd pay the bill."

"Well, all right then," she answered. "But you're big enough to go by yourself. You don't need that man totin' you to no doctor's office."

"Come on," said Aaron in a low, gentle tone, "get in my car. I'll be going right past Doctor Patrick's office."

Hugh got in, but after considerable hesitancy.

"Too bad about your accident," began Aaron. "Will it keep

218

you from working for any length of time?"

"Maybe a day. I hope not longer."

Aaron saw the boy eying him with uneasiness out of the corner of his eye.

"Did—did she call you to come up there?" Aaron could hear Hugh's irregular, anxious breathing.

"No, Hugh," he answered. He drove on.

"Did Dave—tell you—where I lived?"

"No." Aaron debated uncomfortably long before selecting his next words. "Does he know where you live?"

"I—I hoped he didn't." Hugh looked in the opposite direction. "You can let me out here, Mr. Loomas." His hand was on the door handle.

"I'll take you on to the office, Hugh. I'm not going out of my way."

"Bet she told you I'm not good enough to be playing ball on the same team with your boy," ventured Hugh, searchingly and with tenseness.

"No," replied Aaron, "she told me nothing of the kind. In fact, I think she feels you're too good to chum with our David."

Hugh gave Aaron a sharp sidewise glance. "But you know she's wrong, Mr. Loomas. It's the opposite. She's most of the time wrong." He shifted. "I hope—" He couldn't finish what he started.

"You can't help wondering why I was there, I know," said Aaron, drawing a long, deep breath.

"You sure got me on nettles, Mr. Loomas. I—I just can't imagine. I'm worried. I'm scared."

"Don't be, Hugh." He reached over and touched the boy's knee.

"But I am." Hugh moved closer to the door.

Aaron was on the spot and he knew it. He waited unbearably long, searching for something to say.

Hugh got limp. Hot and limp. Aaron could see it.

"I guess your Aunt Vi—" Aaron knew at once he had said the wrong thing.

219

Hugh bristled. "She's not my aunt. And I want you to tell Dave never to come up there where I stay. I didn't aim for you to know either. Who told you where it was, Mr. Loomas?"

Aaron hesitated. "A friend of yours."

"A friend told you? My friend?"

"Miss McClure told me."

"Oh, no," cried Hugh. "Not her. Then she's not my friend."

"Yes, she is, Hugh."

"What else did she tell you?"

"Nothing bad, I assure you." Aaron stopped in front of Doctor Patrick's office.

"Even if I'm colored, Mr. Loomas," panted Hugh, getting out of the car, "I care about some things. And I care real much. I'm not as lucky as Dave to have a nice home and folks who really care. But just the same, someday, after I'm on my own, I'll—I'll strike out and—"

"Of course you will, Hugh. You'll make a contribution for good in the world."

"Thanks for the ride, Mr. Loomas."

"Just this yet, Hugh. Why didn't Vi know you've been in our home?"

"Did you tell her?" Hugh looked alarmed, almost sick.

"No. I didn't Hugh. But where did she think you were those times you were over?"

"She didn't need to think anything. She probably never came home all night anyhow, and if she did, she might have been so full she wouldn't have known if I was there or not." Hugh looked pitifully distressed. His eyes got glassy. "I'm—I'm terribly embarrassed, Mr. Loomas," he said. "Vi had too much in her today. When she's that way, she talks too much."

"Would you rather I wouldn't let Dave know I was up there?"

"Please, Mr. Loomas. Please."

"Okay, Hugh."

"If it won't cause you to tell a lie, I'd rather you wouldn't mention it."

"All right, Hugh. I won't."

As Aaron watched Hugh walking up the steps to the doctor's office, he was almost convinced his good intentions to help the boy would get no further than intentions.

He was altogether convinced after his interview with the third party, the one and only Negro minister in town.

"I know all I need to know about that situation, Mr. Loomas. And I'd thank you and Miss McClure if you'd both kindly let your hands out of it. Hugh and Miss Vi are both under my pastorly care. Vi's not able to come to church often, but I pay her calls when she's not. Hugh's been coming right often and I see no reason why any white person need think he's being neglected. Hugh is smart enough that he'll soon be making his own way through college if he wants to go on. Miss Vi's done real well by him, I think, considering everything."

Dave rode his bicycle over to the greenhouse a few evenings later to catch Hugh.

"He left five minutes ago," said Mr. Gregory. "He usually cuts out across the field."

Dave went around two blocks and overtook him. "Hi, Hugh. How's your hand?"

"All right. Why? How'd you hear about it?"

"Dad said he saw you going into the doctor's office and it was bandaged. What happened?"

"Didn't he tell you?"

"No. He didn't know, did he?"

"Look, Dave, what more did he tell you?"

"Nothing," answered Dave. "I don't understand. What's up?"

"That's what I now ask you. What's up?"

"Nothing that I know of. When you didn't come over to play ball last Friday, I wondered. Dad told me you hurt your hand. So I thought I'd track you down and find out if you were able to play tonight."

"Go on back," snapped Hugh. "I can't play yet. It's too tender. Doctor put in three stitches."

"How did it happen?"

"Broke a piece of glass out there on the old hotbed. Go on home. You know about it, and you probably know too much about some other things too."

Dave was dumfounded. "What in the world are you referring to, Hugh?"

"Count me out for good."

"For good? Why do you say that?"

"It's best I drop out. Best for you and best for me too."

"I don't understand, Hugh. What's happened?"

"I told you once that's what I'd like to know." Hugh started to walk on.

"Wait." Dave rode up beside him and caught him by the shoulder. "Have I offended you? Tell me, please."

Hugh made no answer.

"You've got me stumped, Hugh," said Dave in a hurt, sorrowful tone. "If I haven't, who has? Will you tell me that?"

"I won't ever tell you, nor anybody else, anything again," answered Hugh. There was bitterness mingled with repulsion in his answer. "Just because Vi lies a lot doesn't mean she lies every time. And I don't think Reverend Parks would if she did."

"What in the world, Hugh? You've got me completely baffled."

"Then you know how I feel exactly," retorted Hugh. "You can let your rich dad cover up and frost over everything for you, but I'll work my own way out of my own mess if it takes me the rest of my life. I'm never going to trust anybody from now on. And I have a good notion to throw that book right straight into Miss McClure's face. She's in it too."

"Hugh," cried Dave, "wait. Please explain. This makes me feel awful. Don't let something come between us."

"Well, it already has. You're double-faced like everyone else."

"No," insisted Dave. "I'm not. I've been a true friend to you, Hugh. I've never told a single soul what you confided in me."

"I don't believe you. I can't."

222

"I'm telling you the truth, Hugh. And I challenge you to ask anybody you want to. Anybody in the whole wide world."

Hugh tried desperately to withhold tears. "Everything in the whole wide world is in one rotten mess," he cried, half sobbing, "and everybody white and black and half white is rotten too, or getting rotten fast." His breath came in gasps.

"I've thought that myself already, Hugh. But I remember you said—well, I have no idea what you're driving at, but you said you weren't going to worry over what you couldn't help and couldn't change, after you read that book. Remember?"

"I said that, yes. But if Miss McClure can't be trusted, then nobody can. And I've made up my mind nobody can." Hugh walked on.

Dave followed close behind. "I wish you'd come over tonight and we could talk this over."

Hugh walked faster.

"If you come over, I won't play ball, Hugh. I wish you'd come."

Hugh started running.

Dave didn't even open his Bible that night. He sat by his table for an hour with his head on his arm. Then in the bottom dresser drawer he found the valentine on which he had printed, "To my mother, Shana Grant." He held it a long time as he read and reread the verse he had so painstakingly printed, what seemed now nearly half a century ago.

> I love you for so many things
> I don't know where to start,
> So I'll just say, I love you, Mother,
> From the bottom of my heart.

Dave shook his head. Was she—somewhere? He held another paper and studied what he had written.

Found paper in file Sept. 22, 1923.

He lived it all again. Joy—anticipation—hope.

Mailed letter Oct. 8, 1923.

More anticipation—disappointment.

Stood for Christ July 28, 1924

New joy—relief—prayers—Mamma—Papa—love.

Baptized Aug. 7, 1924.

Promises—Mamma—Papa—love.

Janet died July 10, 1926.

Shock—sorrow—sympathy—concern.

Moved to town July 16, 1926.

Papa—love—new interests—Dug.

First letter July 24, 1926.

Sister Lora—love.

Second letter July 30, 1926.

Sister Lora—love—forgiveness.

Went to Philadelphia July 4, 1929.

Dave relived it all. Through it all he felt, woven in, that warm, comforting cord of love. A love he could see—touch—taste—hear—feel. Poor loveless, fatherless, motherless, Lora-less Hugh. Dave sat in deep study. He put the papers back in the dresser drawer. He paced back and forth across the room. Everything rotten? Everybody rotten? How could Janet be rotten? Sweet, tender, beautiful Janet? How could Mother Loomas be rotten? Rotten inside, yet so sweet and lovable outside? And Sister Lora?

Dave found a sheet of paper. His pencil moved swiftly, as though some evil, unseen hand might grab it from out of nowhere, anywhere, and stop it before he was finished.

Dear Sister Lora,

I wish you would call me up the day you get this. But please don't let anybody know I asked you to. I get home from work around five-thirty.

David.

"David hasn't been turning his radio on much of late," Rose remarked to Aaron two days later. "He seems unusually quiet. Haven't you noticed it?"

"Of course I have. He looks at me sometimes as though he doesn't know quite what to make of me. I'm puzzled."

"Why don't you ask him if something is wrong?"

"I wouldn't want him to think I fear such a thing. There just dare not anything ever come between us."

"He hasn't mentioned Hugh for several days that I recall," Rose said.

"Maybe that's it. Dreads going away to school unless Hugh can go too. I wish I had some way of letting him know I tried, without breaking any promises. Isn't it awful how human beings can live under the same roof, eat at the same table, go to the same church, pray to the same God, and yet one have to wonder what the other is thinking and be afraid the other is misunderstanding?"

"Well, Aaron," said Rose thoughtfully, "after all, one has to respect the other's right of privacy of mind and heart. We have no reason to complain about Davy's conduct. I guess every boy gets quiet spells."

"I'm not complaining, Rose. You brought up the subject. Mothers are usually more quick to notice such things. But just the same I've noticed and I wonder."

"Have you seen Hugh lately?" asked Aaron at the table that evening.

Dave trimmed the fat off his steak. "I saw him going home from work the other night."

"His hand must be better then?"

"He's working, but it's still taped," answered Dave.

"Help yourself to the corn. You and Dug will be glad when he's able to bat a ball again, I dare say."

Dave took a drink. "Sure. He was a good batter. But," he added at length, "I think he aims to take pretty good care of his hand for quite a while." He gave Aaron a hasty glance.

"Don't you think, Dave, it would be best to wait a year and see what we can do about helping him go to college?"

"Yes," agreed Dave. "I—I think maybe." He looked up. "Dad," he said, "do you know Reverend Parks?"

"Yes."

"Who is he?"

"The Negro minister."

"Did you ever talk to him?"

"Yes. Why?"

"Recently?"

"Yes. Why?"

"I just wondered. Does he tell the truth?"

Aaron dropped his fork. "I sincerely hope so. Why? Do you have reason to think he doesn't?"

"I don't know, Dad. But I have plenty of reason to think someone doesn't."

"What do you mean?"

The phone rang. Rose answered. "It's for you, Dave. I'm not sure, but it sounds like Sister Lora."

CHAPTER 27

"David?"

"Yes."

"I got your letter."

"Yes."

"You told me to call you."

"Yes."

"Any particular reason?"

"Yes."

Rose looked at Aaron. Aaron looked at Rose.

"I'm anxious to hear what it is."

No answer.

"Are you there, David?"

"Yes."

"Is it something you can't tell me now?"

"Yes, Sister Lora."

"I see. Because others are listening?"

"Yes."

"That complicates things, doesn't it?"

"Yes."

"Well, I tell you what, David, how about coming along home with me Sunday after church. Will it keep until then?"

"Yes."

"Will you say yes then to that question also?"

"Yes."

She laughed. "All right then. Are you well?"

"Yes."

"Then good-by, David. See you Sunday."

"Good-by."

"I'd call that quite a *yes* conversation you had," laughed Rose good-naturedly.

"That was Sister Lora," explained Dave, "and she wants me to go along home with her for Sunday dinner."

"How sweet of her!" remarked Rose. "Before you leave for school. I suppose she will always feel like a big sister to you. She loved you so dearly when you were in her care at the Home."

"May I be excused?" asked Dave.

"Not done eating already!" objected Rose. "No pie tonight?"

"Not tonight, thanks." He noted her look of disappointment. "It does look good, Mother, but I'm full."

"Just a minute, Dave," began Aaron, holding out one hand. "You have me puzzled over what you said a few minutes ago. Sounds to me like someone is trying to muddle up or destroy your confidence in certain people. Do you care to share with us what this is about?"

Dave looked at nothing but the hem of the tablecloth.

Aaron tried again. "Is Hugh at the bottom of this?"

"I don't know," answered Dave, drearily, "who is at the bottom of what. All I know is that I'm—" his voice was a trifle unsteady—"I'm so disappointed and puzzled too, I just don't know what to think."

Aaron got up from the table. "What about, Son?"

"About almost everything. And so is Hugh."

"When did all this happen?"

Dave looked at Aaron a long time. "Dad," he began, "Hugh has been told something. That's for certain. What, I don't know. I don't know who told him, but it must have been either Vi or Reverend Parks. Whatever it is, he's terribly upset and cross. He's lost confidence in everybody. Even in Miss McClure, and that hurts. He thought a lot of her. He believed in her. He trusted her. What's been said? He's disgusted with you. And with me, and I can't imagine what I've done. What have I done, Dad?"

"I don't know that you've done anything, Son."

"But, Dad, things just don't add up. Surely—surely you must not be telling me something I should know."

Dave walked to the stairway. "I think I'd better leave if I'm a disgrace to you."

"A disgrace?" exclaimed Aaron.

"Leave?" cried Rose.

Dave fought tears. "You've been awful good to me," he faltered, "but I can't stay if I'm—if you know something that you need to cover up and frost over about me."

"Cover up?" asked Aaron. "Dave, what is this? I'm really confused now."

"Hugh said Vi tells the truth sometimes, but if she didn't, Reverend Parks would. Is this about me?" Dave hid his face in his arm and leaned against the door casing.

"Come," said Aaron. "Sit down, Son. I think Mother and I would both sooner die than see you leave us. I'd sooner die than lose your confidence. We want you to know we have confidence in you. I have a feeling now I've taken the wrong step. I must be at fault. Dave, I'll try to explain as best I can without breaking any promises."

"Don't break a promise, Dad. Please, don't do that," pleaded Dave.

"Well, let me see. How can I tell you to help clear up something? Someone has misinformed Hugh, without a doubt. I don't know him very well. I've talked with Reverend Parks but once, and that was recently. I've spoken to Miss McClure but one time. I've talked with Miss Vi once. I'm tempted to break a promise to clear things up for you, Dave, but—"

"No, don't break a promise, Dad, just to do that. Please."

"Well, how can I set your mind at rest, Son? I can't let you go on in this state of bewilderment. You see, I got the idea I would like to surprise you and Hugh both by helping Hugh go to college."

"To college?"

"That's right, Son. So first of all I wanted advice—counsel—encouragement. So who did I call on first of all?"

"Reverend Parks?"

"No."

"Vi?"

"No, Son. Don't guess any further. But I was informed by someone where Vi lived. Dave, never go there. Hugh doesn't want you to."

"I don't know where it is."

"I know you don't. And I am not telling, because Hugh doesn't want you to know."

"He's embarrassed. That's why."

"Exactly."

"Hugh is ashamed of Vi, too, I know."

"I'm sorry now I ever went there. She's a—a different sort of person, Dave."

"I pity Hugh."

"So do I, Son. I promised Hugh I wouldn't tell you where he lives."

"Then you did talk to him?"

"Yes, I did. The day he hurt his hand. That's when I promised I wouldn't tell you."

"Then don't do it, Dad."

"I'm not going to, Dave. Vi had been drinking. Now what she told Hugh or Reverend Parks about me, I don't have any idea, or what Reverend Parks told Hugh I have no idea. But it in no way could possibly have anything to do with you, Dave, except that she doesn't want him associating with you."

"But why?" exclaimed Dave. "What does she think is so wrong about me that I'm not good enough?"

"What she thinks has nothing to do with it," cried Rose. "You are you and what she says doesn't change anything. She says things because she feels inferior, I suppose."

"But Miss McClure. Hugh said he'd like to throw that book in her face. Why? What has she done?"

"What book?" asked Aaron.

"A certain book she gave Hugh to read once."

"I have no idea, Dave. Do you?"

"Partly."

"Can you figure it out then?"

Dave studied the floor by his foot for a long time. He rubbed his hands. He shook his head.

"Then I'm as stumped as you are," said Aaron. "Miss McClure spoke very highly of Hugh."

"She did?"

"And she's glad you've befriended him."

"She is?"

"And she wants to help Hugh all she can. She feels sorry for him. She told me some things about him that I promised not to repeat."

With knitted brow Dave looked up sharply. "Then keep it, Dad," he said. "If there's anything I despise, it's a broken promise."

"Well, Son," said Aaron, "I'll never need fear sharing a secret with you, will I?"

"I hope not." Dave smiled when he spoke.

"Now do you feel a little better? Have I cleared up anything for you at all without betraying anyone's confidence?"

"Well, for me, a little, yes. But poor Hugh. What awful lies is he believing about you and me and Miss McClure? He's mad at the whole world and everybody in it. And all because somebody has twisted the truth. It's not right. I don't like to see Hugh so worked up. He has enough to feel bad about. He might do something desperate."

"I'm sorry, Dave. I did what I did because I knew you were interested in the boy, but I've only made matters worse. I've failed you, Son."

Dave jumped up. "No, you haven't," he said. "Don't talk like that."

Just then Dug whistled. "Get your bat and come on, Dave," he called.

"Just a minute, Dug," he answered. "I want to eat a piece of pie first. May I, Mother, after all?"

"May you eat a piece of pie?" she smiled. "You may eat two pieces if you want to."

He sat up to the table. "Would I dare ask a question, Mother?"

"I dare you to. What is it?"

"Do you and Dad get paid for keeping me?"

"Paid!" exclaimed Rose as if horrified. "What makes you ask such a question? Of course not. Paid for keeping you?"

"Did you ever?"

"No, never. Now who put that into your head, pray tell?"

"I didn't think so," he answered. "I just wanted to hear you tell me it wasn't true."

Rose pulled ever so gently on Dave's one ear and said, "What else could I say to make you feel loved and wanted and one of us? What all goes through that wonderful working head of yours, we'll never know."

"Aren't you going to eat dinner with me?" Leon called as soon as he saw Dave going up the walk beside Sister Lora.

"He's my guest today," she answered. "My," she remarked glancing up at him, "I can hardly believe it how you keep growing. Here I am looking up to you already." She laughed softly.

Dave's cheeks colored. "But I'll always be looking up to you," he said, "no matter how much taller I get."

She seated him opposite her at the round guest table in the big dining room with its many low tables. He watched the fifty-two children file in and take their places. Not one did he know. A strange feeling of mingled wonder, loneliness, strange comfort, and awe swept over Dave. He knew he had once been just as helpless and ignorant as the smallest little boy sitting at the lowest table in the corner. He wondered if the child understood at all why he was there or where he had come from. He wondered instinctively if he had a mother and one who cared. Vaguely

232

he remembered sitting at the table in the room on the low bench.

"Aren't you taking care of the tiny ones any more, Sister Lora?" he asked.

"I do, yes. But for this one meal I asked Mildred Ann to take my place because," she smiled up at him, "I have you to take care of today."

"Well, I do hope I won't spill any food or cause you any trouble."

They both laughed softly.

The dinner was a simple one, but tasty and satisfying.

"You had a special reason for sending me the letter, didn't you?" Sister Lora touched his arm.

"I guess it was rather bold of me," he confessed. "But I was —well, sorta lonesome that night." He took one deep breath. "I just thought I'd like to talk to you. You must have thought I was stupid on the phone the way I answered, but—"

"No, not stupid, David. I understood."

"You did?"

"Of course. As soon as I read your letter I felt you were trying to tell me something."

"That's why you asked me to come?"

"Of course. Wasn't that what you wanted me to do?"

"Yes," he admitted.

"Where shall we go to talk? Up in the little room off the nursery? We might be least disturbed there. If we go into the reception room, someone is apt to come in."

"Wherever you say, Sister Lora."

As Dave listened to the children sing their song of thanks for the food and file out, he lived in those few minutes portions of fifty-two young lives, wonderings, fears, laughter, tears, longings, prayers, and with it all, the sweet satisfying presence of Sister Lora.

Beds. Rows of white painted beds. There it was in its proper place—his bed, like a comforting prayer, waiting with white outstretched arms for another tired but happy little boy who was still blissfully ignorant of the cruelties of life.

He followed her through the room on tiptoe, for it seemed like a hallowed place where an angel of love hovered.

"How does it make you feel to come back now?" she asked, as she motioned to him to take the chair by the west window.

"Well," he said, "it's hard to express how it makes me feel, but mostly happy, because I never knew anything but happiness when I lived here with you."

"You don't mean you haven't been happy since you left the Home?"

"Oh, I've had a great deal of happiness, Sister Lora. It's nobody's fault when I'm not."

"Aren't you happy now?"

"Yes. Oh, yes, Sister Lora. I don't know how to try to tell you what I mean. Mother and Dad Loomas are the nicest people a boy could ever know. Sometimes I almost worship them, but—"

"But what?"

He clasped one hand over the other. "It's the fact that I'm not their own. That's all."

"But I'm sure they love you as much as if you were, David."

"But how could that possibly be?" he asked with seriousness.

"Can't you feel it?"

"I feel it, but—but is it really true? Couldn't I imagine they want me? Will they actually miss me when I'm away in school?"

"I know they will, David. And so will I. Rose has already—I mean Mother Loomas—has already told me how they'll miss you."

"Has she? I'll miss them, I know. But—" He gazed far out across the new-mown fields.

"But what?"

"Why doesn't someone *else* miss me *more*? I've—I've been wanting to talk to you for a long time, but I—I couldn't make up my mind to do it. And now I don't know how to begin to make you understand."

"Just try, David. I'll understand, I think."

"Well—do you think if you were me you'd—you'd care at all where you came from?"

234

"I think I'd care. Yes. But I think I'd try not to let it trouble me. I know that's easy to say and quite another thing to do. There's a difference between trouble and bother, David. I suppose it would bother me at times."

"You wouldn't ever—ever—" he hesitated—"be a little anxious or upset?"

"David," she answered, "I'm sure I would feel many times exactly as you do."

She heard him give a sigh of glad relief.

"Listen, David. Many, many times when you were a baby and I held you in my arms I wondered where you came from. I've tried to imagine what a sweet, beautiful mother you must have had, and wondered often why you were taken from her."

Dave hardly breathed. "You think—" he bent forward— "I might have been stolen from her?"

"I didn't mean stolen." Sister Lora hurried on. "Mr. Kolb tried to find out where you were born, but he never had any success. Have you ever talked to him about this matter?"

David shook his head. "Is my real name Grant?"

"It was the name we found in your little stocking when you arrived."

"Can't you tell me more, Sister Lora?" He sat on the edge of the chair.

"You must remember I'm only a worker here," she said kindly. "I am never to give any information to any of the children. Even if I did know the answer to this mystery, I would not be the one to tell you."

She saw his look of disappointment. She saw his shoulders droop.

Should he tell her about finding the card in the file? Should he? He sat debating.

"David," she went on, "there is but one thing I know to do about your problem, and that is the one thing I've been doing every day since I first picked you up in my arms. Commit you to God. I have never missed a day praying for you. When Rose and Aaron took you, two more people started praying for you. I've observed you from Sunday to Sunday growing up. I knew in my heart all along you were trying to discover yourself and fit yourself into this mystery and this maze of society. I feared some of your same fears with you."

"You did?"

"Certainly."

"But how? How could you guess?"

"Have I been here all these years without learning from all these children? David—" she looked him straight in the eyes— "you wonder where your mother and father met, don't you?"

"Yes."

"You wonder where they were married."

"Yes."

"And you wonder, pardon me for saying this, but I know you wonder if they *were* married. Don't you?"

"Sister Lora—" his eyes got blurry— "how did you know?" He stood up. "Who told you?"

"Nobody told me."

"Do you know if they were?"

"No, David. Please sit down. I'm going to talk to you like a sister to a brother."

"Oh, please, do. That's why I—"

"I understand. I'm so glad you came to me. You wanted to get this off your chest before you go away to school."

"How did you know that?"

"How? Well, I guess God put it in my mind, David. I've always asked Him to help me understand you because somehow you were extra close to me and seemed to need it." She saw a faint smile cross his face. "And even though you've been confidential with Leon—"

"Has he told you things?"

"No. Not one thing, David. We've never at any time talked about you. But I know you've been close friends. I was about to say that since I do know how you must wonder about your parents at times and wonder how you came to be, I know too that the uncertainty of it all gives you a dangling, unattached sort of feeling that can be distressing. You long to know where you belong by birth."

He smiled.

"You're in a home where you say you feel they love you. And I know it's true. I know they love you, want you, appreciate you, plan for your happiness, plan for your future. They adore you, David."

"No."

"You won't let yourself believe it? All right, then, doubt it if you insist."

He smiled.

Lora smiled with him.

She hurried on. "Their love for you is not dependent upon any of your circumstances. If sometime you would learn your parents were of an altogether different culture or even nationality, it wouldn't affect their love for you."

"Not even a different race?" He laughed at his own question.

"Nor that." She returned the laugh. "It's human nature to feel as you do, David. You have every comfort of a good home; you have friends, a chance to get an education, foster parents who provide for you good things many boys never enjoy. Yet you lack that one special kind of security every normal person craves, the security of knowing who your real parents are. But, David—" she bent forward— "you can't know what you can't know. Are you following me?"

He nodded.

"So unless God somehow in His all-wise, all-knowing way brings it about, we must live without knowing. We've got to learn to be happy and content in spite of the mystery. Live on top of it. Count our blessings. Praise God, there is no mystery too hard for Him to solve. He sees our end from the beginning. He planned your life before the world was formed."

"You really believe that?"

"I do with all my heart. He knew the very hour you would be delivered here before the first sunrise. And 'way back there He planned to prepare Rose and Aaron Loomas to open their

237

hearts and home to you at the right time. Trust them. They love you dearly."

His smile was spontaneous.

"I want you to go away to school and put everything you've got into it, David. I don't mean just for top grades. But I want you to play hard, laugh hard, sing hard, live a big, full, happy, useful life. Keep looking up with your eyes on the One you do know is your Father by birth and by adoption. David, don't you see how fortunate you are? How very fortunate?"

A tear fell. Then two. "I never saw it like I do now," he said softly. "Oh, I'm so glad you understand and know how to talk to me."

"And listen, David, I think Aaron and Rose understand you too."

"You mean like *you* do?"

"I'm sure they do, David. And if in any little point they don't, I'm positive your love for them will cover if you'll let it. I know they're very sincere and want to understand."

David tried to swallow the lump in his throat. "Perhaps I'd better go over and spend the rest of the afternoon with Leon until church time. Thanks a lot, Sister Lora."

CHAPTER 28

"Hi, there," announced Leon, jumping up when Dave walked in. "Been expecting you. You really must rate high with Sister Lora."

"Why?"

"Well, I don't remember her ever inviting anyone else in like this all on her own." Leon slapped Dave on the back.

"She rates pretty high with me," Dave returned. "You know that without me saying it."

"I was only teasing. What shall we do? Play checkers?"

"Checkers?" Dave buttoned his suit coat and smoothed his hair as he deliberated.

"Or would you just as soon talk?"

"I'd as soon," answered Dave. "We won't have many more chances to be together before I leave."

"I was thinking that. Going out by train?"

"No. Clif and Lesa have offered to take me in their new car."

"Oh, you lucky guy!" exclaimed Leon. "Come. Let's go up to my room." He opened the door. "Step in, my senior."

"Now cut that out," laughed Dave, stepping inside. "Just because I have a chance to go away to school before you do doesn't elevate me one speck."

"But you are my senior," insisted Leon. "I'm glad for you. But really now, you struck it pretty nice when you got into the Loomas home."

"But I didn't decide to go there. They could have chosen someone else."

"I know. And I'm not jealous. I faintly remember your leaving. I know I bawled. I thought they were taking my brother away."

"I bawled too." Dave's chuckle was a combination of embarrassment and amusement. "That stairway in the big farmhouse. It scared me stiff, I remember. I guess I threw a fit. But we had lots of fun sliding down that banister, didn't we, now?"

"Did we ever! Fun all over the place, and out in the barn too. And man, those meals Mamma Loomas made for a bunch of hungry youngsters. Do you hear from Dennis?"

"Mother and Dad got one letter from him since he's married."

"Married?"

"Guess I forgot to tell you. He's been married about four or five months to a Cloretta somebody. I forget. Mother and Dad sent them a beautiful rug and put my name on the card with theirs."

"See. That's what I mean. Things like that. You're so lucky, Dave. They always count you in on everything just like you were their own."

"I know," mused Dave. "It seems like luck to some folks, I guess. Dug and Hugh have told me the same."

"Who's Hugh?"

"A boy I got acquainted with in high school. But Sister Lora told me today she thinks God planned all this ages ago. I think she actually believes that."

"Yeah? How come she got on that subject?"

"Well—" Dave shrugged his shoulders as he rubbed one hand over the bedpost. "One thing just led on to another as we were talking."

"Did you ever tell her how you got me to borrow that stamp and envelope from her?"

"No. Why?"

"I just now thought about it."

"Did you ever tell her?"

"No."

"Or anyone else?"

"Of course not. And I've never told anyone what we found in the file that Sunday afternoon either. Have you?"

Dave sobered. He walked to the window. He stood quietly. "To my regret," he said at length without looking at Leon. "I confided that to Dug. And we made a trip to Philadelphia together to find her."

"You didn't."

"Yes, we did."

"When?"

"Last July fourth. That's why I wasn't at the picnic and ball game. Dug suggested we go. He meant it well. He wanted to help me find her. But we wasted the whole day." Dave turned abruptly and stepped over close to Leon. "Please don't tell anyone about this wild trip. I think I made a big mistake."

"You mean Mother and Dad Loomas didn't know you went?"

"Sure they knew we went. They said we could go. But they didn't know we went especially to try to locate someone. Certainly not my mother."

"Well, what did they think you went for? You surely didn't lie to them, did you?"

"No. No. We just said we wanted to go to spend the day in a big city. And that's what we did. Spent the whole hot day walking. Sounds crazy, doesn't it? Why, Leon, there's pages of Grants in Philadelphia. As long as I don't know my dad's first name, how could I hope to find her? It would take weeks to look up all those Grants. Anyhow they may have moved out of the state. Maybe she's dead. Both dead. I'm not going to ever try again to locate her."

"Well," said Leon, stretching, "what I don't quite understand is how you and Dug got by keeping all this secret. Didn't your folks ask you questions? All kinds of questions after you got home?"

"No. Dad just asked me if we got to see everything we wanted to and I said that would have been impossible. Mother was sick

241

in bed the next morning and for three weeks. I tell you, during that time I began to realize how much she really means to me. In a way—" Dave shifted his glance— "I was glad I didn't find my real mother." He cleared his throat nervously. "I wouldn't want them to even suspect it's ever bothered me, not knowing. That's why I don't want you to tell anyone. I wouldn't want Mother and Dad Loomas to think I wasn't satisfied, because I am. It's not that I want to do things behind their backs. It's not that I want to deceive them. Maybe someday I'll tell them all about everything. But not now. If a person—" Dave seemed to be struggling for words of justification. "Look—unless you're in my place you just can't possibly understand how it is. Sure I still care where I came from, but," he added with sudden impetuousness, "I'm not going to get upset about it. Not even if I'd find a dozen Shana Grants in Philadelphia and I didn't belong to any of them. I—I sorta think she's dead."

Leon stood in blinking silence.

Dave lowered his voice near a panting whisper. "Yes, I agree I have it pretty nice. And I thank God every day for all the good things I'm sure I don't even deserve. Especially since I know how some other fellows have it. And," he added as a concluding afterthought, "I'm glad Mother and Dad don't imagine all the things I've wondered about already."

"Leon."

"Someone's calling you," said Dave. "Sounds like your mother."

"Leon. Lunch is ready."

"Okay, Mother. We'll be right down."

The following Sunday evening quite a number of people shook hands with Dave after church and wished him well in school. There was only one extended hand he felt like refusing to touch. Something about the woman sent an instant repulsion over him. "I hope you'll like your studies," she was saying, slightly squeezing his hand, "and make many friends."

Dave managed a feeble thanks, but he felt like shouting, "Go on. Hurry out of my sight." For he was almost certain hers was the voice that had stabbed him with that disreputable word on a Sunday morning years before. For a dreadful moment a sickening exhaustion possessed him as it did when he found the word in the school dictionary. He wanted to run to the basement and wash his hands and ears, but another hand was gripping his. Stanley Wingard's father was speaking with warm sincerity. "We'll all miss you, David. But you'll be the kind to help make the college a good place for us to send our boys to later on."

"Thank you, Mr. Wingard. I wish Stanley were going along with me."

"I wish so too, David, but he'll have to work a year first. He's plenty young yet."

The day of final packing, Mother Loomas was up in Dave's room checking the list once more: "2 sheets, 2 pillowcases, 1 blanket, 1 dresser scarf, 5 towels, 3 washcloths, 1 pair curtains, 2 throw rugs, 1 bedspread, 1 table lamp, book ends. We'd better go over your list of clothes too. Check your dresser drawers once more."

"Mother," said Dave, "in the bottom drawer there I have a few personal things in a box. I want to leave it here. A couple of letters I got from Sister Lora and some Sunday-school things from long ago. Maybe it's silly to keep them, but—"

"I wouldn't call it silly. That's all right. Nobody will ever get into it."

"It's tied shut. And I've marked it so no one will throw it away by mistake."

"Who would do such a thing? This is your room and no one is going to tamper with a thing in it. When you come back, everything will be exactly as you leave it."

"Thanks, Mother."

A playful gust of wind sent the lace curtain sweeping across the small table beside Dave's bed, brushing off the doily. On the floor face up lay the paper with the list of names on it. If Rose saw it first, she gave Dave a chance to think he did. She noted his startled look and heard him catch a breath. She looked away and gave him time to pick it up and stick it in his pocket.

"Mother," he said, "I'm going to put my radio downstairs for you and Dad to use."

"I'm sure we'll enjoy it."

After supper Dave went over to see Dug. "You be sure to write to me once in a while."

"We'll compare schools."

"Okay."

"I still wish you were going with me to Philadelphia, but I suppose you're going out there to satisfy your folks."

"No. Not altogether. Of course I like to please them, but they never said I had to go there. We decided it together."

"It's going to be pretty nice for me to get to come home weekends if I want to. I can take eats along back. But maybe if you went to school in Philadelphia, you couldn't concentrate so well on your lessons."

"Why couldn't I?"

"Well, maybe you'd be tempted to strike out and look up some more of those Grants."

"Dug, you know I said I wasn't going to try that any more. Now don't go poking fun at me."

"I'm sorry, Dave. I don't mean to poke fun."

"I wish you wouldn't bring it up any more. I try to forget that day, and believe me, it's not been easy."

"I hope you're not sorry for what you told me."

"Well," faltered Dave, "I can't take it back. But I hope I've learned my lesson."

"What about?"

"About keeping such things to myself."

"Well, now," exclaimed Dug in a hurt tone. "I've never once betrayed your confidence."

"And I do appreciate that too. I didn't mean to infer you did. But when I get out there to school, I'm not telling anybody anything. I've made up my mind on that. I came over to listen to records. Want to play a few for me? I can't stay long."

"Sure. You pick out what you want me to play."

The two spent a pleasant half hour together, and Dave left smiling.

Aaron seated himself opposite Rose at the table and handed her the letter:

Dear Dad and Mother,

My schedule is getting full. I can't take on much more. I enjoy A Cappella Choir and Men's Glee Club practice very much. I was really scared when I tried out. I kept watching the bulletin board for the list of names chosen. Ed, my roommate, tried out too. He didn't make it and I felt sorry for him. He laughed it off, but I know he was badly disappointed. That's one thing we all have to learn in college—be happy when the other fellow succeeds. So I'm especially happy for him when he beats me at ping-pong.

I believe Ed's a little homesick. He talks a lot about his three brothers and what all they can do together. He fusses a lot about the skimpy meals too and keeps saying what a wonderful cook his mother is. Well, I fuss a little with him and remind him my mother is a good cook too. [Rose blushed a warm pink.]

Where are you working now, Dad? They could use a good carpenter like you around here. There's a lot of building going on in the community.

Some of the trees have turned color and it's a beautiful view from my dorm window. It makes me think of those fall days back on the farm. When I come home, I hope we can drive out past the place again. Just think, only forty-eight more days until Christmas vacation begins. I'll pity those who won't be able to go home. A boy from Ohio fell while playing basketball yesterday and broke his leg in two places.

I had a letter from Dug and Leon this week and one from Lesa. She said they saw Janet's little boy last Sunday and he looks a lot like her. I'm glad he has such a good home.

I don't suppose you ever see Hugh, but if you do, wave to

him for me. I'm thankful I had a chance to talk to him before I left and get things at least partly straightened out. I hope he can get away from Vi before long. I think it's mighty wonderful of you to help me be here in school this year. Someday I hope I can pay you back.

Guess I'd better get busy and read some more in the Old Testament now. The professor gives such long assignments. I enjoy math classes best.

Oh, yes, thanks for the box of cookies, Mother. A few were broken, but I devoured every crumb.

With love,
Dave.

"Well," remarked Aaron, trying to control his emotions, "sounds like home has a real pulling."

"Sounds like he feels he's our very own," added Rose. "Now the soup has cooled off. I'll warm it up."

"Never mind, dear. I have work lined up and I must be going soon. After a letter like that, who minds eating cold soup? You return thanks."

Less than a week later Dave received the newspaper clipping with Mother's letter. It made him weak all over.

Youth Fatally Injured

Hugh Latimer, eighteen, who resided with his aunt, Vivian Tiller, 115A Carr Street, was struck shortly before noon today by a Reo truck driven by Sam Kragell of 2105 W. High. Young Latimer, on his bicycle, evidently did not see the oncoming truck, for Mr. Kragell reported the boy rode in front of him without looking up. Mr. Kragell was unable to stop in time to avoid the crash. He is not being held.

The youth suffered a fractured skull and a compound fracture of the left arm. He was pronounced dead upon arrival at the hospital. His body was taken to the Whittigar Funeral Home.

This shocking news was not the only reason Dave had little appetite at dinner. Something he read in the Bible that forenoon was definitely disturbing. He hadn't succeeded in shaking it off when the mail came.

"No rice pudding?"

"No thanks, Phil."

"All right, fellows, if Dave's not taking any, we each get one more teaspoonful. What's wrong? You getting sick?"

Dave rested his chin on his hand. "No. I'm just not hungry. Go ahead, take my share. I'd like to be excused if I may."

Five boys gave nodding consent.

Hurrying to his room, he reread the torturous statement. Would God make such a law? There it was in the Holy Bible. Twenty-six words of no hope, no mercy, no love, but horrible anguish for the perfectly helpless. Yes, helpless.

Was he?

Was he one of those?

One of those "can't-help-it" victims, branded with such an unjust segregation! Would he ever know? Whether he was or wasn't, the infliction was a most grievous one. What anxiety, this unsureness! And was he the only one in the class who was plagued by this tormenting statement?

What torture, this aloneness!

The week passed. More chapters were read, but not a student raised a question on the verse. Certainly he would not, and expose his secret misgivings. Dave couldn't help dwelling on poor, helpless Hugh.

It was wonderful to be at home for two weeks. Not a day with nothing to do. If it wasn't skating with Stanley and his brothers, it was being entertained by Leon, or Dug, or Clif and Lesa, or someone else. Mother invited his Sunday-school class for a meal one evening. Another time Sister Lora and the Kolbs were there.

"He looks so well and so happy," remarked Sister Lora to Rose. "But reserved too."

"He's maturing," added Melvin Kolb. "I think Leon notices it."

"Dave, are you anxious to go back?" asked Mrs. Kolb.

"Oh," he deliberated. "I guess so. But not quite as anxious as I was to come home."

But something happened to make Dave anxious to go back. The following morning he noticed a magazine on the living room table. *The Layman's Faith.* He picked it up and leafed through it.

"Mother, where did this come from?"

"We subscribed for it. There's some very good articles in it. You'd be interested in the one in there on evolution."

But it was the note at the bottom of the question and answer page that held Dave's attention. "Send your questions to Dr. Jonathan E. Young, Westminster Theological Seminary, Chicago, Ill. If you wish a personal reply, enclose a self-addressed envelope. Other questions with answers will be published."

For three weeks he waited for that self-addressed envelope.

Did Dr. Young get it?

Did he take time to read it?

A fourth week went by and Dave was beginning to despair of ever hearing.

The day it came, his question had been weighing especially heavy. He put the letter in his notebook and hurried to the library to read it.

CHAPTER 29

Dave spotted a vacant chair at the end of a table nearest the windows. With bated breath and shy, almost dubious, expectancy he placed the unfolded letter inside his open notebook. His eyebrows twitched.

Dear Inquirer,

You have requested an explanation of Deuteronomy 23:2. You are not the first person who has raised a question on this same passage. [What? He shifted as a queer sensation went down his spine.] A bastard is one born out of wedlock or from an illegal marriage, which makes him an illegitimate offspring. It was one of the Levitical laws to exclude such persons from the assembly of the Lord, even to the tenth generation. Another law was that children who were disrespectful to their parents were stoned to death.

The coming of Jesus Christ changed all this. We are no longer under law, but under grace. I see no point in explaining further those laws and regulations of the Old Testament that do not apply to anyone since the death of Christ. [Dave drew a quick breath of relief.]

The sin of bringing illegitimate children into the world is no less a sin than it ever was. Children often have to suffer because of the sins of their parents, but they are never held accountable for the sins of other persons. The blood of Jesus Christ cleanses from all sin, the moment it is confessed and repented of. Sin still condemns. Sin separates us from God.

And separation means death. But God, who created us to be in union with Himself, bridges over this great gulf that separates us from Him because of sin; not by condoning sin, but by Himself, Jesus Christ, bearing the sin. God loves because He *is* love. God pities the sinner even while His law condemns the sin. Read John 3:16; Romans 5:6-8; Ephesians 2:4, 5; I John 9, 10. [The rapid thumping of his heart made Dave warm all over.]

We are living under grace, which the New Testament joyously contrasts with law. Read John 1:17; Romans 6:14. When we receive Christ, we are no longer judged as sinners, but justified by our personal faith in Him. Acts 13:38, 39. We are not only justified, but have the right to fellowship with Him. Romans 5:1, 2; Hebrews 10:19-22. So you see, this excludes *no* one. There is no segregation or partiality in Christ. He sees not race, not rank, not color, not birth, but the heart of man; so that every believer, regardless of circumstances, is a partaker of His divine nature.

You did not state your age nor circumstances, but I trust this answers your question.

Sincerely,

Jonathan E. Young.

A lightsomeness encircled all of Dave's conflicting resentments, even before he read the single-sheet tract clipped to the letter:

He was abused that we might know love.

He was rejected that we might be accepted.

He was forsaken that we might be claimed.

He was condemned that we might be justified.

He was made to be sin that we might be free from sin.

He sweat blood that we might inherit eternal life.

He died that we might live.

A dozen reviving pulses throbbed all through Dave's body. Color brushed his cheeks. All the smoldering embers of past victories suddenly burst into glowing, animated flames, transforming apprehension into deliverance. He wanted to laugh, shout, leap. He lifted his head, and with eyes clear and sparkling scanned the faces of the fifty students seated at tables. For the first time since he arrived on the campus David Grant felt he could face any one of them, with freedom from that secret, tormenting abashment. How glad he was he hadn't raised the question in class! No one need ever guess his unrevealed tensions. He closed his notebook and with quiet confidence walked out of the library.

In his room he looked up the references. There it was, plain as daylight. True as truth. Words of freedom, happy, unfettering.

"O God, why have I let this bother me? I'm sorry. I want you to forgive me."

The release put new stimulus in everything Dave undertook. It was no longer a pretense to live up to Sister Lora's code of behavior. He played, he sang, he studied, he prayed, he laughed with spontaneous enthusiasm. With bright countenance he moved among his classmates and without hesitancy took part in the Sunday-school discussions.

A happy tear trickled down her face when Rose opened the hand-painted Mother's Day greeting.

> For each mile between us
> > This greeting has brought
> An affectionate wish
> > And a warm, loving thought.
> A wish for much happiness
> > Always for you,
> And thoughts of how dear you are
> > All the year through.
> > > David.

"I'll never part with it," she said to Aaron.

Dear Dug,

School will be out in three weeks. What are you going to be doing this summer? I applied for a job at the Lancaster Airport and what do you know? Yes. I start working in the hangar June 12. My answer came yesterday. I wrote to Dad to be looking out for a good, inexpensive used car for me. He said he'd help me get one if I needed it. Can you imagine how excited I am?

I've enjoyed my year here very much, but I'm thinking of going to Philadelphia next year. I still think I'd like to be some kind of a mechanic. I wouldn't mind being a radio technician. Guess we get our education first, don't we?

Mother wrote they got a record player and twenty records. That's only one reason why I'm anxious to get home. Ha. Dad and Mother plan to come for me. If you don't have time to answer, I'll understand. Be seeing you soon.

Dave.

Much too quickly the summer months passed. Dave enjoyed his job at the airport even more than the six-mile jaunts in his 1925 Essex Coupé. The thrill of watching those planes take off and return would never diminish. He swept, he dusted, he oiled and polished; he even worked overtime with hearty satisfaction. Wasn't he part of an elaborate organization of national significance? Perhaps someday he'd learn to manipulate one of those powerful engines. Perhaps someday he'd fly one high above the mountains.

"Dave," remarked Mother one morning, "I think your voice has dropped another step overnight."

He broke his bread and smiled with his whole face.

"And I've lengthened those trousers you have on to the limit."

"I noticed. And my Sunday coat sleeves are an inch too short. But otherwise it's still a good suit."

"Maybe one of the Wingard boys could wear it. You'd better get a new suit. Do you want to pick out your own clothes from now on?"

"Mother," exclaimed Dave, with sudden surprise. "Now I think you're overestimating my ability, if you think I could do that." There was a glint in his brown eyes, however. "What do

I know about quality and prices and all that? Don't you want to go with me any more? Perhaps by another year."

"Sure I'll go with you if you want me to. You say when it will suit you. Tomorrow evening after work?"

"All right."

Rose stood at the screen door humming a gay little tune as she watched Dave dash to his car and drive away.

"A penny for your thoughts." Aaron slipped up behind her and placed a hand on her left shoulder.

"Well," she said, "I was thinking—what you'll have to agree is the truth—that that boy is on the verge of being a very handsome young man."

Aaron chuckled softly. "And we can't claim any of the credit. Wonder if he favors his mother?"

"Have you noticed his hair? It's getting prettier every day."

"You notice everything." He pulled her ear teasingly. "But listen now, do you actually expect that boy, at eighteen, to go to town and select his own clothes?"

"Well, I just wanted to hear his reaction," replied Rose. "As long as he requests my assistance on such matters I know he's still an adolescent. But I'm thinking he won't be for long. I wonder if he's thought much about dating?"

"What don't you think of, Mother Loomas?"

"Sh, now." She brushed his hand off her shoulder. "I have work to do and so do you. Here's a list of things I want you to get at the market."

"Dad," said Dave after church Sunday evening, "Max Fielder and I want to talk to you before we go home."

"Good evening, Max. What's on your mind?"

"It's this, Mr. Loomas. I'm driving out to California week after next, and I have room for another passenger."

"Of course you mean me, don't you?" winked Aaron.

"Well," laughed Max, "I guess we could squeeze you in too, but I really had Dave in mind."

"Why are you going?"

253

"I've been wanting to take a trip west for several years. Now that I'm twenty-one and have my own car, the folks don't object. I have an uncle who has a cattle ranch at Sky Fork. I haven't seen him for twelve years."

"Who else is going along?"

"My brother Tim, and a cousin of ours, Elsie Fielder."

"How old is she?"

"Nineteen. She works in Washington, D.C., and is getting her vacation. We'd be back in three weeks."

"What about your job, Dave?"

"I'd just quit if you'd say I could go along. I'll be quitting anyhow about the time he'll get back to get ready for school."

"You really want to go along?"

"More than anything I can think of, Dad."

"Well, I'll admit," said Aaron, rubbing the back of his neck, "I'd sooner have you go with an older boy like Max here than for you and Dug to start out."

"Dug and I? We aren't planning such a trip."

"Well, good. I remember what you said when you came home from Philadelphia last summer."

"Oh," laughed Dave, "I was just talking that night."

"About how much would this cost him, Max?"

"Not too much, Mr. Loomas. Elsie and I are going to split the car expense. Tim suggested taking Dave along for company, and I thought it was a good idea. We won't be eating often in restaurants. That would soon count up more than the gas. Mother and Elsie are going to make up a box of eats that won't spoil. Of course he ought to have some money on him. We'll have to pay for lodging. We three boys could bunk together and split the cost. We won't stay in any fancy hotels."

"Well, I tell you, we'll go home, Dave, and talk this over with Mother. Huh? We'll let you know, Max."

"All right, Mr. Loomas. Let me know as soon as possible. If he doesn't go along, we'll find someone else. But don't broadcast this. I'm sorta choosy who I take."

"Dave," said Aaron on the way to the car, "I appreciate this that you didn't decide to go along, then tell us."

"Why, Dad, I—I wouldn't think of doing like that."

"Some boys your age would," remarked Aaron. "That's why I say I appreciate your asking first. Well, Mother dear, did you think we were never coming?"

"No," answered Rose. "It's a pleasant evening and I didn't mind waiting. Looked to me like you three were on an interesting topic."

"I'm sure Dave thinks it's interesting. Here's the key. You drive us home. I'll sit in back with Mother and we'll begin sizing up the situation from her viewpoint."

Dave didn't wait until morning to call. "Max, you reserve that space for me. They say I may go if my boss lets me off."

"Good. We'll leave early on the eleventh. I know Tim is tickled. He's smiling from ear to ear."

"Mother said she'd fix a box of eats too."

"Then I'm sure we won't starve on the way out," laughed Max.

Rose Loomas and Mrs. Fielder shared post-card news items by telephone.

"Sounds like they're having a grand time in spite of rain and heat. Our card today came from Topeka, Kansas."

"Ours was mailed in Kansas City. Dave says, *Everything O.K. Feeling fine. Interesting sights, wonderful trip. Thanks for letting me come along. Max and Tim are nice to be with.*"

"Tim wrote this one. He says, *Made 385 miles yesterday. Almost halfway there. Sure glad Dave is along. Elsie doesn't talk much. She sits in front with Max. Dave and I in back. She bought an ice-cold watermelon. Delicious.*

"What kind of a girl is Elsie?"

"She's my sister Clara's oldest daughter. Very nice. Somewhat reserved. She's not the kind to rattle off just to be talking. I suppose she doesn't feel it's necessary to talk much with three boys in the car," she laughed. "I doubt if we would have been very eager to see the boys go out to Uncle Herman's if Elsie hadn't gone along."

"Why?"

"Oh, Herman's a pretty rough sort. He's my oldest brother. Sorry to say it, but he hardly seems like one of the family any more. He left home when he was eighteen. Went out west and got interested in cowpunching. He soon lost what little religion he did have. He's made a lot of money. Bought a ranch, and I'd say he worships his cattle."

"How about his wife?"

"He's not married. I don't think he ever will be. We were out to see him twelve years ago. Took my father along. He came home heartbroken. Maybe Herman has changed. I hope so."

"Will he welcome the boys? And David?"

"Of course, Rose. He'll be kind enough to them. Don't worry about that. He'll show them a good time. He took a special liking to Max. Took him all over the ranch on a pony. Max was nine then, but he's never forgotten it."

"Has Elsie been out there before?"

"No. But I figure, with her along, Herman will soft-pedal his talk a little. Maybe I shouldn't have told you this. You'll not worry now, will you?"

"No, Mrs. Fielder. But I'm glad I know this. They're probably there by now."

Max hadn't said a dozen words about Uncle Herman on the entire trip. "This must be the place," he announced, as he turned in the long lane marked "Circle A Ranch," south of Sky Fork.

"I hope he has plenty on hand to make us supper," suggested Tim.

"Well, I just hope he got Mother's letter that we're coming," added Max. "And I hope he's not quite as bad as I've been warned he is."

"What kind of a person is he?" asked Dave.

"We'll soon find out. I've almost forgotten how he looks."

256

"My mother says he's a faithless old bachelor," said Elsie. "I don't know what to expect."

He saw them coming and hurried to the gate to meet them. Herman was a stocky, large-boned, chesty man with piercing dark eyes awned with heavy eyebrows.

"Hi," he shouted lustily, raising one hairy arm high. "I see you've got a Pennsylvania license plate; so I reckon you're the Fielders."

"I'm Max, Uncle Herman."

"Can't be."

"This is Elsie."

"Clara's girl?" He let out an oath. "Sorry," he said, clapping his hand over his mouth. "I'm not used to having ladies around."

"That's Tim."

"Naw. Can't be."

"And our friend David Grant."

"Good evening," said Dave. "I hope my being here won't inconvenience you."

"Well, now," said the man, jutting out his chesty chest, "I don't allow saint or sinner to inconvenience me. Mark that down." He laughed boisterously. "Pull your car up beside the house, Max, and all of you come on in. Elsie, you look enough like your mother that I'm going to be real bossy an' tell you what to do."

"I'll be glad to help you with supper or anything, Uncle Herman."

He did have a well-stocked pantry. Not with delicacies, but with potatoes, eggs, canned pork and beans, pickles, hominy, peanut butter, and jams. And on a wire from the ceiling hung a large country-cured ham.

The four-room house was soon saturated with the delicious odor of potatoes and meat frying. The kitchen table was not set with fancy dishes. In fact, no two were alike. But with mouth-watering eagerness the boys seated themselves to Uncle Herman's steaming and bountiful supper.

"Hot food will surely taste good again," beamed Elsie. She

bowed her head. The three boys bowed their heads likewise.

A moment of silence.

"Now what's this?" remarked Herman, tapping his knife against his water glass. "Pass the food and cut out such tomfoolery." He picked up the meat platter and helped himself, then thrust it at Elsie.

Dave glanced at Elsie. Elsie glanced at Max.

"It's not tomfoolery to thank God for this delicious supper, Uncle Herman," ventured Elsie. "We always pray at home before we eat."

"Maybe you do," he said, knitting his bushy eyebrows, "but under my roof you don't need to bother." He helped himself to the bread and handed the plate to Max. "Understand," he said. "I allow no one [he looked straight at Dave seated opposite him] to inconvenience me."

Dave winced.

CHAPTER 30

For a moment the four sat almost paralyzed. The only sound that broke the embarrassing quiet was Herman masticating his food.

"Eat," he shouted, pointing his fork at Max. "I was good enough to furnish it for you." He gulped water, then glanced at Elsie again. "Thank me, young lady, if you feel you must thank someone. But I don't go for any of that simple-minded pious stuff."

Tim could resist no longer. He started in. They all did eat. The food was, without question, exceptionally delicious. The boys took second helpings. Herman asked Max a few ordinary questions about the trip, which he answered without elaboration. He seemed afraid or unable to launch a relaxing conversation.

The tenseness during the meal was uncomfortable, to say the least. Dave chewed the man, he swallowed the man, he drank the man seated across from him. It made a great knot in the pit of his stomach.

He squirmed with uneasiness. If Max wasn't going to speak to his own uncle, someone should. He took a drink. He bit the inside of his lip.

"May I—" he faltered. "May I ask you a question, sir?"

"Certainly," answered Herman. "Ask me anything."

"Well, I would like to know, did you never pray in all your life?"

Almost mockingly he laughed. "I did when I was a kid and was told to. But it didn't do any more good than when I said 'Ring-Around-a-Rosy' or 'Little Boy Blue.' "

"You think God never heard a single prayer you ever prayed?" Dave was surprised at his own words. He tingled all over. The knot in his stomach loosened a trifle.

"He did not. And what's more, He never heard any of your prayers either."

"But I'm certain He did," replied Dave, sitting on the edge of his chair.

"You imagine He did," returned Herman, jaws twitching. "That's all baloney. Fairy-story stuff they teach little kids in Sunday school. I remember. Bash all that stuff."

"What do you believe?" asked Dave.

"I believe there is no God. That's my belief."

"Uncle Herman," gasped Elsie. "You can't really mean that."

"Yes, I do," he said emphatically. "You can't prove there is a God. Not one of you can." He pointed his finger at Max. "You say there's a God? You're the oldest here."

"Of course there's a God, Uncle Herman."

"If there is, where does He keep Himself? He certainly never spent any time looking after me. All I have I've worked for. I've earned it with these two hands and by the sweat of my own brow. You—" he said, getting up and pointing at Dave across the table. "You name one thing God has ever done for you."

"Why, He's done lots of things for me. More than I could mention, I suppose."

"See, you're not quite sure. You suppose. I dare say you've prayed many a prayer He didn't answer. Isn't that so?"

Dave was sure his face was getting red. The letter he mailed to Mrs. Shana Grant years before. It hung tantalizingly in front of him. The fruitless trip to Philadelphia. It also flashed before him with disagreeable, sickening freshness. He began to feel a little dizzy.

Herman was leaning over the table riveting Dave, ridiculing

him, with those grueling dark eyes. "See," he grinned triumphantly, "you admit you only imagined some prayers were answered, don't you? Well, all the other times you think your prayers were answered, things would have happened just as they did without your praying."

"I beg your pardon," objected Dave. "I did not admit that. I'm just trying to think."

"But you're not sure. If you were, you wouldn't need time to think. What are you sure of?"

Dave studied his empty plate. Dad, evolution, Mother, Lora, the recent letter from Jonathan Young, all spun through his mind in a split second. "I'm sure there's a God, sir," he said, looking up, "even though I don't understand all His ways."

"No, you're not sure of it. You prove to me there's a God. You can't."

Dave got to his feet. He squared his shoulders and looked the man full in the face unflinchingly. "I'd like to challenge you to prove there *isn't* a God," he said. "I don't see that He needs to be proved. God is God and therefore He cannot lie about Himself."

"That doesn't prove anything," laughed Herman. "Come, let's clear this table. Elsie, over there is the dishpan. Guess you know what they're used for."

"Of course I do."

"I have chores to do. You boys can go along out with me, providing you stay off the subject of religion. I don't want to hear another word about it."

"We'll help Elsie with the dishes first," answered Max.

"Listen, Max," began Elsie, "did you know he'd be like this?"

"Mother reminded me he was an unbeliever and rough, but I never supposed he'd talk up like this. I felt awful. How about you, Dave? I'm glad for what you said. You see, he feels beaten and doesn't want to hear any more."

"I'm not so sure he feels beaten," differed Dave. "He may think we're beaten."

"Well, what are we going to do at breakfast?" asked Elsie. "Go ahead and eat without giving thanks?"

"I don't want a fuss over saying a little table prayer," put in Tim. "After all, this is his house. He just almost scared me."

"Is that the way you feel about it, Dave?" asked Elsie.

"No. He did shock me, I'll admit. And it wasn't the most pleasant experience, but he didn't scare me. And I don't think we ought to let him think he did."

"Neither do I," agreed Max. "But what shall we do? We've got to agree and all do the same thing."

"Well, as far as I'm concerned," said Elsie, "I bow my head before I eat in Uncle Herman's house or any place else. Look, we came all the way out here without a bit of trouble. And I think it's because we prayed and our parents back home did too. Remember those two narrow escapes we had? We could all have been killed. Now if we put God on the shelf while we're here, just because *he* says we should—well, I'll go back home on the train."

"Elsie," exclaimed Max. "You don't mean that. Go back on the train?"

"I certainly do mean just that."

"Elsie has a point," put in Dave. "There's a verse somewhere that says if we're ashamed of God, He'll be ashamed of us."

"Yes, you're right," admitted Max. "We'll all bow our heads in silent prayer. You too, Tim. And if Uncle Herman objects, we strike out tomorrow after breakfast."

Out by the barn Herman showed quite a different personality. In spite of his frequent profanity, he was friendly, talkative, even jovial.

"This isn't the pony I rode twelve years ago, is it, Uncle Herman?"

"Goodness no, Max. I've had Goldie there only two years. Take her out and try her. There's Dock and Dol. One for each of you guys, if you care to ride around. I won't guarantee they won't show off, you being strangers. Maybe, after all, I'd better take the lead on Dock, if one of you won't mind waiting. I don't want any broken bones out here."

"I'll wait," offered Dave.

"Now I've got only two beds in my house," Herman explained on the way back to the house.

"Give one to Elsie," said Max. "And you keep your own bed. We three boys can sleep on the floor."

"Or in the barn," suggested Dave. "Which would cause you the least trouble?"

"I'll give you each a blanket and you can make your own beds wherever you want to. We eat breakfast at six and no later."

The boys were on hand before six. Elsie had prepared a platter of bacon and eggs and a bowl of hot cereal, by order of Uncle Herman.

All four bowed their heads.

"Okay, okay," panted Herman, in a tone of agitation. "Go ahead and pray to your make-believe God if you want to. But I say it's downright ridiculous." His countenance was surly, and his lower lip quivered.

They ate in awkward, self-conscious silence, each honorably preferring the other to break it.

At length Dave made his voice heard. "This has been a very good breakfast, Herman." And the other three gave their "yes, yes."

Dear Mother and Dad,

I hope you got all the post cards I mailed on our way out. I hope this reaches you before I get back. We may cut our visit here at the ranch short. This Uncle Herman is a very busy man and Max sorta feels we're in his way, and Elsie wants to start back. We've seen lots of country and all kinds of houses and people and there's no place like home. We may come back by a southern route, even see a little of Texas. I hope everything has been going well for you while I've been away. It seems like a month since we left. I guess that's because I haven't heard from you. I think we all appreciate, more than ever before, what our homes mean to

263

us after being gone like this. It's different from being away in school.

Dad, just how would you go about it to try to prove to an atheist there is a God?

Don't worry about us. We're all just fine.

Lots of love,
Dave

"We're going to keep that one too," said Rose after Aaron finished reading it. "There must have been a special reason why I woke up so early one morning and felt an urge to pray for that boy."

Three days later Dave walked in, suntanned, dusty, and tired. "Hi, Mother." He caught her in his arms and kissed her. "Where's Dad?"

"He just left for the store to get milk. Maybe I'd better call and tell him to bring extra. Oh, Dave, it's so good to see you safe and sound. You'll have interesting things to tell us, I'm sure."

"Lots of things. Whew." He stretched. "Am I glad to be home. I want to take a bath and get into clean clothes and just relax and listen to all those new records. I mean after we get through eating and talking. Is Dug at home?"

"He went with his folks to Chicago."

"Good. Then I can relax tonight."

As Dave lay on the sofa enjoying the music, he found himself comparing and contrasting Aaron with the godless California rancher. Dad's face, perhaps not the most handsome in the world, but the gentlest, the most peaceful, the most genuinely sincere he had ever seen. With eyes almost closed he studied that face. Never had he seen it offensive with anger. Not once had he heard those lips speak harsh or crusty words or use profanity in any form. What sordid imaginations, what haunting emptiness would have to govern the life of a man who did not believe what Dad believed about God.

The Roger Wagner Chorale was the next record Mother put on. It reminded Dave of one of the songs he helped to sing in A Cappella Choir in college. He put his hands behind his head and gazed at the ceiling. Why was he on this sofa, in this home with these gentle, believing people, enjoying this beautiful music? Why?

Why did they choose him? Why did they love him, and seem to take special delight in doing things to please him and make him happy?

Is that why they got the record player? Did they love Dennis and Janet as much as they did him? They didn't have to love him. His thoughts took a sudden turn. Didn't his mother ever love him? Ever care for him at all? Or his father? Was he an atheist? Was it God or the devil or fatalism that kept him in this state of ignorance? Didn't he have a right to wonder? A right to ask? A right to know? He sat up.

"What's the name of that record, Mother?"

"It's Bach's *Magnificat*. We got it while you were gone. I hope you'll like it."

"I'll see." He lay down again. The music sent him drifting into a sort of wild romantic dream of someday discovering his attachments in this strange mystery of life. Into the cloud of his dream laboratory questions and imaginations floated faster than he could classify them. He must. But how? He would. But when? He will. But where, and when, and how? You can't know what you can't know.

But the majestic music was doing something new and strange to him. He had never before heard such a rare and rich combination of beautiful melodies and beautiful words.

For He that is mighty hath done great things to me
  And Holy is His name.
His mercy is from generation to generation
  To them that fear Him.
He hath shown strength in His arm,
He hath scattered the proud and exalted the humble.
Glory be to the Father and to the Son and to the Holy Ghost
As it was in the beginning, is now,
  And ever shall be, world without end, Amen.
For some inexplicable reason the unfairness, the injustice,

the long-standing frustrations about himself began to fade as he absorbed the profoundly moving music. It stirred the deepest soul-feelings of his manhood. "In the beginning [my past], is now [my present], and ever shall be [my future]." If someone did give him away over eighteen years ago, surely God had not— He who was part of his past, his present, his forever. That must mean every longing, every heartache, every disappointment had never been his alone, but God's. With his eyes closed, Dave viewed his entire existence.

Little did Rose or Aaron Loomas imagine the emotional experience going on in the mind of that fast-growing, relaxed boy on their sofa.

A keen appreciation for good music grew on Dave as he matured. He refused to listen to anything but the best on his radio, and Rose and Aaron were pleased with the observation. Every free moment Dave had, he spent hovering near the record player, often with a book or magazine in one hand.

In June Aaron purchased a house next door to Lesa and Clif in Lititz, and they moved in July.

By September Dave and Dug were rooming in the same college dormitory in Philadelphia. His most enjoyable extra-curricular activity was participation in the college choir. Basketball, soccer, volleyball—these rated second preference. He attended all the musical events of the school season on the campus and an occasional concert in the city.

During the following summer months he worked at the Hamilton Watch Company, saving every cent he could toward another year of education. What he lacked Dad agreed to supplement.

It was near the end of the next school year when he noticed an announcement in the *Philadelphia Times* of a double-feature concert to be given in the Civic Music Center.

"Dug," he said, "I surely want to go hear this concert coming up Saturday night. The sixty-four-voice Concordia Seminary Chorus and the sixty-two-voice Teacher's College Choir will give a four-part joint concert featuring men's and ladies' quartets,

266

solos, and climaxed with a group of Johann Sebastian Bach's most loved chorales by the double choir. Let's go."

"Let's do," agreed Dug. "Let's take dates this time."

"You go ahead and date if you want to. I'm not ready for that."

"Oh, come on, Dave. There's plenty of nice girls floating around this place."

"None for me, Dug. You go ahead with a date if you want one. You're under no obligation to deprive yourself of a girl friend just because I prefer not to have one."

"Well, haven't you seen one single girl here in two years you'd like to go with?"

"I haven't paid that much attention to any of them."

"Well, when are you going to start looking around?"

Dave pretended to be reading the paper.

"I asked you a question."

"Oh, I beg your pardon. What's the question?"

"You heard me, Dave. If you can't pick yourself a date for Saturday night, let me do it for you."

"Nothing doing, Dug. When I get ready, I'll pick my own date."

"All right, all right, if you're so positive about it," laughed Dug, slapping Dave on the shoulder. "I may just let you go alone this time."

"And you won't offend me one bit, Dug. I know the way very well by now."

Dug chuckled.

"What's funny?" asked Dave.

"Remember that hot July day when—"

Dave pressed a finger on each ear and shook his head. "Don't bring that up. Please. I've wished many a time I could forget that day."

"I'm sorry."

Dave went early to get a front balcony seat. The program more than thrilled him. Between parts two and three several of the choir members gave short talks about their personal ambitions for postgraduate work. Several were preparing to enter the teaching profession, two expected foreign missionary assignments, and three were studying for the ministry. After the intermission the Dean of the Theological Seminary spoke.

"Friends," he said. "It is my great pleasure to meet you tonight in company with these two singing groups of students who represent one hundred and twenty-six lives dedicated to the express purpose of spreading peace and good will throughout the world. The mixed group are all in teacher training and will soon be in charge of helping direct young lives in the classrooms. There never has been a time in the history of our nation when the need for dedicated schoolteachers was as great as it is today. This need is not only in our high schools and colleges, but in our elementary schools as well.

"This group of young men represent some of our future ministers. It is our sole purpose to acquaint and inspire our audiences with the church's rich heritage of musical gems which express Christianity's greatest truths in such an incomparable manner. No single voice, and no group of voices with ever so much artistic ability, could ever attain a perfect interpretation of these truths. But we earnestly hope our goal is reached in helping you to a better understanding and a deeper appreciation of these sacred musical treasures. These young men and women are expressing their own convictions in song, and we trust the conviction of many of you also. We hope you young people here tonight will be inspired to devote your days and energies and talents, not merely to accumulating wealth which soon fades away, but to the greatest of all professions, spreading the joy of God's free grace in Christ, of whose love these groups so richly sing. I thank you."

Dave's eyes followed the speaker until he seemed to melt into the green velvet stage curtains. Then a sudden awareness of tiny needles swept over him. He could feel his heartbeat pulsing in his neck. He saw himself back in the church basement the night he stood. He felt the warm pressure of the evangelist's two hands clasped over his and he heard distinctly his sincere but modified tone, "He knows how you feel. God bless you, my boy. I believe He has big things planned for you. And because of your experiences, you may be able to help hundreds, maybe thousands of other boys someday, girls too. Who knows?"

"Who knows?"

Help other boys and girls?

Because of my experiences?

Understand a lonely, frustrated, unclaimed somebody like myself?

There's a need? A purpose? A place—for me?

For me?

Dave scarcely moved during the finale.

CHAPTER 31

June, and Dave was back at the Hamilton Watch Company working on the assembly line.

"What are these things we're sending through?" he asked the man at his right.

"Don't ask questions and I tell no lies. What's the difference what we're making, so long as we get our checks? I think," he said in a padded undertone, and with one quick wink, "these don't go into watches, eh? They may go to some place like England. But you ask me no questions."

Nor did he. Dave's thoughts were occupied with other questions. Questions of greater import. For weeks, in fancy, he saw above the edge of his worktable a young lad's face, perplexed and anxious, looking up into his with searching, brown eyes. The face strikingly and ironically resembled his own at a much earlier age.

What do you want, my boy? Something special on your mind? You cannot tell? You will not tell? Not even me? You don't want anyone to guess? You're lonely? Confused? Afraid? Afraid of what? You too? No mother? No grandmother? No brother? I know how you feel. I understand. Oh, yes, I do. You wouldn't have guessed? That's because I've learned to hide my feelings. How? I've been doing it for a long, long time. For as long as I can remember. You're trying to? It's not always easy. What first frightened you? I see. Mine was a stairway. Long and high. And a black bed. What trifling fears, my boy! If only you had a Janet, or one like her. They come into a boy's life only once in a hundred years or so. Or foster parents like Mamma and Papa Loomas. Poor child. There should be a million, I know.

Sometimes in his fancy the lad's face resembled Hugh, sometimes Dug, sometimes a face he had never seen. Sometimes he found himself soliloquizing to a dozen or more imaginary children, playing ball with them—jumping, racing, winning, laughing.

"Dad," said Dave one Sunday evening just home from church. "I'd like to talk with you and Mother about something."

"All right. Let's take our pie and ice cream and sit in the living room. I believe it's a little cooler in there. Shall we have some music while we talk?"

"Let's do," answered Dave. "You sit down. I'll put something on we all like. Now," he began, turning the volume on low. "I hope you two won't think I'm forever changing my mind about schools, but I'd sorta like to go to Elizabethtown College this fall."

"I noticed you were talking with Stanley and Leon for quite a while. Did you just come to this decision tonight?"

"No, Dad. I've been thinking about this for about eight weeks. I'd like to get ready to do something worth while. I mean something with human beings, like teaching school. Even if it was in a small country school to begin with, I think I'd enjoy teaching a lot more than spending my time and energies on machinery. I thought I'd mention this to you and see what you'd have to say."

"Well," replied Aaron, thinkingly, "I'd say you could make a lots worse choice than that. I've thought more than once there ought to be more men with real convictions and high standards behind our public school desks."

"I think you'd make a good teacher," commented Rose.

"Don't brag on me, Mother," blushed Dave. "I'd have an awful lot to learn."

271

"But I think you'd be kind and sympathetic and understanding. It takes all of that besides a degree to be a good teacher."

"Well, I doubt if I'd have all those qualifications, Mother," remarked Dave, turning the record, "but I'd try—that is, if I'd make the grade. I have a big notion to drive over to Elizabethtown next Saturday afternoon and get one of their catalogs."

He had left the Hamilton parking lot and was headed toward home when he suddenly remembered the pair of trousers he had purchased at Yorges the week before and left for cuffing. It wouldn't take long to go back to Lancaster and get them. At the corner of Second and Jefferson his Essex and a vegetable truck struck fenders. One basket of carrots fell into the street.

The vexed driver of the truck got out faster than Dave did. "What do you think you're doing?" he demanded.

"I'm not sure whether I hit you or you hit me, sir," said Dave.

"Well, you hit me. I had the right of way. Look, you dented my fender, and you'll pay for it."

"My fender is dented too," observed Dave. "I'm glad neither of us was going faster than we were. It could have been a lot worse. You say you had the right of way? Are you sure, mister?"

"Well," puffed the man, gathering up the carrots, "we'll stay right here until a cop comes and we'll ask him."

Before a cop did come along, a small crowd had gathered.

"Give the old duff the works," one man said to Dave over his shoulder. "His old rattletrap's only junk anyhow. I know him. He'll get every cent he can out of you. You gotta be tough with him."

"I want to treat him fair," answered Dave, "but I'm almost certain he hit me."

"You can see he did, boy. Look, yours is bent worse."

"You'll pay for this," declared the trucker again, stepping close to Dave. "Look," he said. "You give me forty dollars and I'll let you go. I'm losing time here."

"I haven't forty dollars on me, sir. And I'm not sure it would cost you that much to straighten your fender. I think I

272

could do it for you myself."

"Not on your life, young man. That goes to a body shop."

Several onlookers laughed outright and the man's indignation mounted.

A motorcycle policeman soon came and viewed the mishap, asked questions, took a few notes, and said, "As far as I can see, you are equally to blame and my suggestion is you each pay your own damages. So please move your vehicles right away."

The policeman left.

"No, you won't get by that easy," scowled the trucker. "You will pay my bill or else. You know you hit me. Don't you have insurance?"

"No, I haven't."

"This ought to teach you a lesson then. Give me your name and address."

"Very well. I'm David Grant, and I live in Lititz. Now give me yours."

"Thad Tapperoli, and I live on West Baker Road. Now what you going to do?"

"I'm going to treat you right, Mr. Tapperoli. This is my first experience of this kind and I'll get some advice."

"Pshaw," said a man over his shoulder. "Go by what the cop said and forget it. I tell you, that guy's an old skinflint."

Dave got into his car and drove away. He picked up his trousers, and directly across the street from Yorges he noticed the gold-lettered sign on the window:

R. T. Dillon, Attorney
Notary Public
D. A. Cornelius, Realtor

He crossed the street. Perhaps it was unnecessary, even uncalled for, but he'd feel better if he got some legal advice.

"May I help you, sir?" The young lady at the typewriter turned on her swivel chair.

"Is Mr. Dillon busy?" asked Dave.

"Mr. Dillon just stepped out for a cup of coffee, sir. He should be back any minute. Won't you have a seat?"

"Thank you."

"Did you have an appointment? I can't recall your name if you did." She got up and glanced down the list of names on the open appointment book.

"No," said Dave. "I didn't have an appointment. Must I in order to see him?"

"Not always," she answered pleasantly. "If it's a matter that won't take long, he may be able to work you in before one o'clock."

"It won't take long, I'm sure. I just had a slight accident and I want a little advice."

"I see." She smiled ever so faintly.

From the chair he chose, Dave, without staring or seeming rude, could easily observe her, busy at her typewriter. There was something refined and graceful and unordinary about the young lady that held his attention. What was it? She had a kind of womanly charm or sweet sincerity he had never particularly noticed in any other girl. He could not quite define it. She had a natural, delicate beauty that seemed to radiate, without effort, from within.

Dave squared his shoulders. For the first time in his life he felt a sudden desire for the acquaintance of a woman. Perhaps it had been there lying dormant, and he did not realize it until now. A distinctly new feeling possessed him. For a moment he forgot why he was there.

She looked up. Their eyes met.

"That is Mr. Dillon coming now," she said. "Mr. Dillon, this man wants to see you for a few minutes."

He glanced at his watch. "Step into my office," said the man.

In less than fifteen minutes the door opened and Dave stepped out.

"Pay the lady at the desk," explained Attorney Dillon. "Janet, give Mr. Grant a receipt for two-fifty."

Janet?

Dave's heart stood still for a beat. What a combination! Grace and charm and a name that had spelled warmth and love and comfort over the years. Janet? Gentle, protecting, thought-ful, playful, sweet.

"Grant?" she asked.

"Yes. David Grant." He noticed her eyes were a soft warm blue and there was something unpretentious about her manner. He watched her write the receipt and below R. T. Dillon's name she wrote her initials, J. W.

Much as he wondered what her last name was, would he dare ask? Emphatically, no. What an absurd thing to be wondering about! All the way home Dave reprimanded himself for such sheer foolishness. The girl was probably engaged. Or even married.

He related the reason for his lateness, ate a quickly re-warmed dinner, and started toward Elizabethtown. It was the last Saturday in July, a most beautiful summer afternoon to be taking a drive through the farmers' flourishing paradise, past fields of mature tall corn, ripening grains, carefully cultivated white-fenced gardens, melon patches, and apple orchards. Wild flowers and new-mown hay scented the balmy air. Contented cattle were grazing in green grassy pastures, and sheep were drinking from still mirrors of water or happily nibbling close by. All the serenities and splendors of full-grown summer seemed to be kissing the earth with power, with plenty, with peace.

For some strange reason Dave found himself taking par-ticular notice of these beauties of nature on either side, as he drove up and over the rolling hills. Something quite apart from himself was magnifying beauties in the simplest things: a lawn swing, a garden gate, a bed of yellow daisies a little girl playing with a collie, the old-fashioned, unpainted covered bridge he drove through. There was music in his car motor. A forceful something, a deep inner urge like nothing he had ever felt before, was demanding him to be nothing less than the best man possible.

With quick steps and motives fixed, he walked toward the registrar's office.

Dug acted somewhat disappointed when he first learned Dave would not be going back to Philadelphia, but he had to admit (when Dave put it to him) that friends of the fairer sex would most likely be occupying a good deal of his thoughts and attention during the coming school year.

Love of music had become so much a part of him that it was not long until Dave was a member of the tenor section of the East Petersburg Community A Cappella Choir. Each rehearsal was a pleasant and relaxing deviation from the mounting study requirements made by the professors.

"Say, Joe," began Dave to a favorite classmate who also sang in the choir. "I have an idea floating around in my head."

"Let's hear it."

"It's this. I wish we could form a smaller singing group, say a double octet, and practice all sacred numbers; and maybe get good enough to sing someplace. Perhaps at Christmas or Easter time, give a program in a home for the aged or at a children's home or—well, maybe in a small church if a big one wouldn't want us."

Joe did a quick tossing with the idea before he spoke. "Why not? I hadn't thought of such a thing, but why not? I'd be ready to help. You mean you'd do this on your own without consulting our director?"

"Well, hardly. We ought to ask him, out of courtesy, what he'd think of the idea."

"He might suggest that you be the director."

"I could hardly do that," answered Dave. "But do you suppose there would be eight girls and six other fellows beside you and me in our big chorus who'd be interested in such a project?"

"Surely in a group of fifty there ought to be. I'm quite certain if this idea of yours materializes we'll get at least one invitation to give a program."

"Where's that?"

"In my church in Manheim."

"Why are you so sure? Is your father on the official board of directors?"

"Well, he's a trustee," grinned Joe, "but more than that, my

276

fiancee is on the Sunday evening program committee."

"Happy day," exclaimed Dave, gripping Joe's arm, "and congratulations. So that's why you like to run home weekends?"

"That's the biggest why," nodded Joe, smiling. "And it's a happy situation you can't appreciate unless you're involved in it yourself. Ever been involved?"

"Me?" chuckled Dave. "No. I'm not involved in anything of that sort."

"Yet," added Joe teasingly.

With eagerness Rose and Aaron looked forward to weekends when Dave would be at home. Invariably he'd have his favorite records playing while he plowed through pages of outside reading. At the table, news items of common interest were exchanged.

"I had a letter from Leon at Eastern Mennonite College this week."

"Does he like it out there?"

"I guess he does, Dad. He says he has a girl friend. I can hardly imagine it."

"Why not? He's older than you, isn't he?"

"Even so, I can't imagine Leon being serious with a girl."

"Just because he goes out with a girl isn't saying he's serious about her," suggested Rose.

Dave took a drink. "Well," he said, "he wrote as though it's more than a passing fancy."

"By the way," said Aaron, "that man—I can't say his name right now—the man you had that accident with last summer, stopped here last week."

"What did he want?"

"He wanted to collect ten dollars from you."

"What did you tell him?

"I told you consulted a lawyer and he said since neither of you had insurance and since the policeman said you were equally at fault for what happened, you owed him no money."

"Then what?"

"He wanted to know the name of the lawyer you talked to

and when I said Dillon, that was it. He left without another word. I smelled liquor on him, but he walked fairly straight."

"Well, thanks, Dad. I'm really glad I stopped in to see a lawyer, because I wanted to treat him right. Evidently Mr. Dillon knows him well. I wonder why he waited this long to come to see me."

"He was probably desperate for money to buy more booze."

Two weeks later the sixteen "Melodians" sang in the corridor of the Lancaster City Jail. Crouched on a cot in the corner of one of the cells, with head hanging low, was a man who glanced up but once. Dave was almost certain it was Thad Tapperoli. He lingered after the rest of the group walked out and called to the man. If he heard, he made no response.

Dear Mother and Dad,

On Sunday evening, May 4, our little choir will be giving a program at 7:30 at the East Fairview Church of the Brethren in Manheim. Why don't you drive over? Maybe Clif and Lesa would come along. I'd like my friend, Joe Hanson, and all the others in our group to meet you.

"Well," smiled Rose, "that boy must—"

"Must what?"

"Must either think quite a bit of us or hopes we do of him. We'll go, won't we?"

"Go? You bet we will. Call Lesa right away."

What a blossom-bursting day was the fourth of May! The church was filled to capacity. Dave spotted his folks with Clifs at once.

"After two opening numbers by this singing group," announced the minister in charge, "David Grant will read a Scripture portion and offer prayer. Joe Hanson will then introduce the Melodians and be in charge of the remainder of the program."

No one who came was disappointed. Many lingered to shake hands with the choir members and express appreciation.

"Son, it was worth coming to hear," beamed Aaron.

"I'm so glad you all came. Clif, you drive carefully on your way home. 'By to you all now. They're serving us lunch in the basement before we leave and I see the rest have all gone down already."

"Good evening, Mr. Grant."

Dave stood speechless. In the soft, blue eyes of the young lady offering him the tray he saw a slight twinkle.

"You don't remember," she said, "but we met once before in Attorney Dillon's office."

"I—I do remember," he answered, taking the tray, "and your first name is Janet." He felt himself quivering all over.

"That's right. Janet Walden. Will you have tea or coffee?"

CHAPTER 32

Thrilled by this, the happy, the unexpected, the sweet simple clarity of her words, how could it matter to Dave whether she poured tea, coffee, or pepper water?

"Coffee, please," he heard himself saying, and he knew he'd soon be sipping it as though it were the most delicious thing in the world.

"I enjoyed your program immensely," she said, filling his cup.

"You were—in the audience?" his own voice almost startled him, it was so feathery, unsteady.

"Of course I was. On the back seat with these other girls who are helping serve."

He steadied himself. "Then you belong here?" He looked her full in the face, smiling.

"This is my home church."

As Dave turned to find a chair, Joe tapped him on the arm. "Come over to our table. I want you to meet Lois."

He did. But during the lunch Dave cast more than one lingering glance at the beautiful girl in the pink dress and white organdy tea apron, as she poured more tea and coffee.

It was the next evening before he had a chance to talk to Joe in private. He could postpone the question no longer.

"Your lady friend, Lois, seems like a very nice girl," he began, treading carefully on unfamiliar ground.

"Thank you. Lois is everything I desire in a girl."

Dave hesitated. "What can you tell me about—" he shifted —"that one girl who was helping serve? She was pouring the coffee. Remember?"

"Janet Walden?"

"That's the one I mean."

"What do you want to know about her?"

"Anything you can tell me."

"Well, she's one of Lois's best friends. As far as I know, everybody thinks she's a fine young lady. And why do you inquire, my good bachelor friend?"

"Ah, come now. Who does she go with?" It was out. His own question made his forehead damp with perspiration.

"No one in particular right now, that I know of. Why? Are you interested? You are. Admit it, Dave."

"Well, I think I'd like to know her better. There's something about her that appeals to me. Do you think I'd have one chance in a thousand?"

Joe laughed as he grabbed Dave by the arm. He shook him a little. "What do you mean, one chance in a thousand? Get rid of that inferiority bug. I don't know why she wouldn't at least give you a try. I think I could arrange it through Lois. Just say the word."

"You mean—a double date?"

"That's what I mean. You guessed it."

"Thanks, Joe." Then trying to conceal his enthusiasm, he added, "I'll think it over and let you know one of these days."

"Okay, thinking man."

From Monday evening until Friday afternoon Dave weighed, reweighed, and dissected the idea. Wasn't he old enough to speak for himself? Why should he expect someone else to arrange his dates? She might think for sure he felt inferior or immature. The uncertainties about himself were as troublesome as ever, but Dug was the last person he had confided in, and Dug would remain the last.

He got out a sheet of paper. But before the first word was penned, the feelings he experienced at Lesa's wedding swept over him with tantalizing trepidation. He got up and walked across the room. He must rise above these affrontings. He must. He snapped his finger. What would Mother and Dad think of him if they knew he had these foolish qualms? His dear and highly respected foster parents, who loved him, trusted him, and had faith he'd amount to something worth while. They'd be heartily disappointed. And so would Sister Lora. "You can't know what you can't know. I've given you to God every day—every day—"

With determination he picked up his pen and wrote in painstaking hand:

May 9, 1934

Dear Miss Walden,

May I have the pleasure of your company on the evening of the eighteenth of May? My friend, Joe Hanson, suggests we could double date with him and Lois. I live in Lititz and plan to go home over that weekend.

Sincerely,

David Grant

"Well," exclaimed Joe, running to catch up with Dave crossing the campus. "I'm about ready to leave for home. What's the word we're to pass on to Janet?"

"I've already mailed her a letter."

"But I thought—well! How did you know her address?"

"I sent it to Attorney Dillon's office where she works."

"You knew she worked there?"

"Sure. That's where I first met her."

"Then why didn't you say so? You let on like you didn't even know her."

"I don't know her. I just saw her in there one time. I decided I'd rather do it this way, Joe, but thanks just the same. I told her you suggested we double. Do you still mean it?"

"Of course. I'll be running on. So long, and—happy reply!"

One more feeble breath spent. Spent.

Then a lifetime of silence.

Shana stood fixed. Could it be? At last? At last!

Very tenderly she planted a kiss on the cold hand across his still chest. Two hard-pressed tears fell on the sheet that covered Anthony's wasted body. She waited what seemed another lifetime before she pushed the button at the head of his bed.

"Yes," nodded the nurse. "It's over, Mrs. Drextell. It's been a long siege for both of you, hasn't it? If you'll step out and sit in the lobby, someone will see you there and inquire where to have the body taken."

"All right. But tell me—" Shana pressed one trembling hand against her pale cheek— "did he say anything at all today?"

"Once when I came in around six, he opened his eyes and called me Shana. I think that was the name."

"That's my name. Did he say anything else?"

"No. Not that I understood. He mumbled something about a baby, but it wasn't anything coherent."

"Baby?" whispered Shana, shaking her head sadly. "Oh, my poor Anthony, my poor dear Anthony." She walked wearily down the hall.

The tyranny of memory worked havoc. After Anthony was laid to rest and Bruce and Hazel were back in Iowa, all the bitterness, remorse, and loneliness pressed in upon Shana with fresh severity, until she had no peace of mind about anything. Weighted with grief and shattered hopes, she felt herself stumbling, almost blinded by her thoughts. The unforeseeable future looked as dark as the unforgettable past. Insecurity, both financial and emotional, loomed with sickening proportions.

Alone once more. Alone and everything gone. Hazel and Bruce had spoken every kind word of comfort they could pronounce, and Shana had promised them she'd be brave. More than that, she said she'd be all right.

And now, in less than one week, she found herself the victim of deep despondency, with inexpressible dreads, longings, hurts.

Slowly she paged the telephone directory, lingering among the H's. She had never been good at remembering names, but this one she would never forget. Holcome. Albert—Ben—Claude —Grace—Henry. She held her breath. Reverend John Thomas Holcome, 833 Brentwood. Could it be? Could it possibly be? Would she dare? She drew a long, weary breath and picked up the receiver. Her hands trembled. Then in her excitement she gave the number of the taxicab station instead of the Holcome residence.

"Yellow Cab."

"Oh," she gasped. "I—I, well, yes, yes, send a cab. . . . Mrs. Shana Drextell."

But before the cab arrived, her intentions almost weakened. The intensity of years of mental and physical strugglings showed in her frayed nerves. Time had not lessened the sting of deception and disappointment. The burning was deep. And the flame had been as fierce and irresistible as a blowtorch. He might not want to take time to listen to her story of a burned-out life. Should she go?

The cab driver was honking.

"To the hospital?" he asked as she got in the back seat.

"No," answered Shana. "My husband passed away eight days ago. Take me to 833 Brentwood, please."

"Brentwood?"

"I've no idea where it is. Have you?"

"I do, Ma'am. So he's gone? Well, well. I've taken you over there many a time, haven't I? And when it wasn't me, one of the other drivers did. He was sick a long time, wasn't he?"

"Seventeen years," sighed Shana wearily, and dropping her head she closed her eyes. Was this the thing to do after all? Was she making a fool of herself?

"Here you are, Ma'am."

Her legs shook as she walked up the steps. Half fearfully she pressed the doorbell.

Footsteps. She bit the inside of her cheek. She swallowed.

"Good afternoon." The screen door opened to her.

That was the voice—the voice she had heard once, but hadn't forgotten. It still had that same soft, mellow accent.

Her heart pounded. "Reverend Holcome," she said in a faltering voice. "I—I don't suppose you remember me." Her bloodshot eyes searched his face.

"We've met before, have we?" He held out his hand. "Won't you come in?"

"Thank you. We met once in the hospital."

"Won't you please take a chair? You know I used to be the chaplain, and over the years I visited thousands of people in beds. But when the same people are up on their feet and dressed, I don't always recognize them at once. So, please, pardon me for not recognizing you. My eyesight isn't so good any more, either. I'm sorry, my friend, but you'll have to tell me who you are."

After a brief silence Shana began with difficulty. Her voice was a bit unsteady. "Do you remember a Mrs. Monson with—with a tiny baby?" For a moment she tore her gaze from his attentive gaze.

"Mrs. Monson!" exclaimed Reverend Holcome. "To be sure, I remember sad young Mrs. Monson. Yes. I baptized that nice little son of yours that you were so much concerned about. Of course I recognize you now, though you've changed—as—as I have too," he added apologetically. "Why, that's been quite a few years back."

"Quite a few years," agreed Shana with heaviness.

"Indeed, Mrs. Monson, I've thought of you countless times since that interview. In fact, I remembered both of you in my prayers more than once. And, please, tell me about your son. He must be quite a young man by this time."

"Oh, Reverend Holcome," cried Shana, breathing faster, "that's what I came to talk to you about. I—I mean if you have a few minutes to share. I intended to call you first—but—" she seemed out of breath already. Her hand went to her neck.

"I'll be glad to talk with you. What is it, Mrs. Monson?" He bent forward in his chair opposite her.

"Oh, dear," she sighed, "to begin with, my name isn't Monson. I—I took that name to try to shield myself and my baby."

"I see. Some do that."

She drew a long, long breath. "I know that it's wrong to lie, and when the lady from the office asked for the name of the baby's father, I knew I'd have to tell her the truth. My real name is Shana. Shana Grant it was then. I'm Mrs. Drextell now. A widow just since the ninth. Yes, of this month."

"I see. And the other man you told me about?"

Shana shook her head. "He never came back. He lost his life in France. But my baby, Reverend Holcome, that's what I came to talk to you about."

"Yes, yes. Tell me about him."

"Is there anyone in the house who might—" Shana gave an anxious glance toward the dining room.

"No, we're here alone. My wife has gone shopping. But if she were here, she'd be very understanding, and sympathetic."

"I'll try," began Shana, picking at the corner of her handkerchief, "to control my emotions. I told you I came here from Scotland when I was eighteen. My well-to-do oldest sister from South Carolina came to the hospital to see me and took my baby along back with her and put him in an orphanage." She wiped one trickling tear. "In no time he died."

"He died? And you're telling me you decided to give him up after all?"

"No. No. That's not what I mean. I fully intended to keep him. But she—" her voice broke—"she insisted and overpowered me. I was helpless. I was so sad and nervous and weak, I can't understand what happened to me to let her do such a thing. She was ashamed and furious and—" The words choked her. She pulled the skin at her neck. Resentments flared against her bewildering maze of thoughts and made her face look even more haggard.

"I'm sorry to hear this," said Reverend Holcome.

"What's more, all these years she has refused to tell me where she left him and I have no way of knowing where he's buried. My own son, Reverend Holcome."

"That doesn't sound fair," he remarked sympathetically.

286

"It isn't fair," cried Shana. "Bernice is proud. She's cruel and selfish. I realize I disgraced the family when I married Brandon. But I didn't know he had a wife. Mother died before I left. Thank God she never knew about it. My father says he forgives me and now he wants me to come back to Scotland and live with him." Shana paused long enough to catch her breath, and wipe her eyes, "But I'm determined I won't go back until—" she spoke with great difficulty—"until I find my baby's grave. A week from today," she choked, "my son David would have been twenty-one. I—I would so like to put some flowers on his grave then." Her whole body drooped like a basket of cut flowers wilting in the hot sun. She bowed her head with grief and cried.

"I'm sure you would like to do that, my friend," said the minister. "But your son is where the most beautiful flowers bloom in profusion all the time." He could see the thought gave her momentary relief. He hurried on. "I'm sorry to hear what happened, but he never thought you neglected him. I'm sure of that."

"He didn't?"

"How old was he when he died?"

"Very small. I don't know how old he was."

"Who told you he died, if you didn't know where he was? I don't understand this."

"Anthony, my husband. He went down to South Carolina before we were married, to try to find him for me. He was ready to take him back and give him a good home. But the superintendent—yes, Bernice told him where she left him—but the superintendent told him he died soon after that."

"Then what's the problem, Mrs. Drextell? This is not clear to me what you're trying to tell me."

"That's because you don't know what kind of a man Anthony was, Reverend Holcome. He loved me very much, but it was such a jealous love. He insisted it was for my own good that I never know where she left my baby. He didn't want me to go there or write or anything. He didn't want me to even mention David's name after he failed to bring him back. He did try, but

287

really, as jealous as Anthony was, I sometimes wondered how we would have gotten along if he had brought my boy back. But, Reverend Holcome, the thing that confuses and disturbs me most of all is—why did God let all this happen to me and to my baby? Why? Was I so wicked?" Shana sat on the edge of the chair, rigid, her eyes glassy and demanding.

"I can't answer that question, my friend," answered Reverend Holcome with calmness. "If I could, I'd be God. The mystery of human suffering is as old as man himself. I wouldn't even want to guess why."

"But I took your advice, Reverend Holcome." Shana's voice weighed heavy with sad recollections. "And I gave my baby to God. Don't you remember?" She twisted the leather handle of her handbag. "You dedicated him. You prayed over him. You baptized him, and all that. Don't you remember?" Her voice trembled now and a tear trickled down each sullen cheek.

"Yes, I remember well."

"And you also told me that day," she sobbed, "that God had a solution for my case. For my case," she repeated. "Then Anthony came," she faltered, "but so soon he got sick."

"Mrs. Drextell, I still say God has a solution for your case. In spite of all that's happened, God has not been blind to all that's come to you. I still say He cares about you. He understands all about you, and all things, the Bible says, yes, *all* things work together for good to those who love the Lord. I'm glad you gave your baby to God that day in the hospital. I'm glad I prayed for him. And I believe God went with him and watched over him until He took him. Didn't you often pray for him yourself?"

"Yes," she admitted, half sobbing. "Many times, until I learned he died."

"Then why don't you believe He answered your prayers and mine and did what He knew was best for your baby?"

"But how could it have been best that my selfish, proud sister took him from me like she did?"

"That I cannot answer, Mrs. Drextell. But I still say that,

in spite of it, God overruled, and through it all I truly believe God never left His hand off your child. Your sister, not you, will have to answer for her misdeeds. Listen, my friend, just why did you come here to see me?"

"Well, I thought," began Shana, with a little hesitancy, "that perhaps if you'd write to my sister, maybe—maybe—she'd tell you where she left my baby. I can't forget him," she cried brokenly. "He belonged to *me*, Reverend Holcome. Why can't I know where he's buried?"

He waited until she stopped crying.

"Didn't you say you gave your baby to God?" His voice was mellow and kind.

She nodded.

"Then wouldn't you say he belonged to God before he belonged to you?"

Shana did not answer.

"I'm trying to understand how you feel, but I wish somehow I could help you to start thanking God for something."

She looked up with mingled surprise and bewilderment.

"Do you truly love the Lord above anything else in all the world, Mrs. Drextell?"

Shana simply stared at the man across the room, then dropped her head. She shifted nervously. Both eyelids twitched.

"Have you been reading your Bible every day?" He put the question to her in soft, gentle tones.

Feebly Shana shook her head. "I've tried to at times," she ventured, "but it's very deep and difficult for me to understand." With one hand she rubbed her forehead. "After Anthony and I were married," she continued, "I hoped we'd start going to church together. Then soon he took sick and was in the hospital all these years. That took all my energy and used up everything he had. Now I'll have to go back to full-time work again. I would read my Bible if I only knew what to read that would help me."

"And how about going to church?"

"Well," she said, "I suppose I should, now that I have no excuse."

"Mrs. Drextell, by all means you need the fellowship of victorious, believing, happy Christians. And you need the daily fellowship with God that one finds only in reading His Word. I'll give you a card that will tell you what to read when you feel discouraged or forsaken or lonely or bitter. This, I am confident, is what you need much more than finding your baby's grave. Would that give you real satisfaction? I wonder.

"Mrs. Drextell, you need to get hold of something alive, and real, and refreshing, and glorious, and that is Jesus Christ. Whosoever believes on Him has everlasting life. And, my friend, that begins here on earth. God can give you that sweet peace of mind that passeth all understanding. Peace that comes by believing all our sins are forgiven, and peace because we forgive all those who have wronged us in any way. There's joy in knowing we are His, that nothing in the world can separate us from Him. When we believe on Him, it means we don't fret, or worry, or brood over anything, especially over things we can't help or can't change.

"I hope you understand I'm saying all this in the tenderest, kindest interest, Mrs. Drextell. I'm not scolding you. I want to help you. But I don't know any other way to do it than to talk plain and honest to you. God wants to be your burden bearer. He wants you to trust Him completely. I'm sure He has a solution for your particular case. There is nothing too hard for God. In spite of everything hard and sad and disappointing in your past, I wish you could, right now, cast all your care upon Him and trust Him. Just like you're relaxing on that chair—that's how you should relax in Christ. You're not afraid that chair will collapse. God is able to carry your load, my friend. I wish you could just let go and let God have a chance to perform a miracle in your life."

Shana's smoldering brown eyes studied the minister's sincere face. She felt herself shaking inside, before her tense nerves loosened.

No human countenance was alien to John Thomas Holcome. "Mrs. Drextell," he said with compassion, "first of all, just thank God that His unspeakable love includes you. He died to redeem you. Be thankful He has given you a mind capable of grasping that blessed fact. Thank God you can read. Thank God you are able to work. Thank God you can go to meet your son in heaven someday and live with him forever. In the meantime you can live to be a blessing to other women in like, or even worse, circumstances. It's possible, Mrs. Drextell. You're far from an old woman yet. God wants to make you happy and help you live above your sorrows."

"You—you wouldn't be interested in writing to my sister in South Carolina?"

"Really, Mrs. Drextell, at the moment I don't feel any prompting to do that. I'd rather not get involved. I do want to help you, but I'd much rather pray instead. God can perform miracles."

"Even on a person like my sister, Bernice McCawlis?" There was both doubt and grievance in those words.

"God's ways are stronger than the thoughts of men, Mrs. Drextell. Nothing with God is impossible. If we have faith as a grain of mustard, we can remove mountains."

Her overburdened eyes studied the pattern in the rug beside her chair before she relieved the prolonged silence. Somewhere in another room, a clock struck four.

"I do thank you for your time, Reverend Holcome," Shana said, getting up and moving toward the door.

"Tell me," he said, following her, " have I helped you at all?"

"More than you know," came her prompt reply. "The card you said you'd give me?"

"Just one minute. I have them in my study. Here you are. There are over forty suggested passages to read."

"Thank you, Reverend Holcome. I promise I'll use it. And I will start going to church as often as possible."

"Good. I was about to suggest that if you didn't have one of your choice in your neighborhood, why not come to our church? On the corner of Plum and Tedrow?"

"Thank you so much. There's a nice church much closer for me. In fact, the minister, Reverend Nash, called me up once since the funeral. It may take years, but after I get everything settled financially, I might go to Iowa where my other sister, my sweet sister Hazel, lives."

"Don't you want me to call a cab?"

"I think I'd as soon walk. If I get tired, there's a park half-way where I can rest a while."

Reverend Holcome watched her until she turned the corner.

CHAPTER 33

She was arranging a fresh bouquet of syringas and rosebuds for the front office when the mailman stepped in.

"Good morning, Miss Walden," he said in his usual courteous manner, "another nice day, isn't it?"

"Just perfect, Mr. Smith," answered Janet cheerily, "and to think you can be out in it all day, soaking up that nice warm sunshine."

"Wouldn't trade places with you," he remarked playfully.

Elizabethtown College? Inquisitively Janet inserted the letter opener. "Well," she exclaimed under her breath, then quickly put the letter in her purse just before Mr. Dillon stepped in.

To her secret chagrin Janet had to use her eraser more than ordinarily that day. After supper she decided to make a telephone call.

"Lois, I got a letter from Elizabethtown College today."

"From David Grant?"

"Then you know all about it, do you?"

"I know what Joe wrote me. You aren't going to turn him down, are you?"

"But I don't know him, Lois."

"Well, he doesn't know you either, does he?"

"Tell me what you know about him."

"Well, all I know is what Joe has told me and that's all good. Can't you judge he's a nice clean-cut fellow if Joe offered to double date with him?"

"I'd think so."

"He has nice, respectable-looking parents."

"How do you know?"

"They were at the program last Sunday night."

"How did I miss seeing them?"

"I guess you went to the basement to start the coffee as soon as it was over, didn't you?"

"Yes, I did."

"Well, I'm not going to tell you what to do, Janet, but as long as you can't make up your mind about Dick, you could at least give this young man a try."

"I look for Dick to give me a phone call tonight. That's why I wanted to call you first."

"According to what Joe tells me, David's not the kind to play up to a girl, then dump her. He loves music. He ought to hear you play the piano."

"Now, Lois."

"Well, you started the subject," laughed Lois.

A singular, invigorating feeling possessed David as he parked in front of her house. Rather gently he knocked. He tried to subdue his eagerness, but a fresh surge of happiness swept over him the moment he saw her through the screen door. She was wearing a delicate blue dress of summery material that hung in soft, unpressed pleats below her slender waist. Her sparkling blue eyes, her sincere smile, her graceful manner made his heart pound with a strange new joy even before she spoke.

"Good evening, David," she said, opening the door.

"Good evening, Janet," he answered, smiling.

"I want you to meet my mother. Mother, this is David Grant."

"I'm happy to meet you." Then turning to Janet he said, "I think Joe and Lois will be stopping here very shortly." He glanced at his watch.

"Yes." She looked radiant. "Find a chair. Any one you like."

"I'll be going now," remarked Mrs. Walden. "I'm invited out for tea before church," she explained to David.

"Have a nice evening," he said genially, "and," he added with sincerity, "I'm glad I got to meet you before you left."

"And we're going to eat our lunch here as soon as Lois and Joe come. I have everything ready."

"Good," he remarked, for loss of a better word.

David was almost overwhelmed with her beauty. There was something refined, winsome, unpretentious about Janet that crowned her personality with pure loveliness. An atmosphere of elegance surrounded her as she sat opposite him.

"How do you like your schoolwork?" she asked.

"Very much. But I'm anxious to put to practice all the things I'm learning about teaching. I made two applications yesterday."

"Around here?"

"In the county, but I'm of the impression both those school boards would rather hire lady teachers."

"I never had a man teacher until I was in my third year of high school and he was a perfect crank." She laughed. "I'm sure you wouldn't compare in any way to little old Mr. Pazley, who suffered from stomach ulcers. The pupils, I'm ashamed to say, vexed him often intentionally, just to watch his reaction. When I was in my early teens, I thought I'd like to teach school someday."

"What changed your mind?"

"Well, secretarial work appealed to me too. In fact, there's about a dozen types of work I would thoroughly enjoy. I like to type and keep records, and most of all I like to meet people, all kinds of people in all kinds of situations."

"Like you do in the job you have?" suggested David with a twinkle in his eye.

"Yes."

"Even fellows who drop in without an appointment?"

"Yes," she admitted, smiling happily. "To be sure, that kind too."

"I believe you play the piano, don't you, Janet?"

"Who told you?"

"Nobody. But you do, don't you?"

"Oh," she replied, "after a fashion."

"I do love music," said David. "I'd enjoy hearing what your after-a-fashion sounds like."

"Those two ought to be coming any minute."

"I know. I won't insist. But sometime you will play for me, I hope."

Without another word she seated herself at the piano and with ease and perfection played through most of Beethoven's *Moonlight Sonata* before Joe and Lois walked in.

"You didn't know she could play like that, did you?" whispered Joe, grinning in Dave's ear.

"I have lots to learn," returned Dave in whispered, grateful acknowledgment.

"Now," announced Lois, "we can have a quartet, unless both you boys sing bass."

"First of all, we're going to eat," said Janet. "Come with me to the sun porch."

Not one thing was ordinary; not to David Grant. Not even the water she poured into his plain, gold-rimmed glass. Nothing she served was lavish or extravagant, but every morsel he put in his mouth tasted like manna from heaven, divinely nourishing, miraculously strengthening, pleasantly satisfying, and strangely comforting.

What was this invisible influence, this strange kind of inspiration that so suddenly was making everything in the world rich and beautiful and right? Could a girl make that much difference in a man's life? All the fears and heartaches and pangs of unsolved mysteries, all the personal uncertainties, faded into insignificance as he sat beside Janet Walden and drank in the choice, dainty perfume she wore, and listened to her voice.

What a delightful spring evening it was! The sky was still aglow from the sunset, when the four rode seven miles out through the country to a small village church. There was something interesting to talk about all the way. Seven miles had never been covered in so short a time.

David and Janet sat together in church. They shared the same hymnbook. Together they bowed their heads in prayer. Companionship? David pondered. Spiritual companionship? He pondered more. Was this a divine craving for true, spiritual, soul-satisfying companionship? His thoughts welled up within him.

Was this real?

Was this life?

Was this pure, beautiful, dainty creature at his side flesh and blood like himself?

Could this be—could this be—love?

The kind that made Clif want Lesa for life? The kind that made Clare want Janet?

Janet. From his earliest recollection that name spelled everything that was good and kind and tender and protecting. Now it spelled elegance, grace, purity, culture, refinement, ability, and well-being. Could he ever, ever attain such a one?

The four sang part of the way home.

"This has been the pleasantest evening of my life," David said after Joe and Lois drove away. He accompanied her to the door.

"It's been a most pleasant one for me too," echoed Janet, looking up at him.

"Would I be too presumptuous to ask you now for another date?"

"When?"

"Two weeks from tonight?"

"I'll look forward to it," she said softly.

"You will?" His heart pounded wildly. "Thank you, Janet. And good night now."

"Good night, David. Are you driving back to school tonight?"

"Yes."

"Be careful."

"I will. I'll be very careful."

As he drove toward Elizabethtown that night, David felt somewhat as he did the day he found his mother's name and ran like a young deer to the creek to give secret vent to his happy emotions. Only this was a different, bigger, more profound kind of emotion. He felt like singing and shouting, but with a calm inner voice of holy satisfaction. This priceless treasure! Something powerful surged through his entire being, something moving and deeply spiritual. His heart and soul vibrated like a great organ under the touch of a musician's skillful hands. Could such wonder and happiness go on and grow?

"David," called the hall manager. "You're wanted on the phone. Come down."

"This is Mother, David."

"What's happened?"

"Nothing. I forgot to mention before you left Sunday that we hope you can come this weekend again."

"Why, Mother?"

"Have you forgotten it's your birthday?"

"Oh, that's right."

"I'd like to have something special for you. Supper with a few friends in. Will you come?"

"Why, yes, Mother. Of course I'll come. But don't you go to a lot of extra bother for me."

"It won't be bother, David. It will be my greatest pleasure."

"All right, Mother dear. I'll be seeing you."

What a delicious birthday supper Rose prepared! Clif and Lesa were there with their new baby boy. Sister Lora, Dug, Mr. and Mrs. Yonkers. The house fairly vibrated with pleasant talk and laughter.

"I've never seen David so happy," whispered Sister Lora to Rose in the kitchen.

"Neither have I," agreed Rose.

"He's maturing remarkably fast."

"He had his first date last Sunday night."

"Who with? Or shouldn't I ask?"

"A girl from Manheim. I really don't know her."

"Well, God bless his heart and life," whispered Lora. "Something new to pray about, isn't it?"

Rose smiled and nodded.

The second date with Janet was more wonderful than the first. This time the two went alone for an hour's ride out through the balmy blossom-bursting country before coming back to the evening service at her church. Her radiant smiles simply thrilled him. Her soft voice, her choice of words, her simple sincerity of speech thrilled him. He liked the neat, well-fitting beige dress she was wearing with slender poise and beauty. There was something delightfully refreshing and polished about her entire being that gave David determination to live the best, truest, most worthwhile life possible. He was thrilled to be seen sitting beside her among her home church friends. He was thrilled to be introduced to her pastor and his wife. After church Janet delighted and thrilled him again by playing several piano selections.

"That's wonderful," he exclaimed, beaming down on her.

"You haven't heard many play." She blushed a little.

"I'm perfectly satisfied with the way you perform," he said softly. "I think I should be going now. I've enjoyed the evening immensely."

She looked up into his face. "Can't you stay long enough to eat a little snack with me before you leave?"

"Well," he smiled, "I guess I can't turn down such a pleasant experience."

He watched her disappear into the kitchen. Did God ever create a sweeter girl, one more perfectly endowed with natural beauty? Could there be another who possessed all the fine qualities of the ideal Christian girl of his dreams?

Soon she came in with plates of tiny meat sandwiches, cheese tidbits, and pink lemonade.

"I don't like to go without a promise for another pleasant

evening with you." They were at the door. Rings of happy wonder were circling his heart. He took her slender hand in his.

"All right," she said. Her eyes met his. "When shall it be?"

"Would next Sunday be too soon?"

"Let's make it next Sunday."

"You make me very happy, Janet. Very happy."

"I'm glad, David."

"My school term closes this week, you know."

"Yes, I know. And you're not sure of a school yet?"

"Not yet."

"Don't be discouraged, David. I'm praying you'll find one soon."

"Then I'm doubly sure I will." He seemed reluctant to leave. But he must.

He could not resist stopping at Attorney Dillon's office Saturday forenoon while in Lancaster.

"David," she exclaimed. "Not another accident, I hope."

"No, not an accident this time. An answer to prayer, Janet. I have a school."

"Where?"

"Over near Forest Hill, close to the Ohio line."

"That far away?"

He thought he detected a tinge of disappointment in her voice. "I won't get home every weekend, that's for sure. But—" he stepped closer to the counter between them— "we can write, can't we?"

Her blue eyes answered even before she nodded.

The summer passed all too quickly. Dave worked once more at the airport with a substantial raise in pay. He and Janet were together every Sunday night. Sometimes they attended his church, sometimes hers, and sometimes they visited other churches.

"What do you think of Janet?" Dave asked Rose one morning.

"I surely could find no fault with her, David. You are to be commended for keeping company with such a lovely young lady. Bring her home for dinner sometime."

"Thanks, Mother. Oh, you're a dear, sweet mother to me. I'll do that sometime before I leave."

David did manage to get home once every two months. This took place on his third visit home. The three were eating breakfast and listening to the morning radio news broadcast.

"On this day, March first, three years ago, our entire nation was shocked by the kidnaping of the Charles Lindbergh baby."

Rose glanced across the table at Aaron before she spoke. His eyes gave her the answer.

"David," she said, "did you know we had a scare over you soon after we got you?"

"Scare? What do you mean?"

"Melvin Kolb called me and said a well-dressed man in a black Cadillac called at the Home and asked where you were. Melvin was suspicious and refused to tell him. He just told him you had been placed in a home. Then the man acted disgusted and drove off and headed south toward our farm. Melvin told me to take you inside. And I did."

"Then what?" Dave dropped his fork.

"Then sure enough a black Cadillac came halfway up our lane. I don't suppose you remember we made, or tried to make, ginger men cookies that day. I was excited and flustered until he drove away."

"Then what?"

Aaron took up the story. "I was just coming home from town and I met this man in the Cadillac in the lane and I asked him what he wanted. Well, he muttered something about how hopeless it was to try to find the party he was looking for, and he just asked me how to find the road to Philadelphia. When I got to the house, Rose was all upset."

"You don't remember we took extra watchful care with you

for a long time after that, do you?"

"No," said Dave. "You never told me about this before. Who was the man?"

"We haven't the slightest idea. The whole thing just vanished. We never learned a thing from it. That report we just heard made me think of it. Now that you're old enough to be your own boss, I guess Mother thought it would be all right to tell you."

"It really made us anxious for a while, Son," said Rose. "We sent up many a prayer for you."

Dave sat in deep thought. "Do you suppose," he said, "it could have been my father?"

"We have no idea," answered Aaron. "He refused to give Melvin his name. He just said he was given orders to find you. We've always liked to believe we weren't supposed to know who it was."

"Now that you've told me this," said Dave, hesitating a brief moment, "I'll tell *you* something. Remember when Dug and I went to Philadelphia together?"

"Yes."

"I don't want this to hurt you, please. Don't misunderstand my motive, but I did go primarily to try to find my real mother."

"Your real mother?" exclaimed Rose. "Is she in Philadelphia?"

"I haven't the slightest idea. I looked in the telephone directory at the list of Grants. Of course I didn't find her. Or anyone I could claim as a relative." He tried to chuckle. He took a bite of toast. "I just thought I'd admit that questions about my personal connection used to enter my mind at times."

Rose looked at Aaron.

"To be sure," stated Aaron. "You'd hardly be normal if they didn't."

"Well, it's a relief to hear you say that."

"Don't such questions ever—enter your mind any more?" asked Rose, almost apologetically.

"Well, I—I can't say they never do, Mother," answered Dave.

302

"But—" he took a drink— "I just thank God you two have been so wonderful to me and helped me through school like you have. I'll pay you back as fast as I can."

"That's all right, Son," choked Aaron, trying desperately to control his emotion. "We're the happiest when you're happy."

"A year ago I never dreamed I'd be this happy. But, I wonder—" a shadow crossed his face— "what Janet Walden will say if—"

"If what?" asked Rose.

"Well, if she finds out I have no idea where I—oh, well, you know what all I mean, I suppose."

"You see," said Rose after Dave left. "I'm glad we never asked him about that paper I found in his room. In due time we'll find out what we need to know."

"I hope that Janet never turns that boy down. She's doing something wonderful to him."

CHAPTER 34

The incident related at the breakfast table sent Dave's thoughts soaring and dipping, spinning and cruising into fantastic imaginations. He took his car to the garage for a tune-up job. While waiting for it, he walked to the public library and scanned the morning papers. In every column he saw the same object, a man in an expensive car (a Cadillac, to be exact) driving up to the entrance of the Millersville Children's Home and asking for David Grant. All these years he had fretted because no one had ever claimed him. Not one living soul had even cared he existed. And now, suddenly, to learn that at least one person in the world knew his name and whereabouts! Who could it have been? The man must have been white, or Dad would have said otherwise. Was this providential that he had come so close to being found and wasn't? Where would he be today if the man would have taken him? Maybe there was a woman hiding in the back seat of the car. Might it have been his mother or grandmother? Why did the man ask for the road to Philadelphia? All day, even while he was at home reading and listening to records, Dave's thoughts were running wild, overlapping, zigzagging, but always colliding at last with reality.

Janet. The thought of her sent every fragmentary impression into peaceful abstraction, for she, to be sure, was sweet reality. Had he been found and taken or kidnaped or whatever, would he have met Janet Walden, this girl of his dreams? In his heart he thanked Mother and Dad Loomas for never telling him this before. It would have only added to his frustrations. If he could only win the heart and hand of Janet, all these shifting wonderments would fade into insignificance. Of that he was confident.

After supper Dave thanked God for telephones. With eagerness he called her.

"Janet, Mother would like to have both of us here for dinner tomorrow."

"Would she? I'd like to come."

He was always delighted with the sound of her voice over the wire.

"I fear we won't be together very long, since it's snowing again. I'll have to start back about two or soon after."

"Really?"

The tinge of disappointment in her voice was not a disappointment to him. "You may be sure I won't leave until I have to," he added with warmth.

"Well, why don't you come over to our church for morning worship? That would save you extra driving."

"Thank you. Maybe I will."

"It starts at 9:15. I'll be looking for you."

With that pleasant refrain repeating in his ear, Dave lay awake a long time before sleep overtook him. And then he dreamed he was a small boy again on a bicycle, stuck in the mud in the long lane at the farm; and a man in a big black car was yelling at him to get out of his way. He woke with a start just as the car was about to mow him down.

One by one the people who attended the East Fairview Church of Manheim recognized David with a friendly handshake and words of welcome. But one young man in the Sunday-school class gave him such a look of utter disdain that he could not help noticing it. He mentioned the fact to Janet that afternoon as he was taking her home.

"That was Dick," she said. "Don't let it bother you."

"Dick who?"

"Dick Marshall."

"But why does he dislike me? I don't even know him. I've done nothing against him that I know of."

"I know you haven't, David. And he acted very crude, I'd say. I used to go with him."

"That's it? So he's angry at me because I took his girl friend?"

"But you really didn't."

David almost stopped the car. "What do you mean?" he asked in alarm. "I didn't? Are you still—"

"No, David," she answered gently, touching his right arm. "I'm not interested in going with Dick. I was ready to tell him so when I got your first letter. We can't help it if he's peeved."

"Oh," exclaimed David, "I felt almost weak for a moment."

"But why?"

"Why? Why, Janet," he said, giving her a long, lingering glance, "we've been seeing each other now for ten months." His heart pounded. "Each time I'm with you—I—I realize more than the last time how happy you make me. Surely—" he slowed down a little— "surely you won't be surprised if I confess I care a great deal for your friendship." He glanced at her again.

Janet pressed one gloved hand over the other. Her lashes brushed her coloring cheeks.

"Janet," he said softly.

"Yes." She looked up at him.

"It makes me weak all over to even think someone else might try to take you from me. I might as well tell you now I think you're the sweetest, most wonderful girl in all the world. And I love you." He gripped the steering wheel to steady his trembling hands. "You—you won't be angry with me for telling you this?"

Her voice was low, gentle, but steady. "Why should I be angry?"

"You don't think I'm bold or out of place?"

"David."

He thought he detected a tinge of admonishment in her tone. "Then tell me, dear," he said.

"Tell you what?"

"Something. Anything that my thumping, bursting, hungry heart has to know before I leave you this time."

"Oh, David," she said in almost a whisper, "can't you tell I like you too? Can't you tell you've also made me happy?"

"You're wonderful, Janet," he responded, his heart pulsating rapidly. "The most precious girl God ever created. Tell me you love me."

She hesitated a moment musingly. "I'm quite sure I do, David," she said softly. "I never felt like this toward anyone else."

"Really?" he exclaimed joyously. "Oh, Janet, my love, you've made me extremely happy today. I'm going to mark it in my book of important events. 'March the second, 1935—Janet Walden said she loved me.' You can't begin to imagine what this means to me. Everything in the world looks beautiful, beautiful because of you. It started back there the first time I saw you. No other girl ever made me feel like you did that day."

"Why? What did I do?"

"It wasn't what you did, Janet dear. It was what I saw you were. You gave me a feeling deep down inside I can't explain. Oh, my dear, I've thanked God many times since, that I had that little accident that day. Isn't it strange how God can turn something unpleasant like that into something as wonderful as meeting you? Say it once more in my ear."

Janet turned and, putting her lips close to his ear, whispered those sweet impassioned words that drenched his soul with luxurious serenity. "I love you, David."

He fairly panted with joy. "And to think I probably won't see you again for two whole months. And while I'm away, no Dick will gain ground with the one I love?"

"Never have a fear, David," came her answer. "There's no comparison, since I've learned to know you. Perhaps next year you can get a school closer home."

"I hope so. But you'll never know how I appreciate those nice letters you write to me. They've convinced me over and over what a wonderful person you really are."

"I look forward to your letters too, David," she said. "Do you dread going back?"

"Dread? Only because it separates us. But I'll probably sing most of the way now. I love my job. I love every one of my thirty-nine pupils, even the few I have to punish once in a while. All in all they're a pretty nice group of children. I've been invited for an evening meal into over half of their homes."

"That speaks well for you. They must like their teacher."

"I hope so. I have two little boys, brothers, nine and eleven, who come from a broken home. Their father deserted them two years ago and their mother is in a t.b. sanatorium. The Welfare placed these boys in a home not far from the place where I stay; so I pick them up every morning."

"I'm sure they love you for that."

"They're real nice little boys. I feel sorry for them; so I do what I can to make them happy. I'm glad each has a brother. And I'm glad they know, too, they have a mother who loves them and writes to them, and is concerned about them."

"You never had a brother?"

"No, Janet. Not that I know of."

"I've often wondered about your real parents. Do you mind if I ask?"

"I'm sorry I must admit that all I can tell you is, my mother's name is Shana Grant."

"Why must you be sorry?"

"You mean if I tell you I have no idea where I came from you'll still love me?"

"Why, David. Why would that make such a difference?" Her words were astonishingly sweet and surprising.

He caught her one hand in his and pressed it. "Now," he said, beaming on her, "I know you're the sweetest girl in all the world. And your heart is big, and wonderful, and pure as gold."

They were in front of her house now.

"You've never told me much of that part of yourself. The next time you come home I wish you'd tell me all about it, that is, if you'd care to share it with me. Will you?"

"What makes you think there's much to tell?"

"There must be something." Her eyes, like two blue stars, looked into his. "And I'd love to hear it." She spoke with deep sincerity.

He gazed at her with fond amazement. "My dear," he said, "if you still love me when I get back, we'll have a good long sharing talk with each other."

There was no questioning, no momentary deliberation. Janet Walden had come into his life unsought, like a gift out of heaven, and David knew within his honest heart he loved her honestly, completely. And more, the gracious words and smiles of sanction from Mother and Dad Loomas gave him a satisfying sense of well-being and rightness. It was almost sacred.

He went back to his school duties with greater enthusiasm than ever. There was new meaning in waking each glad morning. There was new meaning in teaching spelling, reading, history, arithmetic; new sweetness in every song they sang; new fun in the games they played. New beauty in the children's faces.

New life in all of living.

Janet loved him!

Each new Wednesday and Saturday her letters repeated it.

Myla, the sweet, shy little blond second-grader, lingered in the cloakroom when all the other pupils went outside for recess. Quietly she tiptoed back into the room and stood behind David, who was busy writing words to a new song on the blackboard.

"Mr. Grant," she said, scarcely above a whisper.

"What is it, Myla?" He looked into her uplifted face.

She twisted her dress belt around one finger. "I want to tell you something."

"Yes, Myla, what is it you want to tell me?"

"I—I think you're the nicest teacher in all the whole world."

David got down on one knee until his face was level with hers. "I'm glad you think that, Myla. But why did you want to come back and tell me this now?"

"I don't know. I just wanted to because I like you."

He patted her on the shoulder. "Well, thank you, Myla dear. I appreciate this very much. I think you're a nice pupil too. And I hope we'll always be good friends."

"I hope so too, Mr. Grant. Will you be our teacher next year?"

"I'm not sure about that yet."

"I hope so, 'cause my brother, Alvin, will be old enough to start to school and I told him you're a nice teacher 'cause you love us lots more than that other teacher did."

"Do I? Well!" He stood up and very gently stroked her blond hair. "You make me very happy, Myla. I do love all my pupils."

"Mr. Grant."

"Yes."

"You remember that story you read to us this morning about that little girl who went to see her daddy in prison?"

"Yes."

"Was that a really true story?"

"I don't know if it is or not, Myla. I just found it in a library book. Why do you ask?"

"I just wondered, 'cause my mother says my old daddy is in prison like that."

"Your old daddy?"

She nodded. "I don't remember him or anything about it. I got this new daddy when I was a baby. I was too little to remember."

"I see," remarked David, running one hand back over his black hair. "Does your mother ever take you to see your—your old daddy?"

Myla shook her head. "Not yet. Sometimes she says she will when she and Daddy get to fusin'; then that makes him quit usually, 'cause he never wants him to see me."

"Why?"

"I don't know. But I'd kinda like to go see him like that little girl in the story did, 'cause maybe he's a real nice daddy

310

too, like he was, but I wouldn't know where to go or anything. Mother won't tell me where it is."

David looked steadfastly into the unreadable blue eyes looking up at him. "I think you'd better be satisfied to stay at home, Myla," he said advisedly. "Don't ever try to—" He put one arm around the little girl's shoulder. "I had no idea when I selected that story—" He could not finish the sentence for the growing lump in his throat.

"I wish," remarked the child after a deep breath, "my daddy was like you, Mr. Grant. I bet you'd take me to see him, wouldn't you?" Her eyes filled with sudden tears.

Astonished, David blinked twice in wordless seriousness. The wistful questioning faces he had envisioned across his worktable at the Hamilton Watch Company flashed momentarily before him. Seven months in the schoolroom, and he had almost concluded that the two brothers, Jimmy and Henry, were the only pupils who needed any special love and sympathetic understanding.

"Don't you want to go out on the playground now, Myla?" With his hand on her shoulder he accompanied the little girl to the door.

Of all the boyhood fears and imaginings about his belonging, not once had it ever occurred to David that he might be the son of a man of crime, serving sentence behind prison bars. Would such a situation make any difference to Janet? Something inside him automatically recoiled. Sincerely he hoped if such was the case he would not live to learn the truth until he was an old man. And yet as he hunted for new stories to read to his pupils, fresh vigor and adventure of maturing manhood sent his adult mind wondering, rationalizing, hoping, searching, reaching for the answer. He knew that in spite of his uppermost contentment in giving and receiving love, there would always be that silent undercurrent of concern. Would his probing thoughts ever come to a standstill?

Myla's sweet, tender face grew in sweetness. Without realizing it, she was the object of David's daily study.

One morning the woman who was mothering and homing

311

Jimmy and Henry came out to the car when David stopped. "Mr. Grant," she said, "Jimmy's sick."

"I'm sorry to hear it. How about Henry?"

"He's not sick, but he says he's not going if Jimmy can't. He's that way about his brother, Mr. Grant. He's in there whimperin' to go, yet he refuses to put his coat on. I thought I'd better explain it's not me a-keepin' him home. If you have a minute to spare, I'd appreciate it if you'd step in an' talk to him."

David turned off the ignition and got out.

"I wish you'd step in and look at Jimmy too, Mr. Grant. He was talkin' wildlike last night an' burnin' up with a fever. He kept callin' for you. I don't know why, but both the boys talk about you a lot, almost like you was their big brother."

When the two stepped inside, Henry quickly wiped his eyes with the cuff of his shirt sleeve and caught David by the arm. "Please, Mr. Grant," begged Henry, "don't make me go without him. He'll cry, and Mamma said since I'm the oldest I'm to look after Jimmy and never make him cry."

"But wouldn't Mrs. White here take good care of Jimmy?"

"I guess so," answered Henry, looking very forlorn, "but she's not like his own brother."

"That's true," agreed David understandingly. "I know what you mean. I'll have to mark you absent, but I'll give you homework to do so you won't get behind. All right?"

"Sure," nodded Henry, smiling with relief.

"He's in there," pointed Mrs. White.

David gave Jimmy one startled look. "Have you called a doctor?" He felt the boy's forehead.

"Do you think I should, Mr. Grant?"

He nodded.

"Jimmy, do you know me?"

The child's glassy eyes opened. Faintly he smiled, then his eyelids closed.

My dearest Janet,

The sun is brilliant this morning. The lilac bushes are

312

beginning to bud and it's springtime in my heart for the one
I love.

This is a special letter written in haste because I want you
to pray for one of my pupils. Little Jimmy is a very sick boy.

David

Saturday brought her this letter:

Sweetheart,

I sat up all last night with Jimmy. The doctor is puzzled.
Has not diagnosed it yet. His fever keeps coming back. Please,
darling, don't judge my love by the length of my last two letters.
When things are back to normal, I'll make up for it.

All my love,
David

The next one came on Wednesday.

Darling Janet,

If I don't get home Saturday, it's because Jimmy is too
sick for me to leave. Please, dear, understand you come first
in my affection, but these little boys—they have a father, but
where? And their poor mother is a hundred miles away, flat
on her back in the hospital. They have somehow wrapped
themselves around my heart and I can't leave unless Jimmy
turns for the better. I stop in every morning on the way to
school and every evening, and run over during the noon hour.
I stayed all night again last night, partly for Henry's sake.
This is very hard on him. If anything would happen to Jimmy,
I don't know how Henry would take it. I never knew brothers
so close to each other. Please call Mother and tell her not to
worry if I don't get home.

Longing to see you,
David

Janet declined an invitation to go along with her mother
to visit ailing Aunt Mary. She would rather stay at home and
read, and write David a long letter.

She was standing at the west window, pencil in hand, gazing
at the row of first yellow daffodils along the neighbor's fence. But
her thoughts were much farther west than the fence. For eight

313

Sundays she had been looking forward to this one. Why was David so attached to his pupils? Why did they love him so? There was within her lonely heart a sweet, sad stillness in waiting, anticipating, praying for Jimmy's recovery before the next Friday.

A gentle rap on the door.

"David!"

He caught both her hands in his. "I just had to come, if for only an hour."

"I never dreamed you'd come now any more. Is Jimmy better?"

"His fever dropped considerably before midnight. Oh, Janet, Janet," he whispered, holding her out at arm's length. "It's so good to see you. Get your coat and let me hold it for you."

"Where are we going?"

"I don't know where," he answered, beaming on her with sheer joy; "anywhere with you beside me will make it the grandest place in the world. Come, dear. We can't be together long this time."

CHAPTER 35

"Just a minute." David already had his hand on the door-knob. "I ought to call Mother."

"You haven't been home yet?" asked Janet in surprise.

"No, dear. I came straight here." His eyes glittered as he smiled at her. "Why? Precisely to see you first. I'll call and tell them we'll be dropping in for lunch in less than an hour." He hurried across the room. "Won't they be surprised? I wouldn't dare go back without seeing them."

Soon the happy pair were out beyond the village, rolling along through the greening country warmed by the sunshine.

"Is Jimmy going to be all right now, David?"

"That's yet to be seen," he answered, frowning thoughtfully. "The doctor is about ready to pronounce it rheumatic fever. At first he called it a severe case of the flu. At any rate Jimmy won't be coming to school any more this term. But Henry will. I've made that plain to him. Next weekend I promised to take him to see his mother. By the way, the school board wants me to sign up for next year."

A sudden shadow flitted across Janet's face. "I thought you were going to—" Blushing, she caught the next words and quickly tossed them aside. "The way the children all seem to love their teacher," she reasoned, "I'm not surprised they want him back."

David gave her an affectionate glance and said confidingly, "There's but one drawback, Janet, my dear, and I'm sure you know what that is."

"But you must do what your own best judgment tells you to do, David." She smoothed the pleats in her navy skirt. "I'm just glad you're not going 'way out to California or up to Alaska." She tilted her head and, looking up, smiled consolingly. "We can keep on writing."

"Bless your sweet, unselfish heart," exclaimed David. "And that we will. I must admit I'm quite attached to those children. I'll get a raise if I go back and that'll help me get my debt to Dad paid off. And I should trade this old car in on a better one." He drew a deep, deep breath. "But the next year—" he felt touched with a surging, glorifying power—"darling—" He reached over and turned her face toward his. "If I go back, I'd like to take you with me."

Her blue upturned eyes were candidly sweet, but serious. "But I have no teacher's certificate," she said, fresh color creeping into her cheeks.

"But Janet, my love," said David with ardent tenderness, "I'd give you a certificate to be my wife. My wife, darling," he repeated as though he wanted to bathe himself at last in the sweet liquid glory of the sounded word that for days and weeks shouted insistently in his heart. "No one else could take that place, sweetheart. If it's true God has a plan for my life, and I am believing more and more He has, then He must have included you in that plan, darling." He held her hand. "Do you believe God brought us together?"

"I could never believe anything else, David," she admitted. "You know I love you and you only."

His heart leaped. "Then you will marry me someday?"

"Someday David," came her radiantly bright answer. "I promise."

David drank in one long, gloriously happy breath. There were no eyes to see, unless those of the birds in the nearby trees. A quarter of a mile away, the nearest building was an empty schoolhouse. "Darling." He stopped the car. He drew her close to himself. He folded her in his arms and kissed her once and again.

316

"How can you make me so happy?" he whispered, looking steadfastly into her glowing eyes.

"How can you make me so happy?" she echoed.

"We'll seal the promise with one more." He kissed her again. Reluctantly he started the car. "We must turn back," he remarked, glancing at his watch. "Shall we tell the folks we're engaged? Think of it, darling, we're engaged."

"I see no reason why we should keep it secret. We're not teen-agers, you know."

"I should ask your mother first, don't you think?"

"I'm sure it would please her if you would. Maybe the next time you come home. Oh, if my father were living, I know he'd love you."

"Janet, dear, does she really approve of me?"

"Approve? Can't you tell?"

"But, darling, I mean because I don't know anything about my identity. I won't have one single relative at our wedding. Did you think of such a thing?"

"But you have Mother and Dad Loomas. And Clif and Lesa."

"Yes. And thank God I have them."

"Remember, you were going to tell me all about yourself."

"But that will have to be some other time, dearest. Can't you wait until the next time I come home?"

"Of course."

"The next time I'll be coming home for the summer, my love."

"Oh, David. Happy thought."

"If I don't find a good job, Dad will help me get in with a carpenter gang."

"Would you like that kind of work?"

"For the summer I would. I want to learn everything I can about building. Just think, Janet, someday I might want to build a house for us."

"Oh, David." She squeezed his arm. "You think of the nicest things."

317

"And you will help draw the plan. It'll be your home. Our home, Janet. Just think."

"Just think, David." She squeezed his arm again. "I'm sure no girl was ever happier than I am. How could you possibly be so wonderful if you didn't come from wonderful parents? I'm just sure you did. And what does it matter if you didn't when you have such lovely foster parents?"

"I owe much, much to them. Janet, we're nearly there. Tell me this yet. If—if sometime I'd—" he rubbed one hand over the steering wheel—"I'd come to find out my mother never was married, would it bother you—at all? I know I shouldn't think of it, but—but I've wondered already."

Janet turned and with undisturbed dignity looked David full in the face. Reaching up, she touched his chin with the tips of her fingers. "Not at all, David dear. Not at all," she said, "and please, don't ever bother to wonder about it again."

"Darling," he choked, gripped with sudden emotion. "I'm so thrilled and overjoyed I can scarcely keep back the tears. Come," he said, clearing his throat. "Let's go in and tell the folks."

"Will they accept me?"

"Dear me," he laughed, opening the car door, "I'm terribly scared they won't accept my beautiful little queen."

Dearest Janet,

I will always be glad I took Henry to see his mother. She could not get done thanking me. And she appreciated all I could tell her about Jimmy. If we still lived back on the farm, I'd be tempted to take Henry along home with me for the summer, but it would never do to separate the boys, and Jimmy will be in bed at least six more weeks, maybe more. We're making up a sunshine box for him here at school.

The children found out when my birthday is, and they say they're going to have something special for me. Little Myla let the cat out of the bag by telling me the parents are coming and bringing good things to eat. I'll have to act surprised.

318

I had a letter from Joe yesterday giving me an assignment from the program committee to speak in your church the second Sunday evening in June, on how God leads in choosing a vocation. Also he asked me to serve as best man at his wedding. I'm going to tell him I'll be glad to, since he added you'll be the bride's maid of honor. Darling, little did I dream a year ago such would be my happy lot—but, yes, a year ago, I confess, I was beginning to wonder and dream romantically. But not about Joe's wedding. And today I'm caught in the strangely majestic, the sweetly impelling, the completely satisfying experience of love. What a romance with a dear, talented, beautiful girl like you!

Your true lover,
David

"Look, Mr. Grant," said Jimmy one evening when David stopped to see him. "I got a box in the mail today from somebody I don't even know. These two storybooks, a puzzle, a package of gum, and this little pocketknife with a fingernail file in it."

"How nice, Jimmy! You must have more friends than you realize. Wasn't there a name on the box?"

"Show him, Henry. It's there on the table."

"From Janet Walden? I know her very well, Jimmy. She's a good friend of mine. And when you were very sick, I wrote and told her to pray for you. She did, Jimmy. She asked about you the last time I was home. I'll tell her you got the box. And what else shall I tell her?"

"Tell her thanks a lot. And I like what she sent me."

"I certainly will. Maybe someday when you feel stronger you can write her a little note and I'll mail it for you. My, I'm glad to see you smiling and looking so bright. You rest now, like the doctor said you should."

"He's eating better too, Mr. Grant," called Mrs. White from the kitchen.

"You keep that up, Jimmy my boy, and when I come back in

September, you'll be riding along to school with me again."

Before the wedding reception was over, everyone present had learned that the dainty, attractive maid of honor in whisper-soft blue, and the handsome black-haired best man were betrothed.

The busy summer was highlighted with memorable events. There were happy strollings in the moonlight in the park, suppers sitting opposite each other in some cozy restaurant, concerts, special meetings, rides through the wide open country, long talks on the porch swing in the quiet of a Sabbath after church, boat rides on a lake singing love songs, or David listening with admiration while Janet played the piano.

"It will be September all too soon," remarked David, lingering at the door one evening.

"I know what I'm going to do to make the year go faster."

"What, sweetheart?"

"I'm going to start making things we'll be needing, like towels, and linens, pillowcases, dresser scarves, and some of those crocheted frilly doilies, too, just to pretty up a home."

"Wonderful. Wonderful. Good night, my love."

A few days later Janet was surprised when she found an exquisite cedar-lined walnut chest in her room when she got home from work. On the attached card were the words: "From your promised one, with deepest love."

And before the busy, romantic summer reached its climax, David had accepted a second request to speak on a Sunday evening program in Janet's church.

"David," said Pastor Hardy, drawing him aside after the service, "I'd like to thank you personally for the fine contributions you've been making to our congregation. I know I express the feeling of all the members when I say this."

"Thank you very much," replied David with modesty.

"I understand you're engaged to our Janet Walden."

"And I'm happy to say it's true."

"Would you like to bring your letter and transfer your membership to our fellowship. We'd be glad to have you."

"Janet and I have been discussing the matter," answered David. "We've been attending over at my church the Sundays we haven't been here."

"That's what I figured. Please understand, I'm not trying to pressure you at all. We only want you to know our doors are open. I think it's best Janet either join your church or you hers before you marry."

"We agree on that, Pastor Hardy. And thank you very much for your interest and kind invitation. I'm glad I can honestly say you've all made me feel at home here, and I've enjoyed the fellowship very much."

"We need more young men of your character and ability." Pastor Hardy gripped David's arm. "You think it over."

"Thank you. I will. But we're not getting married for a while yet."

My dearest Janet,

Jimmy is back, but he's not to run or get overtired; so I'm keeping at watchful eye on him.

Already I've been asked to teach a class of twelve- and thirteen-year-old boys in the community church here. The superintendent stopped at the school yesterday to talk to me about it. I told him I'm willing to help them out, but I'll be going home several weekends during the school term, and I'd want a good substitute ready to handle it when I'm gone. If I take the job, I want to put everything into it. That's an important age in the life of a boy.

I had a big surprise this evening. You remember Dug Yonkers, the boy I told you about who lived next door and went to Philadelphia with me? Just as I was locking to leave, he drove into the schoolyard and introduced "Lady Carmel, my bride." They're on their honeymoon, and drove ten miles out of their way to look me up. I knew he was getting married, but never expected this. He has a good-looking wife and I'm glad for Dug. But imagine how thrilled I was to be able to open my billfold and say, "Lord Douglas and Lady Carmel, the picture of the beautiful, adorable princess Janet, my wife-to-be." Of course he asked when, and I told him that wasn't for publication yet.

A driving rain, high water, and several detours delayed David's April trip home by nearly eight hours. Several times he had to stop and wait until the blinding downpour subsided. Then he had to inch along through miles of treacherously dense fog. But before he entered Lancaster County the rain stopped abruptly and the sun was soon shining in regal splendor.

He dashed up the steps, opened the door, and found the living room full of women seated around a quilting frame.

"David," exclaimed Rose, looking up in surprise. "I thought you must not be coming after all."

"What's going on? Am I intruding?"

"Of course not," said Rose. "Now that you've seen it, you might as well know it's going to be yours when it's finished."

"Mine?"

"For you and Janet," smiled Rose.

"Mother," he exclaimed, stepping closer, and placing his hands on her shoulders. "You mean you made this beautiful quilt for us?"

"That's what I said, Son. Why not? Let me introduce these ladies to you." She did. He smiled and nodded graciously.

"I've helped quilt a lot of pretty ones, David," said one of the women, "but this is by far the loveliest I've ever seen."

Out in the kitchen Aaron said to David in undertones, "And that's not the first quilt Mother's made for you. She won't be satisfied until she's done the same for you as she did for Lesa and our little Janet."

"Well, I know *my* Janet will be more than pleased."

First of all David called her, then ate a bowl of hot soup and slipped up to his room to sleep until evening.

Rested and refreshed, he was unusually talkative at the supper table. There was much of the unusual to talk about—detours, happenings at school, his class of boys, Dug and his bride, Jimmy, a letter from Leon about his love affair, and to be sure the subject of pre-eminence, Janet. He freely discussed tentative plans for the wedding, where they might live, and what he might do in the future.

"You know," said David, resting his chin in his hand, "first of all Janet and I must decide which church we're going to attend regularly. We can't keep this up much longer—going back and forth, I mean. Dad, you tell me what you think we ought to do. Mother, what's your opinion on this?"

"The only opinion we have, David," answered Aaron, "is this. You two decide. We'd be glad if Janet would see her way clear to come over to our church, but if she'd be happier if you'd join hers, then you two decide. We want you both happy."

"You mean you wouldn't be disappointed if I transferred my membership?"

"Disappointed? That's not the word to use, Son," remarked Aaron. "Why would we be disappointed? We know we can't always keep you close to ourselves. You could do things that would be a lot more disappointing than that."

A few minutes later David was whistling softly while he massaged his face, combed his hair, and brushed his coat.

"Have a nice time," called Rose as he went out the door, "and give our love to Janet."

It was the first day of June. Under one of the brilliant eight-tier crystal chandeliers hanging from the ceiling of the gold room in Hotel Brunswick in Lancaster sat Mrs. Lewis McCawlis, idly tapping her diamond-laden hand on the arm of the tapestry-covered chair. Now and then she leaned forward and glanced anxiously toward the elevator in the lobby. Nervously she worked the heel of her one black, brocaded slipper into the pile of the thick gold carpet, and patted a lacy handkerchief against her damp forehead.

The man who had been sitting on the opposite side of the small table between them folded the paper, as he had been reading it inside out. He put it down, lit a cigar, and walked away.

Bored at waiting, Mrs. McCawlis picked up the paper, and listlessly scanned the boring "about people" columns. She knit her brow. She held her breath for a moment. In bold, black ink she read, "Janet Walden and David Grant engaged to wed," and below in smalled print she read, "Mrs. Curtis Walden of Manheim has announced the engagement of her daughter Janet Marie to David Grant, foster son of Mr. and Mrs. Aaron Loomas of Lititz. Miss Walden and her finance are planning a December wedding. She is employed in the office of R. T. Dillon, Attorney, and D. A. Cornelius, Realtor. Her fiance, a graduate of Elizabethtown College, is a teacher at Forest Hill."

"Bernice."

She jumped. "Oh," she said, frowning, "there you are. What kept you so long?"

"I didn't think I was gone long. I'm ready now. Aren't you?"

"Why—yes—yes, of course I am," she said quite breathy.

"What's wrong?" asked Lewis. "You look funny."

"Nothing is wrong," she declared. "How do I look? Well," she said with mixed emotions, "if you think I look funny, just read that."

"Read what?"

"That," she held the paper in front of him, "right there, Lewis."

He read. "Well," he blinked, "I guess if you're looking for something to feel funny about, that's your privilege. There could be a thousand David Grants in the world. Here, take it and put the stupid paper where you got it, and quit looking stupid. Let's go. Our car is waiting."

She caught him by the arm. "You don't really—"

"Bernice McCawlis," said Lewis in disgust, "are you going crazy? Why has Hazel been wanting to know where that kid's buried if— If you start on this again, I'll take you to a doctor for sure."

"I know it's perfect ridiculous and silly," laughingly admitted Bernice, and bravely gathered herself together. "Just for a minute there," she said, following him, "it sorta got me, and for no reason in the world, Lewis. For no reason in the world," she repeated insistently.

CHAPTER 36

Outdoor work was a pleasant diversion from teaching school, and David felt a definite sense of satisfaction working with Dad at carpentering during the summer. To be sure, it wasn't an easy matter to say good-by to the pupils at Forest Hill, but he had been preparing himself for it for months. The contract to teach close to Lancaster the coming year had already been signed. Janet was delighted.

David also felt a definite sense of rightness in asking for his church letter. He was received into the East Fairview Church of the Brethren in August.

The wedding plans had been discussed from every angle and viewpoint, and the decision was made. It would be neither elaborate nor expensive, and it was not because Janet's mother was tightfisted or lacked any degree of pride in the man her daughter was going to marry. She was proud of David and admired him the more when she learned he wanted to save what he could toward further education.

Wednesday, December 30.

When Janet woke and looked out the window, she was simply thrilled. During the night the drab winter ground was whited clean with a blanket of new fallen snow. "Oh," she breathed. "What a beautiful day for our wedding! A surprise straight from heaven."

In the Walden living room the relatives and friends waited in silent expectation while one of Janet's friends played softly on the piano. David, strikingly handsome in his perfectly tailored black suit, took his place beside Pastor Hardy at the bottom of the open stairway. With an overwhelming joy, his swelling heart started pounding the instant he saw his bride in her soft blue velvet dress, eyes shining, cheeks delicately flushed, slowly, gracefully stepping her way closer, closer to him.

Janet was beautiful, radiantly beautiful. A holy hush filled the room.

Together they took their place between two baskets of long-stemmed red roses. Both looked their wonderful best.

Man and wife.

Two made one for life.

So soon, and the uniting of years of anticipation was completed. A sweet, simple ceremony it was, but impressive in its sacred simplicity. After the congratulations, a lap luncheon was served, and then came the opening of gifts.

It was midafternoon before the happy couple started on their honeymoon trip to New York City.

Two weeks of never-to-be-forgotten happiness, and the joys of full, purposeful living had only begun.

Their three-room apartment in Manheim was as adequate as it was cozy. Since David needed the car to go to school, Janet rode the city bus to the office. Theirs was a sharing, busy life, but a supremely happy one.

It was Easter Sunday, and they were dinner guests at the pastor's home. "David," Pastor Hardy said, "I've had a conviction that I should approach you about something. Have you ever considered dedicating your talents to the work of the ministry?"

David looked up sharply. "Well," he said slowly, rubbing one hand over the arm of the chair, "I can't honestly say I've never thought about it. But I'm not so sure I have talent for that."

"I think you have, David. And we need more young ministers of vision and vigor. Would you be willing to find out if you have such talent?"

"How?"

"Well, how about filling the pulpit, say once a month or so, and see how it goes? You've proved to me you're a man of both conviction and ability, and I don't say this to make you proud. I'm not a man to flatter anyone."

"I'd prefer to think it over before I give an answer," said David. "I was planning on taking some work at Elizabethtown sometime. But," he hesitated, "if you honestly—" he shifted. "Really now, you take me by surprise. I'll talk it over with my wife."

"Of course. Of course. I wouldn't want to rush ahead of God. Haste has ruined many a plan I'm sure He had for certain individuals. But if you have any conviction at all to give yourself to such a calling, don't stifle it, David. You know you could take seminary work in Lancaster, and I can't help thinking God has His hand on you for a special task sometime in the not-too-distant future."

David sat in deep thought. When was it he had heard a similar statement?

Long after Janet had fallen asleep that night, David lay wide awake thinking.

Rose was never happier than when David and Janet came home for a meal. And they both knew they were to feel free to walk in uninvited at any time and as often as possible. It was after a delicious brown flour potato soup supper (David's favorite) on a Saturday night weeks later, the four were lingering at the table, when David said, "Dad, do you think I'd ever make a preacher?"

Aaron studied a long moment the face opposite him before he spoke. "Son," he said, "I think you've got it in you to do whatever you put your mind to. How about it? Do you think you'd make a preacher?"

328

"I'm asking you," answered David.

"But you've got to have a feeling all your own regardless of what anyone else thinks. Yes, Son, I do think you would. Why do you ask?"

"Well, someone approached me about it some time ago, and I've been thinking maybe—maybe—"

"Tell them," said Janet. "He's afraid, I guess, you'll think he's being presumptuous."

"We wouldn't think that," offered Rose. "Surely you know us better than that, David."

"Well, it's this. Should I enroll in the seminary in Lancaster? What do you think?"

"If it's financial help you need," remarked Aaron, "don't hesitate to say so. After all, what good is money unless we do something good with it? I never had to spend one dime on you to get you out of trouble like a lot of parents have had to do, and I can honestly say you never caused us to lie awake at night wondering where you were or what you were into. And a lot of parents have done that too. I could go on and on. But this is what I want to say, David. If God is calling you to work of this kind, I would be the last person to discourage you, and more than that, I would hope to be the first person you'd look to for moral support or financial help or whatever. I can't think of anything you could do—" Aaron had to hesitate, and he cleared his throat—"that would bring Mother and me more real joy." Quickly he turned and brushed away a lone tear.

"Janet," said Mr. Dillon. "I have a letter here from a Jonathan Wells of Cleveland, Ohio, who needs a birth certificate to get a passport. He says he was born in Lancaster County and he's been told by an aunt that his mother's attending physician was E. P. Barneby. I don't know the doctor. Look in the directory and see if you find the name. If so, call him, please, and ask him if he can come to my office. I tell you, some of these people who need birth certificates have to get a lot of people involved in the search before it's all ironed out. Especially people

329

who don't know who their parents are. E. P. Barneby's that name."

"Yes." Janet looked back. "Mr. Dillon."

"Yes."

"I just thought about something."

"You mean about this Doctor Barneby?"

"No. I mean about my husband."

"What about him?"

"He's one of those who doesn't know about his parents."

"Not anything?"

"All he knows is what he found in the file in the Children's Home. He was there three years when Mr. and Mrs. Aaron Loomas took him. They raised him, Mr. Dillon."

"Was he adopted?"

"No. But they're just like parents to him. All he knows is that his mother's name is Shana Grant, and her address Philadelphia."

"Well, does he know his birth date?"

"Yes. May 24, 1913."

"Well, why don't you write to the Bureau of Vital Statistics in Harrisburg and see if they have any information on him?"

"Mr. Dillon," exclaimed Janet, "why haven't we thought of that before?"

"I never knew about the situation."

"No, no, I didn't mean you, Mr. Dillon. I mean, why didn't David, or his folks, or someone think of doing this? All his life he's been wondering—wondering where he came from. Once he even made a trip to Philadelphia to try to locate his mother. Imagine. Of course it was a fruitless search."

"Now, don't set your hopes too high, Janet," warned Mr. Dillon. "I'm only suggesting this one possibility, but it's the place to start."

"Would you dictate a letter for me?"

"I'll do more than that. I'll sign my own name," he added with a wink, "and there'll be no fee."

"Thank you, Mr. Dillon. I'm not going to say a word to

David about this until you get a reply."

In less than a week it came. Janet read it out loud to Mr. Dillon.

David Grant, born May 24, 1913.

Birthplace—Philadelphia, Pa.

Mother—Shana Grant.

Mother's birthplace—Glasgow, Scotland.

Father—Brandon Gray.

Father's birthplace—Leeds, England.

"So," she said with just a faint tinge of disappointment, "then she wasn't married. Not that it matters to me, Mr. Dillon; I just hope it won't to David."

"Sounds to me like she came over here just to have her baby," suggested Mr. Dillon, removing his glasses, "but that may not be the case. Only a guess. So don't jump to any hasty conclusions, Janet."

"Of course not. Oh, won't David be surprised? And now what is our next step?"

"Well, shall we try to get your husband a passport to Scotland? She very likely left him here and went back, don't you suppose?"

Janet shrugged her shoulders.

"Or," went on Mr. Dillon, putting his glasses on again. "You could go to the Philadelphia City Hall and see if the name Shana Grant is listed in their 1913 census. That is, if you think it's worth the trouble."

"Worth the trouble? Oh, I'm sure David will want to try. You see, Mr. Dillon, it's not that his foster parents aren't wonderful people. They're perfectly grand. But all his life he's—"

"I know. I know," said Mr. Dillon. His desk phone was ringing. "That's human nature to want to know who you belong to."

Saturday morning at daybreak David and Janet started for Philadelphia. They were the first to enter the City Hall when the doors opened. It didn't take the lady long to find the name.

"We have here a Shana Grant, 426 North Malca Street. That's out there in the Scottish settlement, you know."

"Thank you very much," said David.

To find North Malca took most of an hour. But there it was —426, a very small modest frame dwelling, painted brown, and somewhat battered. Janet waited in the car.

A young girl answered the door. She shook her head. "Never heard of anyone by that name."

From door to door David stopped, the whole length of the block, but no one knew a Shana Grant. He went back to the car. "What more can I do, Janet?"

"You might try the other side of the street. But rest a little, sweetheart. You look tired."

"I'm not as tired as I am disappointed. Maybe that woman at the City Hall gave us the wrong number."

"Or," suggested Janet, "maybe your mother only rented a room for a short while. Here, eat this candy bar. It'll give you some energy."

Once more David started on his search from door to door. Janet watched from the car, her lips moving at times in silent prayer.

A little white-haired lady was picking up a few twigs from the narrow strip of grass between her house and the sidewalk.

"Madam," ventured David, "have you been living in this community very long?"

"Over thirty years, sir."

"I'm trying to locate a Shana Grant. In 1913 her address was listed as 426 North Malca. That's down there a block on the opposite side of the street. Do you remember anyone by that name ever living there?"

"Well," studied the little old lady, "that's more than twenty years back. Lots of people have come and gone in that length of time. City folks shift a lot. But a—let me think—a—yes—there once lived a young lady in that house or near there, a real pretty miss she was, with such beautiful auburn hair. My husband often spoke of it when she passed by, because he takes a fancy to redheads. She used to pass by our home every morning; so I up and asked her one time what her name was an' where she went every day."

"And—and what did she say?" David was almost panting now.

"She said her name was Shana. That's it. I remember now, Shana Grant, a Scottish girl like we all are along here. And she said she was working in a hotel."

"Do you remember which hotel?"

"No, sir, that I don't. Is she some kin to you?"

"That's what I'm interested in finding out, Ma'am," answered David excitedly. "At least now I know such a person did actually live here. How long did she go by, would you say?"

"How long? Well, several years I'd say. The pretty miss got married, that I remember."

"Married?"

The woman nodded. "Some wealthy-looking man in a big fancy car started paying attention to her. I saw them going by and I was glad for her, because she always looked sad and seemed so alone in the world. I never could get her to open up and talk much to me. Always in a hurry she was."

"Do you know the name of the man she married?"

"No, I couldn't tell you that, sir. But now wait a minute. I think I know someone who used to live on this street that might be able to tell you. Is it important you know right away?"

"It's very important," exclaimed David, trying to hide his excitement. "I'd like to find that out today if at all possible."

"Well, if you want to, you may step inside while I use the phone."

"Thank you. I will."

Breathlessly he listened.

"Olive, this is Aletris. Say, you remember that pretty Shana Grant who used to live over here on our street? Who did she marry? You say Drextell? What's his first name? Anthony? Anthony Drextell. Thanks, Olive. There's a gentleman here who wants to know."

David tiptoed across the room. "Ask her where she lives," he whispered.

"Olive. Wait a minute. Do you know where she's living now? I see. All right, I'll tell him. Thanks." She turned to David. "She says she doesn't know where she's living now, but you might ask the minister of that church over there on the corner of Marshall and Harris. She said that would be her best guess."

"I don't know how to thank you, Ma'am," said David. "I was about ready to give up."

"You're very welcome, I'm sure. What's your name, by the way?"

"My name happens to be Grant. Thanks again."

He all but ran back to the car where Janet was patiently waiting.

"I found someone who knew her," cried David, quite out of breath. "Now to the church on the corner of Marshall and Harris. She's not Shana Grant any more. She's Mrs. Anthony Drextell."

"Calm yourself, honey," said Janet, touching his arm. "You're shaking."

"Well, who wouldn't be excited after all these years?"

"I know, dear. I'm almost as excited as you are. Look!" She held out both hands. "I'm shaking too. But the minister will hardly be in the church today, will he? We'd better find the parsonage."

"Just breathe a prayer, darling."

"I've been praying all morning. Look," she said as they neared the church, "the side door is ajar. There's a man. The janitor sweeping. Ask him."

"Pardon, sir," said David. "I'm trying to find the pastor of this church."

"He's up in his study, I think. At least he was fifteen minutes ago, and I didn't notice him leave."

"And where is his study?"

"Up those stairs and to your right, sir."

"Thank you, mister. Will I dare bother him for just one minute?"

"Well, now, I reckon what some calls bother isn't considered bother by Reverend Nash."

David felt like tearing up the steps two at a time, but he did no such thing. With forced calmness he walked up slowly and tapped lightly on the closed door.

Chapter 37

"Reverend Nash?"

"Yes, sir."

"My name is David Grant."

"Come in, Mr. Grant. What can I do for you? Won't you be seated?"

Thank you. I won't take but a minute of your time, for I realize you're a busy man. I'm trying to locate my mother, who was Shana Grant, and I've been told she married an Anthony Drextell. Can you give me any information about her?"

"You mean Mrs. Drextell is your mother?" The minister eyed David curiously.

"Yes, sir. She must be, even though I've never seen her. Do you know this woman?"

"I've come to know Mrs. Drextell quite well since she lost her husband. I had charge of his funeral."

"Then she—is a widow now?"

"Yes, and Mrs. Shana Drextell belongs to my church. But pardon me, sir, I must ask for an explanation. You say your name is David and you're her son?"

David sat on the edge of his chair. "I was separated from my mother when I was a baby. You see, I've never learned why or how it happened. All my life since the day I realized children have mothers I've been wondering, hoping to find her. I live in Lancaster. Just a while ago I found a woman on North Malca Street who remembered her and was able to shed some light on

336

this mystery. Would you please tell me where she lives?"

The minister looked at David, then opened his file. "I know the street," he said, "but I don't recall the number. Yes, here it is, 1221 East Kent. It's not far from here. Are you going there now?"

"Do you know of any reason why I shouldn't?" inquired David, moving toward the door.

"Well, first of all she may not be at home. She's the house-keeper at the Castle-Jinsen Hotel. And another thing," he added hesitatingly, "if she is at home, I can well imagine this will be quite a shock to her. Yes, quite a shock," he repeated.

"Would you tell me why, Reverend Nash?"

"I'd rather not, rather not."

The color suddenly left David's face. "You—you—mean," he said, scrambling awkwardly for words, "you think—she wouldn't want to see me—or—or even claim me?"

"Not exactly that, Mr. Grant. But I'm sure she doesn't think you're around. Let me call first, and see if she is home."

"Please do."

David felt a bit unsteady for a moment. A weakening sensation swept over him. He caught hold of the doorknob and gripped it.

"Mrs. Drextell? This is your pastor. Yes. How are you today? That's fine."

David scarcely breathed.

"There's a young man here in my study who would like to come to see you. No, he's not a solicitor. No, not a salesman. A friend of yours. Yes. I think you'll be interested in meeting him. Then it's all right if he comes over. All right, Mrs. Drextell."

He turned to David. "She said she's had her lunch, but have you had yours?"

"We've snacked a little, yes. My wife is in the car. Tell her we're not coming for a meal."

"Mrs. Drextell, the gentleman says they won't be there for a meal. Yes, his wife is with him. I'll tell him."

"She said she goes to work at four."

337

"1221 East Kent," David repeated the number. "Thank you from the bottom of my heart, Reverend Nash." He held out his hand.

"God bless your meeting," he said, "and I'll certainly be interested in learning her reaction."

"Go with me," David said to Janet.

Somewhat baffled and half fearfully now, he approached the heavy glassless door. What was this thing the minister wouldn't tell? He heard footsteps, then the turning of the brass knob, and the door swung open.

"Brandon!" Shana's face turned white. She stared at him in shocking surprise. Her hands went to her face.

"Mother," said David softly. "I didn't mean to frighten you. Please. I'm your son David."

"Not David!" she gasped, looking at him with unbelieving eyes. "My—my baby David!" She might have fallen, but he caught her arm to steady her.

"I am David, your son—and this lady with me is my wife, Janet."

"But—but my baby," cried Shana. "David—he—he died, I thought."

"Died! When?"

"Let's sit—all sit down, please." Shana was next to exhaustion.

David led her to the nearest chair.

"But he told me my baby died." Her tired, frightened eyes filled with sudden tears. "How can this be? David!" She looked at his face long and searchingly. "If you," she cried, "if you weren't the very image of—your—father, I—I couldn't believe you were mine. I—I thought at first I—was seeing—" she bit her lip. "Where have you been all these years? Anthony tried to find you, and they told him you died in the orphanage." Tears of strangely mingled surprise, and joy, and doubtings, trickled down Shana's colorless cheeks.

"You mean you never knew where I was?" asked David.

338

"Never. Oh! Oh! How my heart and soul cried out to know where she had taken my baby! I would have gone to the ends of the earth to find him. If you are my David," she cried, "then tell me where in South Carolina did she leave you?"

"She, who?"

"My oldest sister."

"Your sister? I have no idea what you're talking about. I never knew I was in South Carolina. I was in the Millersville Children's Home until I was three."

"Where's that?"

"About seventy miles from here."

"No, no," she choked. "How can it be—so close and I never knew. And then what?"

"Some wonderful people came and got me, and took me home with them. Listen, tell me. Did you write my name and birth date and your name, Shana Grant, on a piece of paper and put it in my one stocking?"

"I did. I did. Why?"

"That's what the nurse at the Children's Home told me. She found that paper. I saw that paper once."

"You did? Oh, David!" Shana crossed the room and, taking his face in both her trembling hands, kissed him on the forehead, on each cheek, then on his lips. "Now," she cried brokenly, "I know, I know. I know," she smiled through her tears, "you *must* be my son. If you care to hear what happened, I'll tell it to you at once."

"Indeed, I do want to hear it."

"And so do I," added Janet.

"Yes," said Shana, turning to Janet. "I don't mean to be ignoring you, dear, but I'm so—so completely overwhelmed about my boy."

"I understand," answered Janet sweetly. "I'm just so happy he found you at last."

Shana moved her chair a little closer to David. She wiped her eyes and drew a long, long breath. "Just this once," she began, "I'll go through my story. It's going to be hard—to tell.

339

Not only heartbreaking—but humiliating." She drew another long breath. "So I don't intend ever to go over it again. I expect you to tell me what all has happened to you since the last time I saw you."

"I will, Mother. I'll tell you everything there is to tell."

For over two hours, with breathless moments, David and his mother pieced together bit by bit the jagged, broken puzzle of their lives. Varied emotions were stirred deeply, and tears ran freely without shame or restraint. As the frustrating unknowns were gently unveiled, one surprise after another merged into amazement, then tremendous relief. The hand of an unseen artist seemed to be brushing from Shana's face the lines drawn by years of grief and bitter disappointment. Gradually she grew astonishingly sweet and beautiful to her son.

"Mother."

"Yes, David."

"What kind of a car was it Anthony drove?"

"A Cadillac."

"Black?"

"Yes. Why?"

"The superintendent at the Home said the man who stopped and asked for me was driving a black Cadillac."

"He did? But it couldn't have been Anthony, David. I—I—no—" she rubbed her hands—"unless the superintendent lied to him about you."

"Melvin Kolb wouldn't lie, Mother," said David with tenderness. He saw the look of dismay cross her face. "It could have been someone else," he added.

Shana bit the inside of her cheek. "If—if Anthony lied to me," she faltered, "I—I just don't want to live to know it. He suffered much and long. And—I—I suffered with him. But," she looked up into David's face and smiling said, "I just thank God I've lived to know someone lied, but it doesn't matter to me now who it was. God knows. And another thing, David, I thank God He let me live to know He had His hand over you all these years. Someday I'd like Reverend Holcome to meet you. Someday,"

340

tears almost blinded her, "I want to meet those dear, kind, wonderful people who have taken such good care of you, and helped you to grow into such a fine young man. I'm sure I couldn't have done so well. Someday I want to thank them personally."

"Would you go back with us now?"

"I couldn't today, David. I have my duties at the hotel. But sometime, after I get a better hold of myself, you and Janet may come and get me." She swallowed. "These emotions in here—are too much right now."

"Mother," said Janet, "wouldn't you like to come to David's ordination?"

"What?"

"He's going to be ordained to the ministry next year. That's not many months from now."

"Ordained? To the ministry?"

"That's right, Mother," said David modestly. "When you dedicated me to God in the hospital, you didn't suppose—"

"No, dear boy, I didn't suppose any of this." Shana smiled through exceedingly happy tears. "This is too much, too much for me," she choked. "I can't understand it all. My heart isn't big enough to contain it. I'm going to call Hazel tonight. She'll probably think I've lost my mind. But I guess I'm only finding it after all these years of bitterness and heartaches."

She held out her arms. David went to her. They embraced each other.

"The searching is over, Mother." He kissed her. "And I'm very, very thankful." He looked into her tear-stained face. "I belong to you and no one else. I love you, Mother."

"And now you have two mothers."

"True, Mother dear. And I shall always love both of you, but God gave me to you first, and we belong to each other."

That sweet sense of satisfying calmness—which those who truly trust God possess—filled their longing hearts. Both God and men call it peace.

The End

341